BITTERSWEET

OCEAN VIEW SERIES #3

MORGAN ELIZABETH

For everyone who wants to have their cake and get eaten, too.

And for Alex. Thanks for supporting my love of writing filth.

PLAYLIST

Shadowstabbing - Cake
    All the Things That I've Done - The Killers
    Look What You Made Me Do - Taylor Swift
    Tiny Dancer - Elton John
    Cardigan - Taylor Swift
    Selfish - Jordan Davis
    I'd Do Anything - Simple Plan
    Love You Madly - Cake

A NOTE FROM MORGAN

Dear Reader,

First off, thank you for choosing to grab my book off of your to be read list and spending some time with my characters. If this is your first time visiting Ocean View, welcome! If you've been here before, welcome back!

Either way, as always, thank you for making my dreams of being an author come true.

Bittersweet contains mentions of gambling, addiction, the expectation of an older sibling, parental death/cancer, infidelity, potential SA, kidnapping, and violence. Please always put yourself first when reading—it's meant to be our happy place.

Love always,
Morgan

ONE

-Lola-

MOST PEOPLE DECIDE to make a significant change when a new year starts.

They spend the entire month of December planning who they want to become in the coming year, searching for ways to lose weight, get a new job, or meet the love of their life.

Some people go so far as to write down the exact path they'll take, the road to success. They need to prove to themselves they have the ability to change, to become someone new.

I don't have time to wait for the new year to roll around.

Six months ago, I decided that change needed to be made, and today I'm taking the final step of my transformation into "New Lola." It's funny to me how things can be toxic in your life, that it can build slowly, so slowly you don't even notice how bad it's gotten, and then one tiny grain of sand tips the scale in a direction that necessitates immediate change.

I guess that's why they call it a "wake-up call." It wakes you up from the daydream you've been floating through and shows you the worst-case scenarios. It shows you what will happen if you don't change and what you'll become.

My wake-up call came in the form of my phone ringing.

It didn't drive me to start my business—no, this has been in the works for years, slowly building to this day.

It was what drove me to say *no more*.

Normal people don't answer numbers they don't know. But when you're the daughter of the mayor and in charge of the "family" and "crisis management" aspect of his image, you answer every call.

But that call? Sometimes I wish I had let it go to voicemail.

"*Hello?*" I had asked, tentative and anxious, like I am every time my phone rings with an unknown number. "This is Lola Turner."

"Lola, *bellissima*." My stomach churned because I knew the voice.

It was a voice I remembered from almost exactly one year ago.

A voice that has never boded well for anyone.

Johnny.

TWO

-Ben-

I WAKE TO LOUD BANGING, metal on metal, and instantly roll over to grab the sock-covered baseball bat beside my bed. It's sat there, blissfully unused for the better part of five years, since I moved into this space. I've never had an issue with someone breaking in, but I always assumed it was a matter of time.

Living on the Ocean View boardwalk, where obnoxious tourists overdrink and let go, means I'm basically begging for one of them to decide what's mine is theirs.

Once my fingers wrap around the cool metal, I swing my legs over the edge of my bed and look at the blinking alarm clock on the bedside table.

That can't be right.

Seven in the morning?

Who robs a tattoo shop at seven a.m.?

Two a.m., when the bars close and the shop is dark, sure.

Three a.m., when the boardwalk lights shut off, the drunks feel comfortable in intoxication, and the cover of the night feels like a welcome mat for shenanigans? Definitely.

But at seven a.m.? When the oldies are already out, power walking the boards and feeding the seagulls before the heat starts? When the rich stay-at-home moms are running with expensive strollers before they make their stop for smoothies and coffee?

It doesn't make sense.

But still, the noise continues below my apartment: a loud clanging, a whirring sound I can't seem to place. A drill, maybe?

Is someone using a drill to break my locks?

Grabbing the bat tighter, I pad toward the front door, opening it and propping it with a colorful door stop my best friend Hattie painted for me when she tired of me calling her at all hours to have her bring my spare key. Not long after moving in, I replaced the door and put in a safety lock, so when the door closes, it locks automatically.

The door stop is hideous, but every time I look at it, I can't help but laugh a bit.

Not today, though. Today, sleep-fogged adrenaline is raging in my veins as I take the first step out of my apartment onto the landing connecting the apartment across the way from me and the stairway that separates the building in two.

On my side is my apartment on top of my tattoo shop, Coleman Ink. The once donut shop next door hasn't been in business for three months.

But as I walk down the first few steps, bat gripped and ready, it clicks.

The sound isn't coming from my shop.

It's from next door.

It's the banging of pans, not the sound of intruders.

The whirl of a mixer, not a drill.

The sign next to my business for the past month flashes in my mind, connecting the last dots in my sleep-addled brain.

A pink sign with girly cursive words in bright white, light- and dark-pink stripes adorning the awning over her front door.

Libby's Bakery - coming soon!

And then a date below that.

A date that, if I pull up my mental calendar, I'm pretty sure is today.

The bakery is opening today.

And between the loud, shitty as fuck music and the banging, it's clear the employees are getting busy.

My tattooed hand scrubs down my face before combing my hair back.

Jesus, fuck.

I hope to God this isn't the norm.

While the shop doesn't stay open past ten most nights, I'm not an early riser. I go to bed late, charcoal and oil paints and designs melding in my mind, keeping me up deep into the night.

Visions that won't let me rest if I don't get them down onto paper leach from my exhausted veins until I can give into sleep.

The Muse is a real bitch that way, if you ask me.

I crafted my life around my art and around the lifestyle that allows me to create, brushing off the responsibility of the family construction business in favor of art and tattoos.

I'm about to head back upstairs and throw a pillow over my head, praying I can fall back asleep, when the singing starts.

It starts, and it starts *loud*, cresting over the sound of the mixer running, pans clambering, and music blasting.

This is where one might assume I'm going to say it was magical. That the singing was like that of an angel, drawing me to the door of the bakery like some kind of moth drawn by flame.

No.

The singing sounds like a dying cat.

It's so incredibly off-key, like they aren't even attempting to make it sound decent. It's the kind of singing you do as a joke at karaoke to get out of having to sing anymore.

There's no fucking way I can fall asleep with *that* happening. A padded cell wouldn't block that noise out, much less a pillow over my head . . .

Still, I should head up. Put on running shoes, work off the lingering exhaustion and irritation and stop in later. Be civil and ask that they keep it down early in the morning.

Or at least put on a shirt and some pants, seeing as I'm in boxers and holding a metal bat.

Fuck that.

Time to meet the new neighbor.

Hattie has met who I assume is the owner once or twice while she was renovating and moving in, but each time I've either been out or with a client.

When I hit the base of the stairs, I make a right until I face the backdoor of the bakery. The center stairwell between our business has one main door leading to the road and a tiny hallway. On either side of the hallway is the backdoor to Coleman Ink, my tattoo shop, and now, Libby's.

I knock on the door with a paper that has a logo and reads "Employees Only" written under it in a woman's careful handwriting. I knock once, twice, three times, and I do it loud, pounding on the solid metal door.

But having the same thick back door, I know that if there is any kind of noise in her place, she won't hear my pounding.

I should just go upstairs. Be a normal human being, take it as a sign that I should talk to her when I'm in better head space.

Unless . . .

I push on the handle. I assume it will be a lost cause because who doesn't lock their door? Especially if you're not used to the area. But low and behold, it moves, clicking with a mechanical thunk I feel more than hear, and I push open the door.

Apparently, my new neighbor didn't lock it.

Who is that level of comfortable with their surroundings to leave a door unlocked? Especially if, from what Hattie told me, it's a woman who moved in.

Jesus Christ, I hope it's not some kind of ditzy, dumb woman opening up a store with her rich daddy's money, no idea how to run a business or keep herself safe.

That thought souring my mind, I push open the door and step in.

And I freeze, still holding the bat in my hand.

Because there is, in fact, a woman standing in front of me, maybe seven or eight feet away, her back to me, facing a stainless steel work bench.

Music is pounding—some kind of pop that my brother's girlfriend Jordan always blasts when she comes down to visit—and her hips are moving to the beat. She might not have a singing voice, but she has rhythm. Full hips sway, encased in tight black shorts that stop at midthigh.

Thick thighs.

Thighs that beg for a man's fingers to leave impressions in.

My eyes move up until they hit long blonde hair with a hint of red, pulled back into two braids down her back, and fuck, there are little, innocent bows tied at the bottom.

Goddamn bows, for Christ's sake.

Her skin is fair and flawless, her arms bare, and a light-pink tank top not quite hitting the top of the high-waisted shorts stops at a small waist. She's not what you'd call a classic hourglass, with a small waist and narrow rib cage, but the way her hips flare out tells me she's not skin and bones, like so many women feel the need to be these days. At her lower back, another pink bow is tied, the strings to an apron grazing the bottom of her ass.

On that ass are streaks of flour, like at some point it coated her fingers and she moved her hands along the fabric without realizing.

But it's the *ass* I'm fixated on.

It's the ass that has me mesmerized, has me leaning in the doorway like some kind of psychopath waiting for her to turn around and notice before I brutally murder her.

I've always been an ass man. It's a weakness, even. A pair of pretty eyes and a fat ass can get a woman anywhere with me.

It's as I'm staring at that ass, my mind trailing off to places it absolutely should not be, when the bat falls from my grip.

It clangs on the linoleum tile, the hollow metal making a sound that finally cuts through her horrific singing and the music and the mixer and my own inappropriate thoughts.

She jumps and turns.

And then she screams.

THREE

-Lola-

MY NERVES ARE at an all-time high today with opening day.

Last night, despite how exhausted I was from cleaning the grimy apartment I could finally move into last minute and moving all of my things from Sam's to the new apartment above the bakery, I could not sleep.

Everything that could go wrong flashed every time I closed my eyes.

What if everyone hates what I'm selling?

What if no one shows up?

What if *too many* people show up?

What if I make someone sick?

And then it moved to a more generalized anxiety about my life.

What if Sam can't handle it all?

What if there's more that Dad hasn't been telling us?

What if Lilah finds out everything we've been shielding her from all these years?

What if someone tells the press?

Then there was the outright strangeness of being somewhere new keeping me awake. Every creak, every blow of wind coming off the ocean, every shout outside from a tourist down on the boardwalk—it all had me on edge.

Suffice to say, I'm exhausted this morning, having only caught two hours or so of sleep by the time the sun came up.

But I would not let one little sleepless night ruin the first day I start to live my life for *me*.

The first day of New Lola.

The day I've been building up to for years and years, whether or not I realized it.

Libby's started in the cookbook I found in a pile of my mom's things my dad hid after she passed away.

The memories were too painful, he'd said. He lost the love of his life when my mom died, and with her went all sensibility and structure from the lives of my sister and me.

It turns out there was so much that Mom had hidden.

So many secrets.

So many promises.

But while my dad might not be the most honest, the most reliable, or the most fatherly, it can't be said that he didn't love my mom. He loved her more than anything on earth. An obsession, even. But do you know what happens when someone with an addictive personality loses his addiction?

It transfers to something else.

That's what happened when his only tether to normalcy, the only tether keeping him from going too far, snapped.

Regardless, I recognized the cookbook instantly, the yellowed cover spawning memories of baking with her before she got sick.

Memories of me at six standing on a chair as my little sister sat in a bouncer. Memories of her showing me the proper way to scoop flour into a measuring cup to make sure you don't overmeasure.

How to scrape the top off and level it, measuring flour to make Lilah's first birthday cake.

"*Such a good sister you are!*" I remember her saying as we decorated the cake during nap time. "*Making it perfect for your sister. Remember this, Lola. Friends will come and go, but you'll always have your little sister. It's your job to keep Lilah safe, okay?*"

Even before the world came crashing down, she was telling me her secrets without my knowing.

It's like she knew, even then.

She knew she wouldn't be around to keep her safe, that Dad might crumble if she wasn't there, and it would become my job.

My burden.

The cookbook brought back memories of me at seven, dumping chocolate chips into dough and scooping the cookies onto a baking sheet while my mom watched with a serene smile.

Memories of her jotting a new recipe she found in some magazine she bought as an impulse buy at the supermarket.

"This one would be perfect for your father's 50th birthday!" she'd said of some incredibly intricate cake with multiple layers and homemade fondant. I remember that one most of all because we never tested that recipe.

She was gone before his 50th birthday.

When I found that cookbook, I realized I had found a lifeline to my mom. I could bake and I could bring her to every major event in our lives. Birthdays and holidays and graduations. Cookies for good grades and brownies for breakups and stupid boys.

In high school, it turned into a way to treat my friends.

When I graduated, it morphed into coworkers giving me some cash to make their kid a birthday cake. Some spending money.

In my twenties, it turned into farmer's markets on Saturday mornings and renting a commercial kitchen, hand-delivering orders.

And at thirty, Libby's Bakery came into fruition. The bakery named after my mother, who inspired this love, the town my father oversees, in the location she loved most of all.

The Ocean View boardwalk.

The downside of being in Ocean View is that my business has

turned into a great PR campaign for Dad: the mayor's daughter keeping her mother's memory alive by opening up a shop in town. Once again, it has put me into the spotlight.

The entire town—the state, even—is watching me now, watching my business to see if I'll make it or if I'll flop.

And they all have their opinions about me starting my business. Many along the lines of, "It must be nice for your rich daddy to bankroll your bakery in a high foot traffic area on taxpayer dimes."

If they only fucking knew.

The thought of the press showing up in just a few hours to record my father coming as my very first customer has me nauseous with adrenaline.

It has been for days.

That adrenaline alone is what drove me to get out of bed despite the lack of sleep, take my shower, and dress in the outfit I laid out the night before. It's what made my hands move as they tied my hair into braids, as they pulled the apron on over my head, and as I walked downstairs to pull out doughs and parchment and cookie sheets.

But different adrenaline is running through me now—not the anxiety of a first day, but the fear of an intruder.

I can hear the clatter over my music and the industrial mixer beating butter and sugar, and when I turn, he's standing here.

A man—a *tall* man—is standing in the backroom of my bakery, a metal bat at his bare feet.

And he's *shirtless.*

And pantless.

The man stands, covered in tattoos with a scruffy beard and messy dark hair in just a pair of tight-fitting underwear, staring at me with a face that, at some point later, when my heart rate returns to a semi-normal state and I'm running through this entire interaction with a fine-tooth comb, I'll realize is a mix of shock and awe.

But all I can see at this moment is a man—a built man, who is much larger than myself—standing in my business that I haven't even opened yet, nearly naked.

And I *scream.*

"Oh my God!" I grab the nearest weapon, a French rolling pin, and arm myself with it, using both hands around the end and pointing it in his direction. "Oh my GOD!" I yell. Panic is causing my brain only to say those three words. "OhmiGod, ohmiGod, ohmiGod!" *Okay, maybe it's just one word now.*

But as I'm standing there, panic flowing through me as I try to think of what to do next, something strange happens.

He seems to snap out of his own daze.

And the man *smiles.*

He fucking smiles.

Clearly, he's a psychopathic murderer.

He is standing in my bakery in his goddamn underwear, smiling at my complete and utter panic.

And while I'm sure my brand of panic is entertaining to watch from an outside perspective, who stands in a woman's presence in his underwear while she has a full-on panic and *smiles?*

Psycho murderers, that's who.

"Get the fuck out!" Finally, my brain finds my mouth and synapses fire. One hand continues to hold the heavy rolling pin as my other hand moves to the side, slapping scoops and measuring cups, knocking things over as I try to find my phone. When my hand touches the device, I grab it but refuse to look down.

I don't want my eyes off this man in front of me.

And *not* because of how he looks.

"Get out! I'm calling the cops!" My thumb keys in my passcode, fumbling over the screen, and I instantly regret even putting it on. Why would I do that? Why wouldn't I just make it easy for myself?

If I make it out of this alive, I vow to take any lock off my phone.

And then the man fucking *laughs.*

"No need to panic, babe. Not here to cause trouble."

What?

Babe?

No need to *panic!?*

Uhm, is this man for real?

"Sir, you are nearly naked and in my business."

"The door was unlocked." My brows come together as confusion joins the soup that is my emotions right now.

"Excuse me?" My arm is getting tired of holding this heavy as fuck rolling pin, but I dare not lower it. It's the only form of a weapon I have right now, even if it's a dumb one.

"The door was unlocked. Dumb move, leaving that door unlocked. The back door doesn't always catch. I could be some drunk kid or a creep trying to rob you."

I stand there confused, blinking at him.

He doesn't seem like he wants to kill me. Maybe he's just a weird peeping Tom?

"Uh, sorry to say this, but you *are* a creep."

"I'm not a creep." I open my mouth to further accuse him, but he beats me there. "Nor am I trying to rob you."

"Oh, so you're just a creepy flasher? Get OUT!" As shock and panic wear off, it melts into frustration and anger.

But again, despite my pissed tone, he smiles.

And fuck, if he wasn't giving me heart palpitations as is, I might have more—different ones, though.

The smile is bright white teeth with full lips and a dark, well-trimmed beard surrounding it.

It's a good smile.

Ted Bundy also had a good smile, though.

My eyes travel to tired eyes, circles underneath like he just woke up, and dark, dark hair. The sides are cut shorter, the top flopping over to the side, and my mind can't help but wonder if he styles it combed back or if it's always a mess.

Either way would suit him.

Jesus Christ, *stay on topic, Lola. Potential fucking murderer!*

"I'm not a flasher, babe."

"I'm not your 'babe.' I'm a woman terrified because a huge tattooed man is in my place of business!"

"You've got that right." He crosses his arms over his chest.

It's a nice chest.

"Excuse me?"

"You're not mine."

"I'm sorry, you've lost me." And fuck me if my polite politician's daughter isn't kicking in, apologizing for things that are *not my fault*.

"You're sure as shit not mine because if a woman of mine had her door unlocked in a new place like you did, I'd turn her ass red." My entire body flushes, anger and something I refuse to look at too closely burning deep inside of me as my mouth opens in shock and surprise. "You should have locked the fucking door," the man says, finishing his attack on me.

"Who just opens a door?"

"Doors were quite literally made to be opened."

"You know what I mean! Who opens a door to a place that *isn't theirs?*"

"A lot of people. People who are a lot worse than me, babe. And for what it's worth, I tried knocking. Shit in here is too loud for you to hear."

"So you just . . . came in?"

"The door was open." Okay, I have no time for this back and forth. I have a business to get going and a scary, strange man in my bakery.

"Gah! Fine! I get it! Note taken. I will lock my door from now on! Now, seriously. Get the fuck out! If you don't, I'm going to call the cops."

There. That should do it. No one wants to deal with the cops.

"Good, let them come," he says, and confusion rolls through me. "I'll file a complaint for this fuckin' noise." That stops me, the rolling pin dipping, my arm screaming for me to drop it. But I easily ignore the ache when his words register in my mind.

Excuse me?

"What?"

"Woke up and thought I was being robbed." I blink at him.

The rolling pin dips again, and my arm finally drops, leaving it resting at my side.

I still hold the rolling pin in my hands, though.

"Your fuckin' noise traveled all the way to my apartment. I thought someone was in my shop robbing me. You need to keep it the fuck down."

"I'm sorry?"

"You should be."

A new feeling flares.

Rage.

Absolutely rage for this man.

Who the fuck is he?

"Are you kidding me?"

"I can hear it in my room."

"Your room . . ."

"Live upstairs, babe."

"Stop calling me that!" I drop the rolling pin down on the metal bakery table, my heart rate still high, but either I'm becoming numb to it or understanding is hitting me. I'm out of imminent danger, I think, but now stepping into a different danger. "I live upstairs," I say, because I do. I just moved in the last of my stuff yesterday.

"Looks like I'm your new neighbor."

The world stops.

The ringing starts in my ears.

My gut falls to the ground.

That would be my luck, wouldn't it?

Day one of New Lola is going just dandy.

And although there is a case to just apologize, make nice, and tell this man I'll keep it down in the future, that kernel of New Lola that's stubborn as fuck, the part that refuses to let people walk all over her anymore, pops up.

"Do you do this a lot, just come into random businesses through the backdoor in nothing but your underwear with a baseball bat? Introduce yourself as the new neighbor?"

"I haven't needed to recently." Annoyance is starting to fester now. It seems like I can't get a single clear answer from this fucking man, like he's trying to be a pain in the ass.

"Who *does* that?! Just breaks into someone's business and harasses them?!"

"I told you, I didn't break in. Thought *you* were breaking in."

"You shouldn't just open doors! That's fucked up."

"I tried knocking. Three times. Was going to ask you to keep it down, but your noise is so loud, you didn't even hear." He's not wrong. I didn't hear him, so wrapped up in trying to scare away my anxiety that I drowned it in music and got lost in sugar and butter and flour.

"Look. I need to go back to bed. You gotta keep it down." He scrubs his hand, tattooed and tanned and way hotter than I should recognize, all things considered, before he steps back, still facing me but moving toward the door.

"Uhm, excuse me. This is my business. I'm working."

"Got it. My business is next door. You gotta keep it down in the mornings." That stops me. I blink at him.

"What?" His eyes widen, and his head tips in a *yeah* movement. "No, a woman owns the business next door. That's my new neighbor."

"Hattie? No, Hattie works for me. You should do your research more carefully." I blink again, confusion and a touch of embarrassment running over me. I've met Hattie, the tattooed woman that *works* next door, a few times and just assumed since she was sweet and welcoming that she was the owner. I should have googled it. I should have researched who my new neighbor would be. He's right.

My mind tries to pull up the name of the business, but I fail. His hand goes out, and I stare at it.

A hand shouldn't be that hot.

Annoying, asshole men in their underwear who may or may not be my new neighbor *should not be that hot*.

"Ben. Ben Coleman. Welcome to the building. Now keep quiet

before eight." I open my mouth to argue. To tell him to fuck off, to say that I pay rent just like him and I need to work when I have to work. That this is a bakery, and bakeries are open *early*. That's the nature of a freaking bakery. People get *baked goods* to enjoy in the mornings.

But then the beeping starts.

It's the fire alarm.

Because cookies are burning to a crisp in the oven. I didn't see the alarm going off on my phone because I was arguing with this *stupid* man, and now an entire tray of chocolate chip cookies is burning.

I run to the oven, opening the door and coughing as smoke flies into my face. Grabbing a pink oven mitt, I start waving at the smoke to clear my vision before grabbing the pan and tossing it straight into the big sink.

"Well, shit," I say before turning back to talk to the intruder.

To my *new neighbor*.

But he's gone, the door closed behind him. The only proof that he was here is the metal bat still lying on the ground, abandoned by its owner.

Coleman Ink.

That's the name of the tattoo shop next door, I remember as my brain kicks in.

And Ben Coleman is the owner.

And I just made the world's worst first impression on my new neighbor.

FOUR

-Lola-

I DON'T HAVE time to overthink the interaction with my new neighbor and what ramifications there might be because I'm on a time limit. It's seven fifteen, and my dad, along with a team of press, will be here in less than forty-five minutes to help me open my bakery. So I keep working, filling the case with things I made last night and this morning, and continue to scoop batters and doughs and put them into the oven.

The rush feels good, the constant movement and calculations taking away any space I might have for stress or panic or anxiety. I only have time for the absolute necessities.

I know that what happens in the next few hours could decide my fate. It could determine if my business flourishes or flops and if New Lola has what it takes to survive in the real world.

And when my phone rings and I look down and see Sam's name, a text telling me they're outside, I know it's game time.

My "politician's daughter" smile goes into place and masks the anxiety that's brewing in my stomach.

Never let them see beneath the mask, I tell myself, walking toward the front door to start the show.

————

The press stays for a full thirty minutes, taking pictures of my dad cutting the wide pink ribbon, wearing a Libby's apron behind the counter with a huge cheesy smile, serving a cookie to a sweet little girl, and taking a bite of a cupcake topped with a cloud of swirling pink frosting on top of it.

There isn't a single picture of me smiling in my business unless my dad is also in the shot. Not one of me behind my counter, and not a solitary question is asked about the bakery unless it has to do with the headline they are spinning: "Beloved Mayor's Daughter Opens Bakery in Hometown to Honor her Mother."

I could be bitter, but I'm used to it. There's an election coming soon, after all.

There's always an election coming up.

Once the press leaves, cameras and lights and shouting reporters giving me room to breathe, my dad places a small, swift kiss on the top of my head, says his goodbyes, and leaves right behind them.

Such is life when you're the daughter of Shane Turner.

There's always a baby to kiss, always a bill to sign, always a hand to shake.

But as always, one of my favorite people on the planet stays behind, his thick dark hair combed back respectably, a suit jacket I know he's dying to toss into a dumpster somewhere, perfect pressed, a white button-down underneath, and a light- and dark-pink striped tie finishing the outfit.

A tie I know he chose simply because it goes with the color scheme of my new bakery.

For context, my dad wore a bright-red tie.

But Sam? I can always count on him to cheer me on and support me.

He's leaning on the counter I stand behind, looking at the four small round tables I have inside the bakery filled with customers munching and chatting. There are more customers outside, mingling and eating baked goods, some at the small wrought-iron tables and chairs I put out front and others sitting on the boardwalk benches.

It feels amazing to see this all, knowing I built it and people are *enjoying* what I made.

"Proud of you," Sam says, his voice soft. When I move my eyes back to him, he's staring at me, and his eyes are as soft as his voice. "Your mom would be even prouder."

And fuck, here come the waterworks.

In another universe, Sam would be my brother.

Instead, he's the son of one of my mother's childhood best friends. We grew up together; photos of him, me, and my sister Lilah sitting around in diapers litter my family room and his parents' house. Over the years, he found his own foothold in politics, most recently being elected as a councilman, but he'll always just be an annoying boy who chased me around with a worm when I was ten.

And apparently, he has a death wish.

"You make me cry in the middle of my bakery on opening day, I'm going to get you back," I say with a threat, but it's hollow with the words scratching through a closing throat.

He smiles his wide politician's smile.

People think that's a learned smile, that it's something you practice and perfect, but I think some people are just born with it. The smile that says, "Trust me. Vote for me. I'll lead the way and better your life," with just the shine of teeth.

But then the smile falters. This, unfortunately, I've seen before, too.

This is the look the public doesn't get to see, but I have many times.

Too many fucking times.

My gut drops.

"What?" Sam looks around, checking to see if anyone is listening.

In a small town like this, whispered conversations can turn into the front page of the *Ocean View Press* the next day. When he determines we're in the clear, he leans in a bit closer, lowering his voice.

"Have you . . . heard anything?"

I don't like where this is going.

So I don't answer the question I know he's asking.

"I hear things all the time." He rolls his eyes.

"Don't be a smart ass."

"I can't help it," I say. I don't know why I'm playing this game—I guess because I know something *not great* is coming. Something I probably don't want to hear, especially on a day like today.

If today is sunshine and rainbows, Sam is about to bring on the rain cloud. And the look on his face tells me he doesn't want to be the one to do it, no matter if he has to.

"I've heard whispers." Whispers are never good. "About your dad."

Fuck.

Fuck, fuck, fuck.

"What kind of whispers?" He sighs.

"Nothing concrete." He pauses, looking over his shoulder then at me. I stare back, waiting for him to finish. He brings his hand up to rake through his hair, a tick he's had since he was a kid, but stops before he ruins his meticulous style. He sighs. "Talk of Johnny Vitale coming into town recently. I can't confirm anything, though."

My stomach falls to the floor.

Johnny Vitale, right hand to Carmello Carluccio of the Carluccio crime family, in theory, has no reason ever to come down to Ocean View other than to enjoy a weekend with the family at the shore.

But a simple, early summer vacation wouldn't be cause for whispers. Whispers of him down this way are bad fucking whispers.

"Why would he be down here?" I say, my voice lower, eyes scanning the bakery the same way Sam's did minutes ago.

"I don't know, Lola. Could be anything. Could be nothing. But the council just struck down a contract for Carluccio Disposal last month." Acid churns in my throat, creeping up slowly. "And your dad fought with the council to get us to approve it." Shit, fuck, goddammit. This is bad. This is *so fucking bad.*

"He's done with that," I say, but even I can feel the uncertainty in my words. Is he? Is he ever done with it?

A year ago, when I told my dad I was *done,* he agreed. He agreed he was done too, that things had gone too far, and that he'd change.

A year of no calls.

A year of no whispers.

A year of peace.

Was I just naïve?

"I haven't heard of anything in a year." I feel sick. Sam looks at me, face going into recovery mode. He knows. He knows what happened when I had the sit down with Dad.

"I'm done, Dad."

I thought that had been a wake-up call for him, the same way it was for me. After all these years, when I finally sat him down and had that intervention I should have held years ago, I thought he would have seen the error of his ways.

Now I'm wondering if maybe it wasn't what it seemed. If maybe it was just a reason to keep things quieter. To keep me out of it.

What use was I anymore, anyway?

"I'm sure it's nothing, Lola. Seriously. I haven't heard much of anything other than that contract being denied."

"Much of?" For a politician, Sam is a shitty liar. I'll never know if it's because I've known him my entire life and I can read him better than I can read myself, or if maybe he really is a shitty liar and his honesty sells him to the people, but he's never been able to keep anything from me.

"Nothing big, I swear." My eyes scan the bakery again, keeping an eye out for listening ears.

"Sam—" His phone rings on the countertop, and I feel the vibration running through to my wrists. It feels like a bell, signaling our time is up.

"Shit, I gotta take this, Lola. Seriously, don't stress. It's nothing. I just wanted to see if you'd heard anything. But I gotta go." He grabs the bag I made him, filled with baked goods for his office, even though he'll probably hoard them and skip lunch and dinner, eating baked goods instead of a real meal. "Thanks for this. I love you. Proud of you. We'll do dinner soon." I smile, but it's weak, partly because he's leaving when I already feel like I never see him, and partly because a rock has taken root in my gut.

"Love you too." He backs up, a new customer coming up behind him as he does, but he pauses.

"She'd be proud, Lol," he says, tipping his head to the smiling photo of my mother I have behind the counter, the namesake of the bakery.

I smile a weak, watery smile,

"Go, before I cry and someone gets a photo." He returns the smile, winking as he walks out, putting the phone to his ear.

———

The rest of the day goes smoothly, with a near constant stream of customers and baking. It's a dream, really, though I might need to look into hiring someone, even if it's just for a few hours a day. Some uninterrupted time to bake or, you know, pee would be nice.

I fully intended to take a tray of items next door as a peace treaty and attempt to make a better first impression, but the time just never came with opening day here, and now that the bakery is closed, my bones ache with exhaustion.

I'm finishing up closing down when my phone rings in my apron pocket, the bluetooth headphones in my ears allowing me to answer as I finish mopping.

"Hey, babe."

"Hey, big-time business owner," Lilah answers. There's a lilt to my baby sister's voice that's always there—sunshine and honey and pure happiness.

Untouched by the chaos.

The baby.

I could feel bitter about it, but that was my goal all along.

"Ahh!" she shouts, and panic enters my chest. What is—

"Lilah!"

"Stop it! No!" The panic creeps through my veins as I pause my mopping. What is wrong? Is she in danger?

"Lilah! What is going on?" My heart is in my stomach.

"My cat is hunting me," she says, and both relief and annoyance flood me.

Her stupid fucking bitch of a cat.

"Jesus, Lilah. You scared the shit out of me."

"Well, she's scaring the shit out of *me*."

"The cat is a menace. She's always hunting you."

"She looks angrier today." I roll my eyes, rinsing out the mop and pushing the bucket to the supply closet.

"She's always angry."

"Angrier, Lola."

"I don't think that's possible." Molly, the calico cat Lilah rescued from a Craigslist ad, hoping to have something cute and cuddly and low maintenance to keep her company, is the meanest cat I've ever met. When she says the cat hunts her, she means it. I've seen her stand on a couch while Molly acts like she's hiding in the savannah grass, ready to pounce. "Have you fed her?" She sighs like I'm an idiot.

"Of course, I've fed my damn cat." The cat is also overweight, and her only joy comes in eating.

And, of course, hunting.

"So what did I do to deserve the pleasure of my baby sister calling me?" I ask, going back to my mopping. I am exhausted, but I'm still running on the fumes of excitement from opening day. It was a complete success, and I even got two catering orders and a cake order for next weekend.

At this rate, I'll be able to pay off the bank loan I had to take out in no time.

"I hear congratulations are in order," she says, her voice singsongy. Lilah is the sweet one, always put together, always amicable. Friendly, the kind of person who you meet and instantly decide she could be your very best friend.

She was that way even when she was a kid, and I always assumed that was why mom was always so careful with her when we were young. She and I would joke that if one of us was going to get kidnapped, it would be Lilah, because she'll talk to any stranger and tell them her life story, for better or worse.

I try to speak, but she keeps going. "I saw the pictures in the *Press*! You looked so cute! The article says it was a huge success."

I roll my eyes and can't fight a smile.

"Thank you. It was . . . pretty awesome."

"I so wish I could have been there, but I have stupid work." There's an audible pout in her voice. "I'll head down soon, though, and eat you out of everything!" Lilah works up north as a pharmaceutical rep, going from doctor's office to doctor's office, using her charm and striking looks to help pay for fancy shoes and exciting outings with friends.

"Of course! You're welcome any time. You can stay with me in my new apartment!"

"We'll have to sneak me into town though. Dad keeps trying to set me up on dates with his friends' sons. I'm like, do I *look* like I'd make a good politician's wife? Ugh." I can almost hear the eye roll and head shake she'd make, her dark-blonde hair in a perfect blowout swaying from side to side. While I got Dad's Irish heritage, red-tinged hair and fair skin, Lilah looks like mom, a short, curvy thing with long blonde hair and skin that tans perfectly.

I hated her for that for a time, the fact that I got the ass and none of the boobs. I got the sunburn and the strawberry-blonde hair and the height and the jokes about being a leprechaun when I was the one who kept Mom's promises and secrets. Lilah got all the good parts of our family while getting the least of the pressure.

Sometimes it just felt unfair.

But I also got *Mom*. Lilah was only 10 when she passed, barely eight when she first got sick. I have fifteen years where Lilah had to scramble through her formative years with me as her womanly guide.

But it also reminds me of my talk with Sam earlier. I can't help but wonder if she's heard similar rumblings. Her crew is different, so far out of Ocean View, most people don't recognize the name, but she still has friends in town.

"Hey, have you . . . Have you talked to Dad lately?" I ask, trying to be subtle.

I suck at subtle.

Thankfully, Lilah is pretty good at not *seeing* subtle in any form.

"Uh, no, not this week. I called him . . . last week?" She pauses like she's picturing the days of the week in her mind. "Yeah. Last Thursday because I was getting ready to go out and he was jabbering on about how he wanted a family dinner. Some kind of photo op. I've been out of the town for like, three weeks total. He's so dramatic."

For a split second, I think about spilling to her.

She's old enough. Old enough to bear the weight of this drama, this stress. And who knows, maybe she'll have a solution that I haven't been able to see.

But if I did that, other secrets would be revealed. Other secrets that could change her life forever. So as with every other pain point in the strained relationship between my father and me, I don't tell Lilah.

I've worked the last fifteen years to keep her in the dark, keep her from being touched by the frustration and insanity that is my father's addiction. Why would I threaten that now?

"Did he . . . say anything?"

"He said lots of things, Lola. He always does." A fumbling comes through the line, then she yells, "Bye, Molly! Be good!" before there's the slamming of the door and the beeping of a car fob coming through the line. "Alright, sis, I gotta go. I love you! I'll come visit soon, yeah? Shoot me a text. I'm so proud of you, babe."

"Will do. Love you!" I say and then stand in the bakery all alone, staring at the wall as the phone goes dead.

FIVE

-Lola-

EVERY BONE, muscle, and tendon aches with exhaustion, but I'm wide awake.

After a day of baking, handling the press, and doing interview after interview, smiling next to my father without grimacing at the fact that he only said a handful of words to me (all carefully chosen and within the earshot of reporters), then a full day of running my own business and cleaning said bakery and prepping for day two, every single atom of my body is tired.

But day one is done.

New Lola is here, and we're starting with an exciting clean slate.

While I've been in and out of the bakery for the last month, making it my own and perfecting everything, the lease for the apartment above it didn't start until yesterday, meaning the day before my new bakery opened, I was moving things from Sam's place, where I was staying between apartments since he's rarely ever there, and the storage facility I had rented to my new home.

I had to drag everything down the three flights of stairs at his place, into a box truck I had rented, and then back up the narrow steps separating my space from my neighbor's. Sam offered to help, but with how busy he is, I didn't want to bother him. So it was just me and my not very present muscles lugging boxes until I wanted to collapse.

Then I ran out to the distribution center to get the hundreds of pounds of flour, sugars, butter, eggs, and whatever else I would need to feed the sweet tooth of the Ocean View boardwalk.

And as I lay in my bed (that I had to painstakingly push up the stairs and then assemble), everything hurts. Exhaustion weighs me down like one of those weighted blankets.

I think moving my toes would be an impossibility.

But despite the whole body exhaustion, and the knowledge that I have to wake up bright and early to get baking, I can't sleep.

Not because I'm overthinking every moment that brought me here.

Not because I'm panicking that day two will be a flop.

Not because I'm terrified that I won't be able to live up to the expectations laid upon me, both by my family and myself.

These things are true, but they aren't the source of my insomnia.

Instead, it's the bass of Cake's "Shadow Stabbing" pounding through the walls of my new apartment, which I'm learning at this moment, are incredibly thin.

Don't get me wrong—it's a great song. In fact, I even have it on my "Shitty Day" playlist, which I play to get myself out of a funk.

But when it's midnight on a Friday and I need to be up at five, it becomes even less appealing.

Panic floods me.

I think I may have made a *huge* mistake.

When I saw the ad in the paper, I barely questioned a thing. The advertisement stated that a commercial kitchen and storefront were up for lease with a small one-bedroom apartment above it. I called up the owners, came to see it, and put the deposit on the lease all in the same day.

They advertised the location as a "bakery on the quiet end of the Ocean View boardwalk," and when I came here to tour the space, it was just that. It's on the far end of the boardwalk, nearing the homes valued at millions of dollars each and far away from the bars and amusements that draw the rowdier crowds.

It was *perfect*.

Once I signed the lease, I only came to do work on the bakery and make it my own during the day, spending my mornings working on making the bakery my own, then afternoons at the commercial kitchen I was still renting, and evenings doing in-person deliveries of what I baked to my existing customers.

The apartment wasn't available to move into for another month after I signed the lease, but I was okay with that, so long as I could get a jump start on the bakery.

Now I'm seeing this may have been a terrible choice.

When a loud cheer comes through the walls, I scratch out the "wondering" part.

It was *absolutely* a shitty choice.

That's because it is 12 a.m. on a Friday night and music from the apartment next to mine is blaring so loud, I can barely think straight.

When I found this location in the paper just days after that wake-up call, I saw it as a sign that this was the direction I needed to go.

In some ways, I saw it as a push from my mother that it was time. That I had done my duty and I could live for *me*.

I'd been quietly planning for a storefront for years, scrimping and saving the money, telling no one about my dream. *Mom's dream.* It had been a donut shop in a past life, but when the other half of the donut shop couple left, the remaining owner closed the business and stayed in the apartment while figuring out what to do next—hence the apartment lease not opening until *last night*.

While last night went fine, despite my inability to fall asleep in a strange place, it seems I never had the chance to find out the neighbor is loud.

And when I say loud, I mean when I went to make myself a glass of chamomile tea an hour ago, my dishware was rattling against itself in the cabinets.

That kind of loud. The kind of loud you can feel in your bones.

After a long day, I was hoping to go to bed early, get rested for another early morning. Except this noise is fucking with that plan.

The noise started at eight. At eight, I was fine with it—it's about what I expected, moving in next to a tattoo shop on the boardwalk. And considering I woke my neighbor up early with my own work schedule, I figured fair was fair. We'd eventually figure out a schedule that worked for both of us. Tomorrow, I'd come over and deliver some treats and have an adult conversation.

But now it's four hours later and the muffled sound of alternative rock is shaking in my brain.

When I signed the lease, I knew getting a place on the Ocean View boardwalk would be loud, especially during the warm months. Sure, I thought situating myself on the quieter end would be better, but I never came into this thinking I'd have a sound, silent sleep every night.

In fact, for the first two hours I told myself this was just training for what's to come when the real summer crowds hit.

At ten, I got ready for bed and realized the sound wasn't dulling anytime soon. I washed my face, did my grounding routine of skin care and teeth brushing, and put on my lucky pajamas—the silky nightie Lilah got me for my birthday last year. She spent way too much, but it's one of my favorite luxuries. I wore it the night I put in my application for the bakery and woke up the next morning to a voicemail telling me I got it.

I secretly think it's lucky—and I could use some luck right now.

Once that was all done, I lay down.

And I stared at the ceiling.

And tried to block out the music.

But still, it's unnerving settling to sleep in a new place that isn't completely yours yet. You don't know the strange shadows, the way the wind creaks the walls. Every sound makes my eyes pop open, and the feeling that started last night is only intensified as the music continues, both adding to and covering the sounds my new apartment makes.

I check the clock on my bedside table. I check my phone. I check the watch I wear, which in the morning will tell me how many hours of deep sleep I had.

It's never enough.

Each time I glance at a clock, I do the math for how many hours of sleep I'll get if I fall asleep at that moment. It's a habit—a bad one.

Why do we do that? Why do we count down the damage instead of making a change?

For me, I've spent the entirety of my thirty years avoiding confrontation. I'm a fixer, not a problem maker. For as long as I can remember, even when I was too young to be relied on as such, friends and family have come to me for help.

I've never stopped any of them, always doing whatever it took to make life easier for them, even if it meant a sacrifice on my end. I hate to be a pain, a nuisance.

This trait is what I'm warring with at midnight when I start questioning if I should just go over there and kindly ask my neighbor to turn down the music.

I can't, I think. *That would be rude.*

This morning was unbearably embarrassing. We already got off on the wrong foot, but I signed this lease for five years, and I can only assume my neighbor has a handful of years left on his lease as well. I want him to like me, especially since I plan to be here for a long time, and I know the tattoo shop is well loved in the community.

But also because I've learned that you can avoid so many issues in shitty housing situations if you befriend your neighbors.

Regardless of my commitment to not start drama, I *can't sleep.*

This has to be God's version of payback for being so loud this morning. I swear it. And I swear, if I had known that I was being so loud, loud enough to wake him, I definitely would have been more considerate.

New Lola might be committed to taking names and getting shit done, but that doesn't mean she's an inconsiderate bitch.

On the other hand, while I don't want to bug him *again* on my first full day here, there's the chance that if I let this go, it might become a regular thing, and that would be worse.

I war with this for a while, trying to balance the need for sleep with the need to not stir the pot.

I *hate* to stir the pot.

Except, this is my new page. New Lola. When I signed this contract, using the money I saved for the vision I selfishly let myself dream up, I told myself I could only do it if I was doing it for me.

Not to give Lilah a glimpse at what ambition looked like.

Not to pay off debts I didn't earn.

Not to create another marketing tactic for Dad's campaigns.

Not to honor Mom in some obtuse way that doesn't even matter, not in the grand scheme.

But for me. Because when was the last time I really, truly did something *for Lola?* I need to take more initiative. I need to work on change over acceptance.

And maybe even more, I need to work on not being such a damn pushover, letting everyone get their way at my expense. I proved I meant business on *that* aspect of personal growth when I went through the lease for the building. The owners wanted a ten-year lease—I demanded five. They told me I'd need to pay extra for the ovens and equipment already here. I refused and told them I wanted to get the place outfitted with extra ovens. I demanded an extra parking spot out back for an employee when I hire one and even managed to get a decreased leasing rate for the first six months.

I'm pretty damn proud of myself for *that* one.

I don't know why the fact that I can negotiate and demand what I need to shocks me, but it did.

It shouldn't.

Ever since our mom died when I was 15 and Lilah was 10, I've had to fill that space.

I was the one who remembered permission slips that needed signing and homework that needed checking.

I was the one who called the utilities and negotiated lower rates or extensions on bills, despite coming from assumed wealth.

I was the one who made sure things were kept quiet and under wraps, kept within the family.

I was also the one who made sure Lilah stayed safe.

I sigh, realizing the difference that I ignored.

All of those things protected the people I love. *Not me.* Advocating for things my family needed, that part was easy.

Advocating for myself?

That's apparently a lot more difficult.

I'm stewing on this thought, the realization uncomfortable, when the music stops for a blissful moment.

Aching muscles I hadn't realized I was tensing loosen, and I sigh in relief.

Sleep should come easy now.

And then the track changes, and the music starts back up.

"Noooo," I groan out loud, reaching for a pillow to lay over my head.

It drowns nothing out.

In fact, I think all it does is keep in the negative thoughts and memories. Like being stuck under the pillow with them is giving them the gas they need to grow.

Memories I keep hidden.

Emotions and feelings I don't let out. Ever.

I'm a *new person*. I don't need to address these.

But stuck here, unable to sleep, my thoughts my only companion?

Yeah. They're lashing out to wreak havoc.

I need to do something.

Rolling off my bed, I sit on the edge and look toward the door, trying to decide what to do.

The thought of going over there, talking to complete strangers who I'll be stuck working and living next to for at least a few years, puts me into utter panic.

A deep laugh breaks out over the music, and a mix of panic and guilt overtakes me.

They sound like they're having fun.

Do I want to be the person who ruins that? The voice in my head telling me if I do that everyone will hate me gets louder.

But then New Lola comes out and smacks that voice straight across her face, sending her spiraling into oblivion.

Don't you deserve a good night's sleep? Why should their fun come above your own comfort? New Lola, remember?

New me is right.

People pleasing is *so* yesterday.

I stand up, slipping my feet into a pair of slide sandals, and walk to the door, ready to go. I am going to go next door. Politely ask them to keep it down. I'll be nice about it. I'll . . .

Then the thought of knocking on the door guts me, and I'm back at square one, the square where I'm wondering just how much sleep do I *actually* even need to run a bakery, ya know? They'll probably be done by . . . oh . . . two?

I turn back around.

But New Lola smacks me again.

I head to my kitchen counter and grab the paper box holding cookies I brought up to celebrate my first day, but then I became so overwhelmed with exhaustion I skipped it entirely.

There. That's a good peace offering, right? A good neighborly hello?

Fuck. Or does it seem like I'm trying to bribe them to be quiet?

Oh God, get over yourself! inner me yells, and that does it. It pushes me to grab the box off the counter and walk to the front door, opening it up and propping it on a moving box I need to unpack.

That's when I realize the noise isn't coming from the apartment next door.

No, it's so loud, yet it's coming from the *tattoo* shop, traveling up and over into my new home.

And now that the sound buffer that is my door is gone, I can hear it's not just two or three people having fun.

It's an entire party.

Jesus Christ.

New Lola shrivels at the task in front of her.

So does Old Lola.

Standing up to one person who you've already technically met, despite it being an embarrassing catastrophe, is one thing.

Interrupting what sounds like an entire party? That's another.

Shit.

I slowly walk down the stairs separating the buildings, trying to get the nerve until I'm at the entryway between them. There are three doors there—the back entrance that leads to the street, an entrance to the bakery, and a door that leads to Coleman Ink next door.

I lift my hand to knock on the tattoo shop but freeze. Panicking.

Maybe I'll let it go another twenty minutes, an hour. I mean, how long could it be? I bet it's settling down and—

A loud, jarring round of laughter interrupts me, and I head back to the door, reinvigorated.

I lift my hand and . . .

Nothing.

I can't do it.

Shit.

What am I doing? I'm standing here ready to, what? Interrupt a party? Be *that neighbor?*

I can't do it.

Fuck.

But also, I can't *not sleep.*

It's then I decide.

I can't do this forever, pacing in a hall like a crazy person, mumbling to myself, trying to get the nerve to ask a party to keep it down.

I need to go talk to them.

This can be another version of day one. The first day of the rest of my life, where I refuse to let my concern for making others feel uncomfortable mess with how I live my life.

I'm just as important.

It's crazy that I feel the need to remind myself that.

I lift my hand to knock, to bang on the door, and I feel a breeze.

As my arm lifts, the silk moves too, and I realize I'm still in my nightie.

What is wrong with me?

I need to go upstairs, change, and then bring the cookies around to the *front* of the shop like a normal person. Try to get their attention, kindly ask them to turn down the music, and start a great friendship.

So what if we started off poorly? We both were taken aback. He probably was tired and cranky, the same way I am right now.

Yes, that's it. I'm sure my new neighbors are perfectly kind and reasonable.

Understanding, even.

Maybe we can create some kind of partnership—get a tattoo and a free cookie!

But first, I need to turn around and put on actual clothes. I start up the stairs, getting up two steps, eager to hide away with my new plan.

Then I hear it. The click of the door.

No, no, no, no!

"You okay?" I hear, my back to the voice, and *fuck, fuck, fuck.*

I can't believe this is happening to me!

Why does the world fucking *hate me?*

"Hey, uh, hi," I say the words up the stairs, trying to pretend this isn't happening.

I can feel the cool air from the air conditioning in his shop leaking out through the door and licking up my legs and the underside of my *fucking asscheeks,* which I'm 99% sure are sticking out and now staring straight at this man.

Jesus fucking Christ.

"You okay?" he repeats.

I turn around slowly, holding the cookies like an idiot and trying to stretch a calm smile on my lips.

"Uh, yeah," is all I say, like some kind of idiot who can't use words.

Some kind of idiot who is standing in an entryway, in a nightie, holding cookies at nearly midnight.

Dear brain, please reconnect with mouth. Immediately. Thanks. Signed, Upper Management.

"What are you doing?" He looks me up and down, and panic and embarrassment flow through me. Why did I not think about these stupid fucking pajamas before?

"I uh . . . I have cookies."

"I see that."

"There are uhm . . . flavors. A few?" Oh lord, what am I *saying?!* "Chocolate chip. Oatmeal raisin . . . There's a monster cookie in there. It's chocolate chip and cookies and cream. That one's a home-made Oreo," I say, pointing to the sandwich cookie. "A black and white—"

"I don't need your cookie menu." I blink at him. His voice seems . . . annoyed.

Well, that snaps me out of it.

Why is *he* annoyed?

I'm the one who can't freaking sleep because his music is shaking my *brain!*

"I was going to bring them over. As a peace offering?" I gulp. *New Lola, come back. Remember that this guy is a fucking asshole. Not only did he break into your business this morning, but he's also doing the same thing he bitched about less than 24 hours ago.* "And to see if you might possibly turn down the music a hair? It's just, it's really loud. Like shaking my brain loud, and I'm absolutely exhausted—"

"You would be, how early you were up." I stop speaking. I blink at him. He's not . . . is this . . .

"I'm sorry?"

"Woke me up early as can be and now you're asking me to keep quiet?" Well, shit.

"I'm really sorry about that. I didn't mean to, and I'll try and—"

"I'm not turning down my music." That stops me. Tattooed arms cross the black tee stretched over his chest.

"I'm sorry?"

"I'm running a business. The music is for an event we're having. Adds ambiance."

"Well your ambiance is keeping me up."

"Sucks to be you." My head snaps back.

"What are you, five?" He raises a thick eyebrow. He has attractive eyebrows. I've never been attracted to eyebrows, but his are thick and dark and . . . expressive.

And then I have to remind myself that he's an *asshole.* Like, a big one. Definitely not hot *at all.* And the fact that he's a dick cancels any potential hotness out. "Is this retaliation for this morning? Because that is so fucking childish. I apologized. I planned on doing what I can in the mornings to be quiet. I just—

"Look, I told Brad that whoever moved in next door had to be cool with the music." I blink. "We're not always open late, but some nights we are. And also, I don't do mornings. He told me I wouldn't have to worry about you being loud in the mornings, waking me up." Brad is our landlord, and I'm starting to think Brad is a moron.

"Okay, well, I told Brad that I'd have early mornings as a *bakery.*" Ben looks at me, frustration clear in his eyes when he looks at the ceiling.

"Fuckin' Brad," he says, like it's a curse in and of itself, and honestly, it might be. "Keep telling him to sell me the building. He doesn't want to do the upkeep, doesn't want to deal with me bitching him out about shit. But no. He's a greedy asshole. No one wanted to move in next door because of it." My guts drops.

Well, maybe I'm not a master negotiator like I thought.

"Nothing over there fucking works, and he can't keep up on updating the security of the building. I don't know how you're running a business out of there." I don't tell him that I spend hours watching YouTube videos to fix the ovens in the bakery. My mind drifts to the front door lock that never catches.

My gut sinks.

Fuck, fuck, *fuck*.

"Brad doesn't give a shit. He didn't even want to put someone in there, too much work for him. Wanted to collect the write-off for it being unoccupied."

I feel sick.

"You, pretty eyes and a killer ass, what'd you do to convince him to give you the place?" My eyes widen.

"Excuse me?"

"You don't look dumb. What'd you ask for?" I blink, shock and frustration running through me, the music that's still blaring tunneling into my brain.

The extra parking spot.

The lease negotiation.

The reduced pricing.

The equipment.

My stomach turns.

It wasn't because I'm turning over a new leaf and taking charge. It wasn't because I'm turning into an advocate for myself.

I was his last resort.

I fell into his lap and was so excited that I didn't even question any of it.

"Look, you seem sweet. Probably got conned into this place. But just because you didn't do your due diligence doesn't mean your hours will affect mine. I have a business to run, same as you." My mind is still stuck on what he's revealed to me.

My new self-image has spiderweb fractures along it, ready to shatter.

He's oblivious to this, to my own, new, incredibly fragile sense of self crumbling in front of him.

Someone calls his name, and he looks back over his shoulder, his foot still holding the door open.

"Look, I gotta go. If you wanna talk, come over tomorrow. Happy to fill you in on how Brad fucked up."

And then he's gone, the heavy metal door clicking behind him, and I'm standing in the stairwell, in my pajamas that show way too much ass, holding a bakery box of cookies.

I go upstairs in a daze, eat half the cookies, and then cry myself to sleep, wondering how what seemed so promising is already falling apart.

SIX

-Ben-

LOCKING the door behind me and facing the stairs, all my mind sees is the vision of my new neighbor standing there last night in a fuckin' silky nightie, holding a box of cookies, wide-eyed and confused.

I was a dick to her.

I should have kept the noise down—regardless of the charity event happening, there was no reason for it to be as loud as it was.

Ambiance.

I'd said it was for *ambiance,* like some kind of self-righteous tool.

And I should have been kinder when I told her about what a dick Brad is. I saw it in her eyes, the shock of reality.

But seeing her there, something snapped in me.

A woman like that, walking around in what was essentially lingerie, her ass hanging out for all to see, no idea who would walk out into the shared space . . . It just wasn't safe.

Just like that stupid fucking unlocked door.

In this day and age, what kind of woman is that reckless?

I don't let myself think too long about why the idea of a friend or client catching her there, seeing her exposed like that, got me up in arms, got my blood burning.

It's just a safety issue. A safety issue she is *clearly* ignoring.

That is all, I tell myself as I jog down the stairs and unlock the door that leads to the back room of my shop.

This place was once a pipe dream, something that only came to mind when I daydreamed, drawing designs in the margins of my notes for the business administration class I took. And yet somehow, it defied all laws of science, becoming a reality.

I wave at Hattie, who is already getting her station sanitized and organized before clients roll in, and I'm about to do the same when my phone rings.

The screen shows the name of my younger brother, Tanner.

Shit.

I don't want to do this right now. I have had enough strange and uncharacteristic thoughts and feelings already today. I don't need to add talking with my brother, who, in the eyes of my family, did what I was *supposed* to have done all those years ago.

It also doesn't help that I know why he's calling. I groan, looking at the ceiling before swiping and putting the phone to my ear.

"Brother," I say, leaning my back against the wall and looking down at my boots.

Despite not following the family profession, it seems blue-collar runs through my veins because unless I'm running or attending the yearly charity auction, you won't find me in anything but old, beat-up work boots.

"Ben. I'm shocked you answered," my brother says with a laugh. Two years ago, that sound would have been uncharacteristic. Now, with a good woman by his side and the family business finally making money, he sounds free. My hand moves to my hair, combing through as I laugh at his calling me out.

"Super busy. Don't take it personally."

"Yeah, yeah, yeah. Remember that Hattie and Jordan are friends now. Hattie loves to report on your very empty personal schedule," he says with a laugh.

My coworker and best friend, Hattie Jones, is a pain in my ass, making friends with literally everyone she meets, despite her occasionally scary appearance and always scary excited personality. The last time Tanner and his girl Jordan were down in Ocean View, Hattie made a new best friend.

Apparently, they chat.

"Fuckin' Hattie," I say.

"You know why I'm calling." I sigh.

"Yeah, I know." I move toward the backroom, sitting down at the break table and grabbing a sharpie I keep there, doodling to distract myself. "I don't think I can make it," I tell my brother, juggling the device between my shoulder and ear while I draw a bow on the table in a blank spot.

"Come on, man, are you kidding me?"

"Shit's busy here. I can't just head home for the weekend whenever you make some crazy plan."

"It's not some crazy plan—it's Mom's 60th birthday. And it's in two months. Plenty of time to plan ahead, block off the weekend." He's not wrong. I could—I'm typically booked out for six weeks, with more appointments scattered in there through six months. I could move things around, and it wouldn't be too much of a problem. "Fuck, even just the day. The drive isn't that long."

I just don't *want* to head back to my hometown, and the shop is the perfect excuse.

"It's not that easy, Tanner. We've got a lot going on over here. Summer is peak season. The boardwalk is packed. I can't just close for a weekend; that's not how businesses work."

"That's exactly how businesses work when you own them, Ben. You and I both know that." The knife in my gut turns. We both know that because years ago, I ran out on my family responsibility of running Coleman Construction and never looked back, leaving my younger brother to pick up the slack of the failing business and turn it around.

I don't go to Springbrook Hills for that reason. The reminder that I followed my heart instead of my mind, that I left Tanner to that . . . It's too much.

"I don't see you enough, Ben. Shit's changing. We're all getting older." I sigh. "I want you to get to know Jordan." Again, the knife turns. Somehow, although Tanner spent ten years breaking his back to fix the family business, sacrificing his own dreams and ambitions to make it happen, he found the perfect woman. One he treats like a total fuckin' princess, but who also won't take his shit.

Jordan is perfect for Tanner in every way, and I hate that they're so far from me so I can't get to know her better. Sure, they come down for a night or two, but it's not the same.

And I have successfully avoided Springbrook Hills and the threat of facing my father in his own home since I left for art school.

"You guys come down here for a weekend, and bring Mom and Dad. I'll put you all in a hotel, do the beach thing. It'll be fun." That's usually the best solution. It makes Mom happy to be down the shore, and my dad won't bring up shit that's dead and buried for fear of upsetting Mom. I can also avoid any conversations I don't want to have by heading back to my place or faking an appointment.

"Will you come to the wedding?" The question stops my train of thought.

"Wedding?"

"When I marry Jordan. Will you come?" Jesus Christ. Is he saying . . . ?

"Are you engaged?"

"Not yet, but it's coming. I told you that." He did. Months ago. Shit, not even long after he started dating Jordan, he texted me a picture of her in a Coleman Construction tee, hammering God knows the fuck what, wearing this ridiculous pink hard hat, and captioned it just that. *"I'm going to marry this woman."*

"Fuck. I feel old," I mumble under my breath.

"You are old. And lonely."

"Fuck off." As he laughs, I hear a voice in the background—the woman in question.

"Alright, Princess, calm down," he says, the words muffled like his hand is on the receiver. "I gotta go. Sit on it, okay? I want you there. It's been forever. I know Mom would appreciate it, too." I know that. That's the only reason I ever even entertain any invitation. But . . .

"And Dad?"

"Dad?"

"How would Dad feel about me coming home? Staying at his place like the good old days." Tanner sighs, a heavy sigh that he has from being the monkey in the middle, trying to balance letting me do my thing and Dad's overbearing ambition for the company he no longer operates.

"He's dad. You know . . ."

Yeah, I know. Dad spent my entire childhood expecting me to take over Coleman Construction. As the oldest son, it was my privilege—my duty. It wasn't for me, though. I'll never know if part of me just rebelled at the idea of having my life planned out for me or if this was always where I was destined to wind up.

When I was 10, my mom gave me a sketchbook. She'd always be up early in the morning before any of us, sipping her coffee and doodling on her own. She said it was her own time, time to feed her soul.

I never understood until she gave me my own, numbered with the days of the year, a page for each day.

That first day I drew a strawberry riding a skateboard, and life made sense.

I think a part of me started planning how to get out of my destiny from then on. That same part of me bears the guilt of knowing I forced Tanner to take on that destiny while I lived out my own dreams.

My mom gives me a new journal every year for Christmas. Every morning I wake up and sketch something out, a habit that is as natural now as breathing, as ingrained as brushing my teeth. Sometimes it's stupid, like a strawberry on a skateboard; sometimes it turns into something gorgeous, a new tattoo to put to skin.

But it's a habit that feeds my soul. A precious routine that was given to me by my mother.

"I'll think about it, okay?" I ask, hoping that will appease him. It does. I don't know if he realizes that something will have come up in a month to prolong my grand return home, but either way, he accepts.

"Alright, man. Let me know. If not, Jordan will try to get on your ass." I laugh before saying goodbye and swiping to hang up. I lean back in my chair and sigh at the ceiling, a patchwork of fluorescent lights and particle board ceiling tiles.

"You're so full of shit," a voice says, interrupting my thoughts. My head moves to the break room doorway where Hattie leans against the frame, blunt, black hair to her shoulders, dark glasses framing her blue eyes. Black pants and a tank show off her colorful arms.

"What?" I ask. Hattie is not only one of my best friends, but she's also a pain in my ass. If I feed into this conversation, I will be stuck in it indefinitely.

"You can't go to your own mother's birthday party?"

"How long were you standing there?" I ask, and she rolls her eyes, walking in and sitting in one of the plastic chairs.

"Long enough to know you need to go home," she says, leaning over and grabbing the sharpie and capping it like she's a mom who wants my focus and I'm her petulant child.

"No, I don't."

"I can move appointments around. I can take over for a few days. Shit, we can close. The shop will survive. Go live a life."

"I do live a life."

"Oh yeah? When? And seeing me daily while we're at work doesn't count." My mind glazes through recent months.

"I went to that concert with Vic."

"That was last summer, Ben." Shit, it was, wasn't it?

"I went to Luke's bachelor party."

"Three months ago." Fuck.

"Tanner and Jordan were just down here!" I'm grasping at straws, and Hattie knows it.

"Yeah, you always make them come down here." I'm silent because that one I can't argue. "All of your friends are getting married. Luke and Cassie's wedding is next week."

"Vic and Gab aren't getting married." She just stares at me, knowing the truth. Vic and Gabi are *definitely* getting married, whether or not he's asked yet. The two are attached at the hip, just like Cassie and Luke. And Tanner and Jordan. Shit. *When I marry Jordan, will you come?* Tanner just asked that. Hattie's right. I *hate* when Hattie's right.

"Chris Jacobs," I say, naming the friend who grew up here in Ocean View and then moved to Springbrook Hills to work for Tanner, essentially an Uno Reverse of myself.

"Chris doesn't count. He's a man whore. He doesn't stay in one bed long enough to get tied down." She's not wrong. And honestly, the fact that he was the only person I could think of bodes terribly for my position. She stares at me, reading me in the way she's been able to do since I first met her at the first shop I worked at. I actually didn't even give her the job, to be honest. I told her I was starting a shop of my own, and she told me she was taking the job.

That's Hattie for you.

She sighs. "You can't avoid your dad forever." The shitty part about your best friend being a woman is that they can read you better than any man ever could. A man will hear that, nod, and move on to asking you about sports, plans, or anything other than emotions. Women *read* you. And that sucks.

"I'm not," I defend as if that will change her mind.

"Sure you're not," she says with a sad smile. But just then, the bell chimes over the front door. My next client is here.

"Can you go greet my client and get her signed in while I get settled?" I ask, staring at her. She stares back for a long moment before sighing again, nodding, and walking toward the front of the shop.

Saved by the bell.

SEVEN

-Lola-

I FLIP my sign to "We'll be right back" and straighten my apron. I think I'm going to make it my signature, this pink apron. It's pretty and frilly and perfect for a place with rainbows, sunshine, and frosting.

I should order more and get my logo put onto them, too.

When I finally hire employees, they can wear them as well. Or maybe I'll get theirs in a darker pink so that I can stand out.

Another part of Old Lola I'm throwing away: never wanting to stand out. I spent so many years purposely standing in my Dad's shadow, letting him shine, doing as he asked.

No more.

But I won't let my mind sit on the thought too long—my anxiety is high enough right now as it is.

Because I'm making my last-ditch effort to make nice with my new neighbor.

The first time was a disaster—meeting the owner next door and threatening to beat him with a rolling pin? Not my shining moment.

The second time wasn't much better. Having him find me lurking in the hall in a tiny nightie holding a plate of cookies? Embarrassing.

Third time's the charm, right?

This third time will be crafted by me, though, no shock or surprise or unexpected barbs and jabs.

And hopefully, both of us will be fully clothed this time. I hope this goes well because I signed a five-year lease on this building and I don't believe his is up any time soon, if I remember what the landlord told me correctly. Despite learning the landlord is a dick and useless, I'm locked into this location, and I need to make it work.

Because this is the make-or-break-it moment of playing nice with my neighbor, I went all out with the tray I'm bringing over. It holds cookies in all my flavors and half a dozen cupcakes with various frostings: my signature pink strawberry, vanilla, chocolate, cookies and cream, black and white, and peanut butter.

How could someone see this plate and not want to make nice?

Sugar and butter fix everything, after all.

I'm grateful that today is a bit less crazy than yesterday, giving me the ability to do things like taking a sip of coffee or, you know, pee.

It also gave me a few minutes to think about last night.

I was exhausted. I overreacted, letting my mind and my fear of failure fog up reality. Whether or not the landlord is a dick, and even if the reason I was able to negotiate a decent lease for myself wasn't that I'm turning a new leaf and sticking up for myself, I still did just that.

I still stood up for myself.

I need to use that foothold and keep going, not disappear back into myself and clam up. Project *New Lola* is still on.

That also means I need to channel Old Lola and make nice. With my customers having disappeared for a few minutes, it's time to close up shop and be a good neighbor. He offered to talk in the morning when we met last night, and I need to put on my big girl panties and do just that. No more head in the sand and avoiding people because I'm afraid I'll get a negative reaction.

No more safe, careful Lola. I walk the four steps until I'm standing in front of the door with the logo for Coleman Ink. It's in some kind of elaborate old script font with thorny vines wrapping it—classy but still unique. Dark and ominous, it's the complete opposite of my own bubblegum-pink storefront.

Immediately, I question this decision.

I should turn back.

This is *so* awkward.

Why am I *doing* this?

I'm about to turn around and spend my mini break in the back-room inhaling sugar and butter-filled treats as if it will coat my shame and embarrassment with some flubber when the door in front of me opens.

"New neighbor girl, right?" A woman stands in the doorway, holding it open, a thick black eyebrow raised. It's pierced with a looped ring and she has thick pink glasses on, cat eye style with rhinestones in the corners, and a funky eyeglass chain keeping them connected to her. Straight black hair falls to her shoulders, paired with the same style of blunt bangs. There is a row of earrings up each ear, and both her arms are covered in tattoos.

"Yes. Hattie, right?" I say, unsure of how to act. I've met her in passing a few times but never actually had to interact with her truly.

"Are you bringing those to us?" she asks, tipping her face toward the tray in my hands.

"Uh . . . yes?"

"Killer!" Then she grabs my arm and pulls me in. "I have been dying to try your stuff, but yesterday you were so damn busy, so I figured I'd wait. I was planning to come by and buy something, but here you are!" She grabs the tray and walks toward a reception desk, plopping it there and promptly grabbing a cupcake and removing the wrapper.

"I'm Lola. I don't know if I introduced myself when we met before," I say, but the words come out low and distracted. Because I am distracted. My eyes are hungrily eating up the details of this room.

It's not pretty in a conventional way, but still, it's breathtaking.

Each wall is covered in frames of all sizes. Every frame holds a handful of different drawings, and as I walk farther into the room, I realize they're all tattoo options. Flowers, hearts, an octopus on a sinking ship. Open books and birds and a deck of cards.

They line the walls in a flurry of colors, some all black and white, some a burst of rainbow.

"Oh, no need, I already know who you are," Hattie says, pulling me out of my admiration. She's chewing, a smile on her face when I look toward her.

"What?" My heartbeat is in my ears, my face starting to burn as I wonder what her—boss? Coworker? Oh God, what if he's her *boyfriend*—told her about me.

Immediately, I prepare myself to tell her my side of the chaotic mess. A lifetime of damage control has taught me to act quickly. I need to tell her what happened, that it was all a terrible misunderstanding and I'd love to apologize and introduce myself properly, that—

"Mayor Turner's daughter, right?"

Oh.

Of course.

Of course, that's how she knows me. That's how everyone knows me.

And for a split second, I wonder if I'll ever be known as anything else or if I'll always be doomed to be Mayor Turner's oldest daughter.

Strange how moments ago, I was worried I'd be remembered for some unrelated, embarrassing incident, and now, that sounds almost preferable to what I've always been known as.

Strange how just a year ago, I don't think I would have felt that way.

"Quite the zoo you had there yesterday," she says, wiping her mouth with a pretty white napkin stamped with my logo in pink. "But I can see why. This cupcake is freaking amazing!" I smile.

This I can do. Talking about baked goods and receiving compliments on them? I can do that.

"Thank you. Yeah, it was . . . a bit much."

"It was cool—all those reporters, your dad, the ribbon cutting. That shit's impressive!" She moves to the reception desk, putting both hands to it and lifting herself up on the desk, kicking her feet that are encased in a pair of clunky Doc Martens like she's a kid sitting on the ledge of a jungle gym instead of a heavily tattooed badass.

This woman is a conundrum.

"So you're from here, obviously. You've got your dad and a sister, right? I think?"

"Yeah, Lilah."

"Your mom likes Ls," she says and laughs. Her laugh's a tinkling sweet thing that I can imagine would draw men to her like a dinner bell.

"Yeah, I guess."

"I'm Hattie; I can't remember if I said that already." I nod with a tight awkward smile because I'm now trying to figure out what to do next. Do I ask for Mr. Coleman or . . . "I work for Ben. I have for years. We started at the same shop together. I also do tattoos and all the piercings here." She winks like it's a come-on of some sort.

"Anyway, you're not here to talk to me." I blink. "You want to talk to Ben." Her eyes gleam like she's got some kind of master plan that only she knows.

"BENJAMIN!" Hattie shouts, the words reverberating up my spine and into my brain, ringing there, and that doubt keeps creeping in. "I heard you two already met, yeah?" My entire body burns with embarrassment as I try and decide what to say, how to scrap this entire interaction, when a deep voice calls from the other side of the shop.

"WHAT?!" She smiles, finishing a bite of a cookie.

This is . . . an interesting place. Don't they have, like, clients or something?

"Shops empty. We're all on break right now," she says to me like she can read my mind. "YOU HAVE A VISITOR!" she shouts back. If the tattoo shop is the same as my bakery, there shouldn't be that much room behind her—the businesses aren't huge. I can't imagine shouting is necessary.

"I'm on the phone!"

"Well, when you're done, come say hi!" she says and then smiles at me with a triumphant look. "He hates when I do that." I smile back, unsure of how to respond. "He hates a lot of things. He's like a really grumpy old man." My eyes widen in acknowledgment of that in a "no shit" kind of way.

"Yeah, I've noticed that." Now, why the fuck did I say that? Her eyes go wide with excitement.

"Ohhh, tea! Spill! He said you'd met but didn't give any deets! But that blush? Give it to me." She leans back on her hands, chewing and looking at me expectantly.

Normally, I don't "spill."

I was raised *never* to spill. It's been my job since I was young to keep all stories and secrets close to my chest.

But something about this woman makes me want to show my hand.

So . . . I do.

Kind of.

"I've met him."

"And?" I scrunch up my nose and try to decide just how much to tell this relative stranger,

Without even asking her to, New Lola takes over.

"We've actually met twice. The first time, he came into my bakery to tell me I was too loud, too early. He scared me, and I thought he was going to murder me because he broke into the back room." Her mouth drops open.

"No shit!? How!? Oh, God, did he pick the lock?"

Pick the lock!? It's alarming how she said that like it's something he would do.

"I ,uh, I left it unlocked."

"Baaaaabe," she says with a chin dip to me, like a big sister giving advice. "That's so unsafe!"

"Yeah, I know."

"So the second time?" I sigh.

This one is a bit more embarrassing.

"Last night. I came down to ask him to keep it down. The music in here? It was rattling my apartment. I'm usually pretty chill about that kind of thing, but with everything going on, I was exhausted. But he kind of got annoyed with me and . . ."

"He was a dick?" I cringe, not denying but not confirming. "Interesting. Ben is usually super chill, if not a little stick up his ass-y and broody as fuck."

"Yeah, I got that." I lean forward, feeling a bit more comfortable, and snag a sugar cookie off the tray. She smiles at me with approval.

"You know, it's not usually that loud here. We had an event going on."

"So he said," I say, taking a bit to give my mouth something to do other than continue talking and embarrassing myself. "We're usually only open late on weekends. But even then, doors close by 11:30. Even on the boardwalk, it's a bad idea to get a tattoo after 11:30." I smile because that makes sense. No one should make a decision that will stick with them for the rest of their life at midnight while on vacation. "Once a month during the summer, we do bulk tattoos. People choose from a sheet of 12 options, and we give them a quick, fun tattoo. The money goes to an arts charity that—" She doesn't get to finish because the room is suddenly darkened with a tumultuous presence.

Ben Coleman stands in the hallway, which I assume breaks off into booths for tattooing. Dark jeans, a fitted black tee, and a pair of black boots look way too good on him.

He should not be allowed to look that good.

"What are you doing here?" he asks, eyes running up and down me before moving to Hattie and then the tray of treats.

"I, uh . . ."

"You can't bring food into a tattoo shop. It's supposed to be a sterile environment," he says, eyes fixed not on the tray, but on the cookie that's still in my hand.

"Fuck off, Ben. Don't be a dick. Like you never eat in the shop? Never drink coffee?" She rolls her eyes. "Is this how he was when you guys met?" she asks, and my face burns.

"What does that mean?"

"I hear you were a dick to our new neighbor. *Breaking into her bakery?*"

"I didn't break in. It was open." Hattie stares at him with a "good try" look on her face. "You gossiping with my employee?" he asks, eyes to me.

"No, God, I—"

"Jesus, Ben! Why are you being like that?" Hattie asks, her brows furrowed in confusion. Ben rolls his eyes at her then looks at me.

"Do you have anything to say?" he asks, and although I have lots of things to say—indignation and anger and embarrassment all fighting to speak first—I can't get a single word to move past my lips.

"When my client gets in, send him back, yeah, Hat?" he asks, then he turns around and disappears without a single word to me.

Hattie watches him leave with wide, shocked eyes.

"What an asshole," she murmurs under her breath.

"I heard that!" he shouts back.

"Good! You're an asshole!" she shouts down the hall. Then she looks at me. "I'm so sorry. I don't know what's up his ass. Honestly, he has family pressure that's getting to him. Maybe that's what's going on?" She looks over her shoulder, and I see it now—in her face, there's concern.

She's never seen him act like that.

Hattie takes a deep breath, shakes her head, and turns back to me. When she meets my eyes, that happy smile is pasted on her face once again. "Don't worry about him. He'll get over himself. Next door has been empty for a while, he's not used to having to be personable."

I smile, feeling both rigid and fragile, and then I nod.

"Yeah, I'm sure we all just need to adjust. Anyway, I just wanted to, uh, introduce myself. And say hi. I should . . . you know. Get back to my place."

"For sure!" she says, hoping down from the desk. "Thank you so much for the treats! Let me know if you need anything or if Ben's a dick again. I'll kick his ass."

And then the strange woman pulls me in for a tight hug before I leave and head back to my bakery, still confused.

———

Making the few steps back to my bakery, I curse when I realize that once again, the lock on the front door didn't latch. Knowing that Brad, the landlord, probably won't give a shit, I add "google how to fix a lock" to my impossibly long to-do list.

Before I flip the "Open" sign, I run to the back, use the bathroom, and throw a couple of trays of dough into the ovens before starting a coffee for myself.

Looking back, the next minutes go in slow motion, like one of those horror movies where you know that someone's life is about to be turned upside down.

Because as I walk up to the front door, I see a small white square on the "Open" side of the sign that's still facing inward.

One of my napkins, the swirling pink logo in the corner.

It's stuck to the sign with one of the round logo stickers I use to seal to-go bags and boxes, thick black writing covering the expanse of the white.

And with the words, I'm transported back one year.

Words that read: *Call me. - Johnny.*

Long, torturous minutes pass before I move to take action. Slipping my phone from my apron pocket, my hands shake as I hold it in front of me, trying and failing to open the camera app.

I take a deep, centering breath, and on the third try, my finger lands on the right icon, opening the camera while I snap a picture. Then shaking hands reach forward, grabbing the napkin and ripping it off before I stuff it into my apron pocket. As I do, a couple with a small child approaches the front door. The mother's eyebrows come together in confusion before she mouths, "Are you open?"

I want to say, "No. I'm having a giant crisis of faith and need to demand my father do *something*," but I can't. It's only my second day open, and if I want this business to succeed in any context beyond being the mayor's daughter, I need to put in the work—for myself.

So instead, I nod, putting on my customer service slash politician's daughter smile, and welcome in my customers, flipping the sign to open as I do.

And as I walk to the counter, the little girl chattering about sprinkles and frosting, I type out a quick text to my father, attaching the image to the note.

Me: Fix this.

And though I go on with my day, shaken to the core but burying it in sugar and smiles, I never stop looking at the door, terrified of who will come in.

And I never stop looking at my phone, waiting for the reply that never comes.

EIGHT

-Lola-

ONE YEAR AGO, I cut my father off.

Cut off isn't necessarily the right word, really.

One year ago, the trust my mother left me ran dry, and by default, my father was cut off.

It was an hour after Johnny called me that first time, an hour after Johnny told me that my dad had gotten in too deep. He'd made a bet he couldn't pay. And when the Carluccios required payment, my dear father told them to ask me.

Told them that I could settle his debt.

His daughter.

He told one of the biggest crime families in New Jersey to go to his *daughter* to secure payment for his gambling debt.

That was the wake-up call.

Because there are a lot of things you can forgive when it comes to family. And you can forgive a lot more when illness shows you just how precious and fragile life is, how precious your family is.

But selling out your own child to dig you out of your mistakes?

No. I couldn't forgive him for that.

"Lola, it's just this once. I promise," he'd said. But that's also something I'd heard so many times before. It had started slow, asking for small amounts here and there. He even asked Sam once or twice, and we'd talked about it, trying to come up with a plan. Sam never knew the whole story, but he was aware of how my father coped after Mom. While I was handling the financial end, keeping things settled, Sam had been keeping an ear out on the political side to help keep me abreast of anything that my father might not share that the press might not know of.

When my mother passed slowly and painfully from breast cancer at a relatively young age, my dad dove deep into his work, just like my mom anticipated. I know we both made promises to her in those last few days. Promises I did everything in my power to keep.

But something in me snapped that day. Keeping a promise you made to a dying parent is one thing, but it's different when it's leading you to empty your trust. To drive down to Raceway Park at 11:00 on a Friday to settle a debt that was made behind closed doors.

Things change when you're getting calls from mobsters and they're telling you that your own father told them you'd settle his debt.

I realized then I had become a sure thing for my father. At some point, I had changed from his daughter, whom he was ashamed to ask for help, to a security net he relied on.

The night I got that call, I called my father.

I think a part of me wanted him to be surprised. Or confused. Or embarrassed.

"I got a call, Dad," I'd said.

He didn't sound surprised.

Or confused. Or embarrassed.

He'd sighed. I remember that sigh, a bone-deep, exhausted sigh.

"It was someone from the Carluccios," I continued on. He didn't see that coming, though. "They called me directly, Dad."

When silence hit the line, I realized then he knew. Even if

Johnny had said my father told him to contact me for reimbursement, I held on hope that he'd have that shock. That confusion.

There was just acceptance.

A detached sort of acceptance.

With his acceptance came my own pure form of frustration.

Rage came next.

Frustration and rage.

But those feelings were both tinged in the same type of disappointment I'd been fighting off for years, telling myself it wasn't greed or addiction but grief.

The next night we sat in my father's dining room, the same house my sister and I were brought home from the hospital and raised in, the same dining room our mother served us dinners in, the same house she took her last breaths in, having been released on hospice to spend her final days in the comfort of her home.

It was like her ghost was watching over the proceedings, some unseen judge we knew we'd all have to answer to eventually.

And truth be told, I don't think either of us thought we were doing the right thing in her eyes—not Dad with his thirst for power and undeniable addiction, and not me, with my inability to keep the promise I made her, with my enabling of his problems.

Keep your dad clear, Lola. I need you to promise that you'll help him. He'll be lost without me. I hate putting this on you, but promise me you'll help him.

And keep Lilah safe.

That day I wondered if I misunderstood her words—maybe she wasn't telling me to help him keep things under wraps but to help him learn to fight his demons without her. Maybe all this time, she was sitting in heaven, shaking her head with disappointment that I wasn't doing right by her.

Regardless, that night we sat there in silence, the help having left long before, cold dinners untouched.

"I'm done," I'd said, shattering the silence. And I meant it. "I don't have the money, Dad. I don't."

"What about what Mom left you?" he'd asked, asking about the trust my mother left Lilah and me. My stomach churned, the knowledge that he used my trust as his backup plan burning deep.

Not Lilah's.

Mine.

The sweet, appeasing oldest daughter.

Lilah was there to be pretty and smile and be mysterious, never to make much of a splash.

Hide your sister from them, my mom had said.

I was there to make everything right. To fill in the gaps.

I was the disposable one.

"There's nothing left, Dad," I had said, sick with the knowledge that the financial security my mom thought she was leaving me was just security for him.

He sighed.

I remember that part the most. The sigh was disappointment. He was disappointed in that turn of events. It's a sound that keeps me up at night, echoing in the dark as I try and decode it, try to assign different meanings to it. Meanings that make the situation look better than what it is.

Most parents sigh when their kids spend their money frivolously.

Mine sighed because he spent *mine* frivolously and there wasn't any left.

I remember thinking that was kind of funny, in an ironic kind of way.

"Dad. The *Carluccios* reached out to *me.* Asked me to pay. They told me you told them I'd cover it."

"It's just a small—"

"It's the fucking *Carluccios,* Dad."

"Lola, I'm your father. Don't you—"

"Then fucking *act like it!*" I had roared. It took my father aback, the normally reserved and conceding Lola snapping. "You want to be treated like a father, step up and be one! I'm done with this shit. I knew that after Mom died, you'd need some leniency. I gave it to you.

I gave it *all* to you! You got in deep, and I helped you stay above water. We did that because *you're all we have left, Dad.* And because it's what Mom would have wanted." I paused a beat before I laid that last dig, the final blow to my dad's soul. "This isn't what mom would have wanted. Not you, not what I'm dealing with, and sure as fuck not what Lilah could be facing. The Carluccios, Dad? Seriously?" That one hit, I saw it. The strike.

"Your mother—"

"Grandpa had the ties to the Carluccios. She cut them. She loved Gramps to hell and back but cut those ties when he got in too deep." That's true. The reason Dad would even deign to go to the Carluccios is that there was a time when Andre Santino, my mother's father and a politician in his own right, was looking to build ties with Carmello Sr., the head of the Carluccio family, before his son, Carmello Jr., took over.

He tried to align the family through marriage, offering up his only daughter to Carmello Jr.

It's funny how history repeats itself that way, isn't it? A woman growing up in twisted politics, marrying to get away from it, then winding up right there again, leaving her daughter to that legacy.

When Mom refused to marry into the Carluccios, instead marrying the unknown political science major she met, her family disowned her, cutting ties.

But family ties like that? They don't just break because you will it to happen.

The Carluccios were always a line in the sand for Mom—she'd tolerate a lot, but not that. Not them. It's the true reason Dad getting involved with them was a stab in the back to our mother's memory.

"Lola bear," he'd said. An ice pick hit my stomach at the rarely used nickname. "This once. Please. And then I won't bother you." I sat there, thinking of the small savings I had. "It's what your mom would have wanted."

Looking back now, those words gut me. How fucking manipulative they were, how rehearsed and well thought out.

He knew.

He must have known, then, the promise I made to my mother on her deathbed. Knew and was saving the knowledge for a rainy day.

I still don't know if it was his addiction speaking, that greed he couldn't control, or if he truly never valued me more than as a money source.

That's the part that hurts the most.

New Lola, the one I hadn't met yet, had opened her mouth to argue, face going red with anger and rage, but I spoke before she could jump to my defense. And when I did, my voice—it didn't sound like mine. It was tired, defeated.

Disappointed.

"This is the last time. I have nothing left, Dad. It happens again and you're on your own. Don't ask. I'm *done.*"

That night I went to the bank, emptying the remains of my trust and dipping into my own savings, and drove an hour to meet with Johnny Vitale, who took the money with a strangely disappointing air to him.

It was also the night I decided I was done.

My wake-up call.

Something in my voice that day had to have been clear because he had agreed, and once I sent him a text telling him it was all done, he never asked for more. Never.

I never would figure out if it was the shame of knowing he and he alone had depleted my trust or that he genuinely knew I didn't have the money.

But he never asked again, and I figured that he kept his word, his promise.

Stupid of me, I know, to assume that was it. That he changed without much more than a single push. I let my hope hang on his promises, hollow as I could now see they were. But anyone who has ever loved an addict can tell you that the promises are always there.

It's the follow-through that isn't.

NINE

-Ben-

When I walk around to the front of the store, having spent the entire day avoiding my coworker, Hattie stares at me. I can always tell when Hattie has something she wants to talk about, especially if she's going to tease me about it. It's her specialty, after all.

So much so, I'm pretty sure Tanner enjoys coming down to visit not to see me but to see my assistant and have a partner in crime when it comes to ragging on my ass.

I don't have a sister, but I'm pretty sure if I had had one, this is exactly what it would have been like. Tanner and Hattie against me all day, every day.

I put down the cookie I'd been inspecting, resisting the temptation like if I bit in and enjoyed it, I'd have to confess that I'm an asshole.

Hattie's glare turns into a smile.

Fuck.

I know that fucking smile.

"New girl is hot," she says, her smile growing.

Jesus Christ.

One plate of cookies and that woman brewed up a pot of drama that I'm going to be facing for weeks.

Fucking great.

Trouble. That's what Lola Turner is. It's written all over her.

"Then you should fuck her," I say, picking up a pink cupcake out of the box on the table, trying to avoid her eyes. I want this conversation to end as soon as humanly possible.

The cupcake looks like Lola in food form. Sweet and pink and definitely holding the potential to rot your fucking teeth out.

See? Trouble.

That's all I see when I look at her.

She might be sweet smiles with a thick ass and confections everyone is raving about, but I see it in her eyes. There's trouble in them. And I don't want any reason to get caught up in it.

"Maybe I will," Hattie says, snatching the cupcake out of my fingers.

Frustration and anger roll through me.

It's because she stole your food. Definitely not because of the thought of Hattie fucking the hot baker next door.

"I don't think you're her type, Hat." Now, why did I say that? Why do I care what type Lola is? Why do I assume even to know that information?

"Oh, do you know a lot about her type, Coleman?" Her smile grows, red lips thinning around white teeth.

"Fuck off."

"Ohhh, testy. Why so testy?" Goddammit. I knew this would happen. I took the bait, and now I'm going down.

"She's annoying," I say.

I told Hattie about the first time we met, coming downstairs because I thought we were being robbed, and she knows about me meeting her in the hall last night, cookies in hand.

I conveniently left out that I might have been more of a douche than necessary.

"Last night she was standing in the hall in tiny pajamas holding cookies, waiting for me. I hope she's not one of those desperate chicks, trying to get into my pants."

"Would that be so bad?" Part of me can't think of a single thing worse than fucking the hot—*no, not hot, annoying*—baker next door. Another part of me . . .

"You don't shit where you live, Hat," I say.

"I'm suggesting you *eat where you live*," Hattie says, her devious smile growing even more.

I throw a crumpled-up napkin, hitting her square in the forehead. "You're fucked up."

"And you need to get laid."

"I'm busy."

"You're grumpy." Not this shit again.

"I'm always grumpy, according to you."

"Yeah, but you're grumpier when you're not getting pussy regularly."

"Aren't you all feminist, Hattie? Shouldn't you be against my fucking women just to put me in a good mood?" She rolls her eyes.

"I'm Hattie-ist. If you banging the cute girl next door makes you less of a pain in my ass, I'll take it. Also, I never said you just have to fuck and chuck her. You're not *that* much of a scumbag."

"But I'm a scumbag?"

"I mean, if the shoe fits, babe." She stares at me, but it's not the same look as before. It's her reading me, trying to decode me, to understand whatever she decides I'm not saying out loud. "Why don't you like her?"

"What?"

"The new neighbor. Why don't you like her? She said you were a dick to her when you guys met."

"She's gossiping about me?"

"No, you dumb ass. She just said your first meeting didn't go well." Her eyes stay on me, the look nearly suffocating. "Why don't you like her?" I don't say anything. "She looks sweet."

"She looks like trouble."

"You could use a little bit of trouble."

"Not her kind." Hattie's eyebrows come together.

"You think she's trouble?" I sigh.

"Who knows. But you know the whispers of Turner. Trouble." She opens her mouth to argue, probably to say something about how we don't know her, or that whispers mean nothing, or some other kind of optimistic view that I don't have the time for. Instead, I continue on, spilling it all. "Plus, a girl like her? Comes from money, had everything given to her." She's not buying it.

"She looks like she works hard, Ben. I've seen her there over the last month, fixing shit up, doing it all herself."

"Her daddy definitely bankrolled that place. What does she know about starting a business from scratch? It was basically handed to her, including a built-in adoring fan base from her father."

"That bothers you, doesn't it?" I don't answer. "Why are you so bitter about it?"

"Because I had to work my ass off here."

"But you didn't have to. You chose that." I stop talking, knowing she's right. I didn't have to start Coleman Ink from scratch. I had the family construction company in my grasp, ready to be handed over as soon as I wanted. But I turned it down. Turned it down and became the world's biggest disappointment in my father's eyes.

I shake my head, trying to move that thought out of my mind. This is not the time for a pity party.

"That's not fair. I still did this all by myself."

"I'm just saying, just because you think she was handed every-thing doesn't mean she *was*. You know better than anyone that what you see isn't always what you get."

And with those words reverberating in my mind, tinging my actions with guilt, Hattie stands up. "Just . . . don't be a dick, okay? You don't know her life."

And then she's out the door and I'm stuck with my thoughts and a tray of dessert that looks way too fucking good.

TEN

-Lola-

It's been a week since the opening.

A week since I was caught in my pajamas, holding a tray of treats and trying to win over my noisy neighbor with whom I got off on the wrong foot.

A week since he broke into my bakery at 7 a.m. and yelled at me wearing nothing but his underwear and holding a baseball bat.

A week since the note.

A week since my dad said he had it handled, a text that came close to midnight.

And despite the insane start to my new business, things have quieted down. Business has slowed in a predictable but profitable way, and more bulk catering orders have come in, which has been an exciting turn of events.

I haven't heard anything from my dad or Johnny, and Sam said he hasn't heard any more whispers.

And finally, as Hattie promised, there were no late nights with loud music. I don't know whether that's because she yelled at her boss for being so loud, as she said she would, or because there isn't a lot of noise on any given day. I don't know, but either way, I'm grateful.

Without the loud music, I sleep surprisingly well in this little apartment. Maybe I was always a light sleeper because I never had a place of my own.

It's also been quiet because I've made my own efforts to keep my noise level lowered in the mornings. The bakery opens at eight, but I've been making batters and doughs that can be made ahead of time and baking cookies right as I'm opening. My nights have been late, as I've been staying up to make things that can be baked the night before, like muffins, croissants, and scones.

Once I am in my kitchen baking in the morning, I make an effort to be conscious of how loud I am. My music stays limited to my headphones, and I try to keep the pan clanging and the mixer whirring to a minimum. It helps that I can also refill the cases during the day since the counter opens right to the kitchen, meaning customers can see me flounce from one end of the bakery to the next in between filling orders.

It's not ideal, but it's the least I can do to be neighborly. Granted, there have still been a few times—twice, to be exact—where a deep voice has yelled in the hall to keep it down. Each time I rolled my eyes but tried a bit harder to be quiet.

The neighbor situation might not be ideal, but I love this location with the perfect amount of foot traffic it brings in. My business is already thriving, and it doesn't seem to be just because I'm Shane Turner's daughter keeping her mother's memory alive. The town has noticed I'm good at what I do, and people keep returning because my food is damn delicious.

It's been interesting to feel that success, a success that feels like mine and mine alone.

I'm pretty sure, though, that my favorite day of the week is going to be Friday. I've decided Fridays will be the day I open later, meaning I can have a little more time for *myself*.

This summer, Friday mornings are going to be for walking down the boardwalk and enjoying the warm air. Grabbing an iced latte at the cute little coffee and smoothie stand before walking back and getting to work.

Do I have coffee at home? Yes.

Do I *sell* coffee at the bakery?

Also, yes.

Do I have the money to spend on frivolous things like coffee when I just opened a brand new business?

No.

Am I going to make it my new routine anyway because I need to start living for *myself* and doing the things that make *Lola* happy?

Yes. Yes, I am.

That's what I'm doing now: my hair tied back into my normal braids, a pink "Libby's" tank on, and another pair of black bike shorts as I walk back from the coffee stand with my coffee. It's a hot morning, the cold plastic already sweating in my hand, but it feels good to be out.

My eyes are caught on a pair of seagulls fighting over a pile of bread, headphones in as I listen to music.

The music is loud.

So loud, I don't hear the voice behind me.

Not until it is so close it's nearly right behind me, forcing me to take out a headphone and turn to look behind me.

As I do, the back of my shoulder slams into a body that's coming at me.

A wet, sweaty body.

Someone on a bike flies past, yelling something my mind can't decode in my confusion and overstimulation.

And of course, because my life is a joke, it's the hand that's holding my coffee that goes flying.

"What the—?" I pull out my other headphone and turn.

And there he fucking is.

Ben Coleman.

Fuckin' A.

A shirtless, tanned, sweaty Ben Coleman is standing there, an arm out away from his body, said arm dripping in coffee.

The sun plays on his pecs, glistening with sweat and the light dusting of hair, adding shadows and highlights to tattoos that weren't meant to be there.

I shouldn't be looking, gawking, really, but . . .

I can't stop.

"What the fuck?" his angry voice asks in a gruff tone that knocks me from my daydream.

Coffee is also dripping down my arm that's held away from my body, the position mirroring his own, but once my eyes stop hyperfocusing on muscles and sweat and *man*, I see most of the coffee landed in a puddle at our feet, painting the boards of the boardwalk with creamy, brown goodness. It won't take long to dry up and become a sticky mess.

"My coffee!" I shout, staring at the mess, the plastic cup crushed in my hand. It's like watching the potential of a good day drip between cracks, forever lost to the sand below.

"My *shorts*," he says, and my eyes dip down without my permission to see low-slung basketball shorts which are soaking wet at the crotch.

And *clinging*.

Clinging somewhere my eyes definitely should not be.

Not even a bit.

Oh God, I can't look away, though. Fuck!

It's not *unimpressive*.

Clearly, I've been caught staring, though, and when he speaks, it knocks me from my very inappropriate daydream.

"See something you like?" The words are amused and annoyed, which seems to be his specialty when he's talking to me. I wonder if he talks to Hattie that way, or his clients, or his *girlfriends*.

I'm sure he has plenty.

"What?"

"Eyes are stuck to my dick, babe."

"No, they're not. I'm looking at my coffee that's spilled . . . every-where." I pause, looking at the ice cubes melting on the boards and regretting every choice I've made this morning.

This can't be a good sign for my day.

Everyone knows when you spend an entire day fantasizing about a special, sugar-filled, caffeine-packed drink that you're going to get as a treat, even though you very well could make coffee at home, your day hinges on it being perfect.

The reality of you having a good or bad day depends on whether that drink is good.

And this one was *good*.

Perfect amount of sweetener to espresso to milk ratio.

And I barely got *one sip in*.

"It's just a coffee," he says, breaking into my thoughts.

"I was looking forward to it. Haven't you ever had something that you've been looking forward to?" He looks at me like I'm an idiot.

Men.

"Don't you sell coffee?" I just stare at him, refusing to give in to his taunting. That's what this is, after all. Incessant and unnecessary taunting. I bet he was a bully when he was younger. Or maybe he was bullied and that's why he picks on everyone, teasing until they break.

Too bad for Ben, I'm done with letting other people break me.

"Guess it's not that good, then?" Except I'm finding it increas-ingly hard not to give in to his bullshit and fight him on *everything*.

"If you don't give yourself a tattoo, does that mean you're not a good tattoo artist?" I ask, raising an eyebrow at him. My arm with its empty cup drops to my side, and I feel the sticky liquid beginning to dry on my skin, pulling it taut and begging for me to wash it off. He stares at me.

"Fair point," he says, and it feels like a victory. I fight a smile.

It's not polite to brag about your accomplishments, after all.

No matter how bad you want to "nana nana boo boo" in an asshole's face. "I was calling your name. You almost got plowed by that asshole on a bike who wasn't paying attention to where he was going either."

"I had headphones in. I didn't hear you"

"That's not safe."

"I'm sorry?"

"It's not safe. A woman like you, alone, walking with headphones in. You should be aware of your surroundings."

"What do you mean, a woman like me?" He looks me up and down, taking in my outfit, stopping at places a man who might actually like me would stop, a small smirk on his face.

"Ditzy," he says, and my gut drops out from under me. "A privileged little girl who has lived in her daddy's shelter for so long, she can't see the danger around her."

A mix of humor and anger drips into my veins.

This man has to be kidding, right?

There is so much right there that he has no fucking clue about. So much that he has *so fucking wrong*.

I want to argue with him, tell him he's wrong, to spill my guts like this is some kind of competition to see who is more worthy of their business. Who is more capable, and who has been dealt a shittier hand.

But instead, clarity hits.

Because for the last week, every time I see this man, he glares at me like he thinks I'm the scum of the earth.

Like I don't *belong* here.

When I walk over to bring Hattie a cookie, always bringing something for her coworker because I'm a *nice fucking person*, he glares at me like I haven't showered in a week and the smell is permeating his air.

But it's not that he just doesn't like me. It's not that I made a shitty first impression.

No, Benjamin Coleman is like everyone I've ever met who recognized my last name. Everyone who read "Turner" and instantly thought the sweet, privileged, sheltered daughter of a politician. The daughter of the town's beloved mayor. Every award at school I *earned* because I worked my ass off, I'd hear the whispers—*it's because of her dad.*

I was selfish.

I was privileged.

I didn't appreciate what I had.

And yes, I'm not going to say that being me didn't come with its own outward privileges, the obvious ones that everyone else saw.

But it was what no one could see that made those assumptions burn through me like acid until Old Lola was incinerated, leaving New Lola to figure it out.

He hates me because of who he thinks I am.

"Is that why you hate me? You think I'm some kind of privileged brat? That I didn't earn this?" I put my hands on my hips, the dried, syrupy coffee making my hands stick to the material, but I don't feel it.

All I feel is rage at this man—this man who at this moment, represents everyone who underestimated me.

And it makes me furious.

I think I hate him.

His face goes slack.

I don't think he thought I'd respond. He thought I'd be a spoiled princess, shrivel up and cry to Daddy.

Too bad my daddy isn't good for anything but appearances and disappointment.

"That's it. God. You're fucking pathetic."

"Lola—"

"No. It's fine. You're not the first. You won't be the last. But just know this. Everything I've built?" I jab a thumb into my chest. "That business down there?" I point down the boardwalk where you can faintly make out my pink awning. "I worked just as hard as you did to get that." I jab my finger into his chest now. "Nothing was given to me. Ever. So think what you want, be an asshole. Make assumptions. Make my life hell and glare at me every time you see me, but I'm not going anywhere, Ben Coleman. So you'd better get used to seeing me."

And then I walk off.

And I have never felt more proud of myself ever in my life. Leaving Ben standing there, probably fuming and hating my every sinew as I walk away.

———

But the crazy part is, when I walk in through the backdoor of my bakery after coming back downstairs, a quick shower to rinse off and change my clothes, there's a coffee sitting on the metal countertop where I'm going to be rolling out sugar cookies in just a few minutes.

It's been sitting there for a bit, the condensation dripping down the sides and pooling at the bottom.

But it's not the coffee that catches my eye.

No, it's the note on thick notepaper with a fancy logo on top.

And on the note in thick black writing, it reads: *Sorry. -B*

At the top is the logo for Coleman Ink.

I grab the coffee, staring at it, confused.

Should I drink it?

It has the logo of the coffee shop I visited just an hour ago and looks the same . . .

But what if this is some kind of complex plan to kill me? To get me to stop waking him up first thing in the morning?

Whatever.

I need the caffeine.

And when I take a sip, it's my exact order.

ELEVEN

-Lola-

ON FRIDAY, Coleman Ink closes at 11:30.

I know this because Hattie told me.

That first Friday was a fluke, she'd said—bad timing for my move because it was an event. It happens once a month in the summer and, according to Hattie, they usually give the neighbors fair warning and even invite them to come by for drinks, food, and a tattoo if they want.

But today is Friday night, and my walls are shaking again.

They shouldn't be shaking.

I also shouldn't be awake.

This must be the omen my coffee disaster was warning me of. The reason my day would be shit.

I was shocked when I saw that coffee in my bakery and the apology note that accompanied it. And, to be fair, I had a pretty great day—a good flow of customers, selling out of nearly everything. When I went to make everything I needed for Saturday morning after close, as has been my routine not to wake Ben up too early and be a *kind fucking neighbor*, I had everything I needed. No need to run out and get anything I was out of, as tends to be my habit.

As I was washing my face and getting ready for bed, I was thinking that maybe it was a fluke, or maybe the second coffee was an anti-bad-day spell. Maybe the coffee spill was what we needed to break down the tension between us. Maybe my sticking up for myself showed him I'm not someone to fuck with. Maybe the coffee was a white flag.

But now it's after midnight and my walls are shaking, the sounds of The Killers playing, "All the Things that I've Done" reverberating in my brainstem.

And while I love the Killers and can vibe with them on any other day, fury is brewing inside of me.

That's because the sound isn't coming from the store.

No, no, my kind, sweet neighbor who replaced my coffee after causing me to spill it is blasting his music which I can only assume is intentionally from right across the hall.

It *has* to be on purpose.

I thought maybe we had some kind of truce. That when I called him out, figuring out why he hates my guts so much, he saw the error of his ways. Maybe he had felt *bad* for being such a dick once he realized I wasn't some kind of stuck-up princess, that I had worked just as hard to get to where I am as he has.

But I guess not.

And now I'm lying here, trying to figure out what to do next.

I can't just ignore this.

I need to go over there and ask him to quiet down.

Maybe . . . Maybe he doesn't realize how loud he is like I didn't that first morning. Since then, I've done my best to keep quiet.

Maybe he'll do the same.

Checking myself in the mirror (I refuse to be caught in my pajamas again), my exhausted face stares back at me. My long hair is in a messy bun, but not in the effortlessly chic way Lilah does it—in the way that screams "stressed the fuck out."

A pair of leggings that are worn out from too many washes but a new pair isn't quite in the budget.

A white tank.

Fine. This will do.

At least I'm covered up this time.

Breathing deep to center myself, I open the door, stepping out onto the landing. If I thought the noise was loud inside my apartment, it's about twice as loud here.

How is he not going deaf in there with that music blaring? I'm not saying I don't like loud music. I do. But so loud that it's creating permanent hearing damage? I'm good.

Still, I walk the three steps to his door and bang on it.

Hard.

He doesn't answer.

I put my ear to the door, trying to see if I can hear anything in there, a guest or a visitor.

Instead, I just get a sense of ringing in my ear, it going a bit numb in the process.

I was going to be civil.

I was going to knock politely and ask him kindly, but now New Lola is back in place, standing up for herself once again. I start to bang on the door, pounding like I'm a police officer with a warrant.

I throw in a kick for good measure because the feeling of the bass on his fancy security door, much nicer than my own, makes me even *more* annoyed.

There's no way this is an accident.

What the fuck did I do to this man to deserve this?

And finally, as I'm pounding, I hear the music go down slightly like he's trying to decide if the noise is outside or the music.

It's me, fuckface.

I'm still pounding as the door opens, and it takes everything not to keep knocking, pretending I don't notice, and punch the man in the face.

Instead, I put my fists on my hips, standing there and putting my bitchiest face on.

"What?" he asks like I'm a nuisance to *him*.

What? *What?*

The nerve of this fucking man. There is absolutely no way he doesn't realize why I'm here.

But still, I rein it in.

I won't win anything by being a bitch.

I take a deep breath, put on a sweet smile, and speak. "Hey, I just wanted to see if you could turn your music down. It's really, really loud and I'm trying to sleep." I smile, taking him in.

Does this man ever wear a shirt outside of work?

His torso is tanned and his chest tattooed, but his stomach isn't a brick. His build says he lives life and he enjoys it, but he also wants to be around to enjoy it. His arms are defined and strong, one arm hanging down at his side, the other leaning on the door jam. As my eyes travel down without my permission, there is a band of under-wear sticking out over a pair of loose shorts.

I force myself to look back up at assessing eyes, one eyebrow raised like he caught me taking him in, and the other has a smudge of something on it.

Charcoal, I realize. I remember having to use it in high school and how it would get everywhere.

"No," he says.

I stand there for a moment, confused.

Did he just say . . . no?

"I, uh—I—"

"Music stays up."

Silence.

Silence because I did not expect this response.

I expected, at worst, frustrated acceptance. But not a straight-out denial.

"I'm sorry, what?"

"I'm not turning the music down."

"Why not?"

"Because I like it." Again, I blink at him. "I need music when I draw," he says, lifting stained fingers to show me a small stick of charcoal.

"So use headphones."

"No."

"Why not?"

"I don't like them."

"Are you a fucking child?" I ask, nice Lola melting away.

"No, I'm a man. A man who does whatever the fuck I want. I've been living here for three years and never had an issue. You've been here for two weeks and it's been nothing but."

"Excuse me?"

"You heard me."

"I've been quiet in the mornings before I open up. I've been working late to get things done at night. *I've been a kind neighbor.* But my mornings are early and I need to be asleep by eleven."

"And when you open, it's as loud as fuck circus."

"It's my business!"

"It's loud."

"How is that my fault?!"

"The same way my playing music late is my fault."

"So you agree, you're at fault."

"No."

"Jesus, you're such an ass!"

"Then leave." I blink.

"Excuse me?"

"Then leave."

"Is that your plan? To drive me out?"

"It's not, but it sounds like a good one."

I think . . . I think I hate this man.

I don't know what on earth I did to deserve his hatred toward me, but I hate him right back.

It's then I decide that I'm not backing down. I'm not leaving.

He can blast his music, and he can be an ass.

Fine.

Because I was raised by a woman who took no shit and by a man who taught me to play the game until you win.

And I'll be damned if I don't win. I'll endure sleepless nights and a shitty neighbor, but I'll win in the end.

"Fine. Have your music," I say, turning my back to him and heading back to my apartment. I grab the key I brought out with me, putting it into the lock and turning when I hear his voice. I look over my shoulder and see he's still there, leaning in the doorway, but now he has a small smile on his stupid fucking face.

"What?"

"Sweet dreams, babe."

And with that, I flip him off, go into my apartment and slam the door behind me. The music returns to its previous volume, rattling my brain as I put headphones in my own ears to try and drown out the noise.

And when I finally start to drift off despite the pounding music, I'm comforted by the fact that before I lie down, I set an alarm for five a.m.

I guess I will be doing some early morning baking after all.

TWELVE

-Ben-

THERE's a dead cat whining that wakes me up.

I crack one eye open to look around, half asleep but unable to ignore the sound.

The sun is barely up, and my bedroom window overlooking the ocean glows an orangey pink.

Sunrise.

It's sunrise.

Noises join the whining noise.

Loud noises.

Banging and clanging, and for a quick moment, I reach for my baseball bat, sure it's an intruder, and my fingers meet thin air.

But then I realize it's not a cat dying under the boardwalk. It's music. Whiney fucking girl music blaring, and another voice scream-singing along.

Fucking Lola.

My eyes open fully, and my head moves to look at the clock.

Five thirty a.m.

Five fucking thirty in the Goddamn morning.

Is she out of her damn mind? I know she was up late, knocking on my door at midnight and telling me to turn my music down.

She has to be tired—that was just five hours ago.

Then it hits me.

This is retaliation.

Sweet Lola's form of retaliation is giving me a taste of my own medicine, *loud medicine*, at five on a Saturday.

Last night when she came down, asking for me to turn down my music, I should have agreed. Admittedly, there was no reason for it to be so loud—none at all. But fuck if some part of me wasn't sitting there in front of that damn fucking picture, charcoal in hand, enjoying the fact that I was keeping her up.

She's my own kind of torture.

Even when I'm in my zone, she's on my mind.

I'd be a liar if I even tried to deny that.

So when she knocked on my door, all polite and smiling, clearly trying to be a good human, I should have done the same. Smiled, apologized, and turned down my music.

But I didn't. Instead, all I could see was the image I didn't realize I was drawing on my desk, the image angering me.

Braids.

I was drawing two braids, not quite symmetrical, scattered ends tipping out of the folds where they didn't quite make it in, trailing down a back.

A naked back. Freckles and shoulder blades and the curve of a spine.

An image I've never seen in person, but my mind has mixed, envisioned, and dreamed up.

I was drawing Lola without even realizing it, and something about that, the fact that this woman who infuriates me infiltrated my creative space like that, made me angry at her.

I was an ass because apparently, that's all I can do with this woman. Rattle her cage. Push her until that sunshine exterior cracks and her true self shows—the take no shit, speak her mind side.

Because that's the part of her I just might like. The one she hides. I can't quite pin down why the spoiled, silver-spooned daughter of a mayor has so much venom inside of her, or why she coats it in sugar and spice and everything nice, but I like when it comes out, what it reveals.

Now, that temptation has me paying the price.

I throw a pillow over my head in an attempt to drown out the noise, and while I do, I try to think about why the fuck the old neighbors never bothered me. They weren't quiet by a long shot, and when their business was open, they kept similar hours to Lola.

Never did I care.

It rarely woke me up, and when it did, I either went out to run off my exhaustion or rolled over and went back to sleep.

And the few times they did ask me to turn down my music, I always did, apologizing and being more mindful.

But you didn't turn your music loud because you forgot she lived there, my mind reminds me. *You turned it up because you knew if you did, she'd come barging over.*

No. That's not true. Not at all.

Why the fuck would I want Lola to come over here, to bug the shit out of me?

No.

The sound creeps through the fluff of my pillow, and I release a tired groan.

Despite living on the boardwalk, I don't enjoy staying up super late. I'm usually knocked out not long after the shop closes, especially on weekends when the shop closes later. But last night, I closed and went up to my quiet apartment and just . . . couldn't. Knowing I needed to work on my auction piece, I sat at my desk and got lost.

But not before I put on my music.

Fuck. Am I an asshole?

I hear a clang, what sounds like a baking sheet falling from 8 feet off the ground, and decide no. I'm not an asshole.

The music last night was warranted, especially if she's going to do this shit.

My legs swing out of my bed, forcing me to stand on the wood laminate floors that I hate almost as much as I hate waking up before ten. *Almost.*

My ancestors would cringe at the idea of my living in a shitty apartment without the luxury of hand-sanded wood floors and carved railing posts and huge open windows that allow for the perfect amount of natural light.

Sorry, Great-grandpa. That life wasn't meant for me.

My eyes lock on the shorts sitting in the corner where I kicked them before falling into bed last night. My feet slip into the old Vans with the heels caved in from using them as slip-ons. My hand reaches for the front door, slamming it behind me as I walk out and jog down the stairs joining our apartments and businesses.

Then I knock.

Nothing. Possibly an increase in clanging.

"Lola! Open the door!" I shout over the noise.

I know she hears me. While I replaced the doors to the shop and my apartment not long after moving with a more durable, safer, and sound-resistant style, the previous tenants did not. There are old, cheap doors on both the bakery and Lola's apartment.

A part of me thought about that when I realized a pretty woman had moved in. How I should offer—insist, even—to help her out, give her a safer place.

But when I knock and she ignores me again, I decide I'm glad I didn't.

Because this time, she actually locked the door.

But I also know this is a cheap lock and that my pick kit upstairs will do the trick. I run up to grab it, suddenly more awake than I've ever been this early in the morning.

Then I proceed to quickly work on getting past the simple lock.

She needs to replace this door. It's not safe, a door this easy to pick. But right now, as I feel the lock click and turn the handle pushing it into the room where she stands, I'm happy she hasn't upgraded.

"What the fuck?" she shouts, turning to look at me.

She's kind of cute. A look of outrage covers her face, wide green eyes looking at me. Her blonde hair with that hint of red is in those two braids, flour on her cheek, the mixer going.

Cute.

No, Ben. Not cute. Annoying as fuck.

My first plan of attack is the noise.

I move over to where her music is playing and slam the power button until quiet blankets the room.

"What are you doing?"

"You gotta fuckin' keep it down." My words are calm as I cross my arms on my chest and stare at her. There's a cookie sheet lying on the ground and fuck. I wasn't wrong. She definitely dropped it on purpose.

When her eyes drift to the sheet and meet mine, just a fraction of guilt there, I nearly smile at the confirmation.

Because she might be annoying, but it's admirable the level of payback she's gone to.

"Are you kidding me?" she asks.

"I can't sleep." Lola gives me a look that, even though I haven't been in her presence that much or for that long, I know means something along the lines of "You've got to be fucking kidding me, you fucking asshole." Mostly because she gives it to me every time I'm in her presence.

That, too, makes me fight a smile.

Now her arms are crossing her chest, lifting her small tits so the tops show in the scoop of her tee.

"Oh, like you cared last night when I said the exact same thing?" She's not wrong. I won't admit it, though.

"It's five on a Saturday morning. I didn't go to sleep until after one."

"Oh, trust me, I know. You kept me up too."

"Aren't you tired, then? Why aren't you fucking asleep?"

"Because I have a *fucking business to run*, Ben."

"You've been quiet this week, in the mornings."

"Because I was *trying to be fucking considerate!* I felt bad, you being woken up that first time! I wanted to be a good fucking neighbor! But you still yelled at me. I'm sorry that my business is too loud for you. Really, I am. I'm sorry it doesn't work with your stupid fucking sleep schedule. But that's not *my fault*. I'm just trying to run a fucking business and live my damn life just like you. It's unfair that you expect me to cater to you because, what? You were here first? Fuck that. I pay for this location, same as you." Her face is going red, and her chest is heaving with anger.

I wonder for a moment if she also looks like that in other situations.

My cock twitches, the traitorous bastard.

"I tried to be a good neighbor. I did, really. But it's only been a week and you've spent every moment you can trying to make me hate being here. So fuck being a good neighbor. When I have the cash, I'll buy a more soundproof door." She pauses, looking at the pick in my hand. "And one with a fucking deadbolt, apparently." I can't fight the smile this time. "But believe it or not, I'm not made of money. I can't just get a new door in a space I don't own because my neighbor is a dick and a light sleeper. So fuck off, Ben. When you learn to respect others and treat them with kindness, you'll start receiving it back."

At that moment, it hits me.

I'm a dick.

I'm a huge fucking dick.

But, of course, not a single part of me is willing to admit this to her.

So instead, I watch her turn around and start scooping dough onto paper-lined sheets like I'm not even there.

"You need a man," I say, walking toward her back door. Exhaustion is creeping in now that I've gotten my fill of fucking with her. Okay, maybe more, now that I've gotten my ass handed to me by the little firecracker.

But I couldn't leave without getting in one last shot.

"Excuse me?" I hear her say, a metal clanking as I assume she drops the scoop onto the table. Target hit. I face her once more, crossing my arms on my chest and smirking.

I can tell that drives the anger up.

Lola is like one of those cartoons when it comes to emotions—you can read each and every one on her face at any given moment. Right now, I can almost see one of those cartoon thermometers on top of her head, the red creeping up the lines as her anger rises.

It's going to explode soon.

I bet she's fucking gorgeous when she explodes, lets go of the tight reins she has on being prim and proper and sweet as pie.

"I said, you need a man," I repeat, slower.

"Excuse me?" she says once again. That thermometer keeps climbing.

"I said you need. A fucking. Man in your life," I say, and fuck if I'm not grinning now, full-on stretching my face out because her face has gone from annoyed to full-blown anger. I take a step closer.

"Why would I need a man? And why is that any of your business? For all you know, I have someone in my life." I chuckle at her words and take a step closer. There's a foot between us now, and I can feel the heat radiating off her.

"If you had a man, I would know. The entire city of Ocean View would know, baby. If you had a man, no way you'd be taking your neighbor cookies in the middle of the night wearing a nightie."

THIRTEEN

-Lola-

I GULP at Ben's words, the confirmation I needed to realize he had, in fact, noticed my attire that first night. I think self-preservation had convinced me that he hadn't.

Unfortunately, he doesn't stop there.

"If you had a man, you wouldn't be doing everything yourself, lugging in flour and sugar and butter from a fucking hatchback, getting yourself fancy coffees as a treat on a Friday morning. You'd have someone to take care of you."

This hits differently.

It also makes me angry.

What the fuck does Ben know about men, about having someone in your life?

Here's the thing. Women are taught if they have a man in their life, they help do the heavy lifting. That if you have a man in your life, life gets *easier*.

But you know what? I call bullshit.

Because that's also supposed to be what your father does, putting his daughters first, taking care, protecting them.

Not dragging them down.

And you can't show me a single woman who doesn't know at least one other who had a man make her life living hell.

Men think that women need protection, like back in the day when we had to worry about tigers and bears in the wild. They shout it on news channels and social media, about how women wouldn't be able to handle life without men. Who would protect us, after all?

But these days, the only thing women really need protection from is *men.*

"The only person who takes care of me is *me.*" In a way, I confirm what he said about my not having a man, but I don't care. I tip my chin up, keeping it strong, my shoulders back, as my mom always did when reporters asked delicate questions about my dad.

Never let them see you waver, my girls, she would say to us. *Weak women show when they hit the target. Strong women always keep them guessing.*

Ben ignores my words, moving a few inches so we're close, nearly touching but not quite. Heat radiates in the small gap between us.

"Finally, if you had a man," Ben continues, his voice dipping an octave in a way that I can only see as ominous. He's ignoring what I said, that smile growing in preparation for what I can already tell will be the final blow. "You wouldn't be up early, baking for all the men of the boardwalk." My gut drops. I open my mouth to argue because there is no situation where I would end my dream for a fucking *man.* But he keeps talking, clarifying.

"No, if you had a man, he'd give you a reason to stay in that bed, sleep in late. Change your schedule because he can't get enough of you."

A tattooed hand raises, the tanned arm lifting it until it's at the side of my face, pushing a loose piece of hair back behind my ear. Where his fingers touch, the skin burns, burns in a way I want him to continue. As he moves the hair behind my ear, he runs his fingers down the length of my neck, where my breath is shallow and tense.

Then his thumb runs over the collarbone that's exposed by my shirt and apron.

A chill runs down my spine.

It's not one of anger or frustration, either.

Holy fuck, the look in that man's eyes.

I've read about that look.

It's *hunger*.

And not because he wants a cookie or cupcakes.

The air between us suddenly feels thick, charged in a way I've never felt.

"When was the last time you had a man take care of you, sweet girl?" he asks, and now he's so close, his bare chest brushing the thick canvas of my apron, but I can still feel it. I can feel every brush of him like there's nothing between us.

"What?"

"A man, baby. When was the last time you had one?"

It's been a long, long time.

And a part of me, maybe it's a part of New Lola I haven't discovered yet, can't help but think I would give anything right now to have this man break that streak.

"I want to kiss you, Lola," he says, and you'd think those words would shock me out of this daze.

I hate this man.

He's an ass.

He's a jerk.

He's everything bad about the male species.

But I really, really want him to kiss me.

So . . . I nod.

It's a short nod, quick and concise, nearly imperceptible. But he sees it.

I know he does because the next thing I know, his lips are on mine.

And we're kissing.

His lips are moving on mine, and mine are responding.

It is not sweet.

It is not chaste.

It is *wild*.

My hands move, wrapping his neck and moving into his hair that's mussed with sleep, holding him to me like I'm afraid he'll leave.

His hand moves, one arm wrapping around my waist and pulling me tight, the other going to my ass.

He groans as he does so, a sound that is nearly a resignation, like he'd come to realize a truth.

I understand the feeling.

Because I hate this man.

I hate him and his personality and his shitty attitude, but this kiss? This kiss feels *right*. His lips move against mine, soft and smooth, before his tongue dips into mine, demanding the access I eagerly grant.

A tongue pierced with warm metal enters my mouth, running along mine as he tastes me, his taste filling my mouth, overtaking my senses. The hand on my ass pulls me closer, and I feel his cock hardening against my belly.

Now I groan a low, breathy moan into his mouth.

And with that, my senses come back.

This has gone too far. Way too far.

New Lola wouldn't let a man come in, mess with her morning, and then *kiss* her, would she?

I stop the kiss, gently pushing on his chest, and still, he nips my lip a hair harder than necessary, like it's my penance for tempting him before his head moves back completely.

"Yeah, she feels it too," he says under his breath, voice strangely husky. He's talking to himself.

And then Ben steps back, letting me go, but not before he knows I'm stable on my feet. He turns around and leaves like he was never even there in the first place.

He leaves and I'm left standing there, staring at where he once stood, so confused as to what the fuck just happened.

FOURTEEN

-Ben-

WHEN I GET BACK to my place, I toss my shorts onto a chair as I walk to my bed before throwing myself into it again.

The bedsheets are cold.

Empty bedsheets.

They make me remember what I said to Lola, about her needing a man to keep her in bed.

And for the life of me, I can't figure out why I said that.

But as I lie there, staring at the ceiling and fuming because it seems her noise has actually increased since my visit, I can't help but think about how I can keep my bedsheets warm as the smell of butter and brown sugar wraps around me.

I eventually fall back asleep.

FIFTEEN

-Lola-

Hours later, as I'm trying to keep my eyes open with the small amount of sleep I'm running on, dark hair and a friendly smile walk in.

Hattie.

"Hey girl, you sleeping over there?" she asks and I stand from where I was resting my head in my hands on the counter. I cover my mouth as I yawn the kind of yawn that takes over my entire body before smiling at her.

"No, I'm just freaking exhausted," I say then smile. "What can I get ya? Sugar cookie with sprinkles?" I start reaching over to grab her usual.

"I would kill for a cookie," she says with a smile as I hand over the treat wrapped in a sheet of bakery paper. "You know . . ." A small smile forms on her lips. "Ben's looking rather exhausted this morning too."

I'm sure she's hoping for some scandal.

Instead, I look at her deadpanned and roll my eyes. "Good. He kept me up all fucking night with his music." Her brows come together, confused.

"What? Really? There wasn't an event last night."

"Oh, no, it was in his apartment." I roll my eyes then wonder if I should continue. She's quickly becoming a friend, but she also works for Ben . . . Oh, fuck it. I need someone to vent to about this crap. "I tried talking to him, knocking on his door and asking him to turn it down."

"And?" she presses when I hesitate.

"He refused."

"Oh my God, are you kidding me? What is his *deal*?" It feels good that this seems unjustified. "Seriously. He's not usually like this. Grumpy and kind of a turd? Yeah. A full-on douche bag? No way." She takes a bite of the cookie then dots her mouth with a napkin like a polite lady.

"Don't worry, I got him back." An eyebrow goes up and I sigh. It's only fair to air out my own misguided actions as well. "I set my alarm for five. I've been trying to get to the bakery later, be quieter. But this morning . . . well . . . my music was loud. And so was my work." I cringe because even though I feel it was warranted, it wasn't the kindest thing to do.

I mean, did I need to hold that cookie sheet over my head and slam it to the ground?

No.

But it sure did make me feel good in the moment.

Hattie surprises me by tipping her head back to the ceiling and laughing a deep, whole-chested laugh. It's the kind of laugh that makes you want to laugh too.

When she comes down from her laughing fit, she grabs a napkin and dabs at her eyes, her thick eye makeup magically staying put, and looks at me. "Oh my God, that's amazing. You're amazing. What happened?!" She looks around at the blissfully empty bakery before finding a chair and dragging it over to the counter, making herself comfortable. I sigh.

"He came downstairs."

"And?"

"We . . . argued. He picked my lock."

"He *broke into your bakery?!*" There's a mix of laughter and shock in her tone. "Again!?"

"Scared the shit out of me."

"Babe, you are *under his skin!*" There is a level of joy in her voice, in her statement, that I do not reciprocate.

"No, I don't think so," I say. Then I sigh. If I'm going to tell her, I might as well go whole hog. "I ran into him yesterday. Well. He ran into me. He was running on the boardwalk; I had my headphones in and couldn't hear him. Anyway, we argued because, apparently, that's all I can do in his presence." Another sigh. "I swear it feels like freaking middle school." Hattie's nose now scrunches in confusion.

"I just don't get it. Like, sure, he is so not a morning person, but that's not your fault that you have a bakery. What's his issue with you?" I sigh again.

"I don't . . . Look. I don't want to gossip. You guys are friends. We probably just need to acclimate, or—" I'm cut off again and she gasps.

Shit.

"There's something, isn't there? He said something. Jesus Christ, Ben. What did he say?" I sigh again. It seems like it's all I do these days. I bite my lip, trying to decide if I should tell her what happened.

Then I decide fuck it. If he can yell it on a crowded boardwalk, I can tell Hattie.

"He thinks I'm spoiled and privileged. That I didn't earn the bakery, that my father bankrolled it." Then I stumble over words trying to explain. "Which isn't true at all. I swear. I saved up, got a loan, all the normal things. The only help I got from my dad was a busy first day and a bit of name recognition. But that's it." She's staring at me, and she looks . . . confused. Shocked.

Disappointed.

"Are you kidding me?"

"I'm sorry, I shouldn't have—"

"I'm going to kick his ass. We had this talk—I thought he wasn't this big of an imbecile! Are you telling me he's being a dick because *he thinks you don't deserve your business?!*" She looks like she might actually go kick his ass. "That's insanity! Your baking is *amazing*. You can't help that your dad is the mayor. That's so not fair!" I shrug, unsure of what else to do.

"I'll talk to him."

"No. Please, don't. I don't . . . I don't want that. I don't want him thinking I'm gossiping about him. Again. That would make it worse." I'm panicking over the thought of her running to Ben to tell him what an ass he is.

She stares and I wonder how fucked I really am. Hattie doesn't seem to have any kind of filter whatsoever.

Panic rises in my throat.

This lease is for five years.

Five years.

I don't think I could handle five more years of this man hating me more than he already does.

"Alright," she says. "But let me know if he keeps it up. I'm serious. He might be my best friend, and I might work for him, but that won't stop me from beating his ass." I lift an eyebrow because she's about half the size of Ben. "Trust me, I could take him. He's scared of me."

"Hattie, *I'm* scared of you." She smiles.

"Good. I like it that way." I laugh and shake my head as she winks.

"So did you come over for a cookie? Or do you want a coffee?" I ask, turning to get something for her.

"No, no, you're good. I grabbed something this morning, and I can only do so much caffeine. Makes my hands shake." She wiggles her tattooed fingers in the air.

"Yeah, that would be bad for a tattoo artist."

"The real reason I came over is to let you know about the Coleman Ink auction coming up at the end of the summer." I quirk an eyebrow in interest. "It's a big thing, fancy dresses and a big silent auction, crazy amounts of food—"

"I can donate cookies or a cake if you want." Hattie's smile widens, appreciation and friendliness filling the room.

"You're a good one, Lola. I will definitely be reaching out for that. But we also need silent auction items. Nearly every business on the boardwalk participates and donates something, but since you're new, I figured I'd stop by, get my fill of sugar and butter, and I'd tackle the task of asking you for him."

"For him?"

"Ben is usually the one who does it. It's his cause, anyway."

"Cause?" I sound like a parrot.

But whenever my brain moves to the topic of Benjamin Coleman, it short circuits.

I keep telling myself it's with anger and frustration.

I'm starting to wonder how true that is as I remember the way my body felt when his thumb brushed my collarbone.

The way I felt when he kissed me.

Nope, nope, nope, Lola. We decided we would in no way remember that kiss, even if it was possibly the best one you'd had . . . ever.

"Ben raises money to fund scholarships for low-income kids who are graduating high school and going to college to pursue the arts. Music, art, dance, theater . . ."

"Tattoos?" Hattie smiles.

"That too. Last year we funded four full rides. He's hoping to get six this year."

"Wow! That's amazing." My mind wanders to all of the political fundraisers I've helped run over the years, filling in the role my mother left when she passed. Money that went to ads and lined the pockets of insiders and heavy hitters in the political scene.

It makes me sick to think Ben is doing good with the money he raises. More so when I think of how much I raised has been lost and wasted, trickled down to seedy people.

"No pressure, I swear, but I kind of wanted to see if your dad had anything fun he could offer. Something signed or a lunch with the mayor or some kind of exciting thing people could bid on." My gut drops.

Of course, it makes sense. At an auction in Ocean View, something like that could go for a lot of money.

"Feel free to tell me to go fuck myself. I'm nosy and ambitious, but I was always told you get nowhere without asking. So I'm asking but fully aware that it could be a no, and that won't affect my friendship with you."

She bites her lip, and it's kind of funny to see Hattie nervous because she always seems so confident and self-assured.

I guess we all have our faults.

And I want to tell her yes. I'll set something up with Dad to offer —lunch with the mayor or some fun town relic. But the problem is, I haven't talked to my dad since I sent him the image of the note Johnny left inside my shop a week ago.

And since you're probably wondering: no, that isn't normal for my dad. I know he's okay since he's still making press rounds and kissing babies and Sam hasn't called me to relay a tragedy and Lilah hasn't called with her own worries, but for all intents and purposes, he's ignoring me.

But still, that face? I can't let her down.

And it's for a good cause.

"Yeah. I'll see what I can get my dad to offer, Hat," I say, and she smiles, standing and clapping.

"You're the best, girl! Thank you so much!"

SIXTEEN

-Ben-

THE BACK ROOM between clients is usually my happy place, where I can avoid walk-ins and be alone with my mind and usually my sketch pad.

Except I don't trust my hands with a piece of paper and a pen right now. They seem to be fixated on braids and an eerily familiar collarbone. Delicate bone structure, wide hips, and long legs.

Fuck.

I'm so fucked, aren't I?

I'm even more fucked when Hattie pops her head in, that smile that means trouble on her lips, interrupting me from mindless scrolling.

"Hey, you."

"What do you want?" She rolls her eyes and puts her shoes on the table as she plops in a chair.

"God, you're such an ass. I came by to tell you that Lola's gonna contribute to the auction. Something from Libby's and she's going to try and see what she can get from her dad."

"The mayor?"

"You know about her father, huh?" Hattie says, that stupid fucking eyebrow up, implying that it somehow means more if I happen to know who the mayor of Ocean View is and his relation to my neighbor, even if on her opening day there was a whole charade and the man himself came to cut the ribbon.

"Everyone in Ocean View knows about Shane Turner, Hattie."

"Just interesting, is all." There's a pause and I know more is coming. Shit. "She also said you were up last night, loud as fuck."

"I couldn't sleep."

"And then you were down in her bakery this morning."

"She said that to you?" Why does the idea of Lola talking to Hattie about me both irritate and . . . please me?

"Said she felt bad, waking you up." I sigh because that's not right. It's not on her.

"I was a dick, kept her up, refused to turn my music down. Payback was valid." Hattie looks at me again, that smile coming back in.

"So, why did you?"

"Why did I what?"

"Don't play dumb." I would do anything in my power to avoid this conversation right now. "Why were you loud? Knowing it would keep her up?"

I don't say anything, wondering how much to reveal.

Hattie is one of my best friends.

We met when we were apprentices at the same shop for a few years before I opened up mine. She was the first person to join my team and is still the only full-time artist in-house.

But I'd much rather talk about this to an impartial person.

Or, anyone but nosy, pushy Hattie.

Still, the words spill.

"She drives me insane." Her smile grows. "She's spoiled as fuck. Probably had everything given to her. I've seen her type. Has no idea what it's like to build a business, how to take care of others."

"This is the second time you've said something like that to me. Are you sure about that?" Hattie asks, a strange look on her face. "That she's spoiled, had everything given to her?"

"Does that woman seem like she's faced an ounce of hardship in her life?" Hattie doesn't answer. She just keeps staring at me like she knows something I don't.

I don't want to hear what she says. I just know it.

Nothing good will come from that look.

"You know her mom died when she was 15?" My gut drops. I didn't. She must be around 30 now, and I didn't grow up in this town. "It was all over the news here, tragic story. The new mayor's wife, passing so quickly and so young. Lola helped with her younger sister and took the place of her mom the best she could. She helped her dad with his campaign, helped to keep him sane, from what I know." Her face is solemn, her lips turned up in a sad smile.

"How do you know that?"

"Unlike you, I've gotten to know our sweet neighbor in a way that isn't aggressive and douchey. I've, ya know, *talked to her*. She's sweet, Ben. Really. Not fake sweet, but genuine." I don't like this.

I don't like Hattie telling me what I've secretly worried was hidden behind our incessant arguing. She might fight back with me, but I don't think that's her nature. I don't think that's her first instinct, as shown by her trying to bring me cookies that first night as a peace offering and again the second day.

And each and every time I'm in her presence, I'm an asshole to her.

I can't help it. Why is that?

Because you refuse to get close to anyone you think has the possibility of disappointing you.

Hattie stares at me while I process her words, trying to make them fit into the puzzle I've created in my mind with the pieces of her I've already been given. "Anyway, she's going to donate, as I said."

"Great," I say in a murmur, mind still elsewhere.

"I think you should be the point of contact for her." Thankfully, this knocks me out of it.

"What? Why?"

"Babe, you don't pay me enough to manage an entire silent auction. I do more than I'm paid for as it is. I'm not your secretary."

"Bullshit, the only thing I ask you to do for this fundraiser is the shit you like doing. Going out and finessing businesses, guilting them into giving you shit. You love that," I say because it's true.

"Here's her number," she says, ignoring me and handing me a slip of paper. Ten numbers are written in a precise, feminine handwriting, pink ink scrawling *Lola* in loopy cursive at the top.

Without thinking about it too hard, without thinking about why I'm saving it instead of just tossing the card in my pile of crap, I save it into my phone, another piece clicking into my puzzle.

SEVENTEEN

-Lola-

I LOVE Sundays at the bakery, and so do my customers.

I mean, who doesn't want fresh muffins and scones and coffee first thing on a slow Sunday morning? Some come in and get giant boxes to bring back to families that haven't woken yet; others are couples coming for a treat and to watch the sunrise.

It might be my favorite work day of the week.

And since it's the day I open up earlier than the others, it's also the most exhausting and the reason I'm already contemplating adding on my first employee.

Last week I was sold out of nearly everything before noon. This week, I stayed up late baking muffins and prepping scones, scooping doughs and making sure my case would be full and I could start baking as soon as I hit the bakery in the morning.

But it's so chaotic here by nine, I'm wondering if I should plan to have someone working here by next week—that way one of us could continue to work on filling the case while the other helps customers and makes sure tables get cleared. The seeming success is already overwhelming me.

"You have a great day, okay?" I say to the father and daughter I'm handing a to-go bag to. They smile before walking off, and I turn my head to greet the next customer in line.

And then I see him. He's in a crisp white button-down that's undone at the top, opened to his chest to reveal a sprinkling of chest hair I'm sure is intentional. The cuffs of the dress shirt are rolled up to his elbows, the bottom tucked into perfectly pressed black slacks which end at shiny black dress shoes.

He looks incredibly out of place in my bakery with its bubble-gum pink and lavender touches everywhere.

He's even more out of place on the boardwalk.

You don't wear leather dress shoes to enjoy a day at the shore, where you'll be met with salt and sand.

No, he's here with a purpose.

He's here to talk to me.

Fucking, *fucking* Dad.

"Hey, Johnny. Nice to see you." He smiles wickedly, and for the first time since all of this started, I don't just feel uneasy.

I feel true, all-consuming fear.

That is not the smile of a man who understands that I did not get myself into this mess, that I am being burdened by the literal sins of my father.

This is the smile of a man who knows how this could end and although I might not enjoy it, he would.

Greatly.

Before I let that fear settle, though, I straighten my back.

When I signed the lease for this place with the money I was able to squirrel away, I promised it wouldn't be for nothing. If I was brave enough to start my own business, I needed to be brave enough to stand up for myself.

To end the cycle.

The old me was a pushover.

The old me was a people pleaser.

The old me sacrificed everything to make sure my dad was safe. That our family home was never in jeopardy. That my sister wouldn't be touched by the chaos like I promised my mother.

The new me is a business owner.

The new me puts herself first.

The new me doesn't let people's opinions of her change how she sees herself.

The new me is a badass.

Okay, so I'm still working on making that last part believable.

But a year ago, that first time Johnny came to me personally instead of to my dad, it was my wake-up call.

For years I'd been telling myself it would get better. That grieving looked different for everyone, and my mom hadn't asked me for much. I could do it. I could make this sacrifice.

But something happens when a mobster calls you and tells you your father told them you'd settle debts on his behalf.

Something snaps.

And no matter what I promised my mother or if she told me to keep the family settled and Lilah safe, I knew deep in my bones she wouldn't want that kind of life for me.

There was a reason she didn't opt for it for herself when she was offered, after all.

"Not bad, Lola. Nice place you've got here." I smile a tight, strained smile.

"Thanks. What can I get you?" I ask, reaching for the wax paper I use to grab treats from the bakery case.

Maybe I'm wrong.

Maybe he wants a muffin. Maybe he just got hungry on his way to go hassle some other poor soul and stopped into my little shop . . .

"I'm here to get those rainbow cookies we talked about." My stomach drops.

I don't have rainbow cookies.

I also am sure that he does not want *rainbow cookies*.

"I don't have that kind of . . . cookie. You know that."

"Talked to your dad. He said you did." I feel sick.

When I told my dad to *handle this* and didn't hear back, my dumbass assumed he had, in fact, handled this.

It seems he did not.

"My dad is wrong." My arms cross my chest, not in a power move to prove a point, but because I need that barrier. The way his eyes are on me and his lips are turned up in a smile . . . It has every alarm blaring.

"He said you'd say that. But he also said your bakery was . . . more than capable."

"I don't know what to tell you. Right now, I don't have that." I hate this game, but more so, I just want him out of here. "Can I get you something else in the meantime? Brownie? Chocolate chip cookie? Sprinkle cookie?" All I want is him *gone*. He looks me over, and I think he sees it. His eyes move around the full bakery and he nods.

"I'll take a chocolate chip." He smiles a shit-eating grin like there's some hidden meaning behind that as well, but I don't care. I move to the case, grabbing cookies and tossing a few into the bag, not checking to see how many, not making sure they don't crumble. I don't care. I want him out. Rolling the top of the bag down, I reach out, trying to hand them over.

"On the house." He moves, grabbing my wrist.

The grip isn't just firm.

It's a bruising grip, pain shooting through my arm with the action, and he doesn't let go.

Instead, he leans in.

"You gotta figure this out, *bellissima*. You don't want me here again."

I should tell him off.

I should draw attention to him.

I should tell him to fuck off and call the cops.

But I don't.

"Talk to my father, Johnny," I say, gently trying to pull my wrist out of his grip, but he just holds tighter, causing a small squeak to fall from my lips.

He just smiles before another hand comes over, grabbing the bag and taking a single step back.

It's interesting how he has the confidence to do this in a crowded, small bakery.

He's not scared of getting caught.

But I sure as fuck am scared.

"See you soon, Lola," he says, taking a step back as he unfolds the bag, picking a cookie out and taking a bite. "A great thing you've got going on here. Hope you can keep it strong."

Before I can argue, he turns his back. His dark suit jacket, so out of place in the sea of customers and vacationers, is out of my bakery, already walking down the boardwalk.

And despite having turned over a new leaf, despite deciding I'm the well-thought-out and all-knowing version of myself, New Lola has no fucking clue what to do.

And as I go through my day, I feel the throb of my wrist and watch the fair skin darken into a deep bruise.

This is bad.

EIGHTEEN

-Lola-

MY DAD DOESN'T ANSWER the text I send as soon as Johnny is out of my store or the three others I send him during the day.

He doesn't answer the call I make at noon when I find a moment of peace or the one I make right before closing.

He doesn't answer when I call to tell him I'm heading over.

That's why I'm now sitting outside of my childhood home, readying myself to go inside and figure out what the fuck is going on.

A year ago, I told my dad I was done, and nothing has touched me since.

Until that note in my bakery.

Until today, when a literal mobster came into my business, threatened me, and bruised me in a public, crowded space.

Old Lola would have let this be brushed under the rug and hoped to God that Dad figured it out.

New Lola says fuck that. She says that she's not letting the shitty actions of others impact her sleep, her business, her happiness, or her safety.

New Lola knows that when you sweep something under the rug, it's still there. Just because it's out of sight doesn't mean that you're out of the range of repercussions. You can still trip on a rock you hide under an ugly rug.

And when the rock is a debt to the Jersey Mob, it's better to face it sooner rather than later.

My feet move up a familiar walkway, noting my dad's car in the drive. He's home.

And as I walk up the three steps before reaching his front door, my dad opens it, standing with the light to his back, creating an illusion that almost replicated how I used to see him.

Some kind of awesome higher power. Just. A superhero. Undefeatable.

But the man beneath the glow is exhausted in a way I haven't seen since my mother was on her last days. Wrinkles and lines look deeper, the circles under his eyes are darker, his hair disheveled.

This is not the untouchable father I once thought I had.

This is a man full of errors.

A weak man.

It's strange to finally realize that about someone you once thought was invincible.

"Come on in. I made a plate for you," he says, putting his arm into the house to guide me in. He knew I was coming. He knew I wouldn't just shy away.

Good.

Ten minutes later, we're both sitting at the dining room table. It's just my dad and me staring at each other, dinners cooling quickly in front of us.

It's eerily similar to what happened a year ago, and part of me wonders if there will ever be a time when I can sit here again and eat a meal without remembering who my dad is.

Who he *really* is, beneath all of the pomp and circumstance.

"Are we going to talk about this?" I sit back in my chair and cross my arms. I'm not hungry anyway,

He sighs, running a hand through his hair, the same way he did when I was a kid and I'd spot him and Mom having arguments in hushed tones.

"It's no big deal, Lola."

"It's no big deal?" I say, and my voice is strangely far away, detached.

"It's not."

"Johnny Vitale came to my bakery, giving whispered threats to me in broad fucking daylight," I say.

"You're blowing this out of proportion, Lola. He didn't—"

"Dad, he gave me this!" I shout, lifting an arm to show the angry flesh, skin mottled beneath. It will look worse tomorrow. My skin is fair and always shows bruises brightly.

My dad's eyes lock on my battle wound, going wide.

"Lola, I—"

"He said I was to give him *money*."

"He—"

"And he said *you told him I was good for it!*" I say, shouting now because each time that part crosses my mind, each time I think about what that means, my body seems to float in a sea of chaos for a moment.

"But you—"

"I said I was done! I said I was out of this fucking shit." He blinks then looks to his plate, fork moving around peas like he's a petulant child who doesn't want to continue a conversation where he knows he's at fault.

"How much, Dad?" I ask, my voice strained.

I don't know if I want this answer.

He doesn't give it to me either way.

"Dad."

Still nothing, his face pointed downward. This has to be worse than I anticipated.

Fuck fuck fuck.

"How much, Dad!?" I shout, my voice hoarse.

"Seventy." His words are a whisper, quiet, and I have to wonder if they're also embarrassed. He's never shown that particular emotion before. It would be a novel change.

Still, I feel sick with the words, numbers flashing in my brain like a calculator showing a total as I process them.

"Seventy. *Seventy thousand dollars?!*" My voice cracks as it rises, the mere idea of such a large amount of money being essentially gone, of my father promising it to anyone sinking in, much less that I would fulfill that.

"It was a game."

"It's always a game!"

"I thought . . . I thought we'd be good for it. I never—"

He thought *I* would be good for it.

"Dad, I told you I have nothing left! Mom's trust is *gone*. What were you thinking? What were you—"

"You didn't have a problem opening the bakery." His words are tipped in acid, cruel and unnecessary. My stomach drops. My mouth drops. Shock filters through me, making me lightheaded, making the tips of my fingers feel numb. "You somehow had enough to start your bakery. That wasn't cheap, I'm sure." He says it like it's an accusation.

It's funny how most parents would find that to be an accomplishment. Mine finds it to be an unsavory trait.

"I took out loans, Dad! And I saved! And I worked my ass off! But all of that money is *in the bakery!* It's not just something I can give you to settle some debt with the fucking *mob!*"

"You can help your old man—" My voice goes cold. Cold and steady as I cut him off.

I am done.

New Lola comes back into my body, filling the holes and consuming whatever space Old Lola was still in.

Transition complete.

"My business is not there to become another source for you to dig yourself out of holes. I told you I was done. I'm living my life for me now. I deserve that much."

My feet find the ground, moving to push my chair back.

I'm ready to leave.

His next words are said with intent, sticking me to my chair with remorse and hurt and betrayal.

"Your mother would have wanted it." The intent is to gut me, to weaken me.

But instead, his words strengthen my resolve.

I wonder for a moment if he truly thinks that or if it's just a new tactic. A low blow he's never had to stoop to.

"No. No more of this. That's not true, Dad. The truth is, Mom would be ashamed of this. I have a bruise in the shape of Johnny Vitale's fingers on my wrist." My words are a slow staccato as I lift my arm to show him again, and at least that gets a reaction, a small softening in his eyes. "This is a bruise he gave me in open daylight in a busy bakery. He threatened me without a care in the world. Mom would never have wanted that. She wanted us to steer clear of them! And you know that's for *good reason, D—*" He cuts me off.

"They know about Lilah."

My gut drops.

"What?" *No, no, no.*

"Johnny definitely knows." Acid moves up my throat. "He knows, and lately, there have been talks. Strengthening family ties. He wants a seat at the table, I think. I'm afraid . . ." He swallows, looking somewhere past my head, avoiding my eyes. "I'm afraid that he's using this as his chance. Getting me in deep, more than you can handle, more than I can handle. Threatening you, and then going for her."

This is everything Mom didn't want.

Everything I have fought against.

I gave up 15 years of my life to avoid this moment.

And somehow, here we are.

Because my father is weak and susceptible and addicted to money and power.

To find a solution, though, I need to know what happened. I need to know everything.

I won't do it to help my dad, but I will do it for Lilah.

And once I know she's safe, I'm safe, we're out for good. Whether that means completely cutting ties or getting Dad the help he needs will be up to Dad.

"Dad . . . How—"

"I was set up." He looks defeated.

"What?" He continues to talk as if I didn't.

"I couldn't lose. There was no way, Lola."

"What was it?"

"Closed game. Poker, held by Paulie Carluccio." Fuckin' A. Paulie Carluccio is the grandson of Carmello, around my age, deep into the "family business" and rumored to be in the running for taking over when the time comes.

His father was the man my mother was to marry forty years ago.

"Fuck, Dad. What were you *thinking*!?"

"I'm serious. It was perfect. I was winning big, and then I wasn't. I was set up. They were planning it. They wanted the disposal ordinance passed in order to settle the debt, but I couldn't make it happen without questions. Now Johnny's asking for money he knows I don't have. But I swear, I was winning. It was a no-lose situation."

I snap.

"It's always no-lose! Until you *fucking lose, Dad!* And then your daughter is losing her entire trust to your bullshit to keep you clean, to keep your image clean!"

"I can't—"

"And now Lilah! It was *the one thing she asked for, Dad!* And you're fucking it up! What were you thinking?"

"Don't talk to me like that, Lola. I'm your father," he says, his voice angry in a way I've never heard.

I don't have a chance to register the shock that ripples through me, the shock that he's actually angry *at me*.

As if I'm not the one who had her entire sense of safety and privacy stripped away.

As if I haven't spent my entire life keeping Lilah safe because Mom asked me to and he fucked that up at a poker table.

Instead, I stand, my chair scraping against hardwood floors in a way that my mom would have yelled at me for if she were still here.

But she's not.

And as much as I don't want to admit it, this is just as much her fault as it is Dad's. As it is mine, for letting things go this far. Her secrets, her lies, and her inability to stand up to her husband are, in part, what got us here.

But we're here all the same.

I lean forward on the table, my finger pointing at my father.

"You need to fix this. I cannot fix this for you. You need to fix this and keep Lilah and me out of it." His mouth opens, but the rage has taken over.

New Lola has taken control, and she's not leaving any room for misinterpretation.

"Fix this or I'm gonna start talking." His face drains of color. "To your colleagues, to the press, to whoever will listen. Sam told me there are already doubts, so it wouldn't take much. But I'm telling you now, if I go down, you're coming with me, Dad. If something happens to Lilah, I will make sure that you crumble alongside us."

"Lola—"

"Goodbye, Dad. Call me when this is handled. Until then, do not contact me."

And then I leave, wondering if I just made a huge mistake by putting this in his hands.

NINETEEN

-Lola-

I don't sleep that night, instead going through everything I can think of to get myself out of this mess, to get Lilah out, and trying to figure out how I can stay out for good.

Since Mom died, I've felt alone.

I have Lilah, of course, but she's in the dark.

I have Sam, but he's too close to it. If he knew the whole story, he would cause a riot.

I can't talk to anyone else about any of this—the goal is always to protect the family.

But right now, I feel more alone than I ever have.

And when I'm putting the next batch of cookies in the oven the next morning, I can't help but wonder what I'm doing with my life.

This needs to end.

I need to figure out how.

There was once a time when I felt that if I went to Dad and told him straight up that I couldn't do this, that I couldn't protect him and the family anymore, he'd change.

But now we're here, where he's resentful that I built a business and won't use my own money to bail him out, angry that he's been cut off and setting me up to have to pay anyway.

So now I'm in the bakery, music blaring and trying to both wake myself up because of lack of sleep and simultaneously quiet the demons screaming in my mind. I should probably be a good neighbor, turn it down or use my headphones, but today?

Today I need the noise.

Today, my mental health is more important than neighbor relations.

And fuck, if he can't be courteous to me and my sleep needs, why should I be to his?

At seven fifteen, my phone buzzes, rattling the metal table I had it set on. I think about ignoring it, about letting it wait until later when my mind is less of a mess, but it could be Dad with a solution.

It could be Lilah needing help.

Right now, it could be any number of issues that are so far out of my control.

I check the stupid phone.

Unknown: Turn the music down.

My gut knows who this is—who else would be texting me early in the morning asking me to turn down music?

But still . . .

Me: Who is this?

Unknown: You often have random numbers asking you to turn off your music?

I roll my eyes.

To be fair, I asked for that one.

Unknown: It's Ben.

No shit, Sherlock.

Me: How'd you get my number?

Ben: You gave it to Hattie

Me: So?

Ben: So I have it now. Turn your music down.

Me: Fuck off. It's not even that early.

Ben: Turn the fucking music down.

Me: Get over it. These are my normal working hours. If you have a problem with it, you can go fuck yourself.

I smile to myself, scooping batter into muffin tins for the morning rush, when my phone buzzes in my apron pocket. I roll my eyes as I grab it out of the pocket.

A chill runs down my spine.

Ben: You keep up with that sassy mouth and I'll find a way to shut you up.

Me: I'd like to see you try.

Now, why the fuck would I say that?

I already have one asshole up my ass, trying to make my life hell. Why would I invite Ben to join in on that?

Normally, I don't even let shit like this phase me. I'm a born people pleaser. My entire life, I've been working to make myself a bit smaller to make others more comfortable. It's why I was always the sister who took care of the shit behind the scenes, making sure it didn't impact anything or anyone else.

It's why my mom trusted me with her secrets, with this responsibility.

This burden, my mind says. For weeks now, I've been slowly reframing and deconstructing my mom's words. Her demands, the impossible task she handed me. I've been reimagining what I once felt to be an honorable responsibility to uphold and seeing it for what it truly is.

An unfair burden.

Minutes after that last text, I hear knocking at the door.

For a split second, my gut goes sour, thinking it's my not-so-friendly, not-so-neighborhood bookie back after yesterday's issues.

"Lola, let me in," Ben says, fist pounding on the door.

A chill runs down my spine.

Why is he here?

Okay. That's a dumb question.

The better one is, is it because of the music and my refusal not to turn it down, or is it because of my taunt?

And even more—why do I hope it's the second one?

We've both avoiding each other since that first kiss, but I'd be a liar if I said I hadn't thought of it many, many times since it happened.

Shit.

Christ.

"Go away," I shout, continuing to fill up liners with blueberry muffin batter. It has a hint of lemon zest, and the entire bakery smells like citrus because of it.

He's silent for a moment, and I think maybe, just maybe, he's gone.

That I succeeded in getting him away.

Then the handle twists.

The fucking handle twists.

Jesus Christ, did I forget to lock that stupid door?!

I'm an idiot.

"You didn't lock your door *again?*" he asks, staring at me in the open door, fury in his eyes.

"I didn't expect my psycho neighbor to come barging in *again.*" Never mind the fact that he's done this *multiple times* already.

"It's hardly barging in if all I'm doing is *twisting the knob* and walking in. You don't even have a sign on the back saying not to come in." I've thought of this, especially after seeing a similar sign on his own door.

"Most people know not to come in a business door if it's closed. And you're the only one who has access to that door."

"The front door—is it locked?" he asks, and I don't answer because the truth is, I haven't gotten around to fixing that lock.

Unfortunately, I don't have to answer.

"It's not, is it?" I sigh, turning to the remote that controls my music and turning it down a hair, just enough to hear myself think while having a conversation with this painful fucking man.

"It doesn't always catch. I told Brad, but from what you tell me, he's not going to fix it. I've watched some videos, and I'm going to do it myself when I have a few hours." He looks . . . disappointed in me.

"There's a lot of scum in this world, babe. I know you live in your cushy tower with your Daddy keeping you safe, but learn this now—it'll save you lots of stress. People in the real world? They're shit."

If he only knew the truth. My truth.

"I'm not some kind of protected princess."

"Sure you aren't. You just had Daddy help you buy into a lease, buy your fancy equipment, help stock you, and then make sure it's a success with some sob story in the news about the town's beloved mayor's beloved oldest daughter opening a business in her mom's name."

It's almost funny that this is why he hates me with such a passion.

He thinks I'm privileged, that I haven't earned any of this.

I could be shocked, but truly, I'm not. I've faced this my entire life. Any success, any grain of accomplishment was always downplayed by those around me as if it weren't me who did it.

At least I understand in a strange way—I'm sure Ben came from nothing, built up his business from scratch, and worked extremely hard to have the success he has. And while I did the same, if not as obviously, it's a valid emotion.

That frustration when you have to work to the bone for something that seems to have been given to others—look at my frustration with Lilah some days.

"My dad didn't help with my bakery, Ben," I say, my voice softer than I expect. Like I'm comforting him or explaining something to a hurt dog. "I'm sure it seems—" I start, but then stop when I see his eyes locked to my wrist, the wrist of the hand I just lifted in what was supposed to be a kind, friendly gesture.

I look down at said wrist and see it.

A deep purple bruise on fair skin, and I instantly curse my father's Irish side of the family with their red hair and fair fucking skin and ability to bruise if you just look *sideways* at them.

He steps closer.

I step back.

My ass hits the edge of the table, the cool metal seeping through the thin material of my shorts.

"What is that?" His voice is low, menacing. His eyes are still on my wrist, which, *stupidly,* is still held in the air.

"Ben, I—" I try to drop it, but he wraps his fingers around it.

If you'd have asked, I would have thought he'd snatch it, grab it.

But the hold . . .

It's soft. Gentle. He takes a step closer, less than a foot in between us.

His skin is on mine.

Flames are licking me from where he's touching me, moving down my arm, heat pooling in me.

"What is this?" he asks again, his voice a bit gruffer, angrier.

"Ben, it's nothing, I—"

He closes the gap, pressing his hips to mine, pressing his belly into my hand pinned between us.

"*Who did this to you?*" he says, his voice louder now in the small space, angry and frustrated.

"Ben, you're scaring me," I say, a shiver in my voice.

With my words, his eyes soften.

His grip loosens.

He doesn't move away, though.

Instead, he moves closer and uses his free hand to move the little hairs that always fall from my braids around my ear.

"No. No, Lola. You never have to be scared of me, sweet girl. Ever."

"I have a lot of things to be scared of, Ben." I don't know what makes me say it. It's like when I'm in his presence, my filter melts, common sense goes blank, and I say what's on my mind instead of what I should.

The words I was trained to say.

"Everything is fine."

"I'm happy."

"Our thoughts and prayers . . ."

"My dad is a great man."

Instead, when I'm with Ben, I find myself telling him what I really feel.

Whether it's that he's a total fucking dick or . . . something else.

And that? That's dangerous.

Because underneath my perfect mask is a person who I've never shown anyone. Not completely.

She's a person who would disappoint my dad. That betrays the promise I made my mom. She's a person who isn't perfect and sunshine and rainbows every day.

"What do you have to be scared of, sweet girl?" he asks, that hand now resting on my neck, gripping it, reassuring.

My breathing is heavy, his own a mirror of mine, and I can't help but think about how I should probably be scared.

This man who *does not like me* has me pinned in place in my bakery.

But I'm not afraid.

No, I'm *turned on.*

And honestly? Right now? That's so much scarier than feeling real fear.

"Nothing," I whisper under my breath, the air whispering against his lips. "A heavy bag. I was carrying a heavy bag on my wrist and it left a mark."

He moves closer with my words, and as I stare into his eyes, I know two things down to my soul.

One, not a single part of him believes my story of how I got the bruise.

Two, Benjamin Coleman is going to kiss me again.

And if I want to throw in a third, undeniable fact: I'm not going to stop him.

And then his lips are on mine and everything goes blank.

My mind. The world around me.

The panic that's been slowly creeping into my bones for days.

The pressure of my family.

The frustration I feel toward this man.

It's all gone.

In its place is fire.

Fire everywhere his hand touches my body.

Heat radiates off him and onto me, warming me to the bone.

His lips press to mine, surprisingly gentle, scruff scratching at my chin, and it's not what I expected.

I'd be a liar if I said I didn't think about what it would be like to kiss this man again, despite trying to convince myself that it would never—*could never*—happen again.

I thought it would be rough, like last time.

Demanding.

But this is gentle and kind and . . . exploring as his lips move against mine, softly testing the waters and tasting.

My tongue reaches out, touching his bottom lip.

And then he groans.

A switch is flipped.

The sound reverberates through my entire body, sending a shiver through me. His hand on my hip grips, grabbing me tighter, more demanding.

Another hand grabs my braids, tugging them back to angle my head how he wants me.

And then his lips are devouring me. His tongue is licking at my lips.

I'm reciprocating, hitching a leg around his leg to get him closer, closer in any way I can because some part of my body—some unknown, unidentified, painful part of my soul—wants him.

For the first time in my life, I love my height, five eight and the tallest in my class. For the first time in my life with a man, I hitch that leg and don't have to move much more than to my tippy toes to line his hard cock up with my center.

With the movement, he groans, the sound deep in his chest, and with his mouth to mine and our chests pressed together, I feel the vibrations everywhere.

I moan.

I moan freely and openly, and fuck, the realization hits me: I want this man. His hand has moved to my ass, gripping me at my full hips, the other hand still tight on my braids, the feeling causing delicious pinpricks of pain and pleasure I never thought I'd be the type to crave.

But my moan also snaps me out of my haze.

I can't do this.

I can't get lost in this.

For so many damn reasons, starting with this man is my neighbor who hates me, moving to I get attached and hurt easily, and ending with the fact that I have so much trouble and drama chasing me that I don't need to involve this man in.

Regrettably, my hands move up to his chest, and I push gently, moving him back.

To his credit, he lets go instantly, stepping back to put two feet of space between us.

"Stop. We can't . . . We can't do this," I say, trying to get my words straight, my mind straight. His face is a mask of confusion tinged in lust.

I know the feeling well.

"Did I hurt you?" His brows are together, the confusion morphing to concern. "I didn't mean—"

"No. You didn't. I just . . . I can't do this."

"That was good," he says, still maintaining the distance I asked for, still staring at me, confused.

You and me both.

"Yes. It was."

Mistake.

Huge fucking mistake.

His lips turn up with amusement.

"But you don't want it?" I sigh, trying to decide how to explain that it's not a want or don't want kind of thing.

So I don't.

Instead, I turn from him, as if being in front of him bores me, face my work table once more, and start scooping.

"It can't happen, Ben," I say, portioning batter into lined tins as if nothing happened, as if I'm not working to make my hands stop shaking.

The distance between us shortens, and even though I refuse to turn back, I can still feel the heat of his body seeking mine.

He's so close to me.

A mix of shock and fear runs through me as I realize I want this— I want his body heat on mine, the warmth and the lust and the . . . security.

But that can't happen.

"You keep telling yourself that, sweet girl. That this won't happen, can't happen." Hot breath is on my neck and a finger brushes the nape, moving my braid aside. "But we both know we can only resist this for so long."

Then I feel Ben place a small kiss on the back of my neck before the padding of shoes on the floor hits my ears and the door shuts behind me.

The kiss—which should, in all honesty, have been chaste and simple—burns on my skin throughout the entire day as I try and forget what happened.

TWENTY

-Lola-

THE MUSIC IS QUIET TONIGHT, the night after my strange morning with Ben. It's just a dull, barely there hum.

But this time, I wish there were a loud noise, pounding in my head, the distraction I need.

I can't sleep. Again.

My lack of sleep has nothing to do with Ben and his playing music or deep laugh that I can hear through the thin walls, up the echoey stairwell, through the small corridor between our doors.

No, my lack of sleep is because, for the first time in a long time, I am terrified.

The kiss this morning was a great distraction throughout my day, as was baking and working and then cleaning, but now that I'm lying here, alone and with my own thoughts, I have the space to focus on what's really happening.

Last night I was too scared, too caught up in finding new solutions, but also completely drained from the emotional weight of the day.

Tonight I have the space, the distance my mind needs to over-think and overanalyze everything in my life.

Tonight I'm free to ponder the threat to my sanity, to my safety.

The dark mark on the fair skin of my wrist is a constant reminder of the fucked-up spot I've gotten myself into.

My dad has always made things difficult. I've always made things easy for him, always covered up, always figured things out. When Mom died, Lilah had enough trauma that I didn't want to add more.

So I took it on.

But now . . . I'm here. I'm stuck. I've become the endless supply for my father and have been dragged into his mess, too.

And for what? So that Lilah can live her life of carefree chaos, the perfect Malibu Barbie of the Jersey Shore, galavanting to the city and the beach and off on weekend trips to the Hamptons with her friends, spending the money she earned because she doesn't owe it to anyone else?

To keep a promise that, the older I get, the more I realize it was *wrong* of my mother to ask me to make?

And now it's escalating.

Now they're coming to me when I've told everyone I'm *done*.

I told my dad I wouldn't be helping any more a year ago, and in those twelve months, I didn't hear from anyone about anything related to debts of the seedy underworld of Ocean View.

I assumed that meant it was handled, and I went along with my life, thankful to be starting new, excited to see where it would take me.

Until that note on my door.

Until Johnny showed up at my bakery.

Until Dad told me that he wasn't out like I thought, that instead he'd only gotten in deeper and promised *me* when he couldn't pay.

That Lilah was in danger, too.

And now, I'm scared.

Because what is there to do?

I don't have seventy thousand dollars.

I don't have half of that.

Even if I cashed everything out, let the business fail, and moved back in with Dad, I wouldn't have that kind of money. And I know he doesn't either.

The worst part is that if I did, if I found that money, no matter how much I beg and plead for this to be the last time, he won't stop. It's a sickness that's taken over. Part of me thinks he managed it for long enough to get Lilah out of the house, and now that we're all grown and free, he's snapped. The void that was left with the loss of Mom is now filled with numbers and bets and the promise of something big.

The walls creak and I jump, my eyes moving to the window where a storm is blowing the ocean, rain pelting my window.

Every noise in this place has me on edge.

I need a distraction.

Standing, I check the locks on the door and windows again, grabbing the small white case that holds my Bluetooth headphones before lying back in my bed. I pop in the earphones, trying to shut out the noises.

I close my eyes and toss and turn in the bed for another twenty minutes, listening to soft music, instrumental versions of my favorite songs, but it's no use.

I need something more.

Then I remember my sister and me talking a few weeks ago.

"*I sleep like shit,*" *I'd said when she mentioned I looked tired.* "*Have since I was a kid.*"

"*Not me.*"

"*No?*"

"*Nope.*"

"*What about if you're stressed? Doesn't it keep you up?*"

"*Nope. I give myself a nice little orgasm, then I'm out like a light.*" I'd laughed but right now, after a week of shitty sleep and knowing I have to be up early, I'm desperate.

What could it hurt? I think, and with desperation strong, I decide to go for it.

Sighing to myself, I move my phone to the nightstand and lie in bed, music still playing in my ears quietly. I'm wearing a sleep shirt and a pair of loose shorts, but that's fine. As my hand moves down my body, I try to picture it as a man's hand. Calloused and strong, warm, bigger than mine. Spanning my belly, stretching from thumb to finger, and nearly covering the expanse. My mind fills in the blanks that physically aren't there, creating a shadow of a man beside me. My fingertips slip beneath the waistband, and I sigh, fingering my close-cut curls, then moving down. My breathing is already starting to quicken as my ring finger hits the very top of my slit, pressing in to quickly graze my clit.

A quick intake of breath.

Shit.

It's been a while.

In my mind, I can almost feel hot breath on my neck, the breath of a man, a body larger than mine taking up the space next to me.

My hand dips down farther, my middle finger dipping into my already wet center, and I moan.

Shit, it feels good.

The wet finger comes back up as my free hand moves beneath my shirt, grazing nipples that have already tightened.

My fingers come together on one, pinching hard as I move a finger back into my wet pussy, and I moan louder this time.

My back arches, the top of my head staying on my pillow as I continue pumping, adding another finger.

I'm not full enough.

In my imagination, the mystery man in my mind would have thick fingers, would fill me easily.

Still, my thumb moves to my clit, rubbing hard, and a near animalistic sound comes from deep in my chest, one of frustration and ecstasy and possibly a hint of confusion.

This has never felt as good as it does right now. The finger on my nipple continues to move, pulling and tugging at the flesh, a direct course to my throbbing clit that's being strummed in tandem.

That's my girl. Are you gonna come for your man? the voice in my head asks, the mystery man still made of fog and shadows, but just the thought of it—of a man's voice urging me on, of his fingers fucking me, of the promise of a more that I haven't had in far too long—it has me on the edge.

I'm close.

I'm so damned close to exploding.

The music on my phone quiets, but I'm so far in my mind that I don't register the fact. My breathing has gone heavier. My mind continues to craft the vision of the mysterious man, thumb on my clit, hovering over me, breath in my ear.

That's it. Are you going to come for me, Lola? Are you going to shout my name?

I moan. The man is starting to clear, going from a foggy, vague ghost of a person to a recognizable voice that I know. I know it, but I can't place it.

I don't dwell, though. The feeling is building in my belly, burning bright as I continue to rub my clit, dipping into my wet and dragging it up.

I'm so close.

And right as I reach the top of the hill, as it builds to the point that I have to break, the vision clears.

Dark, old-school tattoos line the tanned arm that's working my clit in my imagination. It's attached to broad shoulders, and a familiar grin is on the face.

"That's it, sweet girl. Come for me," the voice I now recognize says into my mind, and as I come, I make a fatal mistake. I moan his name out loud.

"Oh, God, Ben!" I shout as the heat takes over me, my back arching, leaving only my shoulders still on the bed, ears buzzing. "Yes!"

And as I come down from my high, breathing heavy, I don't even hear the annoying voice of the lady who lives in my phone saying, "Message sent."

TWENTY-ONE

-Ben-
Five minutes earlier

"You NEED to reach out to Lola, ask what she's donating to the auction," Hattie says, poking her head into the break room. My next client isn't due for another 30 minutes, and I'm spending it hiding from the world and trying to forget what happened this morning.

That kiss.

That *fucking* kiss.

That kiss should never have happened.

The first one was anger and rage and frustration.

A simple slip-up that we both could have forgotten.

The second one?

It was none of that. It was none of that and so much more. And then, for whatever fucking reason, she ended it and acted like it didn't matter, telling some lie about the marks on her wrist and pushing me to leave.

That bruise was not from a bag.

It was not from a friend.

It was from a man, and it was not a hold she wanted.

You learn something when you work with people who are trusting you to embellish their bodies in permanent ways. You connect with them, hear their stories, and know their lives. But most of all, you learn to read them.

And the words and tales I read in Lola—in her eyes, in her face, in her body language?

There is more to her story.

Her story is dark and twisted.

She's not sunshine and rainbows and sprinkles and frosting and overwhelming privilege. That's all a facade.

And with that kiss, despite how fuckin' infuriated she makes me, despite that she's full of secrets and frustration, I decided I wanted to know those secrets.

So much so that this morning, instead of going back to sleep, I spent far too long searching her name, researching her until the images started to blur on the screen.

Searches I have fought my hands to make late at night since she moved in.

Searches that lead me down rabbit holes, press photos of Lola in sleek dresses that show off her curves on the arm of her father.

Quotes about how proud she is of her father and how she's devoted to his cause to whatever the fuck they were celebrating.

Each and every photo I found was of the well-off, privileged, dutiful daughter.

The Princess of Ocean View.

Including the press release her father's office seemed to have sent out when Libby's was announced.

"I'm thrilled to assist my daughter Lola in any and every way as she makes her own footprint on the boardwalk by bringing the people of Ocean View a taste of my late wife. Libby's features recipes that Lola and her mother, Libby, created together before she tragically passed, and it's an honor to have a hand in making sure her memory will live on."

It's clear her daddy did, in fact, help build her business.

I'm not sure why that makes me so angry, considering I once had an entire family business tied up in a bow, just waiting for me to take over.

Honestly, this whole situation is so fucked. I can't stand her and her pink store and her stupid delicious cookies and her shitty fucking music and her annoying as fuck work hours.

But also, I'm man enough to see the truth.

She's gorgeous. And she's sweet. And, honestly, she means well. Each time she comes knocking for me to keep it down, it's valid.

And she's right to be pissed that I keep barging in on her place, expecting the same respect I'm not giving her.

But something in me wants to fuck with her, annoy her, get her as angry as she makes me. Something comes out in her when she does. Something I find irresistible.

In another world, another universe, she'd make a good match for me. Sunshine to my dark, sweet to my bitter. A pretty, kind thing to sit in my booth while I work, chat up my customers, cackle in the lobby with Hattie, drive me wild.

Except she's clearly trouble.

I don't need trouble.

I don't know what that bruise on her wrist was, or why she was acting like a scared, cornered kitten. Whatever it is, it's none of my business, and even more, it's not my problem to solve. She made her own bed.

I'm not going to lie in it with her.

Even if I can't get the vision of her shorts-wrapped ass out of my mind.

I shake my head, knocking the vision free before I answer Hat.

"What?"

"I told you. She's donating something to the auction. Not sure what, though. You need to text her and get the listing so I can put it up on the site."

"Why can't you do it?" She smiles her devious cat-like smile that she only does when trying to make me miserable. The one she does when there's a devious motivation behind her words.

"Because it's your fundraiser, not mine." I stare at her some more, knowing there's another motivation.

Is it to drive me insane? Possibly.

But there's *something*.

"You contact all of the potential fundraisers for me."

"Yeah, which is why I think you can handle texting our sweet neighbor and bugging her." Her hand with black, painted nails pushes the phone my way, and I stare at it like it's poisonous.

"You're being a fucking baby, Coleman," she says, looking at me with a taunting look, and I want to strangle her.

Mostly because I know that look, and she knows I can't back down from a taunt.

Friends who know you well are shitty. I don't care what anyone says.

Still, I reach over and grab my phone, scrolling to Lola's contact and opening a new message, seeing our previous conversations in the chat box.

God why am I such a dick to her?

Because it's fun, and she drives you wild in a way you didn't expect.

I shake my head to get *that* thought moving as I start to type. Hattie leaves the room with a smile on her lips like she just won some fight I didn't know we were having.

She's got some master plan, and I'm afraid to know what it is.

Me: Hey, I need to get a final list for the auction. Can you send me a description of what you're donating? Hattie needs to add it to the site.

There.

Easy. Professional. Not a dick.

Thoughts of how Lola reacts when I am a dick run through my mind.

The way her eyes get dark and her jaw gets tight.

The way she moaned when I kissed her. When I finally had those braids that have been taunting me wrapped around my hand, positioning her the way I like, the way I wanted to keep her.

The way she tasted, the way her body fit so fucking well with mine.

Then my mind moves to other parts of this woman who is driving me endlessly insane.

Her fucking stubbornness.

The way she *never fucking locks her doors.*

The loud fucking music and her shitty singing.

That bruise.

That bruise she brushed aside.

That bruise which sure as fuck did not come from a heavy bag, but the fingers of someone bigger than Lola.

There is more to Lola Turner than meets the eye.

I'm starting to wonder if anything I've thought about her was right at all.

From the table, my phone vibrates.

I shake my head, reaching for it and trying to ignore the thoughts about Lola that never seem far from the surface these days.

Lola: Oh, God, Ben!

What the fuck?

For a split second, I sit there and wonder what to do.

Something must be wrong.

She's in danger.

Someone is in her apartment.

My mind moves to the bruises.

The bruises.

My body starts moving, grabbing my phone and starting for the back door.

I don't even tell Hattie where I'm going, slamming the back door behind me and running up the stairs two at a time. Panic is suffusing my system in a way I'll have to look into deeper another time.

Right now, I have to go save my woman.

She doesn't know it yet, but I've just decided she's mine—in every way.

But first, she's mine to protect.

"Lola!" I shout, pounding on the door. "Lola! Open up!" I hear shuffling through the thin, shitty door.

It's now on my list to replace.

"Lola, open up or I'm breaking the door down!"

"Jesus, hold on! Leave my door alone!" I hear her shout, and a small drop of relief washes through me.

She doesn't sound scared or traumatized.

Annoyed, yes. Which to be honest, I should be embarrassed how that kind of turns me on.

Fuck.

Before I can think too long on that, the door opens.

Lola is standing there.

Her light hair is pulled up on top of her head, a messy bun with whisps falling around like she's been lying in bed, moving around with it.

Her shirt is askew, off the shoulder, and through the thin material I can see pebbled nipples.

And her shorts.

Loose sleep shorts that aren't pulled up all the way, stuck on a hip, revealing an expanse of creamy pale skin.

Finally, her chest is moving rapidly.

She's panting.

Trying to catch her breath.

Like she's . . .

She's . . .

Holy shit.

Oh God, Ben! wasn't a cry of panic. It wasn't her begging me for help.

It was her coming.

With my fucking name on her lips.

And with that angry look on her face, I can tell she has no idea.

"What's going on?"

"You called for me," I say, testing her.

And fuck if those already flushed cheeks don't go deeply red with embarrassment.

My cock gets hard.

"I—no. What? No. I didn't. I—"

"You texted me, Lola." Her eyebrows come together, and I can't take it.

She's too fucking cute.

Too fucking sweet.

I need a taste.

Just one more.

Maybe that will satisfy me.

If I just . . .

I step closer until her pebbled nipples are on my chest.

Her breathing goes even more erratic.

"You said, 'Oh God, Ben.'" Her eyes go wide, and the breath that leaves her lips is shaky.

Is it because she just came?

Or because I'm close to her.

Either way, she confirmed it with that blush.

I'm as deep in her as she is in me.

I move the sliver until our bodies are pressed together, so she can feel what the thought of her fingering herself with my name on her lips is doing to me.

My hard cock presses into her belly as I move one arm around her waist, pulling her into me.

My other hand moves down her arm softly until I grab her hand, lifting it between us.

Her eyes go impossibly wider.

And I smile at her.

I smile at her because whether she knows it or not, tonight, I've decided to lean into this fucked-up game and make this infuriating, beautiful woman mine.

And what I do next seals that.

I bring her hand up, up, up.

My grip on her wrist is loose.

She comes to me willingly.

A gentle tug, a "no," anything at all, and I'd let her go. I'd step back and I'd go downstairs.

I go slow, eyes locked to hers, telling her she's making this decision.

I might be doing the action, but she's approving it.

And she doesn't say anything whatsoever.

Instead, she licks her lips, eyes on my own.

I'll take that as a go ahead.

I slip her fingers into my mouth, the first two, and roll my tongue around them, letting my tongue ring hit her nails, her knuckles.

And there I taste it.

Her pussy.

Not long ago, these fingers were inside of her; her pussy was clamping down while she fucked herself, rubbed herself with these fingers that I'm cleaning with my tongue.

She was coming with my name on her lips.

She's sweet. Sweet and musky and all I want is to taste more. I want to live in this taste.

Fuck cookies and cupcakes.

I want to eat Lola Turner until I die.

A small moan, almost indistinguishable through the pounding of blood in my ears, falls from her lips.

Fuck.

I gotta go before I pin her to her door and fuck her right in her hallway.

And really, I would. I'd love to. But I've got a client in twenty.

So I let go of her wrist, let it fall, and put a hand behind her head, pulling her to me and kissing her again.

It's better than last time.

It's harder. It's more impatient.

And it tastes like her lips and her pussy.

When I end the kiss years before I would like to, I step back, letting go of her. She stays standing there, eyes hooded with desire. Desire I don't think I would ever get tired of seeing on this woman's face.

I am so completely fucked.

"Next time, sweet girl, just come downstairs. I'll take care of you." When her eyes flare, a mix of heat and embarrassment and desire flooding those green irises, I know.

"You come find me when you're ready to talk about whatever the fuck this is," I say, putting the ball in her court.

Regardless of the decision she makes, I know at this moment that no matter how much Lola Turned drives me insane, I also want to drive her wild.

One way or another, I'll make this woman mine.

Now I just have to figure out how.

TWENTY-TWO

-Ben-

"Ah, he answers," the voice says, the same tinkling lilt it's always had as I bring my phone to my ear.

My mother.

"Hey, Ma," I say, sitting back on my couch, a glass of whiskey in hand.

"What's the occasion?" she asks, and I wonder how she can see me drinking on my couch on a Monday night.

The truth is, there is no occasion other than the shop closes early on Mondays, and despite my best efforts (and they have been plenty, no matter how many times I tell myself that the late, loud nights and endless walks through the stairwell in hopes of catching Lola were completely *unrelated* to Lola), I have nothing on my mind but a woman with reddish-blonde braids, hips I need to sink my fingers into, and a dark bruise marring her perfect skin.

And yet, somehow, despite my best efforts, she's avoided me all together.

It's been a full week since I've seen her last.

"What?"

"The occasion. Answering on the first ring. Not making me call a few more times this week until I'm worried Officer Garrison's gonna be coming to my door to tell me some bad news." My gut cramps knowing she's not wrong—that is my typical way of handling calls.

"You caught me on a slow night."

"I'd hope so. You're single and your shop is closed tonight."

"Stop talking with Hattie, Mom."

The problem with Hattie being Hattie is she is the kind of person who instantly becomes best friends with everyone, including my mother, and will keep them in the loop of nearly everything and anything.

"At least Hattie answers when I call."

"I just answered."

"At least Hattie keeps me updated on your life." I groan. "On *all* aspects of your life."

"Jesus, what's this call for? To check in or get dirt?" My mom laughs, and the sound is nostalgic, though irritating,

"Hattie says you have a new neighbor that you're enamored with."

"I'm firing Hattie."

"No, you're not." She's not wrong. "So? Tell me. What's going on?"

Another sigh.

I could handle this two ways. I could let her mull on whatever lies or inflated stories and build some kind of chaotic storyline in her mind, or I could give her *my* side and hope she doesn't talk to Hattie again.

"We have a new neighbor. She's the mayor's daughter, opened up a bakery."

"And?"

"And nothing." My mom doesn't say anything for a beat, and I wonder if I won until she does.

"What's this I hear about loud music and you not being kind?"

Fucking, *fucking Hattie.*

"Jesus, Mom, are you this heavily involved in Tanner's shit?"

"Tanner lives in Springbrook Hills and has dinner with me regularly. I don't *have* to be in his shit. He's getting engaged and settling down and living his life. You're a mystery."

"So go bug Tanner about shit."

"I do. I'm bugging you right now." Again, I sigh, taking another deep sip of my drink. My veins feel warm, this being the second one I poured, and I guess that's why I start talking.

"Fuck. I don't know, Mom. She's . . . a pain. She's all pink and sugar and up way too fucking early—"

"You never were a morning person."

"And she never locks her damn doors. Drives me insane."

"Makes sense. You know all about what happened with Jordan and Luna. The world isn't always safe." I feel appeased at her confirmation of my irritation and continue on.

"And she's spoiled. Her dad's the mayor, and he helped her build her business. She didn't have to work for it."

"Why does that bother you?" I don't answer. "Your dad was given Coleman and Sons. You could have had it. Tanner was given it. Does that make the work he's done less important? Or less valuable?"

"No, of course not" Her tone gets firm.

"So it's because she's a woman?"

"No, it's not that, it's just—"

"It's just you're being an ass, Benjamin James." I don't respond. "Tell me what's really going on."

When we were kids, Tanner laughed at me for confiding in our mom. But when someone takes your passion and nurtures it, fighting for it to have room to grow, you trust them.

Hattie says it makes me a momma's boy, but I'm not sure if I care. And so, for the first time, I confess what Lola Turner is doing to me.

"She's gorgeous, Mom."

"She has to be to catch your eye."

"She didn't catch my eye. I barged into her bakery the first day I met her because she was being loud as fuck at seven in the morning singing. She's a terrible singer."

"You broke into her bakery?"

"The door was unlocked!" I don't tell her I thought she was robbing me or that I had a baseball bat and was in just my underwear. "Anyway. We got off on the wrong foot, and it never really . . . righted. Every time I see her, she drives me insane and I say something dickish."

My mother sighs.

"You know, Ben, you got art from me. But the rest? That's all your father. Was an ass when I met him. Still is, which you know. But he made me fall for him. Won me over."

I refuse to look too closely at why that makes me feel a bit better.

"Sometimes people need a push, Ben, darling. Just look at Tanner and his Jordan. He was dragging his feet, trying to do it all. Jordan whipped him into shape."

"I'm not trying to do it all, Mom," I say, taking another deep sip of my drink, it burning on the way down.

"No, you just bury yourself in your art in order to avoid the world."

"What am I avoiding?" I'll never know why I always play into this hand, why when she sets it up for me, I always take a swing. I can hear the smile in her voice, knowing I fell into her trap.

"Home." I roll my eyes at the obvious answer. "Your father."

"I'm not avoiding Dad. You guys were just down here for Memorial Day."

"No, you're not outright ignoring him, but you are avoiding any situation where the two of you would actually have to talk about what happened with you two and Coleman and Sons." She sighs, and I know if she were here, I'd see that crease between her eyebrows that she's convinced Tanner and I gave her. "The two of you. So damn stubborn. Avoiding tough subjects." I don't say anything, instead sipping once more. "He's proud of you, you know. Of what you've built." There's more silence. "It's not what he expected, and he had to mourn that, and I'll tell you—we fought tooth and nail about the way he mourned that. But Benjamin, he loves you. And he's proud of you. He just is too fucking manly to tell you." I grunt. "Sounds like someone else I know."

"I've never pretended I was too manly for anything, Ma."

"Yeah, well. Maybe you should drop the manly act and go ask that neighbor of yours out," she says with a laugh. "Alright, well, I hear your dad's truck pulling up. We're headed out to dinner. Please, consider coming home for the party."

"You know about that?"

"Jordan's got a big mouth." I smile, knowing that there was a time when my brother's girlfriend had to keep secrets for a living and loving that that's so far behind her now. "Please, Ben. Think about it. Maybe bring your neighbor."

"Goodbye, Mom," I say.

"Bye, my darling boy. Remember that sometimes people need the push!"

"Yeah, yeah. I love you."

"I love you too," I say before swiping to end the call.

I sit there for a few minutes before making a decision.

I stand, pour myself a drink, and then sip it as I start to make that push.

TWENTY-THREE

-Lola-

I'VE SUCCESSFULLY AVOIDED Ben for two weeks.

Two weeks of timing my arrivals and departures around his schedule like some kind of reverse stalker. Two weeks of staying at the bakery late to make doughs and batters and bake, so I don't have to be up early and risk waking him up.

Two weeks of doing everything in my power not to give Ben any reason to have to come over to my side of the building.

Unfortunately, he hasn't been nearly as considerate.

More than once, I've slammed the door when I caught him leaving his apartment unexpectedly, waiting long minutes until he left to sneak out of my place.

More than a few times, he's played his music loud late at night, after close.

A part of me can't help but wonder if it's a test.

A test to see if I'll react, if I'll break.

Like this isn't me avoiding him and waiting for the awkward to pass, waiting for the fun of me to wear off so I can move on with my life without having Benjamin Coleman bugging me. But instead, it's a waiting game for how long I can endure his prodding until I snap.

That part of me thinks this is true because it's never loud when he has someone over. It's never the shop having some kind of event, never guests in his apartment.

It's just Ben, our two cars the only ones parked in the lot.

And it stops at eleven on the dot.

I need to sleep by eleven.

My words ricochet in my mind every night when the noise dies out each time.

Old Lola would read into it.

Old Lola would think that's kind, sweet even. Old Lola would go over with a plate of cookies and a pretty smile and daydream about possibilities.

New Lola lives for *Lola*, though.

New Lola has a bookie on her ass that's a little too interested in her.

New Lola cut off her father, is avoiding her sister, and is trying to run a business.

New Lola doesn't have time for games.

Either way, it seems my punishment for avoiding Ben instead of seeking him out as he instructed me to is the noise.

He hasn't made any effort to come to me, but he's made it hard not to go to him.

And it's not that I'd be going to him to do any of the filthy shit that's admittedly run through my mind. No, it would be to *fucking strangle* him. Tonight, as I'm mopping, listening to the already thumping music next door, my fingers curl around the handle of the mop, picturing his throat.

And not a single part of me doesn't think he's doing it with the express purpose of irritating me. Before I moved in, I spent a few early evenings at the bakery, setting up. While I was never here late, I was here when the tattoo shop was open.

I never heard this loud music.

But now it's every night.

Every. Single. Night.

Since that night, I lie in bed and let my mind take over, and my stupid, stupid phone sent a very unwelcome text to Benjamin Coleman. (I actually don't know if his full name is Benjamin, but I don't really care. He seems like a Benjamin. A douchey, privileged asshole who took his parents' money and made a business with it. Someone who turned into a punky, grumpy asshole to piss off his parents.)

Every night since that night, as soon as I flip my sign to "Closed," like he has some kind of stalker sixth sense that can hear the sound of the acrylic hitting glass, his music kicks on.

I guess in some ways, I should thank him for not pulling this shit when I have customers in the store, but also, that's just common decency.

But not for Ben, because he's a giant dickhole.

I giggle to myself at the thought of calling Ben a dickhole when the screen on my register makes a beep as I'm trying to check the numbers for the day, and a notice pops on the screen.

Searching for network . . .

Strange.

It seems like, for whatever reason, it disconnected from the internet.

I tap the screen a few times and try to find the wifi so I can reset it, but the normal network that is for this building is gone.

What I find in its place makes my blood run cold.

"Network Name: COMEOVERFORTHEPASSWORD"

The other networks are random ones, all locked and for nearby businesses.

I remember Brad, the building owner, told me the internet router was based on the other side of the building.

No, no, no.

He wouldn't.

I try the network that I just *know* has to be mine with the previous password.

Nope.

Fuck.

I should just ignore it. Go to bed, ignore his bullshit, and ask Hattie in the morning.

I should call Brad and see if he can add a separate router.

I should go to a nearby business and beg to use their wifi.

But . . . my own curiosity is out to get me.

Why does he want me to come over so bad?

It's a new escalation, more than just taunting and annoying me.

But . . . why?

I wait long minutes, five, ten, fifteen passing as I stare at my computer, occasionally trying passwords to no avail before I say fuck it.

He wants a face-off, he's going to get one.

TWENTY-FOUR

-Ben-

The shop closed at four, and for the two hours between my close and the closing time of Libby's, I sit at my desk wondering what the fuck is wrong with me.

Lola has lived next door, officially, for four weeks.

In those four weeks, she has consumed my mind and overtaken every moment of free time.

When I sit down with paper and pen, it's her I see on the paper.

Braids.

Freckles.

Delicate bones.

Fucking *cupcakes*.

It's her and it's taking over my consciousness.

Last night I dreamed about her.

She's sneaking into my *un*consciousness too.

I need a solution. I need to fix this shit. I need . . . to get her out of my system? Or get myself into hers, maybe.

Except she is somehow ignoring and avoiding me with such finesse that I haven't seen her in two weeks.

So tonight, in a moment of weakness, I pushed.

The router to the internet of the building was flashing at me, a beacon of ideas, and I finally fell into the trap.

I changed the name and the password, making it unable to be misinterpreted, and then waited.

I knew there was a fifty-fifty shot that this wouldn't work, that she'd find a way around it or ask Hattie or call the landlord, but it was worth the try.

And when I hear a pounding at my apartment door, I can't help but smile.

Here we go.

Walking to the door, I switch the sound of the music down—I don't want any interruptions if this goes how I really fucking hope it will. And then I'm there, opening the door and staring at Lola, her face red with frustration and anger, hands on her hips, that irresistible outfit she's mastered of a too-small tank top and skin-tight shorts showing off the curves I've been putting to paper for weeks.

"Change it back," she says through gritted teeth.

I take another step outside of my apartment and cross my arms over my chest as I lean against the door.

Lola takes a step back, maintaining the distance between us.

"Change what?" I say, the smile taking over my face.

She looks good.

I hate to admit it, but fuck, I missed seeing her angry face.

Or maybe I should man up and just start admitting it. Maybe that would make my life easier.

"I don't want to do this, Ben, seriously. I'm exhausted. I've been up late every night thanks to your loud fucking music—"

"It's off every night by eleven," I say, stepping closer to her. She steps away again, her back aiming toward the wall that lines the landing between our apartments.

She licks her lips, her eyebrows coming together in confusion.

"Eleven?"

"That's what you told me. You need the music off by eleven. It's always off." No response. "You also haven't come over to tell me to turn it down."

"Like that would have helped? I've tried that before, remember?"

"But that was before," I say, stepping toward her again. Her back bumps the wall, and while I leave space between us, it's burning with tension.

She feels it.

I know she does.

"Before what?" she says, her tongue dipping out to taste her lip.

Fuuuck.

"Before this started. Before we started."

"There's no—" I take a step closer to her, and while our bodies aren't touching, I can feel her heat.

"Don't start lying to me now, Lola." She doesn't respond, and I put a hand on the wall next to her head, bending low until our faces are close but not touching. Her head tips up, looking at me. "There's something here, Lola. I fought it; you've been fighting it. We drive each other wild, but I know you've wondered if we can drive each other crazy in other ways."

"I—"

"Don't lie, Lola." And then it happens.

Her chin tips up, just enough so her lips graze mine, and I'm kissing Lola Turner again for the first time in weeks.

Like the previous times, my mind goes blank and my body turns to fire. I take the smallest step until our bodies are lined up as I sneak my tongue past her lips, tasting her again. She moans as I slip into her mouth.

Her hand moves around my neck, trying to encourage me to move, to get closer to her. She needs more. I know.

And I want more just the same.

This woman might baffle me at every turn, but here? Like this?

I know her to the fucking core.

But still, I don't.

Instead, I step back.

"Ben—"

"Shut up," I say because I don't want to give her space or time.

I don't want her to talk and, in turn, talk herself out of this.

I've made my mind up.

We're doing this.

It's been a month of dancing around this shit, playing games, fucking around, and pretending that she doesn't make me fucking burn up every time I see her.

A month of her avoiding me and pretending like she doesn't feel it all the same.

I grab her hand and start moving, pulling her toward my door.

"Ben, what are you—" she starts but then she stops as I press her hard to the door of my apartment. I pin her in place with my body, grinding my hard cock into her softness, and she stops her objections.

"Last chance, Lola."

"What?"

"Last chance. You don't want this, you tell me."

"Ben, I—"

"But if you want to forget whatever the fuck has been clouding your eyes and you want to do it by me fucking you out of my system, I'll open my door, bring you in, and make you scream my fucking name. Lola, say yes, and I'll make you forget everything but my cock between your legs."

Her eyes go from wide and confused to hooded and hot, her lips parted as she pants softly.

"Lola. Give me your answer."

She stares at me long and hard, and I wonder if maybe I pushed too far.

If I should have been sweeter and kinder, like the other men I'm sure she's fucked.

But my sweet girl surprises me, just like she does at every damn corner.

"I want to forget, Ben."

"Fuck yeah," I say, the words a growl as I grind my cock into her and reach into my pocket for my keys as my lips meet hers again.

Her hands are in my hair, tugging like she wants to devour me as we kiss and I fumble with the lock.

Click.

We're in.

Detaching myself from her, I move, grabbing her hand again and nearly dragging her toward my room.

I need to get her in my room.

Then I need to get her naked.

Then I need to get my cock inside her.

Those are my priorities right now.

When we reach the door, I nearly fling her into the room and start to kick off my shoes as she looks around, taking in the framed drawings and dark painted walls.

"Shirt, shorts, off," is all I say as I cross my arms over my back, moving to take my shirt off.

I expect an argument.

I don't get it.

Seems that when Miss Lola is turned on, she listens to me.

Good to know.

I also can't help but wonder how far that courtesy goes.

I slow my own undressing as she takes off her top and then shimmies her shorts down, stepping out of them before standing there in front of my bed, a gallery of dark art surrounding her perfect, pale body.

Jesus fuck.

This was meant to be some kind of quick thing, a way to get her out from under my skin and for her to burn off steam.

But seeing her there, pristine and untouched, skin I'd love to mark in so many ways, my mind goes places it should not.

Never.

And definitely not with this woman, all fire and fury and trouble and *bad decisions.*

Not with Lola.

My thumbs go to the waistband of my shorts, sitting underneath antique anchor tattoos at my hips, ready to push them down and let out my aching cock.

Anything to get my mind on the right track.

"Bra," I say, and instantly her hands, not hesitant but sure and eager, go to her back, undoing the clasp and letting her tits free.

Perfection.

Jesus.

Who created this woman?

Whoever it was created her for me. Perfectly sized tits, on the small side, leading to hips a man can hold on to.

"Underwear," I say, my voice husky as I take in her breasts with rosy pink nipples, already peaked and begging for my mouth.

Her hands go to her hips and begin to push down, but I want to savor this.

If this is it, my one chance to get my fill of this woman, I'm taking it all.

"Slow," I hear my voice say, and her face moves, looking at me, locking her eyes with mine.

There it is.

The war in her eyes.

The war where she's trying to decide is she should listen to me or tell me to fuck off.

Sweet girl, trust me. You want to listen to me. Daddy will make you feel so fucking good if you do.

I try to transmit the words to her through some kind of mind meld, my own heart thumping erratically with a mix of anticipation and panic.

What if she fights me?

I don't do fighting.

I do sweet and docile.

The moments span what feels like days but are truly just a few seconds, eyes locked, a battle of wills.

And then her small pink tongue peeks out, wetting her lips and rolling them together.

And her hands begin again, pushing down the lacy pink underwear.

And she does it slowly.

I groan a little. It can't be helped.

"Good girl," I say before moving my eyes to the fabric, savoring every inch of revealed flesh.

But not before I catch her eyes flare just the tiniest bit with my words.

Potential.

There's fucking *potential* there.

My cock twitches again, agreeing with my thoughts.

I move my shorts down quickly when her underwear hits the floor, leaving me in just my boxer briefs. Her eyes move to where my hand is adjusting my painfully hard dick through my underwear, and the woman licks her lips again.

So much fucking potential. My mind is moving without my conscious approval, creating scenarios where I can keep this woman in my bed indefinitely.

I need to move on.

"Sit on the bed, Lola." Again, a flash, the need to disobey.

But then she sits on the edge of the dark comforter. "Open your legs, sweet girl." A sharp intake of breath, another internal panic that she won't do what I say, but there it is.

Thick, milky-white thighs open for me, revealing a perfectly pink, wet pussy.

"Fuuuuckk," I say, the sound coming from deep in my throat without my permission, but really, what else do you say when your dream cunt is just a foot away begging for your dick or your hands or your mouth? "Spread yourself for me." Her eyes move to me, panic clear.

Ahh, this is new for her.

Interesting.

"I know you know how to, baby." We haven't talked about that text, the one that indefinitely changed the track of my mind when thinking of Lola, the one where I realized she came with my fucking name on her lips.

I expect the argument now.

Or at least the denial.

But no.

As seems to be her style, Lola Turner shocks me when two pink-painted pointer fingers go to either side of that wet pussy and pull it open for my eyes to see.

And then she takes it a step further, locking eyes with me and swiping a finger through her wet, from her entrance to where she circles her clit at the top, letting out a breathy noise.

"Again," I say, needing to see that again, to cement it in my mind until I die, a reel I'll replay and jack off to until I'm senile.

And she does, this time moving her hand to dip farther into her entrance, circling her clit more than once, moaning a little louder. "Fuck, Lola," is all I can say.

She continues, this time losing an entire finger inside of herself, moaning as it dips in and grazes her G-spot with the angle, coming out glistening with wet, then moving up, two fingers now rubbing her clit back and forth as she keeps her eyes locked on me.

It's then I realize she hasn't given in.

She's not being sweet, not being docile.

As always, she's fighting me, just in a way I really don't fucking mind.

But it's time to show her who's in charge, though.

My hands move my boxers down, and I kick them to the side, my hand going to my cock and stroking, once, twice, hard and slow.

Lola's eyes follow my hand, moaning as her fingers hit her clit again.

I take a step closer, then two, three, until my knees are hitting the bed between her spread legs. Her breaths pant over my cock as I continue to slowly pump, but her eyes are on me, her head tipped up just the slightest bit.

Such a fucking good girl.

I take my cock in my hand and trace the head on her lips, barely parted.

"Such a pretty, sweet girl you are, my Lola." Her breath hitches, the breath pushing cool air against my piercing.

I rub it on her lips to warm it back up.

Her eyes go wide.

"Oh yeah, baby. That's what you think it is."

I expect her to say something

I expect questions.

What I don't expect is her hot tongue dipping out and touching the warm metal below the head on the underside of my cock.

I don't expect her to tilt her head and suck the barbell into her mouth.

I don't expect her to then take the whole head between her lips.

And I don't expect her to do this while her green eyes lock to mine, a mix of sex fiend and utter innocence burning there.

"Jesus fuck, Lola. I knew you'd be hungry for my cock, but this is better than I dreamed." She moans again, eyes going hooded and drifting shut.

A tick in the pros column.

Women can go either way when it comes to dirty talk.

Lola likes it filthy.

A wet noise has me looking down between us, past her pink lips wrapped around my cock to where I can just barely see three fucking fingers buried in her cunt, her hips moving gently as she fucks herself.

I step back, regretting it instantly as the cold air hits my wet dick, but move to kneel between her legs.

"No. Don't stop," I say as she pauses, looking in her eyes before focusing back on those hands. One holding her thigh open, fingers denting the soft flesh there, the other fucking herself, wetness dripping. "Fucking hell, Lola. Don't think I've seen anything prettier than you fucking your pretty pussy." Breath leaves her lips quickly, her lungs hitching. "You taste as sweet as your cookies, don't you, baby?" Her lips open again, breath coming fast, tits heaving with each breath as I dip my head forward, looking at her.

Her fingers start to move, to leave.

"No. Stay." I use one hand to show her, forcing her to press those fingers deeper. For good measure, I pull the hand out then press it back in, helping her fuck herself.

I could do this forever.

But that clit is calling my name.

"Good girl, just like that. You keep fucking yourself, and Daddy will eat." Her breath hitches, but I'm already moving forward, already reaching my tongue out to taste her.

Fucking heaven.

"Oh, oh God," she moans, hips moving; whether to get her fingers deeper or my face closer, I'm not sure.

But she accomplishes both.

My lips latch to her clit, sucking deep as her hips buck, her fingers moving just beneath my chin.

My tongue comes out to lave her clit before moving, so the piercing on my tongue is pushing under her hood, rubbing the sensitive bud until she's screaming.

The hand holding her thighs open moves, her leg wrapping around to hold me in place as her hand goes into my hair, holding me in place.

But I'm not leaving.

No fucking way am I leaving until we get her to come together.

And once we do, I'm going to fuck my sweet girl until she squeezes my dick and screams my fucking name.

My hands go to her hips, pulling her deeper into my face, while her fingers move frantically, the words coming from her near inhuman.

Until it happens,

"Oh, fuck, Ben! Ben!" she shouts, grinding her fingers that are pumping frantically, her hand tightening in my hair, pulling me closer.

I flatten my tongue on her clit and suck.

"FUCK! I'm coming!" she shouts, the words loud enough that if Hattie were in the break room, she most definitely would hear it.

But its not her words that have me losing my fucking mind.

It's the wet.

The wet my mouth is lapping up as she screams and wails, riding her fingers and gripping my face to her cunt. I move my head back and forth, growling into her pussy as she gushes on my face, screams my name, and rides her fingers.

The woman is a dream.

A dream I need to be inside of.

As her grip loosens on my hair, slowly letting go, her leg that she wrapped around my back to keep me close unraveling, I lick once more before sitting back on my heels. Looking up at her from my spot on the floor, her head is tipped to the ceiling, eyes closed, fingers still inside her.

If I had a camera nearby, I'd take a photo.

One day, maybe I'll draw this from memory and savor every moment.

Her hair falling down her back, chest heaving, tits peaked, fingers in her pussy, wet spot making the comforter beneath her darker.

Every part of it is a dream.

"That good, sweet girl?" I ask, and my voice is hoarse as I do. Her eyes open and meet mine, hazy and hooded, and I feel my lips tip up in a half smile. "Yeah, it was good for you. That's just a taste, though. Now be a good girl and turn around, put your ass in the air." Those hooded green eyes look at me, registering my words, blinking.

Again, I wonder if she's going to fight me.

But once again, the surprise hits me when she just smiles, takes her fingers out of her pussy, and licks them clean, eyes locked on me.

If she were mine, I'd punish her.

If she were mine, I'd tell her she knows damn well that's my job.

Something tells me that if she were mine, she'd do it anyway, the same smirk playing on her face.

But then she's standing, unsteady on her feet, and turning to face my bed.

And then she's kneeling on the edge of it, legs spread, hands on the mattress.

I step back, taking in the scene.

Her full ass on display, her asshole begs for its own special treatment. Her pussy is already swollen and wet. Thick thighs end in the mattress, her back arched, her head looking over her shoulder at me.

An eyebrow raised in challenge.

I stroke my cock and then I step closer, lining my entire body with hers. Then I lean forward, my chest along her back, each vertebra beneath me as I put my mouth to her ear, sucking the lobe into my mouth, running my tongue along it.

I'm about to ask her if she's on anything.

I'm clean, and if she's covered, nothing can stop me from sliding into the wet cunt I've been dreaming about, for better or worse, for the better part of a month.

And then my *fucking phone rings.*

Her body tenses.

My body tenses.

Deep down, I know we're fucked and not in the way I thought we'd be a minute ago.

Because I know I just lost her.

I know when my phone continues to ring and I look down at her, her face tilting to mine with a look like she just came out of a daze, like she just came back to the land of the living.

No, no, no!

"Oh, God. Oh, God!" she murmurs under her breath, and I stand.

"Fuck," I say, because I know that's it.

She's come back to reality, to her senses.

"Oh my God, I should have never—we should have never —we almost—"

"Lola, stop."

"I have to go."

My phone is ringing, the sound vibrating in my mind like a mosquito that I wish would *just fucking shut up*. Lola is moving to her ass from the position I had her in, and her eyes are dazed, looking around the room, searching for her clothes.

"Where are my shorts? I need—"

"Lola, stop," I say, grabbing her wrist.

And that's it.

The last straw.

Her eyes, the eyes that moments ago were filled with heat and desire, go cold, but beneath that, there's a hint of something more: fear.

I let go before she can pull away.

"Lola, we need to talk."

"Please change the wi-fi back," she says, her voice low and embarrassed, as she bends to put feet into the shorts that she found. *Fuck fuck fuck!*

"*Lola!*" She looks up at me once more, snapping a bra behind her back.

"This was a mistake. I . . . I needed a distraction. So, thanks for that. But I'm leaving now."

And with her words, the phone stops ringing, the room silent once again as her eyes meet mine.

"Later, Ben," she says, turning around, her shoes in hand, her shirt somehow having found its way to her body.

And I watch her go.

I watch her walk to the door, watch her unlock it, open the door, and step onto the landing.

And when the door slams behind her, my phone beeps with a text.

I glare over to the wretched thing that just ruined what should have been fucking amazing, my cock still hard despite the chaos of the last two minutes.

Missed call from Tanner.

New Text from Tanner: Bro, stop avoiding me. You gotta come to Mom's party. Hat told Jordan you've got a new girl—bring her too.

I groan in frustration, acknowledging that even though my little brother is on the other side of the fucking state, he still has the ability to cockblock me.

TWENTY-FIVE

-Lola-

THE WORST PART of my new apartment is the roller coaster that is Ben Coleman.

The best part about my new apartment is Hattie Jones, a roller coaster in and of herself.

She's been over a few times to chat, to grab a coffee or a treat. And while she kind of terrifies me with her blatantly in-my-face friendship—something I've never experienced in a life of arranged friends and faked friendly acquaintances—it's been nice to have her here.

A friend.

It's . . . new.

At the risk of making myself sound like a lonely loser, I haven't had many of those. Especially those who have zero interest in using my connection to further their own career.

The downside of Hattie: she's nosy as can be. And now she's invested in the non-relationship between her best friend slash boss and me.

More than once, she's asked me what's going on with Ben and me, like she knows more than I've told her myself.

Part of me wonders why Ben would tell her about what happened between us. The other part of me is dying to know *what he told her* and if that means anything.

But New Lola doesn't dig and doesn't play into the games of annoying men, despite how they might make the butterflies in her belly flutter and her panties get just a little wet every time I think about those kisses . . . and the *other* kind of kiss he gave me.

Regardless of my putting an end to my people-pleasing ways, I don't think there's a single human who can say no to Hattie when she has an idea.

That's why I've found myself out to lunch with her, the "We'll be back" sign on the bakery flipped as we both sit at the little ocean-side bistro, a salad in front of me and chicken fingers in front of Hattie.

"I so wish I could have a drink right now," she says, eyeing some fabulous-looking blue drink in a tall glass that's being delivered to a tourist. I follow the drink to its destination—an exhausted-looking mother sitting at a table with a crew of sun-burned kids and an equally exhausted-looking father.

"I think she needs it more," I say with a laugh.

"Yeah, well, I've been dealing with a very grumpy Ben." It takes all that I have to tame the muscles in my face at her words. Her eyes are locked on me, taking in every small movement like she might replay the tape later and dissect it against some kind of body language manual.

"Isn't he always grumpy?" I ask, uninterested, stabbing at a grape tomato. It slips from the tines, rolling to the other side of the plate as I chase it with my fork, trying to avoid Hattie's burning gaze.

"Yes . . ." She's feeling me out, deciding what else to say. "Except he seems exceptionally grumpy the past, oh, say, two, three weeks." My fork hits the tomato, popping it and causing it to explode on my shirt.

"Shit!" I shout, the mom in the corner glaring at my outburst as I start to dab at tomato goo. Hattie instantly starts laughing.

"Oh my God! Something DID happen, didn't it!?" she asks in a squeal, leaning back in her seat and clapping.

Yes, the woman starts clapping, laughing maniacally like an insane person.

"I don't know what you're talking about," I say in denial, blotting at my shirt in an attempt to get the sticky tomato off of me and also avoid this conversation altogether.

I like Hattie. I can definitely see her being a great friend. But I don't know how eager I am to dish about messing around with her boss . . .

"Shut up. You've been holed up in that bakery for weeks, conveniently never coming out when Ben is around. Never coming over to bring cookies or cupcakes. I need to come to you, which is not a hardship, but before you brought over peace offerings and fucked with Ben's head. It was fun to watch. Now he's pissy as fuck and you're nowhere to be seen." It's been nine days since Ben pulled me into his apartment and made me come on his bed, his phone the only thing stopping us from going further, and I've doubled down on my avoidance tactics.

"He's been crankier than normal?" I ask, but as the words leave my mouth, I realize my mistake.

I showed interest.

Hattie latches on.

"Yes, he has." Her smile grows. "You wouldn't know anything about that, would you?" I stare at her. She stares at me. I spend the next thirty seconds trying to decide the likelihood of her dropping the subject.

It seems very, very slim.

"We . . . kissed."

"OH MY GOD, I KNEW IT!" she shouts, hand slapping the table as her head tips back to the sky. Her straight bob moves with her head shaking.

"Hattie! Shut up!"

"I can't. Not until I get the details! What happened? When!? How!?" I stare at her and realize there's no way out of this.

She is going to dig at this until I give in.

"Two, three weeks ago," I say under my breath. Another screech, drawing attention.

"DETAILS! I NEED DETAILS!"

"What? No. God, no."

"I need details, woman!"

"If you want details about how your boss kisses so bad, why don't you just hook up with him?" The words roll off my tongue.

She stares at me, mouth open, eyes wide.

Jesus, what is *wrong* with me?

"God, Hattie, I'm so sorry. That was way out of—"

And then Hattie starts laughing again, this time even more maniacally, tears streaming from the corners of her eyes.

Any remaining gazes that weren't already locked on us move in our direction.

"Me? And *Ben!?* Oh, honey, no. No, no, no." I continue to stare. "Never in a million years would you catch me with that man." Okay, well, that kind of stung.

"It's not like he's hard to look at," I say, eyes moving to my food and voice low.

Embarrassed, I realize.

Because despite how much I hate to admit it, there's not a fucking molecule in my body that isn't attracted to Ben.

And someone questioning my taste to this degree? Well . . .

"Oh, he's good-looking, that's for sure. You've caught a hottie, babe."

"I haven't—"

"You have. You both are just too fucking stubborn to admit it." She takes a napkin and dabs at her eyes, and I make a mental note to ask what kind of mascara and eyeliner she uses because the thick layer doesn't even budge. "Lola, he's not my *type*."

Not her type.

In what universe would Ben not be a red-blooded woman's type? Unless . . .

"Ding, ding, ding, you've got a winner," she says, winking at me. "You're more my style, babe." I blink. "Don't worry, I don't poach from my bestie. Though, for you? I could make an exception."

"I'm sorry. I . . . That was incredibly rude of me to assume, I—"

"I get it all the time. It's my own fault. I love to mess with people and play along. But you had that hurt doe look in your eyes, and I couldn't do it." She sighs, putting the napkin on her lap. "No, Ben isn't my type, and I'm definitely not his." She looks me over again, red-painted lips tipping as she picks up a fork and then waves it up and down in my direction. "But you? You're fucking perfect."

"I'm . . ."

"Perfect. This is perfect, actually." A French fry goes into her mouth and she chews. "God, I can't believe I didn't see it early. Sweet as sugar, spice lying underneath. I bet you're also submissive as fuck in bed, aren't you?" My eyes go wide, panicking.

My mind also goes back to that night.

Every command he gave, and every time I didn't hesitate.

"Oh my God, you're perfect for him," she says, white teeth bright within the confines of red lips. "Perfect balance. Won't take his shit, he won't get bored. Keep him on his toes and he'll keep you in line. Make sure you take care of yourself." She puts another bite of salad in her mouth, chewing while looking me over like she's vetting me for something. "Fucking perfect. Meant to be."

"I'm sorry. I think you have this completely misunderstood. This isn't . . . I'm not . . . We're not . . . I haven't . . ." I can't finish a single sentence.

The words won't come.

But Hattie just smiles.

"Oh, I know. I know you're not—now. But I see it. You are. You just don't know it."

"It's not like that. It was one time, and that's it, never again."

"I doubt it," she says with a sly smile. Hattie knows more.

"Hattie. The man can't stand me."

"Interesting that you didn't say you can't stand him." A thick eyebrow is raised, and shit if she isn't right.

Why is that? Why did I focus on how Ben feels toward me and not the other way around?

"Well, that too. I can't stand him. But he can't even be in the same room as me without arguing with me."

"You never lock your doors."

"What?"

"Drives him nuts. Hear him grumbling about it. You never lock your door." He's not wrong. And the few times he's barged in, he's mentioned that. But what does that have to do with fucking anything?

"What does it matter to him? The back door to the street locks automatically. It's not like I'm leaving his business or apartment at risk."

"It's not safe." I stare at her. "He . . . He has a thing about safety. Especially safety for women." As I'm looking at her, there's a flash, a memory surfacing. "His hometown. A buddy of his, his girlfriend, was kidnapped. Crazy stalker, obsessed with her. Anyway, she got away, but before that, she was taken to his family's work site. The girl was kidnapped from her own business, her cop boyfriend sitting right outside. You just . . . You never know." Her eyes move to my wrist, bruises having long healed, and I wonder if he talked to her about the mark or if she's remembering when the dark mark caught her own eye. "His brother's girl? She was in an abusive relationship for years. Things with safety just . . . hit too close to home for him." I swallow, not knowing what to say.

I can't deny the bruise, but I also can't tell anyone the real source. Hattie continues talking.

"He doesn't hate you. He . . . doesn't feel things. Locks himself away. Stays in his art, his business. He's separated himself from so many things." She looks at the sky, blue and cloudless, a seagull overhead looking for something to steal. "Anyway. Just . . . give it time. Give him time. And don't . . . Don't shut out the opportunity altogether, yeah?" she says, and her eyes look so genuine, like she really, truly wants nothing more in this moment than for me to give her best friend a chance.

I sigh.

"Yeah, Hattie," is all I say on the subject, but her smile tells me it was enough.

And for the rest of the day, I blame Old Lola for still being present, having a bit of the reins. I tell myself that it's because of the old people-pleasing side of me that I said that.

But deep down, New Lola knows.

That's not why I agreed.

No, that was for me, not Hattie.

TWENTY-SIX

-Lola-

THAT NIGHT, the bell rings over the front door of Libby's and I don't even look up. This is the third time this has happened tonight alone.

I need to work on getting the lock fixed as soon as possible. Tonight, I'm planning on rigging up a chair under the lock, but that can't be a permanent solution.

Right now, I'm ducked behind the counter, organizing white bakery boxes and rolling up the extra rolls of pink twine, closing up for the day before I head upstairs and collapse in bed. And as much as I love my customers, once the bakery is closed, I'm done with customer service. I want to finish cleaning and then flop in my bed, where I'll overthink every interaction I've ever made while trying to fall asleep.

"We're closed, I'm so sorry!" I shout then knock my head into the underside of the counter as I try to stand. "Fuck!"

Great, Lola. Very professional.

No lock on the door, *and* you just cursed in front of a potential customer.

Except when I open my eyes, rubbing at my head where I'm sure there will be a bump, I don't see a potential customer.

Instead, there stands Johnny Vitale.

"I think you can stay open a few minutes later for me, *bellissima*." My stomach churns at his dark hair, slicked back and greasy. It's thinning but combed back in a way to attempt to hide that, and he has a smile on his face that gives me chills.

And not the chills Ben gives me when he gives me a douchey smile.

The kind of chills you get when you're watching a scary movie and everything goes quiet.

The kind of chills you get when something that you can't pinpoint inside of you knows intuitively that something bad is about to happen.

Johnny is bad news.

That much I know for certain. But this? This feels . . . more sinister.

"Leave, Johnny."

"Oh, don't be like that, Lola. I thought we were friends." His voice is sickly sweet, his thick North Jersey accent making a mockery of the kind words.

"I don't even know you. All I know is that, once again, my father fucked up, and once again, I'm being forced to make it better."

"I'd like you to make it better." Acid burns in my throat. He keeps walking closer, hand grazing the top of one of my tables as he moves closer to me. "You talk to your father recently?" he asks, a smile playing on his lips, a thick eyebrow raised. This is a game for him.

A sick and twisted game to pull me into this shit.

My stomach drops.

New me might be putting myself first and saying fuck it to everyone else, but old me? She knows what this means.

And old me knows that no matter what new me tells herself, I can't just ignore this problem.

"I can't say I have," I say, not giving him much of anything.

Though it's the truth. I haven't heard from him. Stupid of me to assume that silence on his end meant his chaos wouldn't be touching me any longer.

"Johnny, you need to leave or I'll call the cops." All joking, any hint of vague friendliness leaves his voice.

"You call the cops and it won't end well for your daddy," he says, and honestly, that should be the expected response.

Even more so, I should say *okay, do it.* I should say *fine, he deserves it.* I should tell Johnny and my father and the world at large that I'm done with this burden. This burden that I've wasted *so damn much* of my life shouldering. But that's the problem, isn't it? When you spend so long taking care of someone, you don't want to see all of your hard work go to waste.

And when you tie your self-worth to keeping someone out of trouble, it makes the way you see yourself—for better or worse—inherently tied to that person.

It might not have always been my job to take care of my dad, to shield Lilah from the messes he always got himself into, from the messes Mom left behind, but I made it that. I took it and never questioned a thing, never said no. It was wrong of my mom to ask me to help when I was that young. But I know to my soul she didn't want *this* for me. She never thought it would go this far.

And for that, I have no one to blame but myself.

"Johnny, please. Leave," I say again, this time firmer, but internally I feel like Jell-O. Terrified. Quaking.

His smile has turned from teasing to sinister.

"What do you have for me, Lola?" I sigh, my eyes looking over my bakery, my small haven.

My dream.

"I have nothing. I built this place on loans and savings. *I have nothing.*"

"He's gotta tab, Lola," Johnny says.

I already knew this.

I already know the total.

You'd think those words, the acknowledgment of what I already knew, wouldn't cut. You'd think that after all these years, I'd be numb to it.

I'm not. It still cuts, even more knowing my dad has a debt that he clearly expects me to settle.

I sigh, the feeling going bone-deep.

The exhaustion.

Anyone who has ever loved an addict knows that feeling too. The bone-deep exhaustion from life closing in on you.

"Not my problem, Johnny," I say, trying to sound tough, trying to sound resolute.

"Unfortunately, *bellissima*, it is."

"I didn't make promises. I'm not in power. I don't have access to anything."

"He says you have the money."

"My father has no concept of my or anyone's financial situation. The money he thinks I have to dig him out of *yet another hole* was spent to open this bakery."

"It's not going to be good for him if he doesn't get this sorted."

"Why do you keep letting this happen? You know damn well he doesn't have the fucking money. And he can't pull any more favors without raising the alarm."

"Not in the business of telling people how to live their lives."

"Can't you blacklist him or something?"

"If we blacklisted every gambler, Lola, we wouldn't have a business at all." I guess that makes sense. I don't like it, but the logic is there.

"Look, I hate to bother a pretty thing like you. Visiting isn't a hardship, seeing you in your cute little uniform with your sweet braids, but it's a long drive to the shore. I have real work to do. I gave you an extra week because I didn't want to come down, but now it's getting a little out of hand." The bile burns when he calls me a pretty little thing. I sigh, trying to seem like I'm annoyed but not scared.

Never show you're scared, not to a man like this.

"I have some. Not all." Since his last visit, I begrudgingly created an envelope, skimming some of the cash each day just in case. In case I was cornered, just like this.

Because I guess even though I left this in my father's court, I knew. A sad part of me knew he wouldn't handle it and I'd be left to pick up the pieces.

"He's not gonna be happy."

"Well, he's gonna have to make due. I just opened this place."

"That's not Mr. Carluccio's problem."

"It shouldn't be mine."

"Your father gave Carmello Carluccio your word, and he expects you to keep it."

Carmello Carluccio.

The head of the Carluccio crime family.

For the rest of the state, the rest of the world, even, the Carluccios are a mix of a tabloid story filled with truths and lies. Something to gossip about at a ball game, but not too loud for the wrong person to hear.

They're what movies and books are written around, exaggerated and glamorized versions of the same story. The Don of New Jersey, with hands in unions and the waste industry. If you listen, you'll hear whispers of money laundering through strip clubs and butcher shops, laundromats, and cigar stores. Cash businesses and imports where money can get muddled easily. You'll hear of quiet handshakes with politicians to get around permits and ordinances or elaborate dinners and wine-soaked smiles at banquets.

But for me, it all became real-life a year ago when I got the call from Johnny on behalf of the Carluccios.

It turns out that the handshakes with politicians part is true.

In the past, my father paid off his gambling debts with permits and by sweeping potential charges under the rug.

But as the world turns, as things change, as every move a politician makes is researched and picked apart on social media, it became harder. The spotlight was bigger, and the mouths that needed feeding became hungrier.

The problem is, my father likes to gamble.

Regardless of whether he could settle his debt with favors and gifts, he continued promising them.

The other problem is he's not very *good* at gambling.

"That was a year ago, Johnny."

"Years ago or days ago, that's how this business works, sweetheart, sorry to tell you. You put your neck out once and you're attached to the debt." I stare at him, wondering how much more of my life will be spent paying for my father's mistakes.

Am I forever doomed to fear the worst and never to grow?

As always, when it comes to issues with my father, my mother's last words come back to me.

"Please take care of your father. He's going to need you once I'm gone. I know it's not fair, but you have to do it for the family. Don't let it touch Lilah, Lola. She'll get dragged in deep."

Lilah.

I always held to that, making sure Dad's shit never touched her.

God. What a fucking mess this all is.

"I can't do this forever. I need . . . I can't keep doing this," I say, speaking to myself but also Johnny.

I need an out.

"Once this is done. Once we settle this, I need to end it. I can't do this forever. I need . . . I need to make it known that my father can no longer do this."

Johnny smiles.

The look is devious. Dangerous.

Evil.

"You know, I could work on that. Talk to Carm. See what I could do." I'm reaching into my bag and grabbing for my wallet where I have the cash I pulled for this reason, but I pause.

I pause because those words don't sound right.

They sound . . . off.

The meaning of them doesn't sit right.

It's never that simple.

He takes a step closer, moving toward the open area between the customer area and behind the register.

His eyes are roaming my body as blood is draining from my face.

This is so not good.

This is *so so bad.*

"It would require some . . . incentive for me, though."

Can he hear my heart beating?

It's going in time with the rhythm of the bass next door, low, steady.

Strangely, the noise is a comfort instead of its typical nuisance.

"What do you mean?" My hand is grasping the envelope with four thousand dollars in it.

"I think you know what I mean, Lola." His voice is low, and his tongue dips out of his mouth, wetting his lips as he takes another step so he's now fully behind the counter.

I'm weakened prey that limped into a cave, and he is a predator who followed the scent of my blood.

My hand goes out, the envelope between us. The white paper is shaking.

Shit.

Keep it together, Lola.

"I think you should take this and go." He steps closer, a hand moving toward the paper.

"I could help you, Lola."

"Do you really think your boss would be happy if I hooked up with you in order to clear my father's debts?" Our hands are now attached at the envelope, but he doesn't grab it away, and I don't let go.

It's the only thing between us.

It feels like a lifeline.

Not just a lifeline to protecting my father anymore. Not just cash that will keep him out of trouble. But a flimsy wall between myself and this terrifying man.

"I could make it work," he says, looking me over.

"I'd rather pay," I say. Johnny's eyes go dark.

"What if I don't care what you'd rather do?" he asks, and the sinister nature of those words curls around me, swirls around us like venom in the air. I can almost see it threatening me. My hand drops the money as I step back, trying to get away.

My back hits the wall.

And Johnny steps forward, locking me in place.

"You know, I can always go to your sister if you can't help. Maybe she could, one way or another."

I have spent fifteen years protecting Lilah from the poor decisions of my father and keeping her safe from the secrets bred from the poor decisions of our mother. I've always been my little sister's protector, always shielding her from this shit.

I won't let this scumbag change that.

"Please, Johnny. Don't. Leave Lilah out of this."

"Lilah is such a pretty name. She looks so much like your mother, too—one of us." Lilah got the most of my mother's Italian, while I got Dad's Irish. She has the curves and the skin that tans perfectly, striking features, and a perfectly sloped nose.

"Johnny. Please. I'll . . . I'll figure it out." I take a deep breath, thinking. "Give me a week. I can . . . I can get more together next week." My mind runs through what I can sell, what I can pull from, and how much I need to sell in cookies and cupcakes to get enough for him.

"At least fifteen grand. His total is up to one hundred." I feel sick, knowing that since I last talked to my dad, thirty thousand dollars have been added to the total.

"I'll figure it out," I grit out. I guess I won't be hiring an employee soon.

"I'll need a retainer. Something so I know you mean business."

"There's four thousand in that envelope."

"I'm not talking money, *bellissima*." He steps closer to me until I back into a wall.

"Johnny—"

"Just a taste," he says, and his breath hits my lips. Panic freezes me.

When you're a woman, you think often about what you'd do in a situation like this.

It's the sad truth of the world, that we all wonder what would happen if we were cornered by a man who had sick, ill intentions.

We all like to think we'd shout, scream, hit—anything.

But I just stand there.

A statue.

My mind is blank.

My body is ice, blood frozen in my veins.

"Johnny, please—"

"A taste, bella," he says, and then his lips are on mine, kissing me, tasting of bourbon and tobacco and smelling of too much fucking cologne, and my senses are overwhelmed instantly.

My mind goes blank with the panic, the rage.

And then I do it.

I slap him, my body kicking into gear and fracturing from the fear, moving to survival.

"What the fuck!" he shouts, holding his ear where I slapped him. The skin there is already bright red. I'd be proud of myself but I don't have time when his hand moves and grabs my wrists in each hand, the envelope of cash falling to the ground, and he pins them to the wall above me.

Oh fuck.

TWENTY-SEVEN

-Ben-

"Can you bring this over to Lola?" Hattie asks, a fork in a salad as she sits her ass on the edge of the reception desk. Her hand lifts a stack of envelopes in a rubber band.

I ignore what's in her hand.

"Is that sanitary?"

"Eating?"

"Sitting on the desk."

"Are you going to tattoo someone on the reception desk?" she asks, a single penciled eyebrow raised. I roll my eyes. "Testy, testy, Mr. Coleman." I ignore her. "Seems every time I bring up our sweet neighbor, you get grumpy. Or should I say, grumpier." This is the game she's been playing for weeks: mentioning Lola, waiting for my reaction, and then reacting to that.

Normally, I would just ignore her.

But Lola herself has been ignoring me for nearly two weeks. I haven't seen her in the hall, haven't run into her on the boardwalk, and she sure as fuck hasn't been bringing me any cookies.

And it's driving me insane.

As much as this woman drives me crazy, I've been enjoying our banter, the back and forth, the frustration. The rush I get when she's around.

That being said, I'm not sure why every time Hattie brings up Lola, I feel the need to argue and change the subject, but here we are.

Yes, you do, the voice in my head whispers. *It has a lot to do with the way she looked sitting on your bed with her fingers in her pussy, coming with your name on her lips.*

The way she left you unsatisfied, stammering that it was a mistake.

The way you assumed that once she cooled down, she'd see reason and come find you—but still hasn't.

That one really got to you, the voice reminds me. Because it's not wrong—I thought after that kiss, she'd seek me out. I thought she'd have felt it too.

I mentally flip off the little voice.

It's also the reason you've done everything in your power this week to piss her off enough to get her to come over and bitch at you.

This time I flick the little voice, which sounds annoyingly like my little brother Tanner, and answer Hattie.

"Fuck off."

"So can you?"

"Can I what?"

"Can you bring over these to Lola? It's mail. Hers keeps getting dropped off here." I look at the stack again. Sure enough, the envelopes have Libby's bakery as the recipient.

"Why would I do that?" Her eyebrows meet in the middle.

"Uh, because they aren't ours? And she might need them? And I'm pretty sure it's illegal to keep someone else's mail?"

"Aren't you friends with her? Couldn't you bring it over to her? You're there all the time." *And I don't want to see the temptation that is Lola.*

"I've got a client coming soon."

"So do I," I say. I know it's pointless to hope that she doesn't know the truth, but . . .

"I know you can't read through the sound of your fucking booming music, which, just to tell you, I know you're doing it to piss off a neighbor. It's also starting to get on my nerves, too, but you can still read your schedule and see you don't have any appointments for an hour."

She's right, of course.

"Come on, Hattie. Can't you just go over and hand them to her? Or bring it the next time you see her?" She shakes her head, her hair moving with it in a pin-straight curtain.

"Nope. It's illegal to withhold mail. And I have a piercing coming in in—" The bell above the door rings. "Oh, look! There she is!" I turn, expecting to see Lola finally here to bitch me out. My heart skips, and I hate the stupid fucking disappointment I feel when it's a cute blonde with a crop top, shyly waving at Hattie. "My six o'clock is here!" The guest looks me over, giving me a head-to-toe that tells me she's the kind of sweet who would love to give dark and dangerous a chance.

Her type isn't uncommon in my line of work: women who will eventually go on to marry accountants and pop out the perfect 2.5 kids thinking they might want to give the broody tattoo artist a try.

Not my type.

Oh, but what about sweet bakers who wear pink and bop around to Taylor Swift? the voice asks.

This time I mentally punch the voice in the nonexistent face.

"You. Go next door. Ask Lola what her display will look like and if she has a photo. I also need a rundown of what she's auctioning off and the retail value." Hattie points to the front door.

"Hattie—"

"Now. Go. Put on your big boy pants and face the big scary bakery owner." She actually rolls her eyes at that.

"I'm not scared of her, Hat—" I start. But she laughs, cutting me off as she puts her hand on the arm of the client, urging her into her booth.

"You might not be scared of her in the traditional way, Ben, but that woman scares the shit out of you. Once you realize that, we'll all be able to live with less of a headache."

And then she's gone behind a closed door, and I can hear her turn down the loud music, almost like she's telling me to man the fuck up and go.

With a challenge like that, I can't stay no.

Saying no would mean she won.

And I don't lose.

When the bell chimes as I leave the shop, I can hear Hattie's laugh ringing out over the sound of the lowered music.

I walk the five feet from my front door to Lola's, and each step, I think about how I shouldn't be doing this.

In fact, I should just drop the mail in her box or slip it under her door and move on with my day.

But the truth of the matter is, this woman has gotten deep under my skin. She's a fucking pain in my ass. Her sass, her attitude, her unwillingness to even listen or reason with me.

I can't stand her.

And even more, her insistence on avoiding me, ignoring me, when we both know something is brewing between us is maddening.

After I changed the wifi and we had what we did together, I knew I was fucked. That ignoring her and ignoring my dick wouldn't get her out of my system. But she's been incredibly successful at ignoring *me* since that day.

Still, something about her has my mind stuck on the way her ass looks in those little shorts, the way her apron strings cinch her waist. The way she moaned my name, the way she came with my name on her lips, the way she pulled the head of my cock into her mouth . . .

And, of course, the way she can bake a hell of a fucking cookie.

Is it normal for your dick to be connected to tastes? There's no universe where the thought of a chocolate chip cookie should get my dick hard.

No, but the memory of her hair tousled, chest heaving, standing in her front doorway does. That glazed look stuck around in her eyes even after she realized her mistake of texting me when she was fucking coming.

Coming saying my name, even when I wasn't around.

And the memory of seeing that in person, my fingers sliding deep into that wet pussy, my tattooed hands on her thick hips, the way she was ready to take me?

Fuck, I think I'll be jacking off to that memory until I die.

I shake my head as I reach for the front door.

A bad place to be.

A man's mind could stay on that thought forever. The thought of sweet, giggly Lola coming with his name on her lips?

Fuck.

I adjust myself as I open the door.

It should be locked—the bakery is technically closed right now.

She still hasn't fixed the lock.

This woman is a fucking mess.

But that thought isn't what has my body stopping, frozen like a bucket of ice was dumped over my head.

It's the sound of a smack, then a man's voice screaming, "What the fuck!"

And as I enter the bakery quickly, on red alert, it's the sight of Johnny Vitale pinning one of Lola's hands above her head.

A white envelope on the floor next to her.

And fear on her face.

Johnny Vitale, the right-hand man to Carmello Carluccio. Everyone on the East Coast knows the Carluccio family and their soldiers. Especially if you're one of the tattoo shops the men get their loyalty pieces at.

It all becomes clear.

The stress, the bakery. Her telling me this place *needs to work.*

She has a loan with the Carluccios.

It all makes sense.

She's right—she didn't use Daddy's money to build her business. No, she just used his connections to get herself in a fucking dangerous position.

A part of me is disappointed in her. For the past few weeks, guilt has started to eat at me. I targeted her wrong. She's not a spoiled brat —she's had hardship and she worked hard. I was a dick by denying that. But what I'm seeing now, what's starting to become clearer . . . It's blurring that for me.

But it's the look of fear on Lola's face has it all melting.

Who cares if she built this place from the bottom up like I built up Coleman Ink? Who cares if she took a shady loan or if her family spotted her cash? All I need to worry about is what's going on now and how I can help her out of this mess.

And I sure as fuck don't have time to wonder why I want to fix her mess when her eyes shift to mine, locking there.

Relief.

That's what I see there.

Sweet fucking relief, and all I want to do is pull her into my arms and make her mine.

Fuck the games, fuck fucking her out of my system. Fuck it all, because that look?

She's mine.

Strange how relief in her raises alarm in me. Strange how her relief cements my place in her life, whether she knows it or not.

"What the fuck is going on here?" I ask, voice booming in the small space, and that's it. That's all I say.

"Ben!" Her voice is weak, fear drenching the single word, but relief is in her eyes. Stark relief.

"Who the fuck are you?" Johnny has dropped Lola's hands but hasn't stepped back, still pinning her in place with his body.

"Her neighbor," I say, arms crossing on my chest like I give not a single fuck. "And her man." And at this moment, I understand the mark on Lola's wrist I saw weeks ago was from this man.

Mixed with the panic on her face moments ago, the panic of which the remnants are still there, I feel my own rage forming.

I step closer to where they are.

"Her man, huh?" I don't respond. Instead, I continue staring.

"You need to back the fuck up," I say. "Right fucking now." I take another step closer, my tone full of venom. Lola's eyes widen as I approach, my hand moving to Johnny's shoulder, pushing him away and back from Lola.

The change is subtle, but her body—it sinks a bit. An ounce of tension leaves her veins.

Johnny's body shifts to face me more, moving to appraise, to see how he measures up to me. If he can take me.

His eyes give me a full head-to-toe before he steps back fully from Lola, letting her free to take a single step closer to me.

Figures.

I've come to realize in my years that men like this? They don't know what to do when another man, a bigger man, questions them.

His kind is all fucking talk unless they're talking to someone they deem smaller, weaker.

I am neither of those.

"We were in the middle of a conversation," he says, arms crossing on his chest, a small smile on his lips. "Weren't we, *bellissima*." The word makes me sick. "Just a conversation amongst . . . colleagues. Trying to get inventive with a solution to a problem."

It's a taunt.

He's stepped back from me once more, three or four feet between us, and it's given a boost to his confidence.

Because men like this, once the immediate danger is gone? They can't resist. And he couldn't resist.

Men like this rarely can deny the urge to poke the bear. I put a hand to Lola's elbow, moving her behind me as I stare at him down my nose.

"Did you ask him to touch you?" I ask the question but don't look to Lola to get the answer. I already know it. "Your conversation is done," I say, staring hard at the man in front of me. In his eyes, there is frustration. Frustration, anger, and a hint of embarrassment.

But on his lips? There's a smile.

And I see why when his hand moves out, reaching for my girl.

Reaching for Lola.

Her body tenses, not fully behind me yet, and instinct takes over.

I can't help it.

My own hand reaches out, grabbing his and twisting, so it's behind his back. My body moves quick, pinning him to the wall where minutes before, he had Lola locked in.

Doesn't feel so good, does it now?

"You even think about putting your hands on her again, we're going to have problems." He tries to push back, to remove himself, possibly fight back, but it's clear that he's not used to being in this position. He's not used to being the smaller man, in stature or socially. "I do not see you here. I do not see you at this bakery. I do not see you on the boardwalk. You come near Lola again, I'll come find you. You might have friends in high places, but I won't need friends. I will find you, and I will make you fucking pay. You leave Lola alone." I push harder on his wrist, digging it into his back until a soft sigh of pain comes from his lips. "Tell me you understand."

Silence.

I press harder, pulling the arm up his back at an awkward angle, his face pressing into the pink wall of Lola's bakery. She makes a distressed noise from behind me but stays put.

For once in her life, the woman is doing what she should be.

Thank you, God.

"Do you understand?" I ask again, pressing harder and knowing that much more will lead to more than an ache in the morning.

Not that I give a shit.

"I understand," he grumbles out, the words muffled with strain.

I don't let go, holding on to the position for a few moments still before letting go and pushing him toward the door.

"Not worth my fucking time, Lola," he says, grabbing something from the ground that fell earlier before I can get a glimpse of it.

"Then shouldn't be a problem then, should it?" I say, moving to completely shield Lola with my body. We move as one, following Johnny's progress to the front door of the bakery.

But a man like that, he can't leave without getting the last word.

"You better figure out a way to settle this, you fucking cunt," he says, spitting at my shoes. His next words come quieter, directed to the shaking woman behind me as he tucks a white envelope into a jacket pocket. "If not, I'll be taking a lot more than a kiss," he says, and then he's gone.

I watch as he walks out the door, pushing it so it slams behind him and the glass rattles, my eyes following as he turns left down the boardwalk. I wonder if he's walking to his car to head back up toward Newark or if he's going to another business on the boardwalk, another business owner who made the wrong choice in their pursuit of the American dream.

Once he's out of sight, I walk to the front and flip the deadbolt, noticing it doesn't stick before I shake my head. "Fuckin' Brad," I mumble under my breath, grabbing a nearby chair and notching it under the handle. It will have to do for now. Then I turn back to Lola.

She's in the same place, back to the wall, staring off at the front door as if I'm not even standing a few feet away from her.

That's not what worries me, though.

This woman might drive me insane, but she's confident. Sure of herself. There's never been a moment when she goes toe-to-toe with me where she's backed down, questioned things.

But right now? Panic runs through me as I look at her.

She's shaking.

From head to toe, she's shaking.

"Come here, Lola," I say, opening my arms as I stand in front of her.

In any other situation, any other woman, I'd pull her into my arms. I'd force her, drag her to me, shield her from the world.

But with Lola, I just don't fucking *know*.

Something tells me I need her to come to me. To make that choice, take that step on her own.

I don't think she heard me, though, her eye still on that door, somewhere else.

"Lola, come here," I say once more, my voice firmer, louder. Finally, her head turns to me. She heard me now, but this is almost worse. Now that she's facing me, I can see her eyes. They are glazed, fear and adrenaline needing an outlet. My decision is made. "Now," I say, my voice demanding.

I'm hoping she doesn't hear the slight shake to it, the sound of uncertainty, because seeing her, this strong, petulant, annoying as fuck woman, broken and shaken like this is killing me.

But then it happens.

I'm not sure what I expected with my demand, but it wasn't this.

It wasn't her doing just as I asked.

It wasn't her moving the four steps until she's right in my arms, where I can wrap them around her, the top of her head nestling right under my chin.

She's tall.

I knew this, of course, but having her here in my arms without some kind of argument or build-up before is . . . nice.

She fits.

Most women, they hit my chest and I have to bend to hold them, to kiss them.

Not Lola. I breathe in her hair, brown sugar and vanilla, the smell that wafts up to my apartment every fucking morning, the scent that haunts me day in and day out.

"You okay?" I ask into her hair.

As always, she surprises me.

"I'm fine," she says, despite the shaking. It's lessened, but her body still moves, wrapped in mine.

It's not the words that shock me.

It's the voice.

It's not fear laced in her words—it's anger.

Lola is *mad*.

Why on earth would she be fucking mad?

She got in bed with the Carluccios. Clearly, she had them help her build this place and she bit off more than she could chew.

What did she expect would happen? That they'd be sweet Girl Scouts, calling her on the phone to politely request their payments?

"No, you aren't," I say because she's not. Angry or scared or any other emotion, Lola is not okay.

"What do you know?" That anger is turning to me, directing itself from the situation she's found herself into the only person in reach to catch the hit.

That's fine, baby. I'll be your punching bag.

"I know that you're shaking and white as a sheet. Look at me, Lola," I say, moving a hand to her chin and tipping it up. Something about my hands, tattooed and tanned against her fair skin does things to me. Seeing the juxtaposition snaps one of the threads inside; the angry wall I've built between us weakening.

Something about the touch must snap something in her, too, shaking her out of her daze.

"Ben, I need you to kiss me." The words aren't breathy and sweet, but fierce and demanding.

"What?"

"I need you to kiss me. I need to . . . Shit, I need to forget this," she says, her hands bunching in the black tee shirt I'm wearing, the same one I always wear for work. Her hand, tipped with light-pink nails, bunches up the old-school white logo.

Another juxtaposition.

Another snap to the tether.

One hand moves to her hip.

Her lips loosen, open slightly, her breath becoming erratic.

She wants this.

I can't tell if it's because she wants to forget or if that's an excuse.

I don't know if I'll regret this in ten minutes or an hour or a year.

But I do know I can't go a single moment longer without kissing this woman.

So my other hand moves to the back of her neck as my lips crash to hers.

It's not sweet.

It's not gentle.

It's not some kind of bond being built, the start of something beautiful and everlasting.

No, it's hot, and it's angry, and it's filled with the tension we've both been creating and avoiding. My teeth clash with hers as her mouth opens to mine, my tongue entering her mouth and tangling with hers, tasting her. Coffee and cookies.

The same as that first time.

My teeth nip her lip hard, probably close to drawing blood, but she is as lost as I am, moaning at the sensation. I take two steps until she's pinned to the wall. My hand on the back of her head gathers her braids, tugging her back hard, drawing another moan from her as my hand angles her head better to get more, to fight her until she gives me everything.

My mind goes back to having her pinned against the hall in the landing between our apartments, how she whimpered my name as she came. About how fucking badly I wanted to fuck her until we both had this attraction out of our systems.

Funny, because right now, I don't think I'll ever actually get this woman out of my system.

That thought should scare me.

Instead, it fuels me.

Every molecule in my body yearns for this woman.

But not here.

And sure as fuck not now.

When I break the kiss, releasing her braids and her body, she mewls in protest.

"Is the back door locked?" I ask, forehead to hers, panting.

"Wha—?" she asks, her voice woozy like she's not all here.

In any other situation, I'd smile.

Right now, I'm fighting the urge to both fuck her and run down the boardwalk and rip someone's throat out.

"The front door. It doesn't lock?" This question I know the answer to.

"It doesn't click. It doesn't . . . not always . . . and I called Brad to get it fixed, but . . ." I sigh.

"But Brad doesn't fucking fix anything." She just blinks.

"Back door?" *That one I know locks.* She just chooses to forget about it.

"What?"

"The back door, baby. Is it locked?"

She bites her lip.

I know the answer. My hand goes to her chin as she tries to look away from me, holding it tight and without any regard for her comfort.

"You. Lock. The. Fucking. Door. Lola. Every time. The back door stays locked no matter what. The front door is locked as soon as you close, and you don't open it until you open up the next day. I'll fix that lock in the morning."

She's silent.

"You done in here?"

"What?" God. Cute. Cute and infuriating, and right now, with her still shaken, scary.

"Are you done in here? Or do you have other things to do?" She looks around, trying to remember where we are. Again, if we were anywhere else, in any other situation, the fact that my lips have her lost like this would make me smile.

"No. I'm done. I was just . . . cleaning up. Extra stuff." I don't answer. Instead, I pick her up. Her legs wrap around my hips, and fuck, I like it. A lot.

She fits.

I knew she would.

I walk us, my hands under her ass to support her as she lays her head in the crook of my neck, to her back door, flipping the shitty, flimsy lock before leaving it behind us. I pull out my own keys to unlock the back door to Coleman's.

Hattie's sitting at the back table, and when her eyes go to Lola in my arms, her face flushes with confusion.

"Cancel my appointments," I say, tipping my chin to my best friend and coworker.

I expect her to argue. Tell me I can't just cancel appointments. Tell me that she's not my bitch.

Typical Hattie shit.

But her eyes move to Lola in my arms.

"Got it. Call me . . . soon?" she says, not even demanding.

And right there. That's the reason Hattie Jones is my best friend. The only person on the earth who would see this, know I have it handled, know when to argue, and let me go.

She's a real one.

"Cancel your appointments, too. We're locking up, and then I'll walk you out."

She stares at me, her face losing color as she realizes this isn't some small issue.

But she just nods, grabs her bag, and starts turning off the lights.

A real one.

TWENTY-EIGHT

-Lola-

Ben's living room couch is shockingly comfortable.

I was only in his apartment for those short minutes, unable to take anything in. I'm not sure what I expected when he carried me up here, but it wasn't dark wood and framed art. It sure wasn't cozy and cool and welcoming.

I guess I would have expected a frat house vibe, pull-out couches for beds and dirty socks strewn about. Instead, I got dark, broken-in leather couches, antique writing desks, and walls of art.

It's been at least an hour since the Johnny situation, and my body has finally stopped shaking. My mind is starting to work on words and feelings and an understanding of what just happened and where I am now.

But because I'm me, instead of, say, thanking Ben for saving my ass or explaining what happened or even just going back to my place, my head turns to the man and says the first thing that comes to my mind.

"I'm not . . . messing around with you," I say. Then I decide to clarify because I am a glutton for punishment. "Tonight." His thick dark brows come together as he turns his head to me.

"What?"

"I'm not doing stuff with you. You know . . . sexual stuff." God, why am I doing this? His brows furrow deeper in confusion and maybe even frustration.

"No shit," he says. "You've been through enough. Plus, last time was a mistake." My stomach churns with what I've been overthinking for two weeks.

He regrets what happened.

And while I left in a flurry, while I slammed the door in his face and never looked back and avoided him since, something about every moment we're alone together has felt *so fucking right* for me.

Including that night in the hallway.

That night in his bed.

I hate this man.

And I want this man.

And somehow, all of those emotions—frustration and anguish and need and desire—feel so at peace with each other when directed at him. Like a part of me knows at the end, it will all settle, that the pieces will fall into place when I least expect it.

He sees the panic in my face, the panic that he *doesn't want this*.

He sees it. I know he does.

As is the way I'm learning, Ben likes to do, he takes care of me, assuaging my fear. His hands go to my face, cupping it until I'm looking at him, into his eyes that are telling me . . . *more*. So much more than I should see in the eyes of the man who drives me absolutely insane and who, I know I drive up a fucking wall as well.

"No, sweet girl. Not that kind. The kind where I should never have messed with you before we ironed shit out. You were stressed, your mind somewhere else. I saw it—I knew. I knew it wasn't right. You said you wanted a distraction, and since that day I met you in your little pajamas, I knew I was fucked. I haven't been able to stop thinking of you, no matter how fucking crazy you make me."

At this moment, I think I could fall.

I could drop off the cliff of sanity and fall into this man, lose myself there and never come up for air. Let him take care of me and comfort me and be there for me the way no one in my life ever has. Not since my mom, at least.

But I can't do that.

I take care of myself.

I am the one person I can count on to know what I need when I need it.

"You're an ass," I say instead, staring at him. His eyes crinkle with a smile, tiny lines at the side of each eye and a crease in his cheek where one side of his mouth tips up.

He thinks I'm funny.

Interesting.

Very interesting.

"Yeah, I know. But I'm not an ass who's gonna fuck you tonight." He stands up, reaching for his phone. "No matter how much I want to," he says, and a chill runs through me. Maybe I should change my stance . . . "You haven't eaten yet, I assume?" I shake my head. "Pizza good?" He starts to scroll before looking at me. My stomach growls at the thought. Another smile, more crinkles, more belly flipping. "I'll order from Three Brothers, have them bring it down."

———

An hour later, there's music playing quietly—I definitely made a quip about his music having the *ability* to be turned down low, which made him smile—and we're eating pizza.

We haven't talked about what happened.

Every bone and muscle and sinew in my body has been on high alert, waiting for it to happen.

And when Ben turns to me, setting his empty plate aside, I know. I know he's going to ask. I don't know what I expected when he saved me from Johnny, chided me about locked doors, and ordered me to stay in his place, but I guess part of me was hoping for him to just . . . let it go.

And while I don't know Ben Coleman *that* well, I'm pretty sure he's absolutely *not* the type to just let things go.

Fuck, he's been blasting music in his shop and apartment at night just to piss me off for weeks.

"Tell me what happened," he orders, sitting back on the couch we've been eating at like he's settling in for some great story.

"I really don't want to," I say, picking at the crust of my pizza.

"Too bad. You have to." Irritation runs through me.

New Lola has been hiding in the shadow of Old Lola, scared and quiet and trying to figure a fix, but as Ben seems to do, she's being dragged out.

"Says who?"

"Says the man who walked in to find a bookie in your business after you closed while you were scared out of your mind. And let's not even mention that you didn't seem surprised he was there, just that he was being aggressive. There's also the issue of that fucking bruise on your wrist." He stares at me, taking me in, his eyes burning my skin. "Heavy bags, my ass."

"It does happen, Ben. Heavy bags . . . I have fair skin . . ." I try to divert his attention, to convince him of some other reason for that mark, but I know that it's bullshit.

"Lola. Stop with the games. You're in some kind of shit." I look away, embarrassed, before his hand reaches out, touching my chin and moving my head to face him "I want to help you, Lola." My heart stops. "No, I'm *going* to help you, whether you want or ask for it or not." My stomach drops. "Tell me what's going on. Why is Johnny Vitale in your business? Why are you giving him money? Is it for Libby's?"

For a split second, I wonder if I can get out of this. Spin some story with the grace of the best PR agent, flip this mess on its head and tie it up in a pretty bow to avoid telling him the whole truth.

But how do you spin something this messy?

How do I tell him I spent my entire trust digging my father out of holes? How do I tell him that when I told my father I was out of money, I decided to follow my own desires and build my business? How do I tell him that my father thinks I'm selfish for not using that money to fix his problems?

No, not fix.

It becomes crystal clear now, for some reason, after all these years, as I prepare to tell a stranger to my family all about the skeletons in our closet.

He doesn't want to fix his problems.

He wants to plug the hole so he can make more.

Every time I told myself it would be the last time.

Every time he told me it would be the last time.

Every time I remember how my mom never truly stopped him.

Every time I remember telling myself it was just the stress of losing Mom.

It was all a lie.

Lies he told me. Lies Mom told me. Lies I told myself.

He'll never change. He'll never stop. He'll never put me first, not me or even Lilah.

The only person who kept the Turner family in line, who kept us safe and free from the chaos, was my mom.

But she's gone.

She's been gone for fifteen years. And for fifteen years, I've been fighting this fight alone. Letting Dad chase his career and feed his addiction without repercussions. Letting Lilah be a kid, and then a teen, and then a twenty-something without that pressure. Letting Mom's lies and secrets go with her to the grave.

And I took it on, made it my job.

I wore it as a badge of honor, my duty to my family.

And I'm realizing at this moment it never changed a thing. Realizing that everything I sacrificed didn't change or fix or solve *anything* breaks me. Once and for all.

And on the couch of the man I'm pretty sure can't stand me but seems to like to save me and possibly likes kissing me, I start to cry.

Not sweet tears.

Not the kind that you take a photo of and then share on social media.

Not the kind you wipe away with a handkerchief.

Kim Kardashian-level ugly cries. Body wracking, chest heaving, painful cries that break a wall inside of me I didn't realize had been constructed.

I cry.

I cry for myself.

I cry for Mom, who never would have seen this coming.

I cry for Lilah, who never had Mom, not really, and who lives in the shadow of her mistakes.

And I cry for Dad, who can't see past his grief to realize what he's doing to us.

And as I'm crying in my puddle of pain and shame and embarrassment, I feel arms pulling me out of it.

Not out of my puddle—off the couch, into his arms. Solid arms, a solid body.

Ben.

And then I'm sniffing into his shirt, crying there and attempting to get it together.

It's easier than I would have thought with him holding me.

"What do you want, Lol?" Ben asks long moments later, his face in my neck, holding me tight as I sit in his lap.

I don't answer for a while, and he lets that happen. That silence. When I finally break it, I ask, "Can I just . . . pretend? For tonight? Pretend I'm carefree and don't have this shit over my head? Pretend that you're just a hot guy taking me home?" I mull my words over. "I've never had that. That's what I want right now." He waits, deciding his own answer the same way I did.

I let him, waiting in the comfortable silence to hear his answer.

"Will you talk to me about it tomorrow?" He's hesitant to agree.

"Tomorrow?"

"Here."

"Here?"

"You're not going back over to your apartment without me until I know you'll be safe, babe."

"My place is fine."

"You also thought your bakery was safe."

"It is," I say. My response is automatic, and I realize even at this moment how dumb that sounds.

It's the furthest thing from safe.

I've been playing dangerous games for weeks, living in my own world and pretending it was sprinkles and powdered sugar.

I sigh.

"I'll drop it tonight, but we need to talk about this. I need to know what I'm dealing with. What we need to do."

"What *you're* dealing with?"

"You're mine now. I have to know what I need to do to keep you safe." I try to leave his lap.

"What? No." He holds me tighter, staring at me. "Ben, no."

"Yes."

"You can't stand me."

"You drive me insane," he agrees.

"How does driving you insane equate to being yours?"

"Who the fuck knows? You tell me. All I know is I've seen this once before with my brother. Him and his girl Jordan? They butt heads like I've never seen before. Same with my mom and my dad. Probably something in my genes."

"That's fucked up," I say, looking at him with a healthy dose of disbelief.

"Are you denying there's something between us? Something that we've both been denying for fucking weeks?"

That much I can't do.

There is most definitely something between Ben and me despite my adamant thoughts to the contrary.

"Exactly. So until we have this shit figured out—" I open my mouth to cut him off, tell him I do, in fact, have this figured out. "—and by figured out, babe, I mean to my standards. Not you telling me you figured it out and then burying the stress of whatever you're working with. *Figuring it out together*." I screw up my nose.

I should probably be flattered.

Instead, I'm annoyed.

I also expect him to keep talking.

And he does—just not on whatever his master plan is.

"How long have you been fighting this battle alone, sweet girl?" he asks, tucking a stray strand of hair behind my ear.

That gets me.

That *guts me*.

His eyes look into mine, and he sees my answer without my having to give it.

"Too fucking long," he says. "Now I'm here to share that burden."

———

"Alright, babe—you go in there. Shirts are in the top drawer. Not your fancy nighties, but should fit about the same," Ben says as he points me to his bedroom long after pizza and a surprising amount of . . . cuddling.

If you'd have asked me a mere six hours ago if Ben Coleman was a cuddler, I would have laughed in your face. But here we are.

His words hold a laugh, and when I look at him with a glare, he's smiling.

"Fuck off."

"Nothing to be embarrassed about, babe. Jacked myself off to the thought of you standing in the hall in that fucking nightie, fighting with me with your ass hanging out, holding a plate of cookies and fuckin' cursing me in your head."

"You jack off to the idea of me being mad at you?" That smile grows. It's almost boyish when he's not pissed at me.

It's cute.

Endearing, even.

"Are you ever not mad at me?" I roll my eyes.

"I can't remember a time when I wasn't."

"That's a lie, but I like you mad regardless. One day I'll fuck you angry." A shiver rolls through me.

Ben fucking me angry.

Jesus.

"Yeah, my sweet girl likes the idea of that." His hand reaches out, the knuckle of his pointer finger tipping my chin up to him in a move that's so smooth, it causes butterflies in my belly to go crazy. And because I'm me, I can't let Ben think I do, in fact, like the idea of him fucking me angry, because that would mean he won some kind of war that we're in the middle of.

Can't let that happen.

So instead, I roll my eyes and slam the door in his face, his laughter trailing down the hall as he retreats.

I find a shirt and put it on, carefully folding up my own Libby's tank and stuffing it in a corner.

I contemplate leaving my bra on, but I just ugly cried on the man's chest. I don't think lift and separation are important right now.

Now the final decision: before I head to wash my face and brush my teeth, do I leave my shorts on? They're soft, but not necessarily comfy enough to sleep in. The shirt hits right about where the nightie did, grazing the underside of my ass, but with thick thighs and full hips, that bit of coverage doesn't do much.

To show ass cheek or not to show ass cheek. I guess that is the question, right?

Staring in his mirror, eyes still puffy, long, loose, unflattering Coleman Ink shirt covering me nearly to my elbows and then past my hips, I make my decision.

Fuck it.

I walk out, heading for his bathroom and hoping he doesn't see me. Opening the cabinet, I'm strangely pleased to only see one toothbrush. I'm not sure why—he doesn't seem the type to mess around, too busy being broody and rude, but still. It's a comfort. I look in the cabinets to see if there is a backup (and, okay, I'll be honest—I scan for hair ties and purple shampoo because girl code, ya know?) and find nothing.

Again, I decide, fuck it.

I run the water, put his toothbrush under, and then paste it before putting it in my mouth, scrubbing at my teeth.

"Like the view," I hear behind me. Ben's voice. When I turn, he's staring at me with that damned cocky smile before his brows furrow in slight confusion. "Is that my toothbrush?" I nod but continue to brush, foam creeping to the edges of my lips. "Why are you using my toothbrush?" I turn, spit into the sink, and turn back to him.

"Dental hygiene is very important, Ben. Your smile is the first thing people see of you." An eyebrow goes up. "Well, maybe not you because all you do is glare at people. But for the rest of us . . ." I pop the toothbrush back into my mouth, scrubbing, but this time with a triumphant smile.

"I could have gone next door, gotten your toothbrush." Now I glare while brushing my teeth. I finish, turn, spit, rinse, and put the toothbrush back where I found it before turning back to him, crossing my arms on my chest.

"You're telling me you would have gone next door and gotten my pajamas?" He smiles. I think that smile could get him very far with me if he just did it more.

He has a *good* smile.

"But then I wouldn't see you in my tee," he says before a thick tattooed arm reaches out, grabbing me around my waist and tugging me into him until my chest hits his. "And I really like how that looks." His voice is low and husky, and it reverberates in places it has no right to. The other arm moves, dipping until the hand lands on my nearly bare ass. I can't do thongs, but cheeky panties? They're my jam.

A groan leaves his chest, vibrating against my nipples through layers of bones and sinew and skin.

"Trying to drive me crazy, aren't you?"

"In any way I can," I say, my own voice whisper soft as I look up at him.

"You're succeeding," he says, and then his lips are on mine again, soft this time.

But soft or hard, sweet or angry, that same feeling clicks into place.

It's just easier to place when it's sweet and soft and full of . . . more.

Comfort.

Sweet comfort in a way I've never felt. Comfort and security, like being rolled in cotton and silk and protected from the world.

His lips glide along mine, unhurried, kissing and moving, tasting and learning.

Like we're discovering what this is, what this could be. Who we are when we aren't at each other's throats.

And I am terrified because I really, really fucking like it.

The kiss stops, and we're both breathing heavily as he moves back, pressing his lips to my forehead and just . . . holding me.

I breathe him in, a mist of sweat and salty air and lumber and charcoal, like the woods meet the ocean. From what Hattie tells me of him growing up in the woods, it makes sense, like the place he was born in is buried deep into his bones.

"I'm not sleeping with you tonight," he says, the words like gravel.

"I know."

"No, I mean, you get the bed."

"What?" I try to pull my head back, but he doesn't let me, arms wrapping around my waist tighter.

"You are a temptation wrapped in sin, and I can't handle that tonight. You had a rough day. The first time I'm inside you, it won't be fogged with high emotions." *The first time I'm inside you.* His words send a shiver through me, causing a chuckle to run through him.

"See? That's what I mean. Too tempting."

"Where are you going to sleep?" I ask his chest, fighting the urge to look at his handsome face.

"Couch."

"Ben, no, that's not right. I can—"

"Absolutely not. My mom would gut me if she found out I made a woman sleep on the couch."

"It wouldn't be making me. I'm willing. Offering. Insisting, even."

"No, Lola."

"Ben—" He moves to pull back, to look at me.

"Please, Lola. One thing. Don't fight me on this one fucking thing. That's all I'm asking."

Every molecule of my body wants to fight him on this.

Partly because he told me not to.

Partly because the idea of sleeping in his bed with him is strangely . . . nice.

It's an idea I like.

But still.

I smile at him.

"Okay, Ben."

And to be quite honest, I think those words shock him more than anything else that's gone on today.

TWENTY-NINE

-Lola-

I DON'T REALIZE I'm dreaming until there are hands on my body, shaking me until I wake up.

"Lola, honey, wake up. You're safe. You're okay." I move to sitting, part of me here, trying to figure out where "here" is.

The other part is still in a dream where Johnny Vitale has Lilah, holding her as compensation, forcing her to dance in one of the Carluccio clubs everyone knows are even seedier than they look.

Forcing her to do more than just dance.

I've heard the whispers.

It wasn't a dream so much as a nightmare.

But then a light—small and bright—flashes and the room is illuminated.

Ben's room.

Framed photos of drawings of tattoos.

Black bed sheets.

His tee on my body.

His face in mine.

His hands on my shoulders.

"Ben," I breathe, and he breathes too, like he's relieved that I'm back here in the land of the living.

Back here with him.

He sits on the bed, pulls me into his lap, and slowly starts rocking me back and forth. His hand comes up, removing the loose pony from my hair and putting his hand into the strands, rubbing my scalp.

Comfort.

Fear melts, vanishing from my body.

"Does this happen often?" he asks, breaking my silence. I don't answer. My mind is still so muddled, half in a terrifying dream world that is too close to a potential reality and half here in an unfamiliar room but with familiar arms. "It happens often." His arms tighten in frustration. "I know you don't want to talk about it today, Lola, but fuck. It's killing me, not knowing. My mind is running off to some shitty fucking places."

I put a hand on his chest.

Warm.

Reassuring.

Comfort.

"The last person who held me after a nightmare died when I was fifteen," I say, fingers tracing the lines of a wrench, then a screwdriver over his heart.

A logo, I think. But not his. Strange.

"Your mom," he says. I don't look at him.

"You've been searching me, haven't you?"

"You've got a thick wall. But you have me tied up in knots. Can't get past that wall without some kind of ammunition, some kind of knowledge."

I don't know what to do with that.

So I do nothing at all.

"When I was little, she'd hold me, put on the music. Tell me the music scared off the monsters. I always had a wild imagination."

"Music helps?"

"Yeah." He moves off the bed, and I instantly miss his warmth, but then his hand is out to me.

"Come on."

I could argue.

I probably *should* argue.

But right now, that hand feels like a lifeline to safety, and my body is still quaking with the remnants of my dream.

He's still holding my hand when he pulls me to an old record player he has set up in the corner next to his desk. I'm assuming it's not what blares music late at night. I also expect him to have to search for the record he wants.

But once again, this man surprises me by just moving the needle and flipping the switch like the last record he listened to is the one he needs right now.

"Tiny Dancer" starts to play, the chords familiar and sweet, but the volume is low, only meant to be heard in this room.

As the words start, his arms wrap around my waist, first one, then the other, as he pulls me in close. My own arms wrap around his neck, getting the hint as he starts to sway us, my head resting on his chest and soaking him in.

I'm sure we're a strange sight, me in his tee shirt, crazy bed head, tear-stained cheeks. Ben with boxers, tattoos on display, both of us swaying to Elton John in the middle of the night, lights dimmed.

"This song reminds me of you," he says, breaking me from my own thoughts.

"I'm not tiny."

"No, you're not. Big heart, big dreams. Too fuckin' brave." I shake that off.

I can't get caught in his words. That's how I always get stuck. Caught in words and promises and pledges. My entire life is a sticky web of should-haves, could-haves, would-haves, and promises that melted like cotton candy.

Instead, I attack his choice of music, as one does. "I didn't pin you as an Elton John fan. Not what you're typically blasting when I'm trying to sleep at night." His cheeks move in what I know is a smile, the scruff of his beard scratching my temple.

"No, not my normal style." He pauses, his thumb sitting just under the fabric of the shirt I'm wearing, brushing my lower back. It's not sexual, but calming. Sweet. Reassuring. "It was my mom's favorite record when I was growing up. She insisted records were better than CDs and tapes even though my dad bought her all the fancy players. She'd break out her old records, set herself up on the back porch, and paint to the oldies. She'd set me up next to her with my own little paints, and I'd copy her. She loved this song best, though." The vision is serene. I imagine a gorgeous, petite woman with Ben's eyes in a sweet dress staring off into the woods from her back deck, peacefully smiling at her son sitting at a table with watercolors.

I can guess that's where he got his love for art.

The vision reminds me of my mom, who lovingly taught me to bake, how to measure, and to add in extra love. Who would grab on tight when the stool would wobble, and we'd giggle wide-eyed at the near fall.

But Ben got to keep his mom, unlike me.

I wonder what that was like, having a mother who encouraged your passions when it truly mattered. When you were old enough to hear the judgment, to feel the doubt creep in.

"Tell me about her," I ask, nearly greedy for the information. For insight into this man.

For anything to distract me.

No longer from my shitty night or my terrifying dreams, but from the past which has started to haunt me at all hours.

When he hesitates, I wonder if I went too far.

But then he starts to speak.

"My mom and my dad are polar opposites. He's a pain in the ass, hard-headed, knows what he wants and won't stop until he gets it." A snort comes out of me, laughter bubbling at the perfect description of Ben. "My mom," he continues, but I can feel his face moving into another smile in my hair. "My mom is sweet. Kind and gentle. Loves art and sees the beauty in everything. They don't . . . They don't fit. But it works, you know? They make it work. Because for some crazy reason, they love each other." My mind moves to my own parents, my mom, who was kind and open and caring, and my father, who is . . . flawed, but she loved him with her dying breath. "I grew up in a small town—tiny fuckin' town up north. My parents grew up there. A town like that . . . there are expectations. A family of boys, a family like *mine* with boys? We were to be . . . men. Not artists. Football players. Homecoming kings, town heroes. My great grandfather started Coleman and Sons Construction there, and eventually, my dad took it over. It goes to the oldest son." My brows scrunch together, confused.

"Aren't you . . . ?" He doesn't answer my question.

"My mom saw I love art. Found drawings in my room, bought me sketchbooks and tools. I'd hear them, late at night fighting about me. She never fought him on anything. Nothing but that—me."

"She sounds . . . amazing."

"She is."

I want to ask more, but that seems like a good place to end it, to close out the conversation before I'm expected to add my own experiences. When we're quiet for a few minutes, the record cutting out but our bodies still swaying, I can't fight the yawn that overtakes me.

"Do you think you can sleep now?" he asks. I don't want to lie, so I don't answer, but my body rebels from my mind, pulling another yawn from my chest. "Alright you, let's get you to bed."

I nod, and I'm shocked when his knees bend, strong arms scooping me up.

I haven't felt small since I was a kid, except for in this moment.

I feel tiny.

Tiny and cared for.

My arms looped around his neck tighten, and he walks us to his bedroom, gently placing me on the bed, the covers already pulled back.

Tattooed fingers grab the sheets and pull them up around me.

"Night, Lola," he says, turning toward the door, one hand grazing the blankets.

I panic.

It has to be the exhaustion or the adrenaline, but the tether that keeps my mind and actions in line snaps, and my hands go out to grab his, wrapping around his thick wrist.

His body turns back to me, confusion written on his face.

He looks from my face to my hands, both wrapped around his arm, holding him in place.

He can't leave.

"Lola?"

"Please don't go." His eyes run over my face, but my mind is frantic.

I know I won't sleep tonight, that every noise in this unfamiliar room will creep into my subconscious, will tell me horrific stories and dredge up bitter memories. "I don't want to sleep alone. Please, Ben." I'm pleading with him now. Any other time, I'd cringe. I'd be embarrassed.

Where is strong Lola?

Where is the Lola who protects, not who needs protecting?

Where is the Lola who comforts instead of receiving comfort?

And most of all, why do those walls crumble when he is near?

"Lola, I don't know—"

"Please." That's all I say.

He doesn't speak.

He just looks at me.

It feels like a millennium.

And if he says no, I'm going to shrivel into a ball and close up my bakery and move back in to Sam's and bake only for school bake sales.

Baking witness protection.

I'll need a new name.

As I'm contemplating how I feel about Ashley, he sighs.

My blood freezes.

"Just sleeping?" he asks. I nod, my whole body anticipating his answer. "Okay." And then he moves, walking around to the other side of the bed and getting in before leaning over and flicking off the one bedside light illuminating the room.

And now it's dark.

So fucking dark.

And we're lying there next to each other.

The darkness fills my throat with panic.

It creeps into my lungs, clouding my brain with the lack of oxygen.

In the dark, my mind can move, remember, bring back that fear—

A hand touches my hip.

Ben.

Ben's hand.

The panic backs away from my body, like that slight touch is a repellant.

Then another hand grabs my other hip, turning me, pulling me.

Pulling me until he's holding me,

Until I'm wrapped in strong arms, his old tee the only thing keeping warm flesh from warm flesh.

If there were light, I'd be looking in his eyes.

I know because his nose brushes mine, his breath mingling with my own. We lie like this for what feels like forever, breathing and exhaling and breathing again, in our own bubble.

I still can't sleep.

It's no longer thoughts and fears and nightmares keeping me awake. No, it's something more sinister. Sinister to my heart and to my mental health.

"You tired?" he asks, voice gravelly and loud in the silent room.

"No," I whisper.

I was, but now I'm not.

In fact, every molecule of my body is awake at this moment.

"Me neither," he replies, but that's it. More silence, more breathing.

I shift.

He's closer now, breaths touching lips.

The warmth of his own lips emanating and hitting mine, but not quite touching.

"Lola, this is a bad fuckin' idea," he says in a quiet whisper, so quiet that if my ears weren't hyperfocused on everything he's doing, I wouldn't hear it.

"I know," I say, because I do.

This might be the worst idea ever.

Ben kissing me when he's frustrated with me is one thing. Kissing me as punishment is one thing. Letting him kiss me because my adrenaline is too high and I need to forget the world is one thing.

Letting Ben take this further in his bed, in the dead of night, while he whispers against my lips and just danced with me to old records and told me about his mother and got in bed with me because I was too afraid to sleep alone?

That's a whole other thing.

A very dangerous thing.

"I'm gonna kiss you anyway," he says.

My heart soars.

Relief washes over me.

"Good," I say back in the same whisper.

And then his lips are on mine, warm and reassuring, and it's like everything I needed to erase this shit night. If that kiss in the bakery was a balm, this one is the cure.

It's like his kiss is a lifeline, holding me to sanity and safety.

In his arms, his lips on mine, I have never felt more at ease.

And then it deepens, his tongue reaching out to mine, and things go from sweet to fire in a second.

My leg hitches up, hooking around his hip, and his tee comes with it to rest in the crease of my waist. This leaves just a pair of boxers and a pair of underwear between where I'm already wet and where he's getting hard.

"Fuck, Lola," he growls, hand slipping under the band of my panties until his warm hand is grabbing bare skin.

I want him.

I need him.

I need this . . . connection to make this horrible day go away.

His fingers dig into the skin of my ass, pulling me tighter to him, and I grind, dying to get him . . . to get more.

"Stop," he says, and I freeze. My entire body goes cold, panicking because *does he not want this? This thing I need to my* core?

"We need to get one thing clear, Lola," he says, his voice full of aching need, the same need flowing through me.

No, it's not that he doesn't want this.

He wants it *bad*.

My hips move, trying to graze his hard cock again, the cock I need inside of me, the cock I haven't had yet but I've had many daydreams about.

"No, Lola. Listen to me." The hand on my hip tightens, almost painfully, but the kind of pain that flows through me in an unexpectedly heated way. "You need to know how I work." His hand moves, goes to my chin, and tips it up until I'm looking at him. We're still in the dark room, still lying side by side, but my eyes have adjusted to the dark now, and I can see the heat in his.

"The way I work, I make the rules." I open my mouth, but he cuts me off. "You don't have to listen to me anywhere else, but if we do this, you'll be a good girl and listen to me." A shiver down my side, and his lips tip up.

Bastard.

"If we do this, that's you agreeing to listen to me, to do whatever I say."

I pause, thinking about his words.

Thinking about what they mean.

Letting go of control, the thing I've been fighting my whole life to have.

Control of my sister.

Control of my dad's addiction.

Control of the family's reputation.

Now, control of my own future.

And honestly?

The thought of handing over that control to this man, of being free of it and the expectations and the need to be on top of everything?

Fuck.

I like it a lot.

It sounds . . . freeing.

So I nod.

And when he continues to stare at me, I speak.

"Okay, Ben. Yeah. Yes." A deep groan falls from his lips, but then he's gone, rolling and moving until he's sitting with his back to the headboard, legs wide.

"Ben—"

"Kneel right here, sweet girl," he says, motioning between his legs. "I've been thinking about this fucking moment for months. If we're doing this, we're doing it right." I pull my lip in between my teeth, gnawing at it with nerves. "Now, Lola."

This is the moment.

Something tells me this will decide everything.

So I do it.

I move, kneeling between his legs, sitting on my feet and placing my hands on my knees, waiting for the next instruction.

I know I did well when Ben growls deep with satisfaction.

"Like that, baby. You listening to me. Like that a fuck of a lot." His hand moves, tucking a loose strand of hair behind my ear, trailing down my neck before grabbing the hem of the tee. "This. I like the look of you in my tee but want to see you even more. Take it off."

Anxiety blooms in my belly, but he's seen me before. Seen my body. Fuck, he's seen me come. I sigh, crossing my arms in front of me and pulling the shirt over my head, before tossing it to the side.

"That's my girl," he murmurs, almost to himself, before big hands trace my curves. Full hips, a smaller waist that could do with fewer taste tests, then up my ribcage, tickling the sensitive nerves there before cupping my breasts.

I hold my breath, old insecurities rising because while I might have thick hips and curves, I've never had the tits to back it up.

But I should have known this man would know somehow and still work to make me love it.

His hands move, palms covering my breasts and rubbing, my nipples hard, and the friction feels delicious.

"Like these," he says, moving his hands back, each hand catching a nipple between thumb and forefinger and pinching just a hair past comfortable.

"Ah!" I moan, the feeling incredible.

"Sensitive," he says, almost to himself, like he's documenting my body and my responses to his ministrations for future knowledge.

I try to move, to get closer, to get this moving, but his hand pushes me from getting closer to him.

"Up. On your knees, baby," he says, and I'm confused for a second before his hands move down to my ass, lifting it a bit until I get the point. I rise to my knees and wait for the next instruction.

His fingers move, running over the waistband of my underwear, and my breathing goes shallow, already ready for whatever he chooses to do next.

"Widen your legs," he says, and I do, adding a foot or so of space until the outsides of my knees are touching the insides of his own spread thighs. When he moved, he must have removed his underwear, because when I look down, I see his hard cock standing straight, as ready as I feel.

Ben must know where my eyes have gone because he chuckles then starts to lower my underwear. "Not yet, Lola. Soon. So fucking soon." The elastic band stops a few inches from my knees, caging me. As much as I want to lift a leg and help them down, I have a feeling Ben wants me like this, bound by my own underwear and even more at his mercy.

His fingers trail gently, feather soft, up and down the inside of my thighs, and I know I was right. This is part of his game.

And I won't be breaking the rules.

"Such a good girl," Ben murmurs under his breath, smiling at my staying still. "Should I reward you for being a good listener?"

"Yes," I breathe, my breath shaky with need.

"Yes, what?"

"Yes, please, Ben." I try to leave any begging out of my voice but probably fail.

Either way, Ben smiles. And then his fingers trail up again, grazing my slit, gliding easily with my wetness but not dipping in, not providing any relief.

I stay still.

I stay quiet.

I lock my eyes on his.

And when I do, Ben holds my gaze and slowly, torturously slowly, sinks a finger in me. A long breath leaves both of our lungs with the moment, and then his finger is out again, moving up, circling my clit. I moan, a small sound.

I fight the urge to rock my hips, to get more.

"Being really fucking good, Lola," Ben says, then his eyes move down to where his hand is moving toward my center again. This time two fingers enter me, crooking gently to graze my G spot.

"Oh God," I whimper.

"You like that? Your man fingering your pretty cunt, sweet girl?" he asks, his voice a low rumble. I nod as he follows the same path as before. Out, up, circling my swollen clit, then back in. This time he adds a third finger, and I'm starting to feel deliciously full.

Then his hand moves.

Not the one inside of me. That stays still, frozen, a tease to end all teases.

It's his free hand moving to stroke his cock, thumb pressing on that piercing I've spent an ungodly amount of time researching since that first time.

I've read that it feels unreal inside of you.

I want to know for sure.

But right now, I'm wondering if I could come this way, his fingers buried inside of me but unmoving, watching him jack himself off, his own breath going low and labored.

"I've been doing this for weeks. Jacking myself off, thinking of this fucking perfect body. Now you're here in front of me, and it's better than I imagined," he says, a needy growl in his voice.

"Ben . . . ," I moan, clamping down on his fingers without intention, but my hips stay still, still on my knees, still stuffed with his fingers.

"You need more?" I nod. "Ride my fingers, baby." I don't question the kindness, instead moving to rock on his fingers.

A low, deep moan falls from my lips with the small movement. I go higher on my knees then back down, fucking myself on his fingers as Ben jacks his cock, moaning gently as his eyes are locked to where his fingers are lost inside of me. He crooks them as he twists the head of his cock, and my head falls back.

"Fuck, Lola. Magnificent."

"Ben, I'm gonna—" I say because I'm right there. Seconds and I could tip over. I grind harder, trying to get more, before his fingers are gone.

I whimper like a child who hasn't gotten her way because that's how I feel.

"When you come, it will be on my fucking cock, Lola. Last time I missed out. Not this time." He moves, so swift I can barely register it, before he has me pushed flat to my back and I'm staring up at him. His feet move between my legs, kicking down my underwear, and I help him, flailing to try and get the fabric off and him inside of me.

I need this.

He moves his hips, one hand grabbing his cock and rubbing the piercing along my wetness, the slick metal grinding against my swollen clit, and fuck, fuck, fuck. It's like nothing I've ever felt. He continues to move over me, one hand planted next to my head, getting me closer again, building in my belly until . . .

He stops. He stops and lifts his hips so I don't have him anymore.

"Are you on something?"

"What?" I ask, confused, my voice breathy, my hips moving back to try and get purchase.

I need this man.

"Focus, sweet girl. You'll get my cock." I moan low at the idea, the thought of his promise. "Birth control. You on anything?"

I nod, then answer.

"IUD."

"I'm clean."

"Me too." I want that. I want this. I want Ben, bare inside of me, fucking me breathless. "Fuck me, Ben," I say, the words a whisper, but that's all I need. That's all Ben needs before he's moving back, sitting on his knees while I lie in front of him. I watch again as he strokes his cock, now slick with my own wetness, the piercing gleaming in the moonlight.

Holy fuck, this man is everything.

"Oh, God, honey," I say, my voice a whisper as he rubs the tip of his cock from my clit, through my wet, dipping into my opening and then repeating the torturous process.

"I know, sweet girl. Daddy's gonna take care of you, don't you worry." My pussy clenches with his words, but I have no time to over-think them as he continues, each time going inside of me a little farther, a little deeper.

"Ben—"

"Wrap your legs around my hips, baby," he says, hands going to my hips and lifting. I comply, and then without warning, he's slamming inside of me.

I *scream*.

I've never been so perfectly full as I am right now in this moment with Ben inside of me.

"Fuuuuckkk," he growls, panting as he stops at the hilt, my body already convulsing around him. "Holy shit, better than I imagined." He's talking to himself, eyes stuck on where he disappears into me before he slowly pulls out and slams in again.

"Oh, fuck, fuck, fuck!" I shout, my body on fire. Each time he slowly glides out, that barbell scrapes at tender flesh and nerve endings I didn't even know existed, creating shockwaves that flow through my body.

"Play with your tits, baby," Ben growls, slamming into me and moaning. My hands move up, cupping my breasts and pinching my nipples hard as he continues to pump into me. My back arches, pushing me farther into him.

"Fuck yeah, Lola. Fuck yourself on me. That's it, baby." It's building, the burning growing in my belly and my lower back as I frantically move, trying to get more.

I move a hand down my belly, reaching for my clit to get me over the edge, but Ben's hand comes out, slapping it.

"No. This time, you come with just my cock, baby. You can have my mouth, my hand, your hand another time. This time it's just us." I moan, exasperated.

I've never come any other way.

"Ben, I can't—"

"You fucking can, Lola. Look at me. Look at me fucking you, making you mine." I mewl a miserable, turned-on sound and look at his face, sweat dripping down onto my belly, eyes hot.

One hand moves from my hip, swipes at the drop of sweat with a thumb, and puts it in my mouth.

"Suck that, baby." My pussy clamps around him as I do what he demands, staring into his eyes as I do. "Fuck yeah, baby, that's it. You're gonna come just from me fucking you hard, aren't you?"

It's building, the crest coming for me, each thrust hitting something new and deep inside of me, hitting the ache in my belly that he put there.

That only he can cure.

His hand moves back to my hips, moving me to fuck me harder, deeper, the angle changing just a hair, and I scream.

"Right there! Fuck!" I shout, the sound going quiet in my ears.

"That's it, baby, come for your man, then I'm gonna fill you, yeah?"

That does it.

The idea of this fucking man filling me has me screaming, my vision blurring and my body convulsing as I clamp down on him and *lose it.*

As I come, Ben growls an animalistic noise, slams in deep, and then I feel him pulsing into me.

And later, when I come down from my high, after he got a warm wet towel and cleaned me off, after he tucked me into the crook of his arm and held me in the dark, I fall asleep with a smile on my face.

THIRTY

-Lola-

WHEN I WAKE UP, there's an arm weighing me down.

When I crack an eye to look at it, it's covered in dark ink.

Ben.

Ben's arm is weighing me down. Draped on my naked skin.

My naked skin.

It comes back to me.

Johnny coming to the bakery. Trying to barter the debt. Trying to force himself on me.

Ben coming in like my saving grace.

I called his name.

I called his name.

Jesus.

What was I thinking?

Ben pulling Johnny off me. Seeing how small Johnny was compared to Ben.

"Did you ask him to touch you?"

The words send a shiver down my spine.

Telling Hat to cancel all of his appointments.

Going to his apartment.

Sleeping there.

The nightmare.

Dancing.

I should not feel the way I do about last night. But listening to a song Ben's mom used to play for him, hearing him sing it in my ear as we twirled around his living room, feeling *safe*.

Everything that came after that.

Shit.

I need to go.

I look at the clock—5:52.

Shit, I really do need to go.

Rolling, I nearly fall when I hit the end of the bed, stumbling to my feet. *Smooth, Lola. Real smooth.*

"Where are you going?" his croaky, sleepy voice asks, and in another world, I think that would be a nice voice to wake up to every day. Another world where I'm not constantly covering for my dad, another world where I'm not struggling to keep my sister in the dark at all times. Another world where Ben isn't my asshole neighbor because, despite the fact that he saved me and danced with me and is *really fucking good* in bed, he is definitely, probably, still an asshole.

Just a confusing asshole.

In another world, I think it's the kind of asshole I could have fun with. One that would frustrate the hell out of me, but I would throw it back at him, always keeping each other on our toes in a way we both really liked.

But this is not that world.

"I have to bake," I say, tugging up the underwear I wore last night. I'll head up to my place before opening and change, but for now, I need to get going.

"No." That has me pausing.

"No?"

"No." I stare at him, tattooed arm contrasting the dark sheets pulled up to his hips.

"I'm sorry, I don't understand. No?" I look around the room, searching for my bra and tank. I spot the bra and put it on as well.

"You're closed today. Not going there, definitely not without someone watching you." I stare. I did *not* hear him say that.

"Excuse me?"

"We have to talk."

"No, we don't," I counter.

"We sure as fuck do. You need to tell me what the fuck last night was, and I have to figure out what the fuck to do about it."

"None of that is your job, Ben. And it's none of your business."

"None of my *business?*" His eyes are wide, incredulous. "Are you kidding me, Lola?"

I need to go.

I need to get out of here.

More importantly, I need Ben to drop this.

"We need to talk, Lola."

He doesn't drop it though.

Of course, he doesn't.

Why won't he fucking drop it?

Why does he live to make every step of the way difficult?

"Why didn't you have your dad back you? Or why wouldn't you have gotten a traditional loan? Hat says you always have someone in the bakery. Income. It seems it would have been easy to get a small business loan. You didn't need to go and get involved with them."

His words dig. It's what anyone would ask in this situation, of course. But I guess a part of me—a small hidden part—had hoped that despite Ben thinking I'm a spoiled princess, he would see through it.

But he's like everyone else.

And just like everyone else, I cannot reveal too much. I cannot show him the truth of my situation. I look for my shorts, stumbling to catch my footing in my fury and frantic need to *get out.*

"I didn't." I squat when I spot my shorts and put one leg in.

"You had an envelope in your hand, Lola. He took it with him. I don't think there were secret family recipes in there." I stare at him, annoyed that he's jumped to a conclusion that I can't build a business on my own.

Sweet Lola, so innocent and kind. She could never have the back-bone to start a business without help.

If he only knew.

My shorts make a satisfying snap as I tug the waistband up over my hips and stare at him, shrugging into my bra.

"I built this bakery on my own. No one's help."

"I'm not saying you didn't—"

"Yes, you are. You're saying what everyone says. There's no way sweet, ditzy Lola, who can't even remember to lock her back door and loves to bake cookies and takes care of her little sister, could scrounge money and get a hefty small business loan to start her business on her own. There's no way in hell Lola could find a space, secure a lease, and renovate a bakery by herself. There's no fucking way she could watch YouTube videos and fix ovens she found on Craigslist, and there's no way she could move everything she owns into her apart-ment single-handedly." Okay, that one wasn't an easy feat, and I regretted it for weeks after when my body could barely move, espe-cially when that body couldn't rest properly thanks to an asshole neighbor, but I did it. "And there's *no way* that there would be another fucking reason that sweet, innocent Lola has to hand an envelope of cash over to some scum of the earth asshole who corners her in her own fucking business, propositioning her and telling her there are other fucking ways to pay off the debt." My chest is heaving as I slip my shoes back on, pulling my shirt—his shirt, which I will not be returning—over my head. Tears are clawing at my throat, but I refuse to show weakness, to cry in front of another person who doesn't believe in me.

Old Lola would have.

Not New Lola.

"No fucking way, right, Ben? Because I'm Lola, the sweet and annoying neighbor you can't fucking stand. Can't stand me, but you sure as hell can fuck me. Fuck me and fuck with me and get your rocks off and fucking *use me* like every other human being on this earth."

Now where the fuck did that come from?

My chest is heaving as I stand in front of him, where he's naked as can be in his bed, sitting up now and resting on his arms behind him, eyes wide.

I need to leave. I need to turn, walk out the door, let it slam, and not worry about this man anymore. Let this have been me getting him out of my system. A reminder that while the sex can be good, it doesn't fix a shitty attitude. Just because he held me after a nightmare and danced with me in his living room and we had our first real conversation that didn't include taunts and frustration doesn't mean—

No.

Don't read into it.

It will only hurt more later.

"I'm going to my bakery. Thanks for everything, Ben," I say, heading for the door, but his voice has me turning back to stare at him.

"You're not going there, Lola." Who the fuck does he think he is?

"You don't control me, Ben. You can't tell me what I can and can't do." His words come quick, like he knew what I'd say.

"Last night tells me otherwise." I blink. Once, twice, three times.

"Excuse me?"

"Last night? You let me control you. Tell you what to do, when to do it, and for how long. You're mine now, sweet girl."

"I'm no one's. We fucked. That's it." His eyebrow raises.

"Is that so?"

"Yes, Ben."

"I'm not buying it."

"Well, too bad. I do not belong to you. You do not tell me what I can and cannot do." He's sitting up now, sheets barely covering his cock, strong arms crossed on his chest like he's ready for battle.

"What happens when I make you mine, Lola? When you stop playing games and admit you've been mine for a while now." My body fights with currents of hot and cold, both rushing through my anger and frustration and something else I refuse to look at too closely.

"Goodbye, Ben. I'll see you later," I say, slipping my feet into shoes as I walk out his bedroom door.

"Do not walk away when I'm talking to you, Lola."

"Fuck off, Ben."

And then the front door clicks behind me.

Adrenaline has me running down the stairs that divide our apartments and our businesses.

THIRTY-ONE

-Lola-

When I walk into my happy place, locking the door behind me, calm takes me over. There's still anger and irritation rubbing at the edges, but this? This is what I wanted. My own place. It's what I dreamed of for years, and knowing I made it happen by myself always grounds me.

All I've ever wanted was to be my own person.

Not Libby's daughter, left behind.

Not Lilah's older sister, the one who has to shelter the innocent daughter.

Not Shane's daughter, the one who will always clean up the messes.

I've always been looked at through the lens of someone else's life, never as me.

It's why I didn't want the fanfare, the ribbon cutting, the extravagant press most every other business would kill for upon opening, because this place is *mine*. They couldn't touch this part of me. Turn it sour.

I am not who the world has told me I have to be.

And I'm *definitely* not Ben Coleman's.

That thought has me cranking the music, the *Reputation* era fueling me as I take out heavy containers of flour, sugar, and chocolate chips.

Unfortunately, I don't actually have a ton of doughs or batters to make this morning, as I've been pretty good at prepping at night to avoid being too loud, but I need to make *something*. The truth of the matter is, I'm fuming, and when I'm mad, I bake. Some people run. Some people read or draw. Some people start arguments or gamble or go shopping. I mix sugar and butter and flour to create a mood-changing experience.

I'm doing just that, creaming butter and sugar and bringing my eggs to room temperature when I hear it.

Feet on stairs.

Please go to your shop. Leave me alone, I think, but another part of me is ready for the challenge.

Craving it.

Something about fighting with Ben is almost as good as baking.

Though neither touches what if feels like to be fucked by Ben, my devious mind reminds me. I swat the nuisance away.

Then the knob moves.

I locked it after I checked the bakery for any unexpected guests.

I smile to myself. He *has* been bitching at me to lock the door, right? Just doing as I was told.

A fist pounds on the back door.

I ignore it.

"Lola, open the fucking door." I don't. Instead, I crank the volume on my music just a bit. "*Lola!*" he shouts. I smile to myself. "Open the door or I'm opening it."

He wouldn't.

Ben wouldn't break my door down. Not to mention, the heavy metal would most definitely cause some damage.

And I'm right; he doesn't break it.

Instead, it just opens.

In his hand is a silver key.

My spare.

My mind moves to me looking for a place to hide the key and deciding under the pink door mat was a good spot.

Why the fuck did I hide it under the mat? That was dumb. It's the first place everyone checks.

He strides in, wearing low-slung gym shorts with no underwear band in sight, no shirt.

This fucking man.

He has to know, has to know how good he looks *at all times.*

I don't have time to dwell on that as he walks toward me, though. I walk backward, silent, his eyes fixated on me as I move. My back hits the wall next to the sink where I clean up after a long day, the one that has the laminated instructions for fire safety and employee rights taped to it.

"Why do you keep doing that?" I ask. There are a million things I could ask, but that's what comes out.

"What?"

"Backing me into things." I'm breathing heavy already, the anticipation of the unknown rushing through me. Will he, won't he?

I never seem to know with this man.

"Because I like to."

"Well, I don't."

"Oh yeah?" he asks, his lips tipping up in a small smile, devious and taunting.

"Yeah." My words are a pant now. *God damn stupid body. We have a fight to win, woman.*

"Your pussy begs to differ." Said part clenches in response.

"What the fuck!" I say, ignoring that clenching. I think he knows though. He has some sixth sense attached to my pussy that knows when it wants him. It has to be that. How else would he always know when to keep pushing me? His voice is low and rough when he speaks, one hand on the wall next to my head as he looks down at me, the other moving from my thigh to my hip and back down. A taunt.

"I bet you're still wet from last night. Is my come still in you, sweet girl?" *Holy fucking shit.*

"No," I answer, not even giving a small second to let my mind decide.

"No?" That smile grows.

"I'm not wet." I spit the lie out.

"Let Daddy test, prove me wrong." *That should not be so fucking hot. There's no universe where a man calling himself daddy should be so fucking sexy, but here we are.* Without the approval of my mind, my legs shift a bit, separating, giving access, and I want to kill my traitorous body. His smile grows as that hand on my hip moves up, under my shirt, and then down, into my shorts, bypassing the nonexistent panties, right to my slit where his finger glides easily.

There's no way to hide it.

I'm already soaked.

There's something about this man. No matter how annoying and frustrating I find him, there's still a part of me that wants him to own me. Shit, he breaks down my door, pins me in place, says a few words, and my body reacts like it is, in fact, his to do with as he pleases.

"Fuuuckk, sweet girl. Soaked for me," he purrs, moving that thick finger up and down, gathering wet and swirling it around the spot that's already aching for him.

I had him last night, came hard, and already it's like I haven't had an orgasm in centuries. His breath is hot on my neck as his tongue starts at the collarbone revealed in Ben's too-big tee, dragging up my neck until he reaches my ear and nips it, all the while his wet finger circles my clit gently, not enough.

"Don't know what it is about you, Lola. You drive me up a fucking wall, more trouble than you're worth. You never fucking listen to me, you—"

"Why should I?" I ask, cutting him off, taunting him. "Why should I listen to you?" He brings this out in me. This need to fight him, to argue. With him, the Lola who takes on too much and says yes to everything disappears, revealing a version of me I've hidden my entire life.

"Because as soon as you start acting like a good girl, I'll start treating you like one." A shiver runs down my spine, a shiver I know he feels. That one finger presses hard on my clit, eliciting a moan from me. "But if you act like a little brat, I'm going to fuck you and come in you before you can finish. Then you'll spend the rest of the day with my come leaking out of you, miserable and needy because you didn't get there. You'll need to wait until I'm done with my last client before I can finish you off tonight."

I want to spit in his face.

I also want him to make me come on his dick.

What the fuck is wrong with me?

Before I can answer, the finger on my clit sinks down again, filling me but not enough. After last night, I know what that could feel like, and I don't want to settle.

Fuck my dignity.

Fuck the fact that he's a total fucking douche canoe.

I need the service he's readily offering.

When I think of it that way, it's easier to swallow. Much easier than admitting I want this man, and possibly for more than just his dick. For a split second, my mind moves to him dancing with me last night, singing Elton John in my ear until I stopped shaking and then helping me forget about my shitty night and my worse nightmares.

Nope. I must move forward. I can't let myself think of the things that make him *not* a dick.

So instead, my hands go to the waistband of my shorts and push down, letting them pool at my feet as I step out of them.

"Good girl it is," he says under his breath, a cocky smile on his lips.

"You're an ass," I say, both as a reminder to him and myself as he crooks the finger in me, grazing my G spot.

"Keep telling yourself that," he replies, and then his hands are on my hips, pulling me up and pressing me to the wall, urging my legs to wrap around him. "I'm gonna fuck you against this wall, sweet girl, and you're going to tell me just how good it feels to be full of me."

Full body quakes.

This man's mouth.

"Someone will hear," I protest. A weak protest, but one all the same.

"No, they won't; you left that fuckin' noise blaring," he says, pushing his shorts down as I hold on to his neck, pinned between him and the wall. I can feel the heat of him already.

"It's music," I say in protest. I don't know why I can't just let it go. The faster this happens, the faster I'll come, and I can go along with my day.

"No, it's not."

"It's Taylor Swift," I say, but my voice is breathy as he lines himself up with me, dragging the head of his cock through my wetness.

"It's shit," he says, but it sounds as half-assed as my own argument.

"I can't stand you." The words are a moan as he slips in a single inch and then pauses.

"Yeah, well, you don't have to stand for what I'm about to do to you." And then he slams into me, filling me in a way I've only felt once before, but even then, it was right and amazing. The heated metal grazes every nerve ending, brushing swollen tissues that are almost sore from last night, and I *moan* at the feeling. "Fuck, sweet girl. So fucking wet. Is that my cum from last night? Just like I said, trying to run from my bed, my cum still leaking from you."

"I hate how good you feel in me," I say, the words tumbling in a train of thought that's gone off the rails. He laughs, the vibrations chafing my nipples under my tee.

"Back at you, babe." Then he draws his hips back, sliding out before he slams in again, so fucking good. "Think this pussy was made for me. Think you and this body were made for me to fucking destroy. If I get my way, Lola, I'll destroy you every fucking day."

"Good luck," I say with a moan.

"Still fighting me. Full of my cock, moaning for me, writhing because you're already close to the edge, and you're still fucking fighting with me. Where's my sweet girl, Lola?"

"Fuck you," I spit at him but tilt my hips to take him deeper. He smiles that smile, the one that both makes my belly warm and my blood boil, before a hand moves from my hip to under my shirt, grazing the skin on my belly and trailing up to my breast, cupping it in large hands.

"These are fucking perfect," he says, rolling a nipple between two fingers. I moan at the feeling, then groan deeper as he tugs on the tender flesh. "I should get Hat to put a ring here, tug on it while I fuck you." My eyes move to his own piercing there.

The thought flares a heat in me unexpectedly, and my hand moves from his neck down, claiming it as my own as my fingers grab the barbell and tug. His mouth pulls my lip into his mouth with a groan before he pinches my nipple hard. I shriek into his mouth, but he slams into me harder, using those fingers to roll pleasure back into the bruised area.

"You wanna play that, I'm more than happy to, baby. I'll make you ache in a way you never fucking imagined." His words send images past my eyes, thoughts into my mind. Thoughts that I would never have considered until this gruff man came into my life.

I shift my hips, needing more.

I'm close.

"Do you want to come, sweet girl?" he says, his words a growl that has me clenching around him.

I do.

I do really fucking bad.

"Yes," I breathe, a quiet acceptance that he has this control over me, this control over my body. He thrusts in again, pushing me against the wall and holding me there, cock throbbing in me.

"Yes, what?"

I know what he wants me to say.

And I also know somehow that if I say it, I'm accepting this. I'm accepting his control over me. I'm admitting that there is this crazy chemistry between us that neither of us can resist.

"Yes, what, sweet girl? Say it and I'll make you come right here on my cock."

But then again, haven't I already admitted it? I'm pinned to the wall in my bakery, his cock so deep in me it's near bruising, wearing last night's clothes after the man saved me the night before.

And with that realization, I accept my fate and give Ben what he wants.

Something I never in a million years would have ever done, but here with him, it just feels . . . right.

"Yes, Daddy," I whisper in his ear, and the groan that leaves his chest is worth every moment of doubt before I said it.

"Fuck yeah, Lola," he says, thrusting in, the hand that was on my tit moving down until a thick finger settles on my clit. I mewl at the feeling, moving to try and get more from him, but he's controlling this, his arm beneath my ass, keeping my hips braced on the wall.

"Stay still and I'll make you come, okay, sweet girl?" I moan, moan because I want that. I want him, and the idea of this man calling himself *my fucking Daddy*, rubbing a thumb on my swollen, abused clit, and pumping into me has me creeping to the invisible edge I'd do anything to crest.

So I do as I'm told.

I stop moving my hips, stop trying to take control, to be the one who does it all.

I let Lola go and let this man take care of me, even if it's just for this moment while he fills me with immense pleasure.

"That's it, Lola, give it to me. Come for Daddy," he says as his thumb digs hard and rolls. And that's all it takes.

My head flies back, hitting the wall as I moan out, my orgasm making the noise in my ears quiet, ringing silence as my voice cuts out. Pleasure racks me in trembling waves as Ben continues to pump into me, groaning and growling words I can't make out, his thumb carrying out the orgasm of a lifetime.

Except it's not.

It's not the orgasm of a lifetime because I felt that same intensity last night.

And as Ben pumps into me, biting my neck hard when he comes, causing my body to shudder with another, smaller orgasm, I wonder if it would be like that a third time.

———

When we come down from our high, my mind comes back to me, my legs start to unwrap from his hips, and he slowly lowers me until my sneakers hit the floor.

And then he does the unexpected.

"Stay there," he says, kissing me softly on the lips, a contrast to what just happened. I listen, not because I want to listen to Benjamin Coleman, but because my legs are shaking and I need to lean on the cool, painted concrete until they steady.

I hear water running, and then he's back from the small bath-room, a wet washcloth in hand. It's warm as he runs it between my legs, and I hiss in a breath as it grazes my still swollen clit. He smiles that shit-eating grin at me, and even though he's annoying and kind of an ass, I smile back.

"Sore?"

"Not yet." He shakes his head at my taunt, tossing the wet wash-cloth to the ground.

"You can't resist, can you?" he asks, and I just smile. He's right. I can't. "Hands on my shoulders, baby," he says as he bends forward, grabbing my shorts. He urges me to lift one foot, then the other, putting my shorts on and then sliding them up my body, kissing the spot right above my shorts and under my belly button with a rever-ence I don't expect.

It scrambles my mind.

This man scrambles my mind.

He stands and then kisses me again, soft and sweet like we do this often—argue, then fuck, then leave each other for the day, calm and ready to take on whatever life throws at us. He pulls me close and presses another kiss to my forehead.

"Now go bake your cookies, sweet girl. Go make the men of the boardwalk's mouths water, but know that I'm the only one who's tasting you tonight." I can almost hear the record scratch, except my own music is still blaring.

"Excuse me?" I ask, trying to pull back to look at him, his smile in place.

"After you close, come to the shop. You'll sit in my booth until we close, then you'll be sleeping in my bed."

"Excuse me?" I repeat again. There's no way I'm hearing this correctly.

"Your music is loud, babe, but you're not deaf." He leans forward and nips my ear. A shiver runs down my spine, and he smiles. *Such an ass.*

"I'm not sleeping in your bed." I move to get away from him, and he lets me. I stand a few feet away, hands on my hips. When I see my mixer is still going, creaming butter and sugar to oblivion, I walk over and flick the switch. The small change in noise level helps my brain to function, so I move to turn down my music, too.

Once that's off, the quiet is near deafening as I repeat myself. "I'm not sleeping in your bed, Ben."

"Fine, I'll sleep in yours then."

"Ben!"

"Sweet girl, you are not sleeping alone. And not just because I plan to get in you again after work, which I do, in fact, fully plan on doing. But also because I know who Johnny is. I know you're in trouble. And I know from what I saw last night you're going nowhere without me for a while until we figure this shit out." My stomach sinks.

He's not wrong.

This whole thing has gotten out of hand.

But still . . .

"Ben, I've got this under control. I appreciate your help yesterday and whatever . . . this is. . . has been . . . fun, but—"

"Fun?"

"Well . . . yeah."

"This?" He mimics the hand wave I made before.

"Yeah. You. Me. Sex. It's been nice. But—"

"Oh, sweet girl." His hand comes to my face and holds me there, looking at me like I'm a child who doesn't understand something. "You don't get it."

"Get what?"

"You're mine now." I feel my eyebrows come together in confusion.

"I'm . . . yours?"

"You're mine. This is not just me and you having fun. Not just relieving stress from the fucked-up situation you got yourself into. This is weeks and fucking weeks of tension building up and finally giving into it. This is me not being able to avoid you since you moved in, no matter how much I tried—and babe, I really fucking tried." That tweaks in me for some reason, like the thought of him intention-ally avoiding me hurts, regardless of the fact that I did the same. "So tonight, when you clean up and do your thing, you'll come over to the shop. I have appointments, so you'll hang out in the shop with Hat and me until I'm done. Then I'll take you back up to my place or your place or wherever the fuck, and I'll make my sweet girl feel real fuckin' good again, and we'll both sleep good, knowing you're safe with me."

And before I can argue, which, trust me, I really fucking want to do, even if my mind is stuck on the words *safe with me*, he's kissing me once on the forehead before he's walking out the back door and heading up the stairs separating our homes.

And all I can think is, what in the fuck just happened?

THIRTY-TWO

-Ben-

At 6:00, I can see from the front window her lights have flicked off.

Closed for the night.

I expect Lola to walk over any minute.

I've texted her a few times today, checking in to make sure she was safe and that her day was going well. Each reply was a mix of sweet and snarky, but each confirmed that she was headed over as soon as she closed.

I can't help but wonder if that pushback is Lola or if it's a special part she holds just for me.

If you'd have asked me three days ago, I would have said it's annoying, a mark against her.

But now? It's my favorite part about her, especially when I found out that part of her doesn't disappear when I'm buried inside of her.

My cock hardens just at the mere thought of it.

Minutes pass. My eyes shift continually from the piece I'm working on to the front door to the back door. I'm not sure which she'll be coming through, but I know she's coming over here as soon as she's done.

There's no way she's not listening to what I told her to do.

After you close, you come here. Stay in my booth, and then we'll leave together.

I want to know she's safe. I fucking *need* to know she's safe. After walking in on that fucker cornering her, I know for sure the bruise on her wrist was not from heavy bags.

I need to know she's safe.

Because as much as the woman drives me fuckin' insane, as much as she is the total opposite of everything I ever thought I'd want or need in my life, I am drawn to her.

And I'm claiming her as mine.

I try not to think about how much shit Hat's gonna shovel my way when she figures out what's going on.

I sigh, shaking my head as I move to the next part of the tattoo, a back piece for a returning client. I like him. He's quiet and doesn't expect hours of small talk.

My favorite kind of client.

Perfect time to overthink everything in my life, though. And soon, Lola will be in my booth with me, throwin' her sunshine around and giving me attitude.

Some part of me fucking loves that idea.

Except, the next time I look up at the clock, it's 6:30.

Still no Lola.

Where the fuck is she?

My gut starts to twist with worry and anxiety.

This feeling is new and terrible, and I can't help but wonder why the fuck my friends get into relationships if this is a regular occurrence. I can't help but think of the time Vic told me he thought that Gabi had gone on a date without her phone once and lost his mind, pacing her apartment hallway for hours. Or the time that Tanner fucked up and Jordan ran off, and he spent all night searching for her.

Is this what my future holds? A lifetime of stressing about a woman who never does what she's told or takes steps to keep herself safe?

Fuck, why is my mind going there? We've had sex twice, not signed a marriage certificate.

I sigh, staring at the clock, which now reads 6:40. I still have about twenty minutes left on this piece or I'd be going over to check on her myself.

"Hat!" I call, summoning my best friend. No reply. "Hattie! Come in here!" I know she's not with a client, just ignoring me because it brings her immense joy.

What will my life be if Hattie is my best friend and I keep Lola as mine?

"You know, I know you think you're some badass who can just boss people around, but a please would be nice," she says, standing in the doorway, arms crossed, an annoyed look plastered to her face.

"Can you call Lola? She was supposed to come over after she closed, and she closed at 6:00." Hat lifts an eyebrow, humorous questioning on her face.

"Oh?"

"Shut it. She's in some sticky shit, and I want to make sure she's okay." She smiles, and I know. I know where she's gonna go with this.

It's where my mind would go if I were in her shoes.

"Sure." The cat smile grows. "So, is the sticky shit—"

"Hattie! I'm with a fuckin' client!" I say, tipping my head to my regular, a big burly guy who eye fucks Hat every time he's in.

"Nah, I love hearing about chicks' sticky shit."

"Jesus fuckin' Christ. Stop that or I'll fuck your piece up," I say to him, and fuck if I'm not even joking. Rage is running through me at the thought of another man even *thinking* of Lola that way.

What in the actual fuck?

"Ooh, Benny's getting angry!" Hattie says in a sing-song voice, and if she weren't one of my best friends and the only one who I trust with my books, I'd fire her on the spot.

"You," I say, tipping my head to Hattie. "Call Lola." An angry dark eyebrow raises in my direction. *"Please."*

"Ooh, a please from Mr. Coleman. Interesting development." I put down my tattoo machine, which is being held in a finger-cramping death grip of frustration, flexing my fingers as I turn to her.

"Hattie. Please call her."

"Okay, okay, don't get your panties in a twist." She walks out, presumably to get her phone, and I hear her talking a few moments later. *Well, at least it seems like Lola answered.* That's good news, I guess. I catch the end of her conversation as I'm wiping the tattoo down, almost done, just looking for final touches and fixes that need to be done.

"Okay, cool. Let's do drinks soon, yeah? I feel like you have a lot to fill me in on." She's smiling as she swipes her phone. "Lola says she's fine, snug as a bug in her own bed. She emphasized that part—her *own* bed. She says thank you for your concern, but she's very tired and going to sleep."

Fire runs in my veins.

In her own bed.

She promised she'd head over when she closed, that we'd stay together while we confirm she's not in any kind of danger.

I wonder for a split second if this woman knows how to do anything other than irritate people and stir the pot to get a reaction.

Air goes into my nose and out through my mouth as I attempt to keep myself under control, images blurring in my vision.

Of her in her bed. Of her face when I caught her cornered, of her crying in my arms as we danced. Of her coming on my cock. Of her stubbornness kicking in when she told me she would not be coming over tonight.

I'm going to strangle her.

And she's going to like it.

Deep breaths. In, out, in, out, the rhythm a comfort as I formulate my plan.

First, I need to finish this piece.

"Thanks, Hat," I say through gritted teeth. "I have one more appointment tonight, right? In an hour?" Hattie nods, snapping her gum.

"Yup."

"When I'm done with this one, are you good to hold the fort down for a bit?" She smiles a devious smile I try to ignore.

"Sure thing. I feel like Miss Lola won't be very happy with that, though." And then she walks away, cackling as she does, knowing full well that I'm raging as I finish this piece.

When my client is done, pleased with the work and making an appointment already for his next, it's like my veins are filled with electricity.

I cannot fucking believe this woman and the hold she has on me. She's infuriating and reckless. Probably more trouble than she's worth. But still, somehow, she's all I can think about.

"Later, Hat," I say, hands fidgeting in my pockets as I wave to her before heading to the door. "Lock the doors behind me."

"Sure thing, big guy. Be nice to her, yeah? I like this one," she says, her laughter following me down the hall. I don't even respond. I walk to the back door, letting it slam behind me as I run up the stairs and try her apartment door.

It's locked.

Of fucking course.

I check under her mat.

No key this time.

If I were in my right mind, I'd go across the hall and get my kit. But I'm sure she has the chain on, too. I can hear it when I jangle the old as fuck, flimsy door.

She needs a new one. A safer one.

My fist pounds on the door.

"Lola! Open the fucking door." Silence. "Lola! Open this fucking door right now!" Nothing. "I don't know why you can't listen to one fucking thing I tell you."

"Go away, Ben!" she shouts through the door. At least I confirmed she's in there.

But why the *fuck* does she have to fight me on *everything*? Is it a game? Is she testing me? Or does she genuinely not want me to bother her?

"Let me in, Lola. We need to fucking talk."

"I just want to relax, Ben. You don't have to take care of me. I'm a big girl." She's closer now, no longer a muffled voice.

"Lola, you open this door or I'm breaking it down."

"You wouldn't fucking dare. Go to your place, Ben. I don't need you over here. You don't need to burden yourself with my drama, I swear. I'm fine." *There it is.* I knew there was something, something bigger that she wasn't saying.

She thinks I'm doing this out of a sense of duty.

She thinks she's a burden, an inconvenience.

God, has anyone ever taken care of this woman? Has she *let* anyone take care of her?

Even more, has anyone fought to be the one to take care of her?

The thought tears at me, thinking no one has ever bothered.

"The fuck you are, Lola. You had a shit dream last night, woke up screaming. Had to hold you to calm you down."

"I'm fine now," she says, her voice softer. Embarrassed.

Fuck. My own voice goes softer in turn, leaning on the door.

"Lola. Let me in. One way or another, I'm coming in there. You either let me in or I'm breaking in."

"Do it. You won't."

And with that, I smile.

She might be the older sister who raised her baby sister.

But I was the older brother who tormented my younger brother.

"Oh, sweet girl. Don't make bets that you'll lose," I say, and if I could see myself, I'd see a devious smile on my lips.

She has no idea what beast she poked.

I back up and slam my shoulder into the door, the cheap, old locks already beginning to give way.

She needs a new one anyway. The front door is fixed, but this door is next. Something tells me she won't let me replace it unless it's completely necessary.

I'll just make it necessary.

"Ben! What are you doing!?"

"I'm coming into your fuckin' apartment. You open this door or I break it down, baby, but one way or another, I'm coming in."

"You're not going to break the door!"

"That's my plan. I'll replace it. Now move out of the way."

With the shit going down, I want this door secure. She needs a new door and better locks.

I need her safe.

I move again, slamming the wood, and it splinters around the lock.

"BEN!"

One more hit and I'm in.

"Oh my God, Ben! I can't believe you just—" She wants to continue arguing with me, but now I'm inside, and in three long strides, I'm to her, backing her up into a wall, my hand, tattooed and tanned, splayed against the pale skin of her chest exposed in her tiny tank top.

"You're safe," I say, quiet, a different kind of adrenaline flowing through me now that I see her in her sweet pajamas, hair in those fuckin' braids I just want to tug, eyes wide with shock.

But safe.

She's safe.

She locked me out because she's a fuckin' pain in my ass, not because she was hiding some kind of danger.

Her heart pumps beneath my palm.

Safe.

"Ben, what the—"

"You don't do that. You don't play games like that. You want to play games, baby, the good kind we'll both like, I'll play." I feel a shiver under my palm, and it almost brings a smile to my lips. Almost.

"But when you're going through chaos, when just last night I saved you from who the fuck knows what, because you still haven't opened up to me about that shit, you don't play games. I want in. I want to see you're safe."

She opens her mouth to argue but stops, taking me in. Her eyes scan my face, looking deeper now that her own shock has wavered.

"You're—"

"I needed to know you were safe, Lola." My chest is heaving, the feeling of panic that I didn't acknowledge until just now subsiding.

"I'm fine, honey, see? I'm safe. I'm fine." Her little hand, nails tipped in that light pink to match her logo, comes up to my face, resting on my cheek.

Her eyes are on mine, bright green and full of . . . not anger. Not anymore. Not panic or frustration.

They're soft.

Sweet.

Lola.

This is the Lola everyone else gets. The one her sister gets; the one her dad gets, I'm sure.

I'm just starting to realize there are so many Lolas in one person. And I want to meet them all.

"You're good," I say then breathe out, resting my forehead on hers.

"I'm good, baby."

"Don't fucking do that," I say, eyes closed.

"What?"

"Any of it. Hiding from me. Thinking you're a burden to me. Playing fuckin' games. Being fuckin' sweet when I want to strangle you."

"I'm not being sweet."

"Yeah, you are. All sweet babies and soft hands and syrupy voice. I'm mad at you, woman."

"You're mad at me?" Soft Lola is slipping away.

Good.

I can handle attitude Lola.

I can't handle sweet, soft Lola.

That Lola, I have no fucking clue what to do with.

"Fuck yeah, I am."

"You just broke my door down!" Her hand is off my cheek, pressing my chest.

That's fine. I don't want sweet Lola right now. Now that the adrenaline is leaving my veins, I need fire. The rest of the world might get sweet Lola, but I get fiery Lola.

And I think I like her best of all.

"What did I tell you?" I ask, the hand on her chest pushing her into the wall.

"Excuse me?"

"I said, what did I tell you, Lola?" She doesn't answer. "Let me remind you, sweet girl." My face goes to her ear, and I speak the words there. "I told you when you were done with work to be a good girl and come next door. I told you you'd be sitting in my booth until I was done, and then we'd go back up to my place and I'd fuck you. I told you we were spending the night in my bed again." A shiver rolls down her spine, a shiver I can feel in my palm. "But you didn't. Fucking. Listen." Her hands push on my chest, and I move back, just a few inches, so I can look at her.

"I don't do what you ask, Ben. I barely know you."

"Bullshit."

"What?"

"You know me. I know you."

"You don't know me, Ben."

"I sure as fuck do. I know you're sweet when you want to be, and you're so fuckin' stubborn that you'd rather put yourself in danger than do the *one fucking thing* I asked you to do to be safe. I know you spent too fuckin' long taking care of everyone but yourself, and you have no fucking idea what to do when someone else wants to take care of you. That person being *me, Lola*." Her eyes widen. "I know you spent a few weeks trying to be quiet in the mornings so it wouldn't wake me up, but I was still an ass because you're under my fuckin' skin. I know you listen to shit music—" She cuts me off.

"No, I don't!" Of course, that's the part she protests.

"I know you're protective over your shit music," I say with a smile. "I know you liked calling me Daddy when I was fucking you." Her breathing shallows, and her eyes go dark. "I know there's at least one time when you'll willingly be my sweet, good girl," I whisper into her ear then pull back to land my final blow. "And I know you made yourself come thinking about me," I say. Her eyes go wide with panic.

"What? No, I—"

"I came up here terrified something bad happened. But you didn't even know you'd sent me a text. Breathing hard, wearing your sweet pajamas all askew."

"I—"

"Your fingers tasted sweet, babe." No response to *that one*. "You know how many times I've jacked off thinking about that? You coming with my name on your lips." My nose dips, running up her neck and stopping at her ear lobe, pulling it into my mouth. My teeth bite hard, making her breathe in quick. And then her breathing goes heavier.

She fucking *wants* this.

"How many?" she asks, breathy. Her eyes are closed, and I move the hand on the wall to her hip, pulling her into me until she can feel my hard cock.

"Every fucking night."

"Ben," she breathes. My hand moves up, up to her neck. My fingers tighten on the sides almost imperceptibly, but she notices. Her eyes open. They're heavy with lust, want, and need.

"Every night, I think about what would have happened if I'd come up a few minutes earlier, caught you in the act, fingering yourself and moaning my name."

Like always, this woman surprises me.

"What would have happened?"

"I'd have kneeled down between those thighs of yours, slapped your hands away, and eaten you until you were screaming my name. No sweet moans or whimpers. They'd have heard you from the boardwalk." My hand grabs her hips tighter, grinding her against me, and she moans. There's a window a few feet away, and I start moving us toward it until her back bumps into it, and then I turn her, forcing her to face the window. Down below, people are walking the board-walk, oblivious to the heat we're building up here.

"And when you were close," I say into her neck, licking her pulse. "When you were close, baby, I'd crawl up that body of yours." My hand moves, dipping below the waistband of her shorts and moving down, in, until I'm at her clit. A finger circles her, and her ass moves back, grinding into my dick. "Then I'd rub the head of my cock down you, getting it wet. Rub my piercing all over this swollen clit. You're so wet for me already, aren't you, baby? So fucking wet." I dip a finger down into her, barely entering to grab more wetness and drag it up to her already swollen clit, circling her there.

"Ben," she breathes.

"Who are you wet for?" I ask, biting her earlobe again, hard. She moans again, hips bucking, trying to get more.

I give it to her, two fingers sinking into her as I use my body to press her deeper into the window ledge.

"Fuck, Ben!" The moan is low and ragged, my fingers drenched as I start to move in and out of her roughly, palm grinding into her clit.

"Tell me, Lola. Who is this wet cunt for?"

"You!" That's not what I want.

"*Who is this wet cunt for, Lola?*" A test. It's a test, and with the way she fights me on absolutely everything, I'm not sure if she'll pass it.

But still, I try.

"*Say my name, Lola.*"

"It's wet for you, Daddy," she says in a weak whisper, and I groan deep in her ear, seating my fingers deep inside of her and stopping all movements.

"Fuck yeah, it is. And you're going to be a good girl and listen to your Daddy. Good, sweet girls get whatever their greedy cunts want, baby." She moans, hips moving, but I just smile.

She's going to hate me.

My hand leaves her shorts, and she whines as I turn her around, still pinning her into place.

"Clean these," I order, putting my wet fingers in her mouth, and like the good girl she pretends she's not, she holds my eyes as she licks them clean.

My cock twitches.

It's *also* going to hate me.

I step back, grabbing her hand and guiding her to the door. Her eyebrows come together, confused.

"Let's go."

"Go?" Her mind is still muddled in sex and lust.

"I have a client. Told you to come to the shop after work."

"But . . . I . . ."

"Be good and Daddy will take care of you tonight, sweet girl," I say then kiss her deep on the lips with a smile on mine, tasting her pussy there as I do.

And although she's dazed and undoubtedly annoyed, she follows me down the stairs into the shop, sitting in my booth and chatting with Hattie for the rest of the night until I bring her back upstairs and fuck her until she can't move, forcing her to, once again, spend the night in my bed.

And as this happens, I can't help but think about how I could get used to this routine.

THIRTY-THREE

-Lola-

THE NEXT DAY I'm listening to music with headphones in an effort to keep the noise down, scooping dough I'd prepped the day before onto baking sheets when I hear a noise.

These days, noises scare me.

My eyes drift to the door behind me, which I locked with purpose after I left Ben's bed (with his permission and a grumpy, sleepy kiss that absolutely destroyed any hope of keeping this casual with the man). I also remembered to take the spare key with me this time. No more under-the-mat escapades.

Because as much as I refuse to let Ben know, he's right. I need to be better about safety, locks, and making sure no one with ill intent can get to me. With my front lock now fixed, I'm planning to head to the store after work to try and figure out a fix for my apartment door, something I will be ripping on Ben for indefinitely.

I take out a headphone, pausing my music, and I hear it—loud thumping, like something is being dragged up the stairs.

What the . . .

My body jolts when I hear another loud thump followed by a voice.

A man's voice.

Ben's voice.

"Fuck!"

I pause, waiting. What the hell is he . . .

"Stupid fucking door." And then I hear more dragging, moving away from the entrance of the bakery.

What is he doing?

I finish up scooping perfectly sized mounds of dough before setting the tray and dough aside, washing my hands, and heading for the back door.

When I step out into the hall and look up the stairs, Ben is standing at my apartment entrance.

With a new front door.

It looks like mine is already off the hinges, dragged down the stairs, and is leaning against the back door to his shop.

As I start up the stairs, I see he also has a drill in his hands, removing the old door hinges. To his left is a red tool box.

"What are you doing?" I ask, even though it's clear exactly what he's doing.

"Putting on your new door."

"I . . . Why?"

"I broke your other one." Fair enough.

"Why aren't you sleeping?" I ask, glancing at the screen of my phone in my hand. It's nearly seven thirty in the morning. He's dressed, clearly went to a hardware store, took a door off, and got everything ready for this project.

"Broke your door. Needed to swap it out."

"What?" He stands, looking at me, clearly annoyed.

"Jesus, babe, your door was broken. I'm the one who broke it. You're getting a new one. Your lock was trash. I was planning on swapping it anyway. That chain does nothing; you need a dead-bolt." I blink at him. "I went to the store, got a better door, a better lock. Putting it on now." I spit out the first thing that comes to mind.

If you were to ask me, it would have been something along the lines of "Why are you doing this so early?" or "What do you know about my lock?" But instead, I ask, "Do you know how to do that?" He stops lining the door in the frame to look down the stairs at me, frustration on his face. "Replace a door, I mean." My dad was never one to fix things, rather he would hire someone or barter with someone or guilt someone into fixing whatever was broken. It's just another reason why when I found the broken equipment and YouTubed through how to fix them myself, I was so impressed that I could do it. If you've never seen someone fix something with their own two hands, it seems impressive. Impossible, even.

He stares at me like I'm an idiot.

"I'm doing it right now, aren't I?" I guess he's not wrong. "I fixed your lock yesterday, didn't I?" He did do that, spending a total of three minutes at my front door until the lock caught on its own.

"How do you know how to do that?"

"My dad owns a construction company, babe, remember? Well, my brother does now, I guess. It was supposed to be mine."

"Supposed to be?" This seems like as good a time as any to get information out of the tight-lipped man.

Ben disagrees.

"Yeah, it was supposed to go to the oldest son. I wanted something else, though. Obviously," he says, waving a hand down the stairs toward me, indicating his shop. I remember him mentioning it the other night. But I also remember thinking there was more to the story. More that my nosy ass wanted to know about.

"A tattoo shop is pretty far from a construction company," I say. He tips his head to the popcorn ceiling and fluorescent lighting that lines the center hallway, exasperated with me. It's a look I've seen from him often, but this time it's almost . . . endearing, a smile tipping up his lips.

"Yeah, babe. It's different. Do you mind letting me finish this so I can get to my real job?" For a split second, I feel guilty. He's doing this in his free time when he could be working or relaxing or sleeping or . . . whatever.

But then I remember he's the one who broke the door, and it's the least the man can do.

"Can you tell me the story later?"

"What?"

"The story about you and not following in your dad's footsteps. The first son shit. Why did your brother get the company? Did you want it? Did you have a choice? Was your dad mean? Do you like your brother? How—" Ben laughs, still holding that drill and propping the door against the frame.

"Jesus, babe. Calm down. How about we make a deal?"

It's kind of strange, this conversation happening up a flight of stairs, so I start walking up them, nearing where he stands at the top.

"What kind of deal?" I ask when I'm halfway up. Ben puts down the drill and moves the door until it's steady with no risk of falling. When I reach the top of the landing, his thick arm wraps around my waist and pulls me to him.

That comfort takes over me.

That feeling that I don't have to do it all, carry it all by myself.

This relationship—or whatever it is—-is new and confusing and so fucking messy, but whatever it is, my body likes it.

My soul likes it.

Both feel happy and warm when I'm here, in his arms.

My head tips back to look up at him, though the distance isn't huge.

He smiles at me.

"Here's the deal."

"Okay," I whisper, not knowing what the deal is, but if it includes being held by Ben, being in his arms, having that rare smile shine down on me, then I'm game.

He laughs, and it rumbles through me.

"I didn't tell you the deal yet, sweet girl." I smile back. I could be embarrassed. And maybe I should be. But I just smile instead.

"Oh." He shakes his head in that way he does, which means he thinks I'm a nut.

"Tonight. After my last client, we go upstairs together. You come over and hang with Hat and me while you wait. You will not be going upstairs alone, not until I'm sure everything is good." I start to object, to roll my eyes or fight him, even if I'm sure if I look through unfazed lenses, all I'll see is a normal request.

"Uh uh. You're doing that part no matter what. But if you're a good girl and do what I say, I'll make it worth your time." I quirk an eyebrow, a chill running through me.

"Oh?"

"Oh, I'll take care of you in that way too. But I mean, if you do what I ask, when we get upstairs, I'll tell you whatever you want. My brother, the company, my dad. It's not juicy, but I'll tell you because you're nosy and it's gonna eat at you. Plus, if I don't tell you, you'll probably ask Hat, and she'll run you some crazy embellished version that is not even close to reality." My gut clenches, knowing instinctively what's coming next.

"And?"

"And you'll tell me about the trouble you've gotten yourself into." I take a deep breath, my chest moving against his.

"Ben—"

"If we're gonna do this, I gotta know what the mess is. I know people, Lola. I can help. I have people I can talk to. Shit, I have money if you need it—"

"It's not that." Confusion clouds his eyes, and I can only imagine what he assumes about me, having a bookie coming to my brand new business and harassing me. "It's not that."

"Will you tell me?" He stares, and I want to say no.

I want to answer the way I was trained to my entire life, not saying a word, not revealing anything.

I want to keep my word to my mom, to protect my dad. To protect Lilah, to protect our *family*.

But then, in a flash of clarity, I see it for what it is.

My mom wouldn't want that.

She would never have wanted this mess for me.

She'd want me to have Libby's because it made me happy, not because it was a photo opp.

She'd want me to shelter Lilah because it was a good thing for a big sister to do, not because there's no need for us both to feel Dad's weakness.

And she'd want me to have Ben.

She'd want me to feel this sense of home and security and, shit, cared for.

I remember my mom gossiping with me about boys before she died. Asking me who caught my eye on ice cream runs after school and if I thought brown hair was better than blonde. Telling me not to get lost in boys but to have fun.

And as I got older and she got sicker, she started to give me advice on what I should look for and what I should demand in a partner. In that last year, she would tell me to set my boundaries and make them firm but know that no one was perfect.

And in those last days, she told me about Dad. About his addiction, about his drive, about how much she had done behind the scenes that none of us ever realized.

My mom was the engine behind my father's success.

But at the end of the day, she did it, this thankless job she had, because she loved my dad down to her bones and she knew he felt the same. He gave her *this* feeling. This mix of freedom and safety and confidence. The feeling running through my own veins right now. I think she knew that they were made for each other, that once she was gone, he'd transfer that passion, for better or worse, to his work.

But I don't think she could see how much it would affect me, affect Lilah.

She wouldn't want me to live for Dad and his sins.

She'd want me to follow my heart.

And I know deep down that before I can have Ben, before I can even have the promise of Ben, before I can accept what he's offering, I need to let him know everything.

So I answer the only way I can think of.

"Yeah. I'll tell you. Tonight."

And when relief flashes in his eyes, when he bends down and quickly presses his lips to mine, I know it was the right decision.

THIRTY-FOUR

-Lola-

"You GONNA TELL me about the pit you dug yourself in?" Ben asks, staring at me over a bottle of beer, Chinese food containers littering his coffee table. I came over to the shop as promised after I closed up and hung out with Hattie until Ben was done. Then we came upstairs together, grabbing essentials from my place and ordering delivery.

The entire time, I both anticipated and dreaded this moment.

On one hand. I'm tired of holding this burden alone.

On the other hand, I'm starting to realize I *like* Ben. And part of me is terrified that if and when he hears my whole story, knows the nitty-gritty of it all, he'll see me differently.

Right now, he thinks I'm silly and careless, but I think he also thinks I'm tough and strong-willed.

I like being that version of me.

It's New Lola.

But with this conversation, I'll be introducing him to Old Lola, the one who isn't strong and isn't a smart ass. The one who let people take advantage of her, who sacrificed more than she should have.

And I'll be honest with myself: I'm scared. I'm scared that once he hears my story and gets the full picture, Ben will look at me differently. See me differently.

But still. A promise is a promise.

"This story . . . It doesn't . . . It can't . . ." I sigh, staring at a wall because the words just aren't coming out. His hands reach out for mine.

"It won't leave this room, Lola. Whatever you tell me, you can trust that I won't say anything to anyone unless you tell me to." Well, I have no excuses left.

So I start at the beginning.

"My mom died when I was fifteen." I stop, the words stuck in my chest.

"I know that."

"Lilah was ten." He nods again but doesn't speak. "Back then, she was . . . Lilah. My little sister. I've always kept her safe." I look at the ceiling, shaking my head at the lie we'd all been told. "My mom was good. She was amazing. Held my family together like glue. But what she did most of all was keep my dad together. When she was on her deathbed, days before she passed, she confessed years and years of lies and secrets to me. Secrets she'd been keeping since before I was born."

I take a deep breath, knowing that it's coming. "My dad . . . he's got an addictive personality and he likes power. The two? They don't mix." Ben squeezes my hands, but I don't feel it. I'm lost in the memory. "She made me promise, Ben. She was dying, and she looked me in the eye and made me promise. I was fifteen. I . . . I didn't know. I didn't *understand*. There were two things she wanted from me, and she was dying, and who was I to say no?" I stare at the wall, committing the art there to memory because I think a part of me is afraid this will be it.

That once he knows, he'll be done with me and I'll never see this beauty again.

"The first promise was I had to keep Lilah safe. I had to keep her out of the papers, away from questions. They couldn't find out who she was. Who she *is*. And two, I had to keep our dad steady. She told me without her, he'd lose his mind, get lost in grief, and transfer that to his work. He'd go power hungry and lose all sense of reality without her." I look to the window, remembering the way her voice trembled with the warning.

She knew. She knew all along that this could happen. And her lies and her secrets contributed to it. "And she was right. And it became my job to keep him on track. I refused to let Lilah help or carry the burden. I needed to keep her *safe*, Ben. I swear I didn't . . . It wasn't like I enjoyed it. But I figured one of us should have the good life without this shit touching them. And I had already promised. And I had gotten Mom for longer. It was . . . fair." Ben's hand squeezes mine, the touch finally drifting into my consciousness.

"Babe, you're not making any sense." He's right. I just need to put it out there.

"My dad gambles." My eyes finally meet his. "He gambles and does it quietly because the sweet, beloved, widowed mayor of Ocean View can't have a gambling addiction. No one would vote for a man with an ongoing addiction. But also, if everyone knows, he can't use it to gain more power, more money, more . . . friends." Another sigh, deep from my chest. Exhaustion. "He doesn't do it above the board. It's . . . dark. He gambles with money, and he gambles with power. But when you gamble with power, your opponents will do whatever it takes to get more."

"Power?"

"Ordinances. Turning a blind eye to things. Permits and laws being passed to favor a seedy underbelly."

"Fuck." Ben's eyes are wide with understanding, the knowledge that this is so much bigger than me and my bakery as he originally thought.

"I was left a trust. Lilah was too, but hers went to college. You thought I had family money, and I guess I did, so you weren't completely wrong. But that didn't build this business." He looks confused, as he should. "I had to take care of him, Ben," I say, and then, slowly, I watch it come over his face. It morphs from confusion to understanding to . . . anger.

"Lola, no—"

"It was what my mom wanted. I used it for a while, helping out. Sometimes tabs would pop up—there were threats about the media and revealing things—but it was mostly fine." I look back at the wall, drawings, and framed beauty I could get lost in for days.

"Until?"

"Until he got mixed with the Carluccios."

"Sounds about right."

"He wasn't supposed to work with them, Ben. Not ever."

"Well, yeah, I can see why. They're ruthless."

"It's not even that. It's more. This. This is what I needed to keep Lilah safe from." His hand moves, and fingers gently touch my chin until I look at him again.

"My mom was supposed to marry Carmello Jr." His eyebrows come together, trying to put this new fact into the story I'm telling. "My mother's father was also a politician—senate. She'd seen this whole show play out once before, but her father was in deep with the Carluccios. They wanted to strengthen ties and bring the families together. Politics and the underworld can go hand in hand if you want them to. Both crave power. My mother grew up in the fold; her parents grew up in the same little town in Italy as Carmello Carluccio did."

"But your mother married your dad?"

"My mom met him at a function for her father. A fundraiser. Just like me, she was to wear pretty dresses and smile. Win the eye of male voters, but beyond that, she was to be quiet. My dad was a councilman at the time and . . . well . . ." I shrug. "Well, I happened. There was a rushed wedding and strict instructions on how to proceed, even though she had ruined their original plan. She was to attend events, to have a proper wedding, and my father eventually got the support of my grandfather. When I was born, I was added to the voter appeal, and when I was two, my father was elected as mayor."

"Jesus, he's been mayor that long?"

"When you have friends in high places . . ." I say, my voice trailing off to allow him to fill in the blanks.

"Fuck," he murmurs, and I smile a tight smile.

"He got into politics because he was made for it. But he stayed in it because no one would try anything if he were in politics. There was no threat to my father to free up my mom's wedding finger if he was the mayor and in the spotlight. They still wanted to strengthen ties, after all."

"Holy shit," Ben breathes, and I just sigh.

"Eventually, he realized that politics lent a hand to his addiction. He could settle a debt or get payoffs by allowing for a permit to pass or giving special consideration to a business. Highly sought-after city contracts. That kind of thing." I fill my lungs, fresh air not quite reaching the bottoms as I look away from Ben and scan the room. I don't like what I think I see in Ben's eyes. Pity? Disgust?

"My mom loved him. I can tell you that much. She told me she tried to talk him out of it in the beginning, but he wanted to give her everything. She came from money. He . . . didn't. She said he did it for love . . ." I pause because this part I've never said aloud. "I think it was an excuse he told her." I shake my head because I see it for what it was now. I used to think it was romantic, my father doing whatever it took to give her what she wanted and my mother standing by his side throughout it.

But it was toxic.

They were *terrible* for each other.

And what I'm about to confess next is a part of history that has never been shared with someone outside of our family—a secret that was told to me in confidence.

You have to protect Lilah.

I look back at Ben, not seeing that pity or disgust but interest.

"Lilah's my half-sister." Ben's eyes widen. "She's Alfredo Russo's granddaughter."

"What—"

"My dad was deep in an election year and never home. I was four or five, but I remember that part: he was never home. My mom cried a lot. According to her, she went out, got drunk, and called an old flame. Nine months later, Lilah was here." My voice is soft and factual as I speak.

"She doesn't—"

"No. She doesn't know." I sigh again. "The Russos don't know. If the family finds out, they'll pull her in. They like to keep their own close. She'd probably get married off to one of the Carluccios, securing ties with the families. She'd be miserable and constantly in danger. A target. Mom didn't want that for her."

"Her real father?" I smile, a sickly sweet thing, because this part is speculation on my own end.

And this part requires I trust Ben with my whole being.

And for some fucked reason, I do.

"The only Russo son died, mysteriously in a drive-by months after Lilah was born." Ben's eyes go wide. "There's no one to take Alfredo's place when he dies. That's why they'd marry off Lilah to a Carluccio. Secure the line and all."

"Do you think your dad—"

"He knows. He knows, and he knew when he started toeing the line with them. He knew the danger of getting involved with them."

"Fuck, Lola. So your sister is in the line of fire because both of your parents fucked up, and it became your job to keep her safe?" I shrug.

Part of me wants to argue, say that my mom isn't fucked up, but the older I get, and the more I look at it, I can't say he's wrong.

Mom married Dad, knowing his issues, then acted out when those things came to fruition. And now it's Lilah's and my problem.

"Dad started getting in with Carluccio Disposal. Waste is strange and needs a lot of permits and approvals. Dad was able to get them. Sometimes it was to clear up debts or tabs, sometimes to earn favor. A couple of years ago, that started getting harder. More eyes, more scrutiny, and then most of it stopped. He stopped working with them. Or . . . so I thought."

"What changed?" I sigh. I see the fire in his eyes, and he is *not going to like* this part.

"The trust dried up." He blinks. Once, twice, three times. I keep talking, unsure if he heard me or if he understands. "I'd been using my trust to spot him money. It ran out. I told him I had nothing more. I had my own savings, but I didn't say anything. Though . . . the guilt of that ate . . . But I—"

"Are you fucking kidding me?" Ben says, cutting me off. His face is going red.

"Ben—"

"No, Lola. No. Are you *kidding me?* You emptied your trust for his shit?"

"It wasn't just—"

"It was, Lola."

"I needed to keep Lilah safe, Ben." He blinks. "I couldn't have them coming to our house, seeing my sister, putting things together. It never touched me. My dad would call and ask for money, but it was never me. Until . . ."

"Until what?" His voice is firmer, losing the soft edge, but part of me knows, even right now, that it's not anger directed at me.

"A year ago, I got a direct call from Johnny. That was my breaking point." He looks confused. "He called me because Dad told him I was good to cover his debt." Ben's eyes go wide. "I paid it, but that night I told him I was done. That's when I started working to make Libby's happen. I needed to set myself free and live my life. I realized then—with the trust empty—that I had been living for everyone else and putting myself in danger. Driving down to Raceway Park to pay off your father's gambling debt in the middle of the night will do that to you."

"Why did you do it, Lola?" My back stiffens with his tone, a mix of sadness and frustration and indignance.

"It was my job. My mom asked me to keep them safe, to keep Dad above water. I did it." My face sets, firm, immovable. As annoying and frustrating and overall draining as this has all been, I don't regret it. I did what I had to do for my family. "It was quiet for a year. Ever since that day. But I don't think . . . I don't think my dad realized I was building Libby's. And now he owes money and sees I have . . . well . . . something coming in. He told Johnny I was good for it again." Ben looks like he wants to crush something. I sigh.

"It's bad, Ben. I have . . . I have no idea . . . I need to keep Lilah safe."

"Why?" he asks, and I'm confused.

"Why what?"

"Why do you have to keep her safe? Why is that your job?"

"Because . . . she's my sister, Ben."

"Does that equate to you having to put your own dreams on hold for her?" Something in me ticks, the need to justify my actions and make him see the truth of everything.

I was born, and for five years, I was alone. My dad had his career, and my mom had my *dad*. But when Lilah was born, I had her. My best friend. My mom put her in my arms when I visited the hospital, and she told me right then. *"This is your baby sister Delilah. It's your job, Lola. Your job to keep her safe."* When I got older, she'd ask me what my number one job was, and I'd puff my chest out and put my hands on my hips and say, *to keep my sister safe!*

And back then, it meant brushing peanut butter from her hair or making sure she didn't shove something up her nose. But over time, it changed.

"It's my *job,* Ben. She's my baby sister. My job is to keep her safe, to make it so she could do what *she* wanted with her life. So what if that meant I had to sacrifice back then? Right now, I'm following my dreams, and Lilah got to be a *kid.* She was a normal high schooler and went to college and works in the city, happy as can be. I did that. I made it so she could chase her dreams." His mouth opens, and I know what he's going to say. "I got to chase mine, too. It just took me a bit longer. It was a trade-off. I had Mom for 15 years. She only had her for 10. Eight good ones, if you add in cancer. I won't . . . I won't have you telling me what I did was wrong, Ben."

When I look back at Ben, my chest heaving with emotion and frustration and hurt and the need to make him *understand*, his elbows are on his knees, his head in his hands.

I'm not sure if this is because of the situation I'm in, but my gut says it's something else.

Something more.

"Ben—"

"God, I'm a fuckup."

"What?"

"I'm a fuck up, and it took a sweet baker to show me."

"Ben, I don't—" His hands go out to mine, grabbing them.

"I told you I'd tell you my shit. What you just told me? It's heavy. Some crazy fucking shit that we need to sort out—together. We need to figure out a plan to get you free of your shit." I open my mouth. "Yes, *together,* Lola. Because I already told you I'm taking care of you." I don't argue. I can't. I see he needs this right now. So I nod. There's a surprised smile on his lips with my acquiescence.

"But the way you love your sister and did everything in your power to give her what she needed?" A hand runs through his hair, frustrated or stressed, I don't know. "I didn't do that. I did everything you didn't." He sighs like he's in the spotlight now. I understand that feeling. I want to tell him to spill, to tell me everything, because right now? After sharing my burden and my story?

I feel miraculously lighter.

I want to give him that relief as well.

"I'm the older brother." He stops and looks at me.

"Okay?"

"The way it works in my family, the oldest son gets the business.

Three generations of it, and I was to be the fourth. Construction, contracting. Big builds, small updates. They do it all."

"You told me that, Ben. I—"

"I didn't want it. It was my duty, but the idea of it . . . It was suffocating." I stop trying to speak. "I knew for a while I didn't want it. I didn't want the company. I didn't like construction. It's all my dad talked to me about. The company. The family name. The legacy. But every time he brought it up, I felt sick." He looks around, a replication of my own actions just minutes ago when I was trying to avoid his eye. I reach over and grab his hand, hoping I can offer him strength or confidence or whatever he needs at the moment.

"I wanted art. I wanted to make things, beautiful things. My dad and Tanner—they can build shit, build a home, and that's beautiful in its own way, but not the beauty I wanted to bring to the world. To my dad, my art was . . . a dumb hobby he couldn't wait for me to grow out of. It was the dumb shit I did with my mom, not a career. When I was 18, I went off to school, supposed to get a degree in business so I could come back and apply it. But the classes . . . Lola . . . I wanted to die. They stole everything good and boiled it down to numbers and figures. So I took an art class."

"Ben, I don't—"

"You're going to hate me."

"After what I just told you, how weak I've been, what I let happen, you really think that?" I know family can drive you to do some crazy things.

"You did everything for your sister. Everything to keep her safe and give her what she deserved."

"I—"

"And your dad. Whatever he needed, you gave him. Your mom—she asked you to be there for your family, and you chose them, even if they weren't perfect, even if they didn't deserve it."

"It's not that simple. I—" He turns to me then, putting the hand I was holding onto my thigh, leaning in and looking me in the eye.

"I didn't do that." I stop trying to interrupt. This is it, this is him telling me his story. He sits back once more, disconnecting from me and looking at the wall. "I knew the family business was a shit storm. My dad is shit with numbers, but he's a good guy generally. When things went downhill, from the recession and just years of money not being managed correctly, he refused to lay men off. They had families; they had lives. The business made nothing. He's also shit at billing—again, he's a good guy, means well. People go through shit. But I remember I'd taken an intro to accounting course my first semester, and during break, I looked at the books." He breathes in deep. "Lola, they were a disaster. So far underwater." He sighs again. "I didn't want to deal with it."

There it is.

"I didn't want to deal with it, so I changed my major, stayed away from home, and told my dad it wasn't going to be me. It wasn't going to be me taking the business.

"He was so fucking pissed. Called me every hour on the hour for three days. Eventually, he stopped. I went home once, over break, and it was terrible. Screaming and yelling, telling me I was shitting on the family name. I left. I never went back to my hometown."

Understanding creeps in.

"Tanner got the business. He didn't want it either, but he's better than I am. He's so much better than I am. He's my younger brother, and he sacrificed everything to make that business work. Wanted to design the houses, not build them. Wanted to go to school for it, but instead, he jumped right in once he graduated high school to try and give Dad a retirement sooner. He lived in a fucking trailer for years, didn't pay himself, worked so fucking hard, and eventually got things to where they're profitable. He saved that business, the business he didn't want, with blood and sweat and tears simply because I didn't want it. He's a better man than me." A hand goes through his hair. "Jordan, his girlfriend—she helped a ton. She's his manager now, but he did it. He took it on. He wanted to be a designer, an engineer. Now he's stuck running a business and doing the fucking labor every damn day."

"Honey, that's not your fault."

"You gave up everything for your family."

"I didn't—"

"What did you want to be?" I look at him, confused. "When you were fourteen, before your mom passed. What did you want to be?" My gut drops. "Did you get to go to school?" I look away. "Lilah did, did you?" I don't answer. "Lola."

"I wanted to be a baker. I am a baker."

"You're avoiding my questions, and I know why." I sigh. Might as well get it done.

"Lilah went to school out of state, got a degree in marketing and public relations."

"You didn't."

"I had obligations that kept me home."

"And I left home as soon as I could to pursue my passion. I left my brother—who was going through his own shit with a bitch of an ex—to work day in and day out to settle the family business, which was not his responsibility."

"He chose that, Ben."

"He wouldn't have, given the option."

"You don't know that." He looks away, and just like he did, I use a hand to pull his face to mine, to look at me. "We all make decisions. I made mine. You made yours. But, Ben, no one held a gun to his head and forced him to work your family's business." He mulls the thought over but doesn't agree still.

"He's loyal. To the family. You're loyal to yours. I went out and did my own thing."

"You have your family's logo tattooed over your heart, Ben." Stillness. "That's not a coincidence."

"Tattoos rarely are." I roll my eyes.

"You know what I mean." I sigh when he doesn't answer. "If he called you right now and said he needed your help with the business, how would you respond?" He continues to stare at the wall.

"I had a man corner me in my business, and you shut your shop down, canceled appointments, and refused to leave my side. I know exactly how you would respond." He doesn't answer, and I don't think he's willing to accept any kind of empathy.

I know the feeling.

So instead, I continue.

"Still, he sounds happy from what you said. Sounds like he likes what he's doing now, even if it wasn't his original plan. He found a girl that makes him happy, right? I don't know him, but I wouldn't say he resents you."

"Yeah," he says but doesn't look at me or add to the conversation. He's not convinced.

"Does he come down here?" I ask.

"Yeah."

"He loves you then," I say with surety. "He wouldn't make the trip knowing you won't come up if he didn't love you."

"I don't know about that."

"I mean, I wouldn't blame him if he hated you. You're annoying as hell," I say with a smile, poking him with a foot. Funny how I thought I would be ending this conversation caught in my head, embarrassed or ashamed, but I'm here trying to cheer up *Ben*.

"Keep telling yourself that, sweet girl." I roll my eyes, avoiding the truth of his statement, and take another sip of my beer. "I'm supposed to go home," he says when the room is quiet for a bit. "My brother planned a big party for my mom's birthday." His finger rounds the edge of the beer bottle he grabbed off a coffee table, lost in his own mind.

"And?"

"I haven't been home, not really, since I left for school."

"But . . . you see your family, right?"

"Yeah. They come down here. Here? It's safe. If my dad starts anything, I can leave. If I feel uncomfortable, I have excuses. If I go to Springbrook Hills, I'm . . . I'm there. I'm stuck there."

"That makes sense." He looks up at me, shocked. "Lilah moved out of town for the same reason. Our dad can't bother her if she's not in town." He keeps staring at me, still mulling before he sighs, flopping back onto the couch.

"I'm a shit son."

"No, you're not. Your mom wanted you to chase your dreams. She made that happen." He doesn't look at me. "Does she bug you about it? Guilt you?"

"No. Never. Except this—she wants me to come home for it. She won't give me shit out right, but she wants that. I know. And so does Tanner." I can see the guilt in his eyes.

"Have you made your decision yet? If you're gonna go?" His head tips back, looking at the ceiling.

"I know I should. I blocked off the weekend for appointments."

"So you're off?"

"Yeah."

"Hattie?" I ask, knowing he doesn't like her being there alone. A big sigh comes from his chest like he's been wanting to avoid thinking about it.

"Shop is closed for the weekend."

"Which weekend is it?"

"This one," he says, smiling at me like he knows he's waited way too long to make this decision.

It's a boyish grin, a new one. I document it, taking a mental snapshot and filing it in with the other things I've seen in the world that bring me all-consuming joy—daisies and puppies and iced caramel lattes and a cupcake with a perfect pink swirl on top.

"You have to go."

"I don't want to," he retorts, like just the prospect of going home makes him a child. My mind flits over my own weekend that is shockingly free of bulk orders.

Do I want to?

I could offer . . .

I take a sip of my drink, liquid courage, and prepare for rejection.

"I could come with you," I say, then my entire body goes hot in panic-filled prickles. Why the fuck would I say that? I'm about to open my mouth to justify or make a joke or *anything* when he speaks.

"Would you do that?" When I look up at him, his eyes are on me, and fuck, there's something new there.

Hope, maybe.

I don't think about the loss of income.

I don't think of the repercussions of closing on a weekend.

I don't think about any of it, except for that look he's giving me.

"Yeah, Ben. I'd do that."

THIRTY-FIVE

-Lola-

"You GOOD?" I ask Ben, who is glaring out the windshield, driving in silence.

Well, *he's* silent.

I'm blaring Taylor Swift on his car radio.

Should I have changed up my playlist?

Probably.

Did watching his knuckles go white when I demanded radio privileges give me a sick joy? *Absolutely.*

I'm not asking if he's okay because he's been enduring Ms. Swift for nearly two hours.

I'm asking because we're passing a green sign that says *Welcome to Springbrook Hills. Enjoy your stay!*

Ben is taking me home for his mother's birthday party.

We'll be there only for the day, making the long but peaceful drive back late tonight, but I can see the stress and anxiety this short day is putting on the man. He hasn't been home to Springbrook Hills in years, avoiding facing his father's disappointment in his domain.

His eyes stay on the road, and I assume that should be my answer in and of itself.

"I'm fine," he says, but not a single part of me is sold with his declaration.

"If you want to . . . talk about it—"

"I'm fine, Lola." I stare over at him and take in his stiff jaw, teeth gritting and grinding.

"That can't be good for your teeth, Ben," I say. "You've got nice teeth. You'll want to keep them for a long time. I feel like dentures would mess with your biting kink, too." I'd love to see that smile of his right now, but his jaw loosens just a bit.

Progress.

"I don't have a biting kink," he says, eyes to the road still.

"Tell that to my neck and my ass and my hips. I found teeth marks on my thigh this morning," I say. "I had to change my outfit plans because you could see them in my shorts." The sides of his lips tip up. "I don't think your family would appreciate knowing your teeth have been on the inside of my thighs."

He groans, a full smile hitting his lips.

Mission accomplished.

"Lola, if you don't stop talking about my mouth being between your thighs, I'm going to have to pull over."

Now I smile.

"I don't think your mom would appreciate us being late or me showing up with sex hair." His smile continues to grow, his eyes slipping to me, and I see he's started to relax.

"My brother would. He'd probably give me a high five."

"Oh God. Of course, he would." I roll my eyes. "Anyway, I think we need a safe word," I say, and the car swerves, just a bit, but enough to cross the center dividing line. "Jesus, Ben!"

"Did you just say we need a safe word?" His head is turned, looking at me.

"Benjamin! Eyes on the road!" My hands reach for the steering wheel, intending to take over if he's not equipped to do so. Thankfully, his head moves back to the road, but that smile on his lips has morphed into something else.

I've seen *that* smile.

"Sweet girl, did you just say we need a safe word?"

It clicks.

"For escaping! This party! A safe word for the party!" That laugh I love, the deep, genuinely happy one falls from his lips, the sound bouncing around in the car and filling up my happy meter.

"Got it. Well, maybe this safe word can be multipurpose. For events and . . . other places."

My body goes hot.

"Did I tell you I didn't wear panties?" I blurt out.

Again, the car swerves.

"Ben!" I say, once again reaching for the wheel.

"Lola, you can't just say shit like that and expect me to be able to keep this fuckin' car on the road."

"Sorry." I stare at the hands I've balled in my lap, now self-conscious. "It wasn't like . . . a sexual thing. I was rushing around and this dress . . . panty lines . . . " I'm wearing a knee-length bodycon dress with thin straps, and while it's so comfy it might as well be pajamas, the only panties that don't show in it are hella uncomfortable.

So I made a last-minute decision.

I'm kind of regretting it.

Until his hand leaves the steering wheel, reaching out to me and tugging a knee until I spread my knees.

The hand slips under the material easily, sliding up, up, up . . .

His pinky finger meets my center first and I start to move, just a fraction to try and get him where I suddenly need him.

"Jesus," he says, ring finger brushing up my center. "Fuck, are you wet?" he murmurs, eyes locked to the road, remaining hand on the wheel turning onto a side street.

"Your hands are on me, Ben," I say, breathily.

One finger moves back down, gently brushing my entrance, dipping in a knuckle deep.

My eyes drift shut, and my head hits the back of the chair.

A soft moan leaves my lips.

And then so does his hand.

And the car stops.

"Ben, what—?"

"We're here, sweet girl," he says, a devious smile playing on his lips before those fingers that were just under my dress move to his lips, his tongue coming out to taste them, that barbell on his tongue that wreaks havoc on my clit glinting in the light.

"Let's go." And then he's stepping out of the car.

THIRTY-SIX

-Ben-

"My baby! He's here!" my mom says, running down the two front steps and walking toward me with both hands in the air. I walk with my hand in Lola's from the street and up the front walk, letting go when we're close and wrapping my mom up. "I can't believe you made it, Benjamin!"

"Hey, Mom," I say. "Happy birthday." She pulls away, stepping back and putting her hands on her hips.

"Let me see you."

"Mom, you just saw me a few months ago."

"When you have kids of your own, Benjamin, you'll understand that a few months feels like a *lifetime*." I shake my head but still smile, holding my hands at my side, appeasing her.

"You've seen me. Now can I introduce you to my girl?" I ask, the outstretched hand moving to pull Lola into me.

"Oh, my goodness, of course!" she says. "Gosh, I'm so sorry! You must know, Ben *never* comes home. Is this your doing?" Lola stands, dumbstruck, and the look is cute on her. "It must be, a pretty thing like you? He'd want to show you off as soon as possible!" My mom pulls Lola into her arms, and it takes everything in me not to laugh as I watch Lola's arms start stiff, confused, before returning the hug. "I'm Ben's mom."

"Lola," she says, stepping back to me with a big smile.

A genuine smile.

"It's such a pleasure to meet you, Mrs. Coleman. I've heard so many lovely things about you." I see it now. The politician's daughter, winning people over with a smile and some sweet words.

My mom is already voting for her.

"Oh, you're too kind!" My mom turns and waves, urging us inside. "Come on, let's go find your father. Everyone's here, your Aunt Joanie and Uncle Dave. Hunter Hutchins is here. Did you know he got married?" my mom asks. Hunter was Tanner's best friend all through school. He left to build a business and then reconnected with my brother when he came back. He's also Jordan's half-brother.

"Jordan told me last time she was down." I look around the crowded living room of my parent's house, tipping my chin at a few people I know. "Where's Tanner?" I ask, looking around for my brother and his girlfriend. They were the masterminds behind this mess.

"Oh, he'll be here any minute," my mom says with a twinkle in her eye. She always has that look when she knows something I don't.

"What do you—" I start to ask, but then I'm cut off by cheers and whoops.

In the doorway, my brother, the brother who is as to himself as I am, the brother who just a few years ago would simply bark yes or no answers when people tried talking to him, is standing, straight up *beaming*. Both hands are raised, fists pumping like he won a game, one holding a woman's hand.

The hand belongs to Jordan, his girlfriend. Her face is red from the attention, one hand over her face like she's trying to hide it, her dark auburn hair pulled into a ponytail, but a smile is on her face. A huge one that mirrors Tanner's.

And on the hand that Tanner is holding is a ring.

A big fucking rock.

Holy fuck, he did it.

"Benjamin!" my mom said, swatting my shoulder, making me realize I said that out loud. Lola's hand tightens in mine and I can feel her face on me, questioning, but I can't pull my own gaze from Tanner and Jordan.

He proposed.

It all makes sense.

Sure, this was a party for Mom. But it was also an announcement, a party for Jordan. I realize now that their friends are here, all cheering and clapping as well. Chris Jacobs and Tony Garrison. Luna and Zander Davidson. Jordan's family, including her sister, Autumn, her nieces, and her brother-in-law.

I get it now.

My little brother is getting married, and he wanted me here to see *this moment.*

And I almost missed it.

I truly am an ass.

I turn to my mother.

"Did you know?"

"Know what?" She's smiling.

"Don't play games."

"Of course, I knew, Benjamin. All these years, never once gave you shit about coming home. This year I did. And for my birthday? I thought you'd have figured it out. I figured that was why you came," she says, eyes moving to Lola.

Because I did not come because I realized Tanner was going to propose to his girlfriend. I did not come because I wanted to celebrate with my soon-to-be sister-in-law.

I came because a sweet woman gave me the courage to make the trip in the form of her presence.

I look down at her, and her lips are tipped up. She knows. She knows, of course.

"Bet you're glad you made it," she says in a whisper.

"Shut up," I reply, smiling at her and catching Tanner bringing Jordan into his arms and kissing her big as the guests take pictures.

———

Hours later, we're surrounded by friends, Lola two drinks in and giggly as fuck.

I've never seen her like this.

Relaxed.

I like it.

Seeing her like this, surrounded by people I know, people I grew up around, people I love, I'm reminded that I wouldn't hate having this in my life forever.

Lola in my life.

We've been able to avoid my dad, a simple greeting and introduction to Lola before he was pulled off to somewhere else by my mother who looked over her shoulder with a wink toward me like she knew what she was doing.

My mother truly is a saint.

Not a saint is Chris fucking Jacobs, who is sitting next to Lola, laughing with her while telling everyone a story about Lola and a student talent show.

It turns out that Chris, who is originally from Ocean View and best friends with Luke Dawson, went to high school with Lola.

Jordan just told a story about falling off a stage while in ballet as a kid, pointing to a scar on her eyebrow as proof, which apparently jogged a memory of Lola for Chris.

"So then she steps forward but she catches the long skirt she was wearing on her shoe, and the entire thing comes down." Chris is laughing and Lola is too, covering her face with a hand.

"Oh my God, no, stop!" she says, giggling that laugh I love to hear, slapping Chris on the shoulder.

His arm goes around her shoulders, pulling her into him.

"No reason to be embarrassed, Lol. Your panties were very cute," he says, smiling. Even though this happened at least ten years ago, my gut churns knowing that he's seen that part of her.

"Oh my God, you flashed the whole school?!" Jordan yells, aghast with second-hand embarrassment.

Lola buries her face in Chris's arm.

Here's the thing: Chris Jacobs is and always will be a flirt. He knows that. I know that. The whole damn world knows it. I've seen him flirt with a brick wall, with Tanner, his boss's girlfriend, and Luke's wife, Cassie, right in front of him.

It's harmless.

It's usually fun to watch.

But fuck it if right at this moment, being on the receiving end of him being on my girl, I don't lose it.

Something inside of me snaps.

My hands circle her wrist and I'm tugging her from the sofa, pulling her away from the party, the noise, the crowd.

As I do, I hear the laughter of my brother and Chris follows us.

I don't give a fuck.

"Ben, what are you—"

"Shut up and follow me," I say, starting up the stairs toward my room.

"Ben—"

"One minute," I say, words thick and gruff because I am trying not to crawl out of my *skin*. Chris flirting with her, Lola accepting it and giggling back. Her words, his hand on her. It's all a movie in my mind; all I can think is how I need to claim her as mine.

Right now.

We get to my bedroom door and I push it open with too much force, tugging Lola in and closing the door, her back to the thick oak as I press my body to hers.

As always, every soft curve lines up with my body in a way that is so perfect, it's like it was meant to be.

"Ben—"

"What the fuck was that?" I say, face in hers.

"Ben, seriously—"

"I said, what the fuck was that?"

She doesn't play games.

Doesn't pretend she doesn't know what I mean.

That's what I like about her best. She might mess with me, tease me, drive me wild and annoy the fuck out of me, but she never plays games the way other women do.

"Are you jealous?" Her words are low, gravely.

"Did you want me to be?"

"Honestly?" She blinks then licks her lips. "A little." I groan. Every moment with this woman is an aphrodisiac, even when she's driving me wild.

"Don't play that game with me, babe."

"I'm not playing games," she says.

"You are. You're playing games, looking to make me jealous, drive me insane. But guess what, Lola? It worked." My knee moves, pushing hers out, her dress creeping up her legs with the help of my hand on her hip, and then it settles between her legs. "I'm wild for you, and I need to know you're mine." Her breathing is heavy, and without saying a thing, she moves, her weight going to my thigh as her head is pressed to mine. She moves in a small circle, tentatively, then a low, breathy moan falls from her lips.

"That's it, baby. Grind yourself on my leg." One of the hands caging her moves to her full hips, helping her, guiding her as she starts to grind on me, more moans coming. "When you were flirting with him, is this what you wanted? Chris to take you somewhere, pin you to a wall, make you come?"

"No."

"Did you want him to slip his hand up your pretty dress, find out there are no panties there? To touch your wet pussy?"

"No, Ben." She continues her grinding, moaning lightly. I'm wearing shorts, and I feel how wet she is on my thigh with how we're positioned.

"Did you want him to fuck you, slap your ass when he's deep inside? Did you want him to beat up your pretty pussy, baby?" The hand on the wall moves to circle her throat, pressing on the sides with just enough pressure to restrict her air and blood flow.

Her eyes go wide, but her bottom lip gets fuller, her grinding more frantic.

She shakes her head against the door.

"Did you want him to eat you? Did you want him to choke you, to hold you down while you shake, coming on his cock?"

Another head shake.

"Why, Lola?"

But she can't answer, the pleasure too high, my hand too restrictive.

I stop, moving my leg from between hers, removing any friction.

Her head shakes, frantic.

I move my hand, and she breathes in deep and moans deeper as my hand on her hip moves, going under her skirt and thrusting three fingers in, not giving her time to adjust. I slam them in and her head falls back with a moan.

"Whose pussy is this, Lola?" I growl in her ear.

An unintelligible moan comes out, but it's not what I want to hear.

"Tell me who owns you." Another press of my fingers, another grind of her cunt trying to get more.

"You do," she says, whisper soft beneath a moan.

That will do for now.

I remove my fingers, stepping back and putting them into her mouth.

"Clean these," I order, and she does, running her tongue over each knuckle, lapping at me with her eyes locked to mine.

Such a fucking good girl. She hasn't even complained that I haven't finished her off yet.

"Go over to my bed," I say, pointing to the tiny twin bed with dark-blue sheets that never got any action. But Jesus, if I had known then what I know now about height and angles and depth, I would have found any way to use it to my advantage.

Instead, I just get to profit from it fifteen years later.

She walks over, lips red from mine, eyes wide and glazed with lust.

"Hands to the bed, knees on the edge. Spread for your man," I say and watch to see what she does with that information. She hikes up her skirt, moving to kneel on the edge of the bed and sliding the fabric up until it settles, bunched on her lower back before her hands move to the mattress. She arches her back, sliding her hands forward just a bit before looking back at me.

Fucking magnificent.

My own hands move to my shorts, unbuttoning the tab and shoving them and my boxers down, just enough so my cock bobs out.

This is going to be quick.

Quick and messy but exactly what I need right now.

But first.

I move until I'm on my knees, and I put both hands to her bare ass. The visual is fucking glorious: tanned, tattooed skin on her own, fair and unmarked.

The perfect example of how our opposites fit perfectly.

God, I want to keep her. Keep this.

Her hips move, trying to get something, anything, and my thumbs move to either side of her, pulling her apart until her wet pussy is exposed to the air. Her breath hitches, a small moan or plea leaving her lips, and her ass moves back to get . . . more.

One hand leaves her ass, pulling back and slapping hard.

"Stay still or you'll never get what you want, Lola." A moan again, deeper this time, but her hips stop moving. "Good girl," I murmur, hand returning to part her. "Head down, baby." Her head moves to the mattress, her ass moving higher with the change in position.

I can't resist.

I run my tongue over her, tasting every inch of what is rightfully mine. She moans deep into the comforter but doesn't move.

That deserves a reward, I think.

Standing, I stroke my cock, groaning lightly at that simple movement. Her head starts to move, wanting to see—my girl loves to see this—before she remembers her instructions and stays put.

"Your man's going to fuck you hard, Lola. Clearly, I need to remind you who you belong to, who gets to put his hands on you." My hand comes down, smacking her again, and I savor the noise she makes and the way her fair skin retains the shape of my hand on her skin. "Do you understand?"

She moans but stays still all the same.

"Answer me."

"Yes, Ben, I understand." I rub my cock down her slit, getting the head wet, loving that there's never anything between us, that I always get to feel her wet cunt on my cock.

"Are you going to tease me again?" I notch the head but remain there.

Torture.

Pure fucking torture.

"I wasn't—" She can't resist. Can't resist the game, the arguing, the fighting.

I fucking love it.

My hand on her hip moves back, slapping her and cutting her words off. I feel the movement in my cock, reverberating through, and it takes everything not to slam in.

"Yes! I won't tease you! I swear, Ben. I don't. God, please, fuck me!" She's mumbling now, nonsense, and I'm living for it, this control I have over her body, her mind.

She doesn't listen to me ever. Even in bed, it's not a guarantee, but here . . . like this . . . she's mine.

"Stay still. Daddy will take care of you," I say, then I move, both hands on her hips, and slam into her.

Her face pushes into the sheets to hide her scream.

"That's it, baby. Scream for your man," I say, pulling out before slamming back in. We're far enough from the loud party that there's no threat of anyone hearing. From this angle, I know my piercing scrapes her G spot with every thrust, know that she's already on the edge, needy, dripping down her thighs.

I don't care.

"Remember you don't come until I say." Her head moves to the side, each brutal thrust pushing her face into the mattress.

"Ben, I—"

"No." I continue to fuck her, hands moving to spread her ass cheeks, watching my cock disappear inside of her, her tight asshole begging for something.

"Oh, God, Ben—"

My body moves as I tip forward, my hand grasping the nape of her neck and holding her there, pressing her deeper into the bed.

I start fucking her harder, animalistic.

"You do not come until I tell you you can, Lola. You need to remember who owns this fucking body. I control it. It listens to me and me alone." A groan falls from her, the vibrations moving from her to my chest that's on her back. "Who owns this pretty pussy, Lola?"

She moans, tipping her ass back, fighting me.

I press her harder into the bed, growling in her ear. "Who fucking owns you?"

"You do," she says, low and quiet.

That's not what I want.

"Who owns this cunt, Lola?"

"You do, Ben!" Her words are frantic now, wetness coating my cock as I continue to ram into her brutally.

She needs to come.

"*Who fucking owns you?*"

It clicks.

In her sweetest voice, I hear it filtered through a moan and a clench of her pussy around me that makes it hard to keep going.

"You do, Daddy," she says.

Fuck yeah.

Fuck yeah.

"Yeah, I do, sweet girl. Remember that next time you want to play these games."

I move, straightening my back, but don't let her up with me, my hand still pressing into her shoulders. Then I guide it back, that hand pressing to her lower back.

"On your hands, baby." She instantly acquiesces, moving to her hands and knees, my hand on her lower back keeping her arched deeply, the hand still on her hip keeping her moving on me, keeping me fucking her.

The hand on her back moves, sliding up fabric, moving her loose waves to the opposite shoulder.

Then I put two fingers into her mouth, pulling her head back, forcing her to look at the ceiling.

She *moans*. One I haven't heard yet, a primal, exquisite one that has my cock twitching, begging for release. Her pussy clamps on me.

"Don't you come yet, Lola," I whisper, bending a bit so she can hear me, using my hold in her mouth to keep her head tipped back as I plant myself deep, then stop moving.

"You are mine, Lola. Do you get that? Mine. What's mine does not flirt with other men, does not let them touch her. You are mine, no one else's, and right now, I'm claiming, reminding you of just how fucking mine you are. Do you understand?" She nods, her tongue licking my fingers.

"Don't fucking forget it, Lola. This time I'm going to make you come hard on my cock, then I'm going to come inside of this wet cunt and you'll have that reminder all night." She moans. "Next time I won't be nearly as nice, baby."

Another moan, and I can't decide if it's because she's throbbing around my unmoving cock or if it's because she likes the idea of me being *not nearly as nice.*

Jesus.

Instead of asking, I move the hand from her hips, placing it on her chest wide and pulling her up toward me. My hand in her mouth holds her head right next to mine, her back perfectly lining my chest before I start my brutal thrusts again.

The hand on her chest creeps down, landing on her swollen clit, and she screams, needing it.

But she doesn't come.

Doesn't let herself let go.

Because I haven't said so yet.

"Such a good fucking girl, Lola." She moans, tipping her hips to get me deeper as I continue to move. "Do you want to come, baby?"

"Please, Ben," she moans, the fingers in her mouth muffling the words, but it's all it takes.

I start to come inside of her, groaning deep in her ear, rubbing her clit hard.

"Now, Lola, come for your man." I moan, thrusting deep as she shatters, clamping down on me and prolonging my own orgasm. My teeth land in her neck, biting hard and ratcheting up her moan. My hand covers her mouth, trying to avoid being caught.

She continues to come on me, her entire body shaking as I slow my thrusts, a wet glide as I come down from my own high,

Gorgeous.

Fucking *gorgeous.*

And all fucking mine.

As she stops shaking, I gently lower her to the bed, leaving her there as I slip out, tuck myself back in my shorts, and slip into the hall.

When I return, I have a wet cloth and laugh to myself because she hasn't moved, still facedown in my childhood bed, no longer kneeling but with her feet holding her up on the ground.

"Quite a sight," I say with a laugh. She only moves to lift her hand and flip me off. As I run the wet washcloth up her bruised, swollen pussy, she twitches and it takes everything not to start over. But there's only so long we can go missing before someone comes to find us. Once she's cleaned up, I help her tug down her dress and settle it in place, holding her as her arms go around my neck. Gently, I give her a soft kiss before resting my forehead on hers.

"Now we're gonna go back down, you're gonna smile real pretty, but you won't brush that hair. I want every man down there to know you're mine and I laid my claim on you." My face gets close to hers, lips brushing with my words, my fingers still gripping her chin. "And when you feel me dripping out of you, I want you to remember what happens to bad girls who try to tease their men."

I expect her to acquiesce.

I expect her to be a good girl.

I expect an "Okay, Daddy."

I don't get that, which, really, that's what I should expect from Lola after all.

"Are you my man, Ben?" she asks, eyes pointed, chin high, words soft.

I don't reply, not yet.

My arm wraps her waist, pulling her body tight to mine.

My forehead moves to hers, but my hand continues to force her face up to look at me.

"Keep playing these games, Lola. Keep playing them and you'll find out. You know that answer. It started in your bakery, yelling at me because I broke in. Shit got real when I tasted you that first time. I made you mine in my bed, moaning my name at two in the morning when I finally slid inside you that first time."

"That's not—"

"I will spend every day, if I need to, reminding you that you're mine. You wanna fight me on it? Baby, I fucking love the way we fight, so bring it on. But make no mistake, sweet girl. You are mine." Her tongue comes out, licking her lips and grazing the thumb I have on her full lower lips.

Every molecule is begging me to throw her back on the bed and fuck her until she understands what this is.

Understands that she drives me up a wall, and we will fight and fuck and make up and I will live in that cycle happily with her for as long as she lets me lie in her sunshine.

Instead, I press my lips to her, cutting off whatever chaotic argument that will inevitably come from her lips before stepping back, letting go of her chin, and moving that hand to her own, twining small fingers with tattooed ones and tugging.

"Let's go before someone comes looking for us."

And to my surprise, her hand twines with mine, and she follows without a fight.

THIRTY-SEVEN

-Lola-

IT's GONE dark despite it being summer, and it's time to head back to Ocean View. We're standing in the backyard of Ben's childhood home, trees lining the large, green yard and lightning bugs blinking on and off.

Ben is talking to his father.

His jaw is tight, his hand stiff as he puts it out to shake his father's hand, and his father mirrors his actions, tight jaw, arm out, narrowed eyes.

It is *so incredibly awkward.*

But at least I can kind of see now where the stubborn, mildly dick-ish streak he has comes from. My eyes drift to where Tanner is sitting with Jordan in his lap, both smiling and chatting with friends I met while here. I wonder if Tanner has the stubborn streak or his mom's sweet side.

"Thank you so very much for coming today, Lola," Mrs. Coleman says. "And thank you so much for the treats! I can't wait for the next time we head down to you guys so I can try one of everything." Her smile is radiant and I wonder if it's the champagne, her birthday, having her whole family in one place, or if she's always like this.

"Any time, Mrs. Coleman, seriously," I say with a smile. "It was so nice to meet you." I put a hand out to shake hers, but her hand swipes the air.

"Oh no, Lola, you're basically family now." A burning blush takes over my face. "Come, give me a hug!" And then she pulls me into her arms the same way she did before, and just like before, I panic for a split second.

I haven't been hugged like this in 15 years. More if you add in the time mom spent in a hospital bed.

And right now, in this kind woman's arms, I realize I never had even the smallest replacement. Not from Dad, that's for sure.

My arms wrap around her in return, and I sigh into the feeling. With my breath, Mrs. Coleman hugs me a hair tighter.

"Thank you, Lola," she says into my hair. "Thank you for bringing him home."

"Oh, Mrs. Coleman—"

"Call me Joyce." That feels . . . too familiar. Too close.

Too nice.

Then her arms are loosening, and I'm being pulled back, a thick familiar arm on my waist.

Ben.

I can't help but burrow just a bit into his side.

"Bye, Mom. Happy birthday again."

"Thank you, my sweet boy. You made my entire year, coming here." His hand tightens on my side. "Now you have no excuse. You've broken the seal," she says with a smile, voice half joking and half serious.

"Mom—" Ben tries to stop the conversation, but Mrs. Coleman steamrolls right past him, speaking to me directly.

"Bring him back to me, okay, Lola? A family dinner. That way, we can actually get to know you a bit more." Her eyes are kind, but behind that is a tone of pleading. Her husband comes up behind her, holding her the same way his son is holding me.

"Oh, I don't know—"

"You did it once. I know all about you. Ben's been talking." My head tips up, taking him in, and to my shock, his cheeks show a light tint of pink.

"Alright, Mom, we're out of here. It was great to see you," Ben says, waving a hand and starting to lead me to the door. His mom's tinkling laugh follows us as we head toward the front gate.

"You telling your mom about me, Ben Coleman?" I ask with a smile as he helps me into his car. He rolls his eyes and slams the door, but I know he hears my laugh through the metal as he walks around, starts the car, and takes us home.

THIRTY-EIGHT

-Ben-

THREE DAYS after our quick trip to Springbrook Hills, Hattie pops her head into my office as I finish my first client of the evening. It's a woman who was here a few months back for her first tattoo, a small music note on her wrist, and now she's getting a second—a heart on the other wrist.

Tattoos are addictive.

"Sup?" I say, wiping the newly inked skin before slathering it in a protectant lotion.

"You talked to Lola today?" My eyebrows furrow in confusion.

"No. Why?" We're not the kind of couple that talks nonstop. Last night I texted her, asking if she wanted to meet up, but she said she was tired.

I ignored the part of me that wanted to ask for more details, the part of me that wanted her to give me a better excuse. But taking a day off for me meant Lola has been hustling to make up the time, staying up late to make doughs and batters, and she's also been working on interviewing employees.

The employees part gave me visions of taking her away for a long weekend, somewhere we could hide away without worrying about work and spend time together, preferably naked in bed for hours on end.

So instead of bugging her, I'd sent a "Good night, babe, see ya tomorrow" text and went to bed.

Okay, I didn't go straight to bed. I jacked off to the memory of fucking her into submission in her bakery, one of my favorite memories as of late.

I'm starting to worry I'm as whipped as Vic. As whipped as Tanner and Luke.

Goddammit.

How did this happen?

"Lights are off next door. Went to go gossip and get a muffin and the sign is flipped to closed."

My gut goes cold.

"Are you sure?"

"Do I have a food belly from eating three muffins?" She rolls her eyes. "Yes, I'm sure. She's closed."

That's not right.

It's eleven on a Tuesday. She normally opens at eight on Tuesdays.

"Can you call her?"

"I did. No answer."

Acid churns in my stomach, even more seeing Hattie's concerned face. Hattie doesn't even know about half the shit that's been brewing over there, the shit with Lola's dad and Johnny Vitale.

Fuck fuck fuck.

Maybe I should have come over last night. Checked on her, made sure she really was just tired.

And what, look like some kind of lovesick loser?

Lola has made it clear that she doesn't necessarily appreciate when I'm overbearing and protective. She's independent, and so am I.

We just sometimes hang out, and there's no way in hell I'm letting any other man get close to her.

But that urge to take care of her . . . to keep her safe. It pangs.

And the way her face goes slack when I do, in the moments between her being annoyed or angry with me. The split second between when she realizes I care and her deciding she doesn't need my help and who the fuck am I to give it without her asking.

That's when I see it. When I know her words about no one ever taking care of her go deeper than just some irritated oldest child bemoaning the fact that they weren't the center of attention.

In that flash, I always see the real Lola.

It's the Lola I could fall for if we both just let it happen.

I put plastic wrap on the tattoo then turn to the woman.

"Hey, Jess—Hattie's gonna settle you on up, okay? It was great hanging out with you. Gotta go check on our neighbor," I say, walking out of the booth before I can even get a response from her.

Then I'm walking to the break room to grab my phone.

I've never regretted not taking my phone with me into the booth, always knowing that my family, the most important people, know the main phone at the shop in case of emergency.

Does Lola?

But when I get to my phone, there's nothing.

No missed calls.

No SOS messages asking for help.

Nothing.

I scroll through my contacts until I find her, her name displayed with a little cupcake emoji.

I really am fucked, aren't I?

Panicked when she's not at work, putting fucking pink cupcakes on her contact.

Shit.

I can't waste time thinking about that right now.

Instead, I hit send, listening to the rings, counting each as I hear

Hattie checking out Jess and scheduling a new appointment in a few weeks.

"Hey, you've reached Lola Turner. I can't come to the phone right now. If you're calling about Mayor Turner, please reach out to Vanessa Scott, his personal assistant at—" Jesus, she has her fucking father's info in *her voicemail?* I didn't realize how deep this went.

The tone beeps, urging me to leave a message, but I hit end. As I do, Hattie comes back.

"Anything?" She looks as concerned as I feel, more than before.

"No," I say, grabbing my keys, the ones that hold a silver key with a duplicate to her apartment. "I'm gonna go upstairs to check on her."

"Okay. Let me know what's up. Your next appointment isn't until three. I can reschedule it if needed." I thank her, but my mind isn't on appointments and clients and schedules.

It's on Lola and debts and mafia bookies who take the words of a dirty mayor and victimize his helpless daughter.

Fuck.

When I get to the center stairwell between our places, I try the bakery door first.

A shiver runs through me when the door is unlocked.

I fucking told her, I think. How many *fucking times* have I told her she can't just leave doors unlocked like this? On the boardwalk, there are so many fucking idiots wandering where they shouldn't be. It is going to get her into trouble.

I pop my head in, reaching over to flick the light on.

"Lola?" I say, loud, my voice ringing in the clearly empty bakery.

No mess.

No signs of distress or struggle.

No Lola.

Nothing.

I'm not sure if I should be relieved or even more anxious.

Before I can feel either emotion, I back out of the bakery, locking the fucking door behind me, thinking about how I need to change this lock to one that automatically locks when it closes.

Then I head up the stairs to her apartment.

I knock.

No response.

I knock again, this time pounding on the door, my heart racing.

This fucking woman.

I'm about to reach for the key and let myself in when I hear it.

A cough.

Followed by a voice.

"Don't knock that fucking door down, Benjamin!" The words are followed by more coughing.

I should laugh. In another universe, I would laugh at Lola calling me Benjamin.

In this one? Not at all.

"Open the door," I shout through the door like an idiot.

"No! Go away!"

"Lola, open the fucking door!"

"What are you doing here?" Jesus Christ.

"Your bakery is closed."

"Yeah?" More coughing. Is she sick? Or is there something more devious causing her to cough? An intruder, poison, a fire. My mind goes to horrible places.

"It's never closed."

"I was closed like three days ago." I bang my head on the door in frustration and make an effort to bring my voice down, to pour calm into it.

"Lola, let me in."

'Why?" She sounds confused.

How fucking dense is this woman?

But moreover, how much do I want to reveal about my feelings to her?

"I need to make sure you are okay." A beat of silence passes before she answers.

"I'm fine." Coughing. Lots of it.

"You don't sound okay."

"Because I'm shouting through a fucking door when I should be resting."

Again, it takes a lot more than it should to resist laughing.

"Lola. Let me in."

"No."

"Lola."

"You break down that door, I'm going to call the cops."

"I'm not going to break down your door, Lola." My hand reaches into my pocket.

"Good. Go away. I'll see you tomorrow."

Fuck that.

Fuck her thinking I'm just going to leave when something is clearly wrong.

I slip the key into the door.

"Ben, what the—"

I unlock the door, turning the knob and pushing it open.

Panic is flooding me as I do so, part of me scared I'll see the worst.

Instead, I see Lola.

Or should I say, a pile of blankets in the form of Lola and a small Lola head popping out from the center. Her braids are gone. Instead, a loose, messy, ratty bun sits on the top of her head.

"Jesus, babe," I say, my voice low as I look around at the mess surrounding her.

"How the fuck did you get in here?"

She looks like death warmed over. Eyes sunken, nose bright red, cheeks somehow both flushed but also pale.

She's sick.

The pile of tissues should be the first clue, but it's the glassy eyes and the cough that she lets out.

I lift the keys.

"You have a key to my apartment?" I raise an eyebrow. I feel like that much is obvious. "How do you have a key to my apartment?"

"I bought the door. Bought the lock."

"And?"

"Came with two keys. I kept one."

She opens her mouth to argue, eyes wide with shock and frustration.

It's fucking cute.

"You kept my spare ke—"

And then she sneezes, her nose scrunching and the sound almost chipmunk-like. I should have expected that even this woman's sneezes would be cute. I reach over to the tissue box next to her and hand it over.

"What's going on, sweet girl?" I say. Now that my anxiety has simmered, my empathy is here. The poor woman is a fucking mess, clearly sick as a dog.

"Thank you," she says, taking a tissue and blowing her nose. "You should go. I'm sick."

"No shit."

"Don't be a dick."

"Babe, what do you expect? You're sneezing and coughing and your nose is bright red. You're in a pile of blankets in July and watching—" I turn my head to check the television. "*Toy Story?*"

"It's a comfort movie, thank you very much. Now please leave."

"Your comfort movie features a clearly mentally unstable kid who burns ants and mutilates dolls being tormented by his own toys?"

"Go away, Ben. What are you even doing here?"

"I needed to see if you were okay. You weren't answering your phone for me or Hat, and the bakery was closed." Guilt floods her eyes, and she looks toward the kitchen where I see her phone, the light blinking.

"Sorry." She cringes, and I reach over, grabbing the phone and handing it to her. "Fuck. I'm sorry." She sees the missed calls, mine and Hattie's, and knowing her, probably others.

Her dad's. Or his fucking associates or who the fuck ever likes to give her trouble.

"It's fine," I say, moving my hand to brush her hair aside.

She's burning up.

"Well, you've seen I'm fine. You should go. I'm contagious."

"What is it?"

"The flu. Got tested last night and feel like a train hit me this morning. Probably got it up in Springbrook Hills. I've been off since then. I'm hoping a day or two with the prescription will be good. I can't stay closed long . . ." She drifts off, no longer here in her apartment but somewhere else, probably doing money math and trying to figure out loss of income and subtracting her fucking dipshit dad's debts.

We need to bump figuring that out up in our priority list. But first . . .

"What do you need?" I say, pulling out my own phone and sitting on the ottoman next to the couch. "I'll call Hattie, get her to deliver it."

"You should leave," she says instead.

"What?"

"I'm contagious."

"I already had the flu in spring. Knocked me out, but I should be good." She stares at me, eyes blank and watery, a bit dazed, probably from that fuckin' fever. "I told you about my friend Vic's girl, Gabi? Her mom is a trip and invited me to family dinner. Her nephews are germ magnets." She nods as if that makes sense. "So what do you need? Soup? Crackers? Gatorade?" She shakes her head then winces like it hurts to do so.

"I'm fine, seriously. You can go."

"I'm not leaving here. You look like shit, and you're burning up."

"Seriously, I'm fine. I've been through worse." Anger bubbles inside of me. "You have work."

"I'm here right now, Lola. I'm not leaving."

"I'm sure you have clients later today." I stare at her, the same argumentative look she always has in her eyes, but it's dimmed.

The fight won't stay.

She's exhausted and sick.

And some part of me is screaming to do this: take care of her.

I don't think that's happened often.

I make my decision and dig in my pocket for my phone. I keep my eyes locked on Lola, looking down only for a moment to find the name I need before hitting send and putting the phone to my ear.

"She good?" Hattie asks on the other end.

"Can you reschedule my appointments? For today and tomorrow morning. I'll call in the morning and let you know about the afternoon."

"Is Lola okay?" Her voice is concerned, and I realize Lola has another person to worry about her and care for her. I wonder if Lola knows that.

When Hattie decides you're one of her people, you can't shake her. I would know. I've tried many, many times.

"Yeah. Flu."

"Oh, shit. That blows."

"Yeah. She's running a fever and looks like shit." Lola scrunches her face in irritation. "Cute shit, babe," I say with a smile, and Hattie laughs.

"Fuck, you're whipped." I roll my eyes.

"Yeah, yeah. You got clients today?"

"Just one."

"Man or woman?"

"Man." She says the word with slight hesitation, knowing what's coming.

"Can you reschedule? Or I can call Luke, ask him to sit in."

I will never put Hattie in a position to feel uncomfortable or to put herself in danger.

"No, I can reschedule. He's a regular."

"Okay. Reschedule. Close up. You need help locking up?"

"I got it, boss man. You need anything?"

"Not sure. I can probably get it delivered. Vic is next on my list to call." There's a pause. Strange for Hattie. "You good?"

"Yeah, babe." Another pause, but this one I don't break. "I'm happy for you."

"What?"

"I'm happy for you. Taking care of someone. You were made for it. You just never had a good one to do it for." Another pause, but because Hattie is my best friend who I spend nearly every moment with, I know what's next. She confirms it. "You found a good one, babe."

"Yeah." I say, eyes locked on Lola's, whose are still confused but getting sleepy.

I wonder how much of the day she's spent sleeping and what I can do to keep her comfortable while she rides it out.

"Go take care of your girl and keep me updated."

"Yeah. Talk to you later, Hat. Text me when you get home." And then I tap the screen to end the call.

And then I take care of Lola like I was meant to from the day we met.

THIRTY-NINE

-Lola-

MY EYES ARE HEAVY, fighting sleep my body most desperately needs hours later. A call to Ben's doctor friend, Vic, necessitated a delivery of an assortment of soups, drinks, and medicines to my apartment by Hattie, and while he set things up and made his calls, I was able to doze a bit. But once he had take-out for himself and a bowl of soup and crackers for me situated, I refused to let my eyes even droop.

Benjamin Coleman is taking care of me.

Right now, hours after our meal, Ben is watching some random movie, an old western (I made fun of him because he is undoubtedly an old man in my mind now), while he gently brushes my hair with his fingers.

At some point, he forced me to put my head in his lap, and I complained how my messy, knotty bun was giving me a headache. He went to find a wide tooth comb and gently brushed out the tangles, rubbing my scalp to relieve any remaining pressure. Now, even though the knots and my headache are long gone, he continues his ministrations, the action lulling me to sleep.

When my eyes droop again, my mind forcing them to open once more, a chuckle rumbles through his chest.

"Go to sleep, Lola. I've got you."

"I'm good."

"You're falling asleep in my lap."

"I'm just resting my eyes," I say, my words a mumble.

"Bullshit. You need rest, You need to sleep to recover." Silence hangs between us as I give into my droopy eyelids and Ben continues to run his fingers through my hair.

Long minutes pass before my fever must get the best of me, letting my thoughts meet reality.

"I don't want to miss it." His fingers pause.

"What?"

"You. Taking care of me. I want to soak it in," I say, snuggling deeper into his lap, pulling a blanket around me tighter.

"I don't understand, sweet girl."

"It's been a while, you know. Since someone took care of me. I do it myself. I don't mind," I say, ignoring him. "It's not so bad. But it's nice having someone else do it." His fingers are still in my hair and my body wiggles, signaling him to continue. He does, and I start talking again. "I was probably . . . thirteen? The last time my mom was able to take care of me. After that, I had to take care of her, and then Lilah, and then Dad." I yawn, the world closing in on me in my exhaustion.

"No one has taken care of you since you were thirteen?" he asks, and it seems almost . . . annoyed.

But that's Ben for you. I wonder if he's ever *not* annoyed.

"I'm really good at taking care of people," I say. "The next time you're sick, I'll make you soup. Italian wedding soup is my favorite."

"You don't have to take care of me, Lola."

"I like it. Taking care of people," I say, and the world blurs more. "But I also really like you taking care of me." And then the world fades to black.

And I think right before I move to oblivion, I hear Ben say, "I'll take care of you for as long as you'll let me."

But that was just the fever speaking.

FORTY

-Lola-

STANDING in front of my mirror in my bedroom, my entire stomach is a slurry of butterflies.

The gala is tonight.

I'm going not as a donor or as the mayor's daughter.

I'm going as *Ben's date.*

I should be fine; I've been to a million of these fundraisers in my life and this, in theory, should be no different.

But it is, of course.

Because everything that has to do with Ben is different and new and exciting.

And just a bit terrifying.

My budget didn't allow for a new, extravagant dress so I ended up calling Lilah who has all of my old gowns in her closet. She picked one and hand-delivered it over the weekend, a smile on her face that I didn't quite understand until after she left and I unzipped the dress bag.

It's not mine.

It's new, the tags still attached—a gift from my sister.

It's black.

And shimmery.

And *tight*.

It has tiny spaghetti straps, a simple sweetheart neckline that makes me look like I have much bigger boobs than I do, and a daring back that dips deep. The rest is skin tight, ending at mid-shin with a slit up the side that definitely would be way too high for a fancy political fundraiser.

But an art charity gala with my tattooed . . . boyfriend?

Perfect.

Is he my boyfriend? I think as I touch up my red lipstick and tuck another strand of hair into the low bun.

I don't really know that answer. He's been sweet, taking me to meet his family and taking care of me when I was sick. Opening up to me about his life, accepting my own dark secrets. He's been adamant, if not suffocating, about keeping me safe, but technically, he holds the same safety standards for Hattie.

We kiss and we fuck any time we're alone, which is amazing. But are we more?

Once you're past the age of "boyfriends" and "girlfriends," do you have a conversation? Do you sit down and go for commitment and exclusivity, or are you just one day laying in a hospital bed with two rings on your finger, popping out babies?

Jesus, Lola. Way to overthink this, I think to myself as I hear a knock on the door.

With a sigh and one last look at the mirror and the killer red bottom shoes I was forced to borrow from Lilah, I turn and head for the door. Standing in front of it, I take one last deep breath, attempting to ignore the nervous energy flowing through me before impatient knuckles meet the new solid door once more.

Ben is halfway through his second, more frustrated rap when I open the door, leaving his hand hanging in midair.

I smile at him, eyes gobbling up his black button-down shirt, the top few buttons undone and the sleeves rolled up to his elbows, displaying his arms proudly like he already went to the event and we're going to the after party. The shirt disappears into black dress pants held up by black suspenders, the whole thing seamlessly ending in a pair of dark, shiny wingtip shoes. He must have had a trim, the sides of his hair neatly cut and the top combed back impeccably, the neatest I've ever seen it. Even his scruffy beard has been trimmed to look perfect.

This man is everything and more.

And his eyes are locked on me with a greedy, hungry look.

I take a step back and then another, knowing that look, and his feet follow my own.

"Ben, I have lipstick on."

"I see that," he replies, and fuck if I can't help a small smile on my lips.

"It's red."

"Got it."

"If you do anything, you will be covered in red lipstick, Benjamin," I say, my back bumping into the wall. This man and his obsession with backing me into things. I don't bother to tell him this is a transfer-resistant lip *stain*. I spent an *hour* on my makeup and another on my hair and I know it would take him less than one minute to ruin it all if he put his mind to it.

"I don't give a fuck about that, sweet girl," he says, and then he proves himself by pressing his lips to mine. Like seems to be the norm, I relax, tension flowing out of parts of my body I didn't realize were stiff. My arms wrap around his neck and his hands go to my hips, a thumb grazing the bare spot where the slit of my dress has parted. His tongue sweeps in, tasting my own before he pulls back, pressing his forehead to mine and panting.

"I really want to fuck you right now," he says, and that sounds like the most Ben way to say he thinks I look good.

"You mess up my hair and I'll kill you," I say, smiling, tipping my chin up to give him another small peck.

I can't resist.

When he's around, my body turns into a magnet and I crave being as close as I possibly can to him.

"I really want to fuck you right now, but if I'm late to this *Hattie* will kill me," he says, that boyish grin spreading.

"Hattie would definitely be a lot more ruthless and painful than I would," I say. He nods, head moving on mine before he takes a step back, hand still in mine, his eyes roving my body.

"Fuck, you look beautiful," he says, his voice a low grumble, eyes warm and full of desire.

Instinct and training tell me to blush, brush off the compliment, explain that the dress is old and the shoes are borrowed.

But New Lola just smiles.

"Thank you."

"Let's get you around other people before I get any ideas," he says, tugging my arm as I grab my bag and head out the door. As he's locking my door behind me with the key he refuses to return, I can't help but tease him.

"Oh, like that's ever stopped you? What about your parents' house?" His hand freezes, his head turns my way, and there is the heat. The heat I absolutely adore seeing in those eyes.

"Don't test me, sweet girl. I barely want to go to this thing as it is."

And with a giggle, I start down the stairs, freedom and lightness filling my soul in a way I've only ever felt with this man.

FORTY-ONE

-Lola-

"I'M gonna go check out what's up for auction," I say, tipping my chin at Hattie. Ben dropped me off with his best friend not long after we arrived, having to run off to meet and greet and kiss babies.

It's interesting and relieving having the freedom to just *enjoy* an event like this, not needing to be a prop. Part of me wonders if Ben knew that and purposely left me on my own. It would track, him always trying to give me things I've never had.

Hattie is in a tiny, boxy red dress with strands of beads connected to every surface, like a fiery flapper dress. It fits her personality perfectly, but the skyscraper height black heels don't. They look amazing, though. With my words, she just smiles. It's the devious one she puts on often.

That look gives me anxiety, I swear to God.

I pop in headphones, intending to try my best and ignore people for the next twenty minutes, perusing the auction room without people asking me to tell my father something or congratulating me on one of his accomplishments.

It's a trick I learned years ago—if I act like I don't hear them, I have a better chance of avoiding them. Because even though I'm not here with him, I've become such an integral part of his image we can sometimes feel like one and the same.

When I enter the room of the silent auction, items are lined up, beautifully put together along long tables with dark tablecloths and clipboards in front of each item. There are bath goods, a spa trip, jewelry, and home decor. I pass my own basket of baked goods and a gift certificate for Libby's and another for a tattoo from Coleman Ink. There's the display for lunch with the mayor, and when I glance at the sheet, it's boasting some big numbers.

But it's what's propped up in the corner that stops me in my tracks.

A set of three paintings, oil paints, I think.

A shoulder blade.

A braid.

Hands with pink fingertips on a wooden piece.

A rolling pin.

There are others surrounding the three, all equally beautiful and breathtaking—ocean landscapes and beautiful tall trees that remind me of Springbrook Hills, but these . . . They stop my breath.

I know the freckles on that shoulder blade.

I've seen that braid nearly every day of my life for years.

I'd know those hands anywhere.

They're all mine.

Strawberry-blonde hair and fair skin and a light wood rolling pin I once held in front of me as a weapon.

They're me.

I don't have to look at the signature to know who made them.

I do anyway.

B.C. is written in dark ink, stoic and strong, a contrast to the light, sweet images in front of me.

He painted me.

And when I glance at the sheet with the bids, my breath falls away.

Five figures.

And a bidding war, it seems—three different handwritings and signatures keep one-upping each other for the set of three.

I look around the room, trying to find him.

I need . . . I need to ask him.

Why?

These can't have been recent—I've been with him every night for weeks. When would he have had the time?

My eyes sweep the room and first they catch Hattie in the corner, arms crossed on her chest, her partner Lacey standing next to her, but her eyes are on me, one thick eyebrow raised. It's the kind of look that says, "your move next," but I can't even begin to understand what that move would be.

And then my eyes hit another person.

It's not the one I want to see.

It's not Ben standing there, broody and beautiful and everything I'm realizing I didn't know I needed.

Instead, Johnny Vitale is standing in another doorway, arms crossed, not much different than how Hattie was standing, but his face is clear to read.

His hand moves to his pocket as I continue to stand there, panic flooding me and making me turn to ice. I force my face to stay still, not to slip, the politician's daughter mask going into place.

He grabs his phone, typing before he stares at me again. My phone vibrates in my hand, and the voice in my ear tells me I have a text from an unknown number.

Do you want me to read it? the tinny, robot voice asks as it always does with new numbers.

I don't.

I don't want to know what he has said.

There is no good reason for this man to be here. But there is one terrible, *terrible* reason for him to be here. Of course, I have nothing for him. Not in the way he'd accept, at least.

Shaking hands move the phone, swiping to see the screen.

Unknown: I know about Lilah.

Unknown: Follow me.

Nausea instantly roils in my throat.

He knows about Lilah.

There is only one reasonable way to decode that message.

He knows who she is and what it means.

And the look in his eyes . . . Jesus. I see it. He has a plan. A plan I am not going to like one single bit.

My eyes move to Hattie as I make my decision. She's already looking elsewhere, chatting with an attendee, her red dress shimmering with her quick, excited movements.

Another quick glance around the room, and I move toward the entrance Johnny disappeared through.

When I walk through the doorway into a still busy but not as much so area, my eye catches him again, moving to another door that says *stairs*.

I follow.

I don't want to.

But I have to.

Old Lola clicks back into place, fitting like an old glove you haven't worn in a while, familiar but just a bit tight, not stretched and worn the way you once thought it was.

I need to protect my sister.

I might be through helping my father, and I might have finally realized that this life isn't what my mother wanted for me, but she absolutely wanted me to keep Lilah safe.

She demanded it.

And if I don't continue that mission, what were the last 15 years of sacrifice for?

So I listen to the way the expensive heels clack on the marble, letting the noise become my purpose as I open the door and start down the stairs.

He's going to the parking garage.

I need to be smart, though. I need to tell someone, call someone, tell Ben or Hattie or—

But as my hand starts for my phone, a hand grabs my wrist while another grabs my phone.

"You think I'm an idiot?"

The painful grip is familiar, one I've felt and feared before.

Johnny.

He takes my phone, tossing it aside, the clatter echoing in the stairwell as he starts to drag me down the stairs. When we reach the bottom, my mind not working even a single bit to try and argue, he flings the door open, dragging me through.

I don't even try to fight him, don't try to cause a scene. Instead, I'm planning, calculating, looking for an exit. I'm thinking of what I can do if he forces me to leave with him, and how to save myself in the worst-case scenario. As he tugs me, one of the headphones falls from my ear to the concrete below.

I don't dare look at it, don't care to draw attention to it. Right now, my hair is covering the other one. I'm praying that although he threw my phone across the parking garage, it will still be within Bluetooth distance.

And as he does, I hear the tinny voice in my ear speak.

"One new text from Ben: 'Where are you?' Should I respond?"

I need to be smooth.

But I also only have one chance at this.

Johnny is tugging me toward the valet, arguing with the man to bring up his car.

"*Call Ben,*" I whisper in as loud of a voice as I dare without him noticing.

"Call Ben?" My phone asks and *relief*. It flows through me.

"Yes!" I say, this time louder.

The phone rings and Johnny continues to dig his fingers into my arm painfully. The valet's eyes keep moving from me to Johnny, nervously.

"Take this. Go get my car." He hands who I now realize is a teenage kid a thick wad of cash and a valet ticket.

I can't blame the kid when he puts his blinders on, grabs the keys and cash with a "yes, sir," and walks off toward the back of the garage.

"Hey, where are you?" the voice in my ear asks.

Ben.

At least that embarrassing experience taught me this trick.

"Johnny, why are we in the parking garage?" I ask, trying to clue Ben in on what's going on.

I just need time.

"Johnny?" he asks, and there's fear there. He knows. Fear in Ben's voice is so out of character that it starts to pull me into a full panic.

"You're not a stupid bitch, Lola. We're leaving."

"Shit. Fuck. Lola, baby. I'm coming." Relief washes away some of the fear.

He's coming.

Ben is going to save me.

"I'm gonna stay, okay, baby? I'm staying on the line. Can he hear me?"

"No," I whisper.

"Good. Good girl. You're so fucking brave, Lol. I'm coming, baby." Stomping and doors and shouting are coming through the other line, a menagerie of rushing.

And then the car pulls up.

The valet steps out and hands Johnny the keys.

"Now leave," he says, tipping his chin to the kid.

He looks from me to Johnny and back again.

It seems Johnny knows there's no way in hell I'll be getting in this car without a fight and doesn't want witnesses.

"Uh, okay," the kid says and starts jogging away to the building.

Again, I can't blame the kid for wanting to get far away from this psycho, but he also left me to fucking *Johnny*, alone and with Ben on his way, but not here.

I can't get in this car.

That much I know.

I don't know his plan. I don't fully know what he knows about Lilah. I don't know what's going on.

But I do know that if I get in the car, my connection to Ben will cut out. And if that happens, something in my gut tells me something terrible will happen to me.

"I'm not getting in that car, Johnny," I say. With Ben in my ear, New Lola has a foothold back into the world, a bit of backbone holding me in place.

"I know about your sister," he says, and my gut churns the same way it did when he texted me minutes ago.

I need to know what he thinks he knows, though.

"What about her?" His hand tightens on my wrist, to where it takes everything in me not to shout out with pain. His lips tip up in a devious smile.

He likes this.

Likes my pain.

I want to vomit.

"Your sister is the daughter of Arturo, the would-be heir to the Russo family." Blood drains from me. "Unfortunately for him, he's been, let's say, out of commission for quite some time now." *The drive-by . . .* "The old man is getting older, needs to step down before he's gone, but the idiots over there are fucking infighting instead of using their fuckin' brains. Capos all trying to become the new Don, but their eyes are closed, can't see what's really goin' on around them."

"You work for Carmello."

"And I'll never fuckin' take over. Competition is too fuckin' high. A son and a grandson, all willing and able to take control." He looks past me, to the car I can almost guarantee he is planning to throw me into.

I need time.

If I get into that car, my life is over. Whether my actual life will meet an end or just life as I know it, I'm not sure.

I don't want to find out.

I need to buy time, need to make a plan.

I need stupid fucking Johnny to talk, run his mouth, and get distracted while Ben comes up with a better plan.

"So you're going to betray the Carluccios? That's your plan?"

"No, you fucking *sciaquadell*. I'm bringin' the families together." He looks at me, his free hand grabbing my chin, tipping it up, and looking me over. "A shame you're a fuckin' mutt. Wouldn't mind having you in my bed." Fear strikes but I know, I know I need to keep my mind stable.

"Bring the families together?" There's a pause as he continues to look at me, and for a moment, I think he knows *my* plan, that he knows I'm dragging this out to save myself. But then his dumb ass opens his mouth.

"A year ago, I talked Carmello into inviting your dipshit of a father to a game. Lured him in, let him win, then made him lose. That was the first time you and I met, beautiful girl. There had been talk, talk about Libby Capone having an illegitimate daughter with Turner. That it wasn't his girl at all, but Arturo's. An affair. And a secret that *buttagots* took to his fuckin' grave.

"But I knew. Fuck, I knew that if it were true, if it were true and I tied her to me? I'd have it all. I'm tired of being a Capo. Don't wanna be doing the dirty work of dumbasses my entire life, yeah? So I planned."

"You set my dad up." Strange to feel relief, knowing now that my father wasn't completely wrong when he said he *couldn't lose.*

"He's as dumb as Nikola Capone. Ambitious politician but filled with fuckin' greed. I figured if Nikola tried to sell his own daughter to strengthen ties, Turner would do the same," he says of my grandfather.

"So you set him up to get Lilah?"

"Catchin' on."

"But you got me?"

"I'll be honest, didn't realize you would be there, payin' his shit. Didn't know Libby left you money for it. She thought ahead, saw this coming." He sighs. "No, I didn't see you coming, Lola. That first time scared him, us goin' to you. I couldn't get to Lilah. Is that your work? Keeping her in the dark?" I scrunch my nose because he doesn't deserve that, to know the lengths I went to keep this from happening, the sacrifices I made.

"It was good work you did. Definitely not Shane. You're not like your dad, loyal to your family to the core."

Unlike Dad.

Apparently, also unlike my grandfather.

God, how deep does this poison of addiction and greed go in my family?

"So you had my father rack up a debt?"

"He offered to pay it slowly. But Carmello wanted more. I was in his ear, telling him to ask for more. More than Turner could afford. Permits and allowances. Kickbacks. Things he couldn't give without raising alarms." He smiles a sick, wicked smile. "I was going to swoop in, offer Turner a way out. Lilah and the connections she would give me, in exchange for freedom of his debts. I would handle them." My mind is racing, trying to line up the timeline.

"But . . . I still don't get it. Arturo . . . He's been dead for years." He died not long after Lilah was born. When Mom died, I spent weeks learning about the intricate parts of her secrets, the people involved, and the threats facing Lilah. "It was all over the news. A drive-by."

Johnny smiles and the look churns everything in me.

"I told you this plan had been in motion for years, *bellissima*."

No fucking way.

"You . . . ?"

"I killed Arturo Russo. I did it to free up space. His father would be scrambling, wanting blood to take over. I heard whispers about the

Turner girl being family. It was all I needed to know. It was a gamble, I'll say that. Could have been for nothing. But here we are. I knew once I married Lilah, he'd accept me. I have good ties to Carmello. I could bring the families together. Less fighting, more money for everyone. Carmello is starting to . . . dip his toes in new businesses. We need allies."

"Jesus fuck," I hear Ben say through the headphone, but I can't focus on that.

I want to throw up.

I want to rage.

I want to shower and scrub my body, every single place where Johnny's vile hands have touched me.

And most importantly, I forget about needing to waste time.

"You'll never have Lilah," I say, my voice low and angry.

"Excuse me?"

"You're sick. I will never let you take my sister."

Rage, unhinged and clearly not mentally stable, sears in his eyes.

Fury.

He is fucking insane. I can see it now.

His hand leaves my wrist, moving to backhand me. Searing pain shoots through my face and I feel skin tearing open. Blood begins to drip down a wound at my eyebrow. But most worrisome, my headphone falls out of my ear, tumbling down my top into my dress.

I have no idea if the connection is gone, but I can't hear Ben anymore, my anchor.

Panic rises as I realize my line to sanity and calm is gone.

I didn't realize how much it was saving me.

Fuck, fuck, fuck.

"You do not tell me what I can and will do. You? You are fucking nothing. Your sister has worth to me, Lola. You are *nothing*. I could fuck you until you were useless to me and throw you off the fucking pier into the ocean. No one would care. Your dad would use your death as a campaign platform. Your sister would know, but what would she do? Nothing, Lola. Nothing at all."

At that moment, I know he is right.

After all these years of sacrificing myself, of doing what was best for my family, for my sister, I forgot to protect myself. I forgot that I, too, need someone to look out for me, to comfort me, to take care of me. And while I don't regret helping my family or keeping my sister safe, it left me vulnerable.

No one would care.

His words echo in my mind.

But those words, inky and dark and terrifying, are shattered by light.

I see the paintings that gave me chills what feels like moments ago.

Ben would care.

I find that comforting.

Unfortunately, Johnny isn't interested in my mental break-through. "Get in the car, Lola," he commands, tired of waiting for me, probably jittery in fear that we'll be interrupted.

"No."

"*Get in the fucking car, Lola,*" he shouts, and his voice echoes.

Ben isn't here yet.

My time is up.

He opens the door and starts to move me closer.

"No!" I shout, grabbing the edges of the door frame.

A fist comes down, hitting my hand. Pain sears through my fingers and for a moment, I panic about a broken bone. But the pain is stifled by fear.

Because Johnny's putting his weight into my back, pushing me inside.

I buck against him, trying to do whatever I can to *stay out of this car.* But the thing is, Johnny Vitale is not new to forcing his way. He's not new to violence, and I know he has ways to get me into this car.

And as I look over my shoulder, he has a gun in his hand. The hand lifts.

I don't think he'll shoot me—not here. Too public. But he might knock me out with the butt of it. And if that happens, the game is over.

I'm gone.

Lilah might as well be gone.

And as that hand comes down, I close my eyes, waiting for it to happen.

In my mind, I apologize.

To Lilah, who doesn't deserve to lose another person.

To Mom, who put this burden on my shoulders, but I still accepted it.

To Dad, even if he doesn't deserve it.

To Ben, who is going to live with guilt he didn't earn.

And most of all, to myself. To New Lola, who thought today would be another step forward when really it was seven back.

But it doesn't come.

That strike doesn't come, because there is a hand to Johnny's wrist.

And when I look, I recognize the hand. Those tattoos.

Ben.

Ben is here, saving me, once again.

And then the gun goes off.

FORTY-TWO

-Ben-

I'm running.

I'm running because time is slipping through my fingers and Lola is in trouble.

"I'm coming, baby," I say into my phone. She doesn't respond, but I can hear Johnny Vitale talking on the other end.

"I killed Arturo Russo. I did it to free up space."

Arturo Russo was killed in a drive-by years ago. I did some research once Lola told me her whole story and this is one of the things I found.

They had no suspects, but as the son of one of the three families in New Jersey, fingers were pointing near everywhere.

And the murderer has my girl.

Confessing this fact to her can't be a good sign.

People don't confess murder to people they expect to be able to tell the police.

My feet move faster as I hear Lola try and drag out a conversation, as I hear his entire plan play out.

Lilah isn't Shane Turner's daughter, and it seems that the secret is out.

I see Hattie, her face confused.

"HAT! Call the cops! NOW!"

"What? I—" She looks shocked, taken aback.

"Lola! Call the cops; bring them to the parking garage!" She stares, and I hope to God she listened because I'm running out the door, down the winding stairs that lead to the parking garage.

Why the fuck are there so many levels? I think as I stare down at least ten flights of stairs.

I need to go.

The sound starts to crackle, the cement walls of the stairwell not helping my reach.

"Drag it out, Lola, baby. You're doing great. I'm coming for you."

And then there's a noise, a sound from her that I know is pain, and my feet move faster.

My mind goes blank, the call going foggy like the mic is being covered, but it doesn't matter now. I can hear voices echoing in the garage below me—only a few more flights left.

They're at the valet.

I see her now. A black car, the door open, Lola's sweet body pressed against the open doorway, her hands on the metal, going white with strain.

Johnny, a crazy fucking look in his eyes, using his body to push her in.

The noise that comes out of her as his hand comes down on hers, trying to lose her grip.

Pain.

Agony rips through me.

Why wasn't I with her?

Why did I ask her to come to this?

It was too public. I put her in this position.

So many different scenarios go through my mind, trying to figure out what I could have done, or should have done, but the truth of the matter is, nothing can be changed at this point.

I need to get her.

I hit the pavement as his hand goes behind him.

I know before I even see it what he's doing.

A gun.

He won't shoot her, not here. Too obvious, too many cameras and witnesses. But he will bash her head in so she blacks out and he can get her to a safe location without trouble. I reach him as he brings the gun butt down to the back of her head, grabbing his wrist.

Lola's head, cheeks tear-stained and scared, looks back with the sound of a struggle, and her eyes go wide with relief.

She knows every inch of the art on my body as well as I know her curves, having painstakingly taken each in over the past weeks, each night an art show of its own.

The relief is short-lived as I pull the wrist back, pointing toward the sky, and the gun goes off.

The next two minutes move in a slow montage, a mix of images and feelings and panic.

So much panic.

Because there is a gun, there is a desperate man intending to do harm, and both are within reach of my Lola.

Rage flows through me, though, when my eye moves to her fingers. Cut and bleeding, one swelling already. Then her eyebrow, which is bleeding in a slow drip down her face.

"Who the fuck—" Johnny tries to say, turning toward me.

My hand stays on that wrist, and my hand goes to his neck.

"What the fuck are you doing?" I shout in his face.

"Fuck off, mind your own fucking business!" His hand moves, trying to move my hand from his neck, but I hold tighter, the gun and our hands high in the air. We're fighting for control.

"Lola is my fucking business. You got in my fucking business, hurt *my fucking woman*!" My eyes quickly move to Lola, who is coming closer.

I might be falling for the woman, but even at this moment, she makes me unbearably angry.

"Run, Lola! Fucking run!" Johnny tries to kick me, to get me unsteady, and I tighten my grip on his neck. He has to be losing air.

"But, Ben—"

"FUCKING RUN! GET HELP!"

But does she do that?

Of course not.

I shake my head, knowing that's a lost cause.

Instead, I move, kneeing Vitale in the balls where I hope I'll cause permanent damage. A man like this should never procreate.

He loses his grip, the gun falling to the ground, and as it falls, I panic that something will happen—that it will go off, that Lola will be shot.

But it just skitters to the ground, and I tackle Vitale down as well, probably breaking a rib as I do, but that's the least of what he deserves.

I flip him to his stomach, the hand in my grip pinned behind him as I grab the other, a knee in his back.

"Stay down!" I hear Lola's voice shout, and there she is as I look up. My hand moves to Vitale's greasy fucking hair to keep him down.

She's standing, knees scraped, her dress askew and eyebrow bleeding, but fuck if she doesn't look like some badass hot chick, standing there holding the gun in one hand.

The other is by her side, clearly in pain.

Fuck.

"Lola, what the fuck are you doing?" I ask, and a part of me wants to laugh, even if not a single moment of this is funny.

It's just so fucking Lola, standing there, bleeding, a mess.

"I'm making sure he doesn't leave."

"I think I've got that part covered, babe."

"I'm just helping." Her hand moves out to her side like she's frustrated with me. As always.

Only Lola would get pissy with me while holding a gun when I just fucking saved her life.

"Baby, put the gun down."

"No fucking way! He might . . . get out!" Vitale's head moves up and Lola's eyes get wide. I slam it down to the concrete, and that seems to be the last strand—his body goes limp, out cold.

Necessary?

Probably not.

Satisfying?

Fuck yeah.

No one puts his hands on my girl.

No one.

"He's not going anywhere. Put the gun down before you accidentally shoot me."

"I wouldn't shoot you."

"Jesus Christ, do you know how to work a gun?" She stares at me, her nose scrunching.

"No. But I've seen movies." Still kneeling on the man's back, holding his arms just in case he comes to and tries to fight, I look to the sky, praying that God will give me the patience and energy to manage this woman.

God answers in the form of my best friend's voice.

"Over there!" I hear Hattie shout, then the clicking of heels that she wears once a year for this event.

And over the hill, I see her, police officers on foot with cars following behind, all jogging our way.

I look up at the sky again.

"Thank you, God," I mumble.

"Damn, girl. You can't go to a single event without bringing the fun, can you?" Hattie says with that dumb-ass smile when she reaches us, and I glare at her, but I don't have time. Because as the officers detain Vitale, taking the gun from Lola, who I instantly tug in my arms, my girl passes out, and I have to use my full energy to keep her from crashing down.

But from this day on, I will use every ounce of energy within myself to keep this woman standing.

FORTY-THREE

-Ben-

LOLA COMES to in just a few seconds, and I can only assume it was the stress and panic of everything hitting her all at once. Either way, I take her to the hospital, a police car following close behind for security and to question her once we get there.

She's strong the whole time as the nurse checks out her hand first, which is blissfully just sprained and in need of a few stitches.

And as this all happens, she tells the police the story.

I'm able to speak as a second witness, and there are also cameras in the parking garage and the kid from the valet who called the cops as soon as he ran off when Johnny paid him—that's how Hattie and the cops got there so fast.

There's no way Johnny is getting out of this.

She told them about the threats that have been coming to her, conveniently leaving out her father. Told them how Johnny took her as a way to get to her sister. That to Johnny, Lilah was the key to Johnny getting control, and the promise of power drove him mad, clearly.

I'm in awe and absolutely hate how well she saves her father.

Even now, after her life was put in danger, after Lilah's life was put in danger, she still feels the pull to protect him. To keep her mother's promise.

And then Vic walks into the exam room.

"Hey, Lola, it's nice to meet you," my best guy friend says. I glare at him, because throughout the entire time Lola's been talking to nurses and police officers, she's been gritting her teeth through pain, the blood on her eyebrow slowly leaking.

And my best friend, who I texted as we left the hotel, the man who is a literal ER doctor at this hospital, has been taking his sweet time to get here.

"Hi, I—" she starts to respond, but I cut her off.

"Can you stop with the niceties and just fucking help her?"

"Ben!" Lola says, her good hand swatting me in the arm from where I sit next to the hospital bed. "Don't be a dick!" She turns to Vic and gives some crazy-looking cringe smile at him, her polite politician's daughter side kicking in. "I'm so sorry. He's super stressed out. It's been a crazy day."

"No problem at all. I'm used to it," Vic says with a shit-eating grin I really want to smack off him.

Knocking Vitale out felt good, but I have enough frustration and anger running in my veins for another person.

"Either way, that's not right. This is your place of work, and patients and their guests shouldn't make that miserable." I roll my eyes at her, shaking my head.

"Seriously, Vic. She needs something. Pain meds, stitches for sure."

"Jesus, Ben! Oh my God, you need to stop!"

"He needs to do his job." Lola turns to me with that chiding, annoyed look on her that I usually love. But right now, it's tainted with a piece of gauze covering her eyebrow and the glaze of pain in her eyes.

"Benjamin!" she says through gritted teeth.

If it were any other situation, it would be adorable.

"It's fine, seriously," Vic says. "I know Ben."

"He's a friend, babe." Lola blinks then her head moves back to Vic, who is smiling at her with a kind look in his eyes. Her head moves back to me, probably to yell at me, but my eyes are locked on Vic as I glare at him, waiting for him to *do his fucking job.*

"He's not looking like he likes you very much, doctor," Lola says under her breath, and it takes everything in me not to let the humor of her words crack through my frustration.

"Gabi's gonna love this," Vic says, tipping his head toward me.

"Let's worry about meet and greets after you fix her?" He just laughs, ignoring me and lifting the cotton that the nurse put on Lola's head.

"Okay, Lola. So it looks like the bleeding has stopped, which is great, but I still want to do a few stitches to make sure it doesn't scar too badly. You'll probably have a small spot where your eyebrow will be sparse, but we'll see what we can do, okay?"

"I can pierce you! Cover it up!" Hattie says. I have no idea how she weaseled her way into the ER room with us, but it's very on-brand for my nosy best friend.

"Absolutely not," I say. "You aren't getting near her with a needle." Lola, God bless the woman, looks over at me with those wide eyes.

"Really? Why not? I was thinking about getting something . . ." The look in her eyes says more than I want anyone in this room to know.

Then she smiles.

This fucking woman will be the death of me.

"You get anything, it's me doing it," I say, face stern and voice cold, but even at this moment, with her barely avoiding kidnapping, I see it.

The look in her eyes.

The tease.

"Oh yeah?" she says, lips turning up at the corners.

"And that's my cue," Vic says, lifting his hand in the air as Hattie laughs out loud. He turns to me. "You've got your hands full with this one." I just glare at him, though he's not wrong. "Okay, I'm going to get a few things, and then we'll get you all patched up and sent home, okay, Lola?"

Lola nods, and then Vic makes his way out the door, but the peace doesn't last for long.

FORTY-FOUR

-Lola-

BEN'S FRIEND is only gone for mere moments before there's a noise in the hall, and Hattie speaks.

"Fair warning, I think the cavalry has arrived," Hattie says, dipping her head out the hallway to check what the noise is. I groan.

The cavalry comes in the form of my father, trailed by a group of advisors, a security guard or two, and my baby sister.

I can see him smile from the doorway of my hospital room, flashes going before he shoos them off, probably to go document some other horror story they can spin into a feel-good tale for the five o'clock hour.

"Hey, baby, how are you?" my dad says, the politician mask dropping and the dad mask going on. The last time I saw my father, I was arguing with him, begging him to take care of a situation that had put my sister and me in danger.

And it escalated exactly how I thought it might.

It's hard because every part of me knows I should be mad at him. I should be furious, in fact.

He is the reason I'm here. His bullshit, his addiction, his greed, that's what put me here.

His complete disregard for me, for my business, my needs, for our *family.*

Fuck. When I play it out like that, it's clear I very much *should* be pissed.

I should tell him to leave. And from the pure venom, I can feel rolling off of Ben, he's three seconds from kicking my father's ass.

Unfortunately, there's the crumb of me who remembers he's my dad.

My dad. The man who taught me to ride a bike and who bought me the fanciest corsage for the daddy-daughter dance in fifth grade. The man who helped me carve pumpkins and killed spiders and told me to put on a sweater when he thought I was dressing too old for my age.

He's the one who brought the order form to the office to make sure I sold the most cookies for Girl Scouts and the one who stayed up until midnight when I forgot about my science fair project, carefully constructing a volcano with me.

He's my dad.

And I think there's something in a girl that will forgive a fuck ton of shit from her dad just because he's her dad.

"It's okay," I whisper to Ben

"No, it's not." It sounds like his words are coming through gritted teeth.

"Hey, Lolly," Lilah says, and it takes a second for me even to recognize her.

She's pale. And not because she's not wearing her war paint of perfectly done makeup, but because she's *pale.*

"You okay?" she asks, coming over to grab my good hand.

"I'm good," I say, grabbing her hand back and squeezing.

"Of course she's good! Our Lola is tough, just like your mother raised her to be!"

In another universe, I'd respond and tell him he's right.

In this universe, this version of Lola, I want to fight.

I want to tell him that's not how Mom raised me. And even if she did, she would never in a *million years* have expected it to be for this. Because my mom loved us, and she loved my dad, but most of all, she loved *family*. All of us working together as one. Not one of us taking the wheel and throwing all of us under the bus to get what he wanted.

I see it now.

Thanks to Ben.

This isn't about loyalty to family.

This isn't about taking care of everyone. This isn't about keeping my promise to Mom. Because when she made me promise all those years ago, this isn't what she thought I'd be facing.

I think if she were here, if my mom were alive and in this hospital room, she'd wish I had taken Ben's path. Valued myself over what my dad wanted, even if that meant I couldn't give everything to Lilah. If it meant I couldn't keep things quiet, keep her in the dark.

But before I can answer, my dad steps closer to me, probably to grab my hand or brush the hair from my face like he did when I was a kid.

Instead, Ben steps in front of him.

Shit.

My eyes go to Lilah, who, in her pale, shocked way, just looks lost. Then to Hattie, who has her eyes bugging out, like she knows what's happening.

Then to my dad, whose brows are furrowed in clear confusion.

I can't see Ben since his back is to me, but I can picture the face he's making. Stern, frustrated, brick wall. His arms are crossed in front of him, the muscles of his back tense beneath the black dress shirt he's still wearing.

"Excuse me, I would like to see my daughter," my dad says, his politician's voice on full blast.

Shit.

"No."

Double shit.

My eyes move to Hattie, who is fighting back a laugh. I roll my eyes and shake my head, then look at my sister, who, to my surprise, has her own lips tipped up in a small smile.

Her head dips close to me and she whispers, "Ooh, I like him," and if my hand wasn't throbbing, I'd smack her.

"Excuse me?" my dad asks, clearly shocked.

No one tells Shane Turner no.

That's what got us into this mess, after all.

"Ben, it's fine—"

"No, it's not. He put you in this position." My dad's face goes pale, eyes moving around Ben's shoulder to give me an accusing look.

But I'm tired of hiding his mistakes.

"What have you told him, Lola?" Dad asks me while Lilah's face goes confused at the same time.

"What? What are you talking about?" she asks. Her pretty face looks so lost.

At this moment, I wonder if it was a mistake.

Maybe all this time, Mom was wrong. Maybe it would have been better to tell Lilah from the start, tell her the full truth. We could have worked together to figure it out, instead of apart. She's been working for years with a fractured vision, a puzzle missing vital pieces.

Regardless, while I'm in a hospital bed, bleeding from my eyebrow and waiting to see if I'll need to stay overnight, this is not the time.

"Ben, seriously, not now."

"What's going on?" Lilah asks.

"Now seems like a good time as any," Ben says, glaring.

"I think I'm gonna . . . take a walk," Hattie says, cringing at me and sneaking out the door. I remind myself to deny her cookies next time she's in the shop, the bitch. My dad moves his eyes from Ben, looking at me and going soft.

"Lola, I didn't know," he says, and that churns in my guts. The truth is, the Carluccios would never in a million years come to me unless they were told to.

By Dad.

"You didn't know your bookie would come for her?" Ben accuses. My dad sighs.

"I didn't think it would go this far."

"He threatened *Lilah*, Dad."

"What the fuck is going *on?*" Lilah asks, and now she is even paler, her tan skin looking more like my own fair shade and her voice raising in an almost panicked way. She knew about Dad's addiction, even if she didn't know how bad it was. She knows some of the secrets, but the big one? It was the one secret I kept from her.

It didn't feel like mine to tell.

"They never would have gotten to Lilah. It was all a bluff."

"What, so you just sacrificed Lola instead? Or did you just think she'd pay it—again—and you'd all move on? That once again, she could bail you out of a tight spot?" The blood drains from my father's face. "After draining herself dry, she told you she was done. And fuck, Turner. It's one thing to have her pay your hidden horse bets off. It's another to send the *fucking New Jersey Mob* to her business."

"You don't understand. She was—"

"Oh, I understand. I understand that Lola has spent her life sacrificing so you could be a child and do whatever the fuck you wanted. I understand that she was your scapegoat, that you used your dead wife and the secrets you both held to keep Lola loyal to you. I understand that she worked her fucking ass off to build herself a business, and you saw it as another source of money for yourself. I understand that while Lilah got to follow her dreams, go to school, and live her life, Lola was stuck making sure that things went smoothly because her mother asked her to, and she took that to heart." My dad doesn't even blink at his words while I feel Lilah's eyes burning on me.

This, she also didn't know.

The sacrifices I made so she wouldn't be touched by it.

There was no need for us both to suffer.

"But you knew that, didn't you? You knew about your wife's request? That she begged Lola to make sure you didn't fall too deep, to make sure that she kept her sister safe."

The floor falls out from under me as I watch my dad's Adam's apple bob with a swallow.

I want to cry.

A part of me, a quiet, hidden part, thought it was a valiant effort on my end. Honorable, something I should sit with in peace but never let out. I thought I was doing this for my mom, that it was our secret. I thought Dad didn't know and that if he did, if he knew I was doing all of this for Mom, he'd have stopped it.

I never told him about that conversation because I didn't want him to feel that guilt.

But he *knew*.

He knew all along what I was doing and used it to his benefit. Drained me dry, sold me out, and let me think I was doing it for her.

"But most of all, I understand that sacrifice is over." Part of me is excited at his words. Part of me is absolutely horrified. Pretty on-brand, to be honest. Then he turns to Lilah and my stomach drops.

"And you," he says, crossing his arms on his chest.

"Ben—"

"Me?" Lilah says, an eyebrow raised in defiance. Pure princess Lilah coming into formation.

"Yeah, you."

"Me what?"

"You let your sister take this shit on all alone?"

"She didn't tell me, not about all of this," Lilah says. "And I didn't know . . . all of it. Or how far it went."

"But you didn't talk to your father about it?"

"No, but—" Lilah tries to explain.

"Ben, stop."

"When I called you, you didn't seem surprised it went this far, that she was in the hospital," he says, and before Lilah can even start to respond, I jump in.

"*You* called Lilah?" I ask, confused. He's never even *met* Lilah.

"Yes." Ben's eyes stay locked on my sister.

"How? You don't even have her number."

"Your phone is unlocked, like every other fuckin' in thing in your life." I glare at the back of his head, and he turns his face to me.

Part of me will probably find this funny one day, getting annoyed with Ben in the middle of a hospital room while I'm having a come to Jesus moment with my family, much less that we're fighting about things being locked.

It's so very . . . on-brand for us.

"We'll talk later," he says, reading my mind because I have quite a few things I'd like to say to him. His head moves back to my sister.

"Are you blind?"

"Ben!"

"What?" she asks Ben, ignoring me.

"Ben! Stop it." I've never been one for drama. It's probably why it feels so good to start it with Ben.

"No, sweet girl. This is enough. This letting people walk all over you shit? It's done."

"Fine. Why don't I start with you?" I ask, and if I wasn't sitting in a hospital bed, I'd have my hands on my hips or I'd be poking him in his big, stupid chest.

"Babe, you've never let me walk all over you," he says, and, okay. That's kind of true. "Probably the first person, too." His head moves back to Lilah. "You're not blind. You've got a good family, even this piece of shit." His head tips to my dad.

"Ben!" Ben ignores me.

"Everyone in your family has spent the last twenty-five years keeping you safe. You might not know why, which, babe, open your fucking eyes, but there's no way a woman like you didn't realize it."

"A woman like me?" she says, Princess Lilah coming out, the perfectly curated, mysterious, and just a bit snippy daughter.

"A woman like you. You let men get away with shit?" She blinks. "You let anyone get away with shit when it comes to you?" Her nose scrunches. "Your dad—has he ever asked you for money?" Her skin goes white.

My eyes move to Dad.

His face has gone white.

"No," I say under my breath. "Dad, no."

"I fucking knew it," Ben says under his own breath. "You said no, though, right? He asked and you said no." Lilah's eyes are watering.

"I had no choice, Lol," my dad says.

"You sure as fuck did!" I say, my voice rising. "From the *beginning,* you had a choice."

"Your mom . . ."

"Mom enabled you because she was fucking riddled by guilt."

Something in me snaps.

It feels good.

Snapping.

That last thread to Old Lola breaking and the new one coming out in full force. The Lola that's been sitting in a chrysalis for three years, the one who started to break out when I signed the lease to my bakery.

Dad looks at me, shock covering his face.

He's never met New Lola. Not really.

Time for him to make her acquaintance.

"Mom loved family. And she loved you, in her own way. But I think she also loved the freedom you gave her." Dad's eyes go wide. "I know, Dad. I know it all. She told me all about it all. About the family and why she needed to get married so badly, so quickly. About Lilah."

"What about me?" Her voice is questioning, but also like she knows. Like she's waiting for the secret to come into the open so she, too, can metamorphose into something new, what she was always supposed to be.

I see it now.

I ignored it, the differences in us. Kind supporters of my father's would just say I looked just like Dad and Lilah looked just like Mom, the perfect balance. But she doesn't look like Dad at all. She's all tan skin and light hair and curves for days. She's short in stature, has a straight nose and full lips. A bombshell.

The perfect Mob Princess.

But that's not what I see now.

I see the truth in her big brown eyes.

She knows.

She knows.

How long has she known?

I stare longer, that connection that we always had as sisters sparking, a silent conversation.

"You know," I say, my voice soft.

Then I see it again.

A quick dash of pain. Pain at my confirming what she suspected.

She knew there was a secret that she couldn't know, that it wasn't safe for her to know. All this time, those small questions she'd ask, leading me in a direction where we could have talked about it. She knew. She knew, and I probably knew that somewhere deep down, but I never told her.

I never wanted to see this face on her.

I also knew, somewhere deep down, that if I confirmed this fact to her, that we weren't full blood but half-sisters, that she would have no required loyalty to Dad.

I think I knew there was always the chance she would want to burn down the world to keep me safe.

But I had already sacrificed too much to keep her safe.

"You were little. Mom . . . She wanted you safe. And I think, in her own way, she wanted you to remember her in a positive light."

"So it's true," she says, her voice soft.

Broken.

So unlike my strong, sassy sister.

Goddammit.

Years of protecting her, over in a few hours.

Then it's gone, that shattered look. Her back straightens, and her shoulders roll back.

"It's true, and you've spent your whole life protecting me." She looks over at our father—my father, really—and a look of disgust crosses her face. "And you knew all along. You used that against her."

"Lilah, no—"

"You're rotting with greed, Dad. Inside and out. It probably started before Mom died, but as soon as your tether to sanity and morality was gone, it took off. Greed and power and greed for power. Corruption. You knew Lola was protecting me. And you knew *what* she was protecting me from." She says it with knowledge, like she doesn't need the confirmation, like this information was brewing slowly for years. "You used that. You used her fear, her promise to Mom to keep your shit under wraps."

"I don't know—"

"I found her journals." The air in the room goes still.

"What?"

"Mom. She had journals." This is news to me. "They were marked in a box for me. There was a note on top. She wrote it. I know everything." She turns to me again, watery eyes shining. "I swear, Lola. I swear I didn't know you were involved. I didn't know . . . I had no idea . . . you . . . I swear it. I would have . . . stopped it. Something." Her eyes are genuine, watery. "I found them two years ago."

I have so many questions.

What did the journals say?

How much does she know?

What has she done with that information?

But before she can even try to say more, a head pops in.

Vic.

"Hey, am I interrupting?" Thick dark brows come together and I can't decide if it's genuine confusion or if he knows and is interrupting on purpose.

"No. They were just leaving," Ben says, looking pointedly at my dad. To my surprise, my dad, suddenly looking older and smaller than I've ever seen him, nods.

Lilah comes over to me, hugging me and whispering in my ear. "We need to talk." I nod against her soft hair. "I love you, sis," she says, and I kiss her cheek, repeating the phrase. She pulls back, looking me in the eyes. "This changes nothing, Lola. Between us. You're still my big sister, and I still love you. I have a lot to make up for."

"Lilah, no—"

But my sister is already straightening, standing, and brushing her hands down her perfectly pressed dress.

Then they're gone.

"So a few stitches and we'll wrap up your hand, and then you'll be all good to leave. Just need to have Nurse Pam help you out of the building in a chair. It's procedure." His face turns to Ben. "You're taking her home?" Ben nods. "Good. I'll call in a day or two, then Gabs and I will stop by. I can't keep her out. Gabi's mind is already going a mile a minute, wanting to meet your new girl."

"Oh, I'm not—"

"Let's worry about getting you home, sweet girl," Ben says, and something about that sounds so fucking nice, I want to wrap myself up in it forever.

FORTY-FIVE

-Lola-

ONCE I'M CHECKED OUT, Ben helps me into the car, waving off Nurse Pam who was a mother hen through my entire stay (Vic says this is very on-brand for Pam, who loves to baby patients and bicker with the doctors), and we start driving toward the boardwalk.

The drive is silent.

I'm ruminating on the crumbling of my family's secrets and mysteries in a hospital room. I still can't decide if it feels good or if it makes me sick to my stomach, knowing that twenty-five years worth of keeping secrets has come to an end.

And even more, knowing that Lilah's life will change forever. I still don't quite know if she knows all of the true secrets, but either way, it's done.

Ben is probably in his grumpy AF Ben head, pondering what his next steps in his quest to keep me safe will be. But thinking about Ben and how this is all done—for real this time— has me contemplating this.

Because the truth of the matter is, although I've been falling for

Ben, we're still always at each other's throats. I can't go ten minutes without making him pissed at me, and every moment seems to be an opportunity for us to argue.

Nothing about us is compatible. The pink, sugar and spice, Taylor Swift-singing baker and the pissy, broody, beautifully creative tattoo artist.

We don't work.

We've worked so far as a point of necessity. Ben felt an obligation to keep me safe, to take care of me. He's that guy, after all. I think, in a way, he's also poured some of the unnecessary guilt he feels for forcing Tanner to pick up the slack he left into me.

I think about this, what the future will look like, for the long minutes on the drive back. I don't even notice we've parked out behind our apartments until Ben is standing outside the passenger side door, opening it. I jump in my seat, panic flooding me.

"Hey, hey. It's me. It's just me, sweet girl," he says, his voice running through me to soothe the panic, the ache. I look him over, taking each bit into my mind and savoring each detail.

This man.

He's gorgeous.

He deserves the world.

His hand moves out, grabbing my arm gently and helping me out of the car. Easing me out until my feet are steady on the pavement.

"Do you need me to carry you?" he asks.

"I'm good," is all I say as I move toward the door, trying to keep my wits, trying to keep it together. He unlocks the front door, his hand moving to my waist as we step in, and I look up the stairs.

That's a lot of stairs.

My entire body aches, my fingers in the stretchy wrap feeling numb and the stitches above my eye starting to throb.

I need sleep.

I need a drink.

I need sugar and butter and carbs.

I need to cry.

And at this moment, I don't know what I need first. They all seem pretty vital.

But what I need most of all is Ben to stop being so nice to me, to stop being helpful. I need Ben to close himself behind his door, turn his music on way too loud, and go back to ignoring me.

That sounds easier than having any kind of conversation.

I start up the stairs, his hand on my lower back, ready to catch me.

When we hit the landing, we stand there for a moment before Ben starts for his door, digging in his pocket to unlock it.

That's it, I guess.

Easier than I thought.

My own hand is fingering the bottom of the shirt he had Hattie bring me. It's my shirt and I can't help but wonder if his coworker also knows how to pick a lock or if he made himself a second spare when he replaced the lock on my door since my bag, and thus, keys, were brought to the hospital with me.

"What are you doing?" I hear before fingers are wrapped around my good wrist.

I don't jolt, though, the feeling familiar and safe.

Ben.

"Going home?"

"What the fuck?" I stare at him, confused. "You're not going in there."

"What?"

"Babe, you were just nearly kidnapped. You got ten stitches in various places and went through an incredibly traumatizing event. Not to mention, we have no idea if Johnny was the end of it. You are not going into that apartment." I sigh.

"You don't have to do this, Ben."

"What are you talking about?"

"Protect me. I'm good now. Johnny's in custody. No one will be coming after me; it would be way too obvious. I didn't do anything at all. Johnny aired out all of his dirty laundry, and even if he somehow gets released, we all know someone else will be taking care of him." A muscle ticks in Ben's jaw.

"You're not leaving my sight for at least two days."

"Excuse me?"

"You left my sight for ten minutes, and you were *gone*."

"Ben, this is—"

"I was scared, Lola," he says, turning me and starting to press me into my door, his body melding to mine. If you'd have asked me, I would have told you that, given everything that happened, this would scare me.

But it's a comfort.

Protection.

"Ben—"

"Your voice came through the line, and I heard his voice, heard the panic in yours . . . I lost my mind. I've never run that fast. Then I see you, *my girl*, pinned to a car, that fuckwad trying to force you in. Heard when he hit you, heard that it caused you pain, and I swear, Lola, I felt it. True, physical pain knowing I didn't keep you safe, that you were hurt." A hand moves to my jaw, gentle and warm, tipping it up until I look at him. "I am not a man who feels fear, Lola. But at that moment? I was terrified." He keeps staring at me, the look intense and clear, no lie or confusion there.

"And you will not be sleeping in your apartment tonight. You will be coming home with me, staying with me until I'm comfortable with you going back in there."

I open my mouth to speak, but he cuts in again.

"And even after that, you will not be sleeping in there alone." My head tries to move back in confusion, but the door stops me, leaving me stuck inches from Ben's face.

"You don't have to do this," I say.

"Do what?" The hallway is silent.

Uncomfortably silent.

I hate it.

I hate even more that I have to fill it.

"Take care of me." His thick brows furrow.

"What?"

"You don't have to take care of me. I can do it myself." I move from looking at him, his eyes burning holes into my skin as I move my eyes to look beyond him at his apartment door across the way.

Strange that I once thought there couldn't be enough space between us. Now, just a few weeks of there being some form of us, it seems like an ocean between our homes.

"I've been doing it since I was fifteen," I murmur, and regret the words. I don't want to sound needy or like I want pity. I don't want to guilt him into anything.

The good part about having a terrifying experience like I did is that it gives you time to think. The downside is that those thoughts, the conclusions you come to, don't just go away when the panic and danger settle. It just gives you a clearer lens to view your life through.

Ben once told me that my mother was wrong for putting that expectation on me. Wrong for telling me I was responsible for the actions of an adult man, responsible for the actions, poor or wise, she made in her own life. Wrong for making me think it was my job to keep Lilah safe.

At first, I was angry at him for saying that. Because who the fuck was he to say. He didn't know my mother, didn't know her life or my life or the circumstances that lead to asking your daughter that on your deathbed.

But the more I thought about it, I realized the truth of what he was saying.

I've always known that Dad should never have put me in that position, but I promised my mother I'd keep him safe.

And even more, Ben's right: that was unfair for my mom to do. I don't hold it against her, not really, but still—the fact that she knew all along about Dad's shortcomings, knew he'd use us to further his career, and knew he wouldn't change his ways?

But Lilah, too.

When she was ten, it was one thing. I kept it hidden. She had enough trauma being a ten-year-old little girl who lost her mother. But as she grew older, she leaned into the act. Leaned into the position of dutiful daughter, sweet Lilah, who went to all of the functions and smiled pretty.

I was the ambitious daughter who got it from her father and started a business in her mother's name. The one he could show off while signing acts to empower women in business, to gain female voters.

Lilah won the men.

The *promise* of Lilah won the men over.

Where I shied away from the role, Lilah leaned into it.

She loved the chess game, loved playing it.

I think a part of her saw herself as the one who was to follow in Dad's footsteps.

And that's where she went wrong—she missed all the clues because she was too filled with ambition. She missed the hints I dropped because she wanted to live her curated life too badly. And even once she knew a part of the picture, she didn't want to risk that life by seeing the rest of it.

"And now I'll do it with you," he says like that's the obvious answer, and, I guess, to him, it is. But I know what it's like to hold the burden of keeping someone else safe. Ben deserves freedom from that.

"You don't have to—"

"I do have to take care of you." His words break me from my thoughts, the mental games of what ifs and assigning faults. My head moves to him, where he's still staring at me, eyebrows together, confusion now covering his face. "I am *going* to take care of you, Lola." I keep staring, confused. "And not just for right now."

I think I know what he means.

In a way, it's an answer to my question.

The question of what will happen once this all settles and the excitement is over.

Once his sense of misplaced duty settles and wears off.

"Ben, seriously—"

"You're mine." His words stun me into silence. "You're mine, and I take care of what's mine."

"Seriously, it's sweet, but I . . ."

"Lola, what the fuck are you doing right now?"

"What?"

"What are you doing? What's your goal here? What game are you playing?"

"I'm not—"

"Are you really telling me you're not mine?"

"I don't understand." My head is a scrambled mess as I try to untangle my thoughts and his words.

"Are you telling me you're not mine, Lola?" She opens her mouth to argue. "Am I yours?" I'm getting annoyed now. This man can't even let me fucking speak.

"I just—"

"I'm not playing games."

"Jesus fucking Christ, Ben, if you let me finish a single fucking sentence!" I shout, and then he does it.

He smiles.

"There she is."

"Who is?"

"Fiesty Lola. *My* Lola."

"What?"

"You give the rest of the world sweet and kind and caring. You give them patience and understanding. But me? I get the real you. The one that wants to rip my throat out and put me in my place."

"See! That's what I'm trying to say! That makes no sense! I am not yours. You don't even like me!"

"Oh, I like you all right, sweet girl."

"You like fucking me," I say, rolling my eyes. I also have to work hard to ignore the flutter in my belly at his boyish, wicked smile. He laughs, that full belly laugh that I love to hear. It's so rare, but when it happens, it's a full-body melting sensation.

His hand moves to his apartment door and opens it before stepping inside. Then he pops his head out to look at me. "I like doing that, too. But that's not all I like." Then he closes the freaking door in my face. I stand there, staring at the door he just closed like an idiot.

The door opens again, and there's Ben again, standing in the doorway.

"Are you coming?"

"Where?"

"My place."

"I'm not going to your place."

"Fine, your place. But you gotta come inside so I can grab some clothes and shit."

"Why do you need to grab shit?"

"I thought you said you wanted to go to your place."

"I do."

"Then that's where I'm going too, babe."

"What? No." His hand reaches out, and he grabs mine before gently tugging, pulling me into his apartment. Before I can wrap my mind around what's going on, he's pushing me against the thick wood door of his apartment and pinning me there with his body.

"No way in hell are you spending any time alone for the next few days. I just watched you almost get fucking *kidnapped,* Lola. Johnny's out of the picture, but who the fuck knows what will happen next. That debt is still fucking out there. It doesn't just disappear because a man confessed to a murder of a mob boss. Who knows what your father will do next."

"My father said he'd handle it."

"I don't trust that man as far as I could throw him." My mind wonders just how far he could throw a man. My eyes wanders to his arms, muscled and thick, and I think that might actually be pretty far. "You're staying with me or I'm staying with you. End of story."

"Why?"

"Jesus, babe. We just did this. Know you hit your head, but Vic said there's no concussion." I stare at him, not answering. "You're mine."

"That makes no sense."

"How the fuck does it make no sense?" And I don't know if it's the drama of the day or adrenaline or pain pills or that I genuinely want to get this conversation over with, but I say it.

"Because . . . you hate me." His entire body stills.

"What?"

"You don't even like me," I say, this time quieter, embarrassed. God, I feel like an idiot. Some needy woman putting it out there in order to keep a man interested.

"Bullshit," he says, and there it is. That anger in his voice. It's not there on his face, but it's in his voice. In his soul, the way it sounds, I'm sure.

"How is that bullshit?"

"If I hate you, what the fuck have we been doing the past few weeks?"

"Hate fucking." The words come out matter of fact, and he actually rolls his eyes at me. It would be cute if I wasn't sure this was an important moment.

The make or break moment.

And I'm terrified it's going to be a break.

"And the days we spend together, the time we're not fucking?" I sit on that, mostly because I haven't been able to figure that out either. Why has he been spending so much time with me, being so nice to me if this is just an enemies with benefits thing? Why would he bring me home and introduce me to his family?

My mind wanders back to those paintings for auction. Paintings of me.

My mind wanders to Hattie's words.

He's different with you.

But what does that even mean?

He answers my unspoken question, always knowing. He can read me the way no one else has been able to.

"I haven't been able to get you off my mind since that first time I saw you, dancin' around your kitchen, stupid pink bows in your braids, flour on your cheeks, screamin' at me."

I feel my mouth drop open.

"What?"

"You heard me." I'm flustered.

"That's just because you wanted to have sex with me." His smile grows.

"That. And more. Fuck, Lola. You know that. It was sex at first. I wanted to fuck you out of my system. That fucking backfired, and then it became more. Then I realized it was always more. It was always more, Lola. *We were always more.*"

"That's not true."

"The fuck it isn't."

"Ben, you can't stand me. You hate me! But then I became a damsel in distress and you got distracted. Everyone knows a damsel in distress does that to men like you. But in a week, you'll go back to hating me, except then I'll also be out of your system." I feel like a strange mix of realistic and self-deprecating, but a lifetime of lies and secrets and half-truths makes me hesitant to take things at face value.

"Not true."

"How is that not true?" He sighs, a hand moving to my cheek as he looks in my eyes, like his mind is replaying a memory they sparked.

"I think I fell for you that first day." My entire body goes still. "Banging pans and playing shitty music like your life depended on it. Singing like a dying cat, not fucking locking your door then yelling at me like it was my fault. Threatening to call the cops. I loved that you didn't take my shit."

"Ben, that makes—"

"Maybe it was when you spilled your coffee on me and looked like your entire day was falling apart."

"*You* spilled *my* coffee," I say because I won't let that one get past me.

"Every muscle in my body needed to make your day better." I

stop breathing. "Or maybe when I saw you pinned, scared as fuck. Knew I needed you to be mine because I needed to take care of you. It was clear no one had been doing it until me."

"Ben, I—" My voice has gone soft, and I don't think he can even hear me, so stuck in his story and my eyes.

"But that first day. I knew it then. A part of me, at least."

"I—" I hear my own voice has gone soft with resignation. There's no way. He's sweet, saying it, but—

"You don't believe me, do you?"

"It's not that—"

"Come on," he says, stepping back and wrapping his fingers on my wrist "Ben—"

"Come on. I have something to show you."

I want to argue, of course. It's incredibly hard for me *not* to argue, but somehow I manage it, and I let him twine his fingers with mine.

He pulls me into his bedroom, to that little desk in the corner.

When he lets go of my hand, he opens the drawer and pulls out a battered leather journal. It's one of those nice ones, the kind with thick paper.

"Do you know what this is?"

"Your journal. Hattie told me about it." She did. I have no idea why, but one drunken night Hattie told me Ben has this journal he draws in every morning. His ritual, she called it. His mom gets him the journal every year. I remember thinking that was sweet since he told me his mom was the one to encourage his art.

"Hat's big fuckin' mouth," he says with a shake of his head and a small smile. "You know what I do with this?"

"You draw in it." Why does my voice sound so weak? Why are my hands shaking?

"Every single day. I date it. Draw tattoos, inspiration. Little things. Gets my creativity flowing." I nod but still don't understand why he's saying this. What does this have to do with anything? "Okay? And?"

"When was your opening day?"

"What?" I feel my eyebrows come together with confusion, hissing as the one tugs at stitches. Ben looks at the spot and moves a hand like he wants to touch it before shaking his head.

"When was your opening day?"

"What does this—" He sighs, shaking his head and cutting me off.

"Jesus Christ, never mind. Do you have to argue with absolutely fucking everything?" He starts to flip through pages, looking for . . . something. "Your opening day was June 5th." He's right, of course.

"How do you remember that?"

"Because I started drawing these," he says then turns the journal to me.

At the top of the page, June 5th is printed in fancy cursive. It's a dated but unlined journal.

And on that page is a little cupcake. It's shaded like an old school tattoo he might have, the swirls and lines in varying shades of gray pencil.

"What? I don't understand," I say, looking from the simple drawing to him. June 4th has an anchor, a flower tangling through the chains. Completely unrelated.

"Take it. Turn the pages." My hands go out carefully, like this might be a test or a trap, but I grab it anyway. The pages shake with the tremble in my hands.

And I turn the page.

June 6th is next to the 7th, and both pages have a cupcake. One is wearing headphones. The other is giving a peace sign. All three drawings are different.

I keep turning the pages.

Cupcakes. Page after page. One on a skateboard, one drinking a cup of coffee, one eating a cupcake.

"That's kind of fucked up," I whisper, looking at him and pointing at the cannibalistic cupcake. He's looking at me, face full of . . . emotion. Some kind of emotion that I can't quite pinpoint is glowing in his eyes.

"I'm kind of fucked up. I also haven't been able to stop thinking about you since the day I met you. You drive me insane, but fuck if you haven't gotten under my skin." I start to open my mouth to argue, but he stops me, grabbing the journal and tossing it to the desk like he doesn't care what happens to this precious thing.

Then I'm in his arms, wrapped tight, his face in mine, one hand on the back of my head, tangling in my hair and holding me still. "If you say it's because I hate you I'm gonna lose my fuckin' mind, Lola." I open my mouth to speak, to argue, but he keeps talking.

"We are fucking volatile. That's what we are. We will pick at each other, make each other angry, and push each other until we break. That's what we're gonna be, Lola. That's what I've always *needed*, baby. You? You're everything I didn't think I was looking for. Exciting and sweet and challenging." I open my mouth, but he *knows*. Somehow he knows every argument I'll make and how to counter it.

"Now you're gonna say that I only want a challenge. That I'll get bored." *How does he do that?* "But that's not it, Lola. Do you think you'll ever sit down and do what you're told? Doubt it. You lived that life and used up your emotional availability to listen to any man telling you what to do. Now you're your own person. But while you're that, you're also going to be *mine*. And you're going to drive me up a fucking wall, and I'm gonna say dumb shit, and it will make you slam a door in my face, and we're gonna fight, and you're gonna wake me up too fucking early, and I'm gonna use my mouth to convince you to stay in bed longer, but we're gonna live the good life, Lola. And we're gonna do it together." I blink at him, his words not processing. What is he . . . Is he saying what I think he's saying?

"I'm saying you're mine and I'm keeping you. I like this back and forth shit. It fuels me. If it ended, I'd be pissed as shit. I'm saying I love what's between us, and you're not just gonna walk away. That your mind isn't going to fuck this up because it's too fucking good between us."

"I drive you crazy," I say as an argument, because I do.

"And I love it. And I drive you crazy, and you fucking love it too,

Lola." I try and think, try to get my brain to work, but I already know. I know he's right.

I do love it.

I love how he doesn't let me just go on my way, doesn't just accept whatever I say, but instead, he tries to understand me and make me see what I deserve.

I love how he seems to genuinely like New Lola, the one who isn't meek and accepting, but who wants to fight back.

But the reality is, a love based on hatred is doomed to fail.

Right? That's how this works.

Relationships based in chaos and destruction, in quasi-lies and half-truths, they have to be doomed to fail.

And when this does end, if I let myself get in deep and believe this could be more, I will be destroyed by it.

"This won't work, Ben. It's . . . It's too filled with adrenaline to be something real."

There. Easy, succinct, but still exactly what my mind is telling me.

Of course, Ben does not accept this.

"Are you so scared to be let down, so scared this will end badly, you can't see it for what it is? Are you—"

"It's not—"

"Let me finish," he demands, his forehead moving to press to mine in a sweet, intimate move. I close my mouth. "You will drive me insane until the day I die, I think." I screw up my nose in irritation, and he laughs. *Not helping.* "You will drive me insane, but baby, it's in a way I fuckin' love. In a way I can't get enough of. You know me. You've met me. Do you think I want some sweet, compliant thing who will always listen to me? Do you think I want things to come easy?" I stop and think about it.

"Babe, I've had easy. I had my entire life planned out for me. Could have taken it and ran, never had to look back or think about what to do. Yeah, I'd have had to fix the mess my father made, but the business was there, and it was mine. But it was too *easy*. It wasn't what I wanted."

"So you want me because I'm difficult? Because you can't just have me?" Then I say what I've been afraid of from the start. What I've always been afraid of. Because I saw my mom give everything to my dad, and it *wasn't enough*. "What happens when I let you have me, all of me."

"I'll never have all of you."

"What?"

"Never. There's too much buried under there. Every day you reveal something new, like a jewel that's just for me. Every day you fall a little deeper, open a little more. But I don't think I'll ever get to the heart of you."

"So you want me because I'm a challenge?"

"Jesus Christ, Lola. I want you because you're fucking mine." That stops me. Stops my mind. "I want you because you're loyal as fuck. I want you because you do whatever is needed for the people you love. I want you because when you stick up for yourself, it's a fucking spectacular fireworks show. I want you because even *you* don't know what's at the core of you. You haven't gotten that deep, haven't let yourself dig. I think your mom had it, but it got buried. And I'll fight day in and day out until you let it free."

"And when it's done?"

"Then I'll have all of you."

"And you'll get bored."

"When a man works that hard for something that beautiful? He never lets it go, Lola. Never. He cherishes that. And that's what you really want, baby, To be cherished. You want me to prove I deserve that last kernel and spend every day until my last breath proving I deserve it."

And with those words, I concede, a small part of Old Lola breaking through my new shell, making herself comfortable. The part that trusted the words people told her, took them to heart, and let them in.

A part that, from now on, would be only for the man in front of me.

"You'll work to get me?" I ask, my voice small. His face lights up with my words, and I know then. I know before he answers.

He means every single word.

"Yeah, sweet girl. I'll work to keep you."

And though it's a small change in the phrasing, it's everything I need to hear.

FORTY-SIX

-Lola-

As PROMISED, about a month after the disaster that was the gala, we're in the car driving back to Springbrook Hills. This time, we're going for an entire weekend. I've spent the last three weeks recovering and training my two—yes, two!---new employees to feel confident in our weekend away, but I know Ben is anxious.

This time, we're not going for a quick eight hours and the excuse of celebration.

This time, we're going to be with his family, to spend time with them, and, from what Ben tells me, inevitably get into some kind of argument.

But with everything we've gone through, I know we'll be fine.

So I reach over, grab Ben's hand and pull it into my lap, where I use my fingers to trace the inked-in lines. When his face turns to me, I smile at him, and when he smiles back, just a hint of the anxiety has melted away.

-Ben-

We're sitting at the kitchen table with my family, and the sound of utensils on china is deafening.

We've been here for a total of one hour, an hour that was filled with Lola and Jordan chatting about weddings and instantly becoming best friends while Mom hid in the kitchen, shooing everyone out until she called us in.

It shouldn't be a big deal. I'm an adult—what should my father's opinions of me mean to me? But still, my gut churns with the knowledge of what's coming.

We're at the long table my father built my mother some forty-odd years ago. Lola is by my side, my brother across from me, his fiancée across from Lola. Mom is on one end of the table, Dad on the other.

Just like when we were kids.

It's strange, being here again, feeling like a kid but being in my thirties. It's like some part of you never truly outgrows the feeling of being small at a family table.

But stranger is the silence.

And my sweet girl, she can't stand silence. Not for a moment.

"So, Jordan, I hear you work with Tanner, right?" I gave her their entire, tangled backstory the other night when we lay in my bed, telling her about how my brother met his new fiancée two years ago when she was running from her country star ex and landed in Springbrook Hills, dropping the bombshell on Tanner's best friend, Hunter, that she was his half-sister. They couldn't stand each other for a while but eventually realized they worked.

Seems like my family has this issue often.

"Yeah!" Jordan says, relief in her eyes. From what I know about her, she likes silence about as much as Lola does. "It's been a blast. I work in the office, books and clients and that kind of thing, definitely not out on the site or anything." She laughs, and it's a pretty laugh, but the look my brother gives her when she speaks? Half amused, half eye roll, but full-on enamored with her? Fuck, it's familiar. "Tanner does that, though. Always out on the site working with the men."

I feel the mood shift before my father even opens his mouth, the chill in the air. Lola does, too, because her hand moves from the table, slipping underneath and resting on my thigh.

"Tanner's doing a great job over there. Really took the reins, did his duty to our family."

I want to argue.

I catch my mom's face, her eyes wide in a way I've seen before.

The battle is warring in her: keep the peace in front of company or rage on my dad.

I look at Tanner, who, now that he's older, has a look I've never seen staring back at me. One that says, *you make the call, I'm backing it.*

Those times in the past, when this conversation erupted in this same dining room, Tanner was young. Too young to jump in and take my side. And for a moment, I wonder what it would have been like to have a Lola in my life. To have someone to have my corner, ready to smash whatever comes my way. I hope Lilah knows how lucky she is.

Jordan's eyes are on her plate, and something tells me she's biting her own tongue.

I've heard about Jordan and her mouth.

But none of them say anything.

Instead, a small warm hand slips into mine, and a sweet voice starts.

"That's really great that Tanner took over the family business for you, Mr. Coleman."

I look over at Lola.

Her eyes aren't on me.

They aren't on her plate.

They are on my father.

My father stares her back down, and I'm prepared to back her, to back her and leave.

Things have never gotten full-on toxic with my father; there's never been a screaming match. He's more about subtle digs and obvious disappointment. But it's always brewing there.

"Did Ben tell you the business was supposed to go to the oldest son?" His eyebrow is raised like he caught me telling a lie to her. "That he was offered this business and, instead of taking it like a man, ran off to art school?"

"Dave!" my mother says, voice chiding. She might be a sweet wallflower, and my house may have been built with my dad's own hands, but the walls are thin, and I spent many nights up, drawing while my mom and dad argued about my choices.

"I did know Ben followed his passion and utilized the amazing skill that was given to him. By you, Mrs. Coleman, from what I hear." My mom blushes, and I kind of see what Tanner was saying—she is a lot like our mom. Sweet but with a backbone of steel. "Did you know that Ben had an auction a few weeks ago? And his art alone was sold for enough to cover two full-ride scholarships?" she counters.

I've seen this.

Tit for tat.

I also see my dad's irritation start to bubble under the surface, Lola knowing exactly how to push him even though she barely knows the man.

Seems I'm a lot like my dad in a way, with the same buttons to push.

"And did you know he's been helping with repairs to make sure our building is safe? He told me you taught him. He did a great job replacing my door and fixing my front lock when our landlord refused." My dad starts to talk.

"And he saved my life."

Everyone at the table goes silent.

I didn't expect her to say this, not at all.

I haven't told anyone in my family this part.

My eyes flit to Tanner, whose eyes are wide, then to Jordan, who is locked on Lola.

She fills the silence she created.

"A few weeks ago, someone tried to kidnap me."

"Oh, dear!" my mom says.

"He would have gotten away with it. I'm not sure what would

have happened to me had he succeeded, but Ben was on the phone with me, keeping me calm. He ran to save me, nearly got himself shot in the process, called the cops, and *saved my life.*" I want to correct her.

She saved her own life, keeping him talking, getting that confession.

She saved her life and Lilah's as well.

Fuck, she spent *years* saving Lilah's life.

But she doesn't stop.

"He might not have gone that path you wanted him to, Mr. Coleman. I get that. My sister and I haven't gone the paths our father would have wanted." *Yeah, like not living for him and his debts,* I think. "But sons and fathers were made to butt heads." Tanner snorts, and I kick him under the table. Lola's hand tightens on my own. "And you might be disappointed, but Ben is doing what he was made to do. Creating art that changes lives."

"No offense, Lola, but he tattoos." There it is.

That's the part he's never truly deigned to say out loud, the part I've been avoiding.

I know that my father thinks my chosen path is simple, useless. That while he, and now Tanner, were out being productive and building homes and businesses, I was *just tattooing.* Not chasing or living my dream. Definitely not *helping* people.

Just drawing pretty pictures on people's skin.

My mom opens her mouth to say something.

I see Tanner's chin tip and know he's about to speak too.

I move to argue, to stop this before it starts, I don't know.

But Lola beats us all.

"With all due respect, Mr. Coleman, I've been in his shop. I've talked to clients. I get it, you're from a generation where tattoos meant something else. It's not like that anymore. Tattoos are . . . a celebration. A tool for healing. I've met clients who get your son's beautiful art permanently etched on their bodies to commemorate a loss. I've met a woman who beat cancer. Clients using tattoos to celebrate their children or glorying in the fact that they beat terrible, other absolutely horrible circumstances that I don't dare bring to this lovely dinner." She stops and rubs her lips together.

Her tell.

She's full of emotions right now, fighting this battle for me.

I move a hand to her thigh, trying to get her to stop, but she keeps on.

"His art heals. It soothes. Just because it's not what you wanted, what you expected, doesn't make it any less valid. You have two incredibly successful sons. You should be blown away by both of them, feel unending pride in that."

Mom speaks up, dabbing at her eyes.

"I know I am. So incredibly proud of both of you."

"Tattooing isn't—" dad starts

"I'm going to stop you there, Mr. Coleman. Respectfully, it doesn't matter what you think. Your son has spent years avoiding this town he clearly loves, this family he adores, because he was afraid to hear this. Hear your opinions. But you know what? I think that's bullshit."

"Excuse me—"

"She's right, Mr. Coleman." My head moves to Jordan, my future sister-in-law whose own shoulders have straightened. "The first time I met you, you were frustrated that Tanner was running Coleman and Sons opposite of how you did. But he saved that company. And now Tanner is doing amazing things, and he doesn't even like to talk about it for fear of you invalidating that." I look to Tanner, whose eyes are on the ceiling. They move to mine, and his head shakes, silently saying, *"Trust me, it doesn't get easier."*

I feel like Jordan and Lola will get along *just fine.*

"What Tanner does is important," Lola says. "What your family built, that legacy, is *important*. But because *you* chose to continue that because of some banal first son rule does not mean that Ben was required to. And honestly, he doesn't deserve having you make him feel like shit for it."

"Lola," I say, trying to slow her down.

"No, I'm serious, Ben. Both times we drove up here, you were a stressed-out mess. The last time I saw it. You didn't want to leave once we were here. You love these people. You should feel free to live your life, come here, and be happy,"

"You made your point, babe," I say, tucking a loose strand of hair behind her ear and praying she just stops.

She doesn't.

"I just—"

"You're right, Lola."

The entire room goes silent with Dad's words.

"You too, Jordan. You're both right." I look to Mom, whose arms are crossed on her chest, a small smile on her lips. "Your mother's been telling me this for years. You ladies are right."

You could hear a pin drop. My eyes meet Tanner's, as wide and shocked as my own.

"You've done amazing at Coleman and Sons, Tanner. Profitable, getting those big contracts, growing. You've done better than I did, better than your grandfather." Tanner's shoulders drop. "I hated knowing that you took what I thought I was doing well with, changed it, and made it grow. It was wrong—this isn't a competition, and you're my son. But I did, and I'm sorry."

Tanner's mouth parts, but he doesn't have time to speak.

"And you. God, Ben. One day . . . One day, you'll see. You have kids, and you have these ideas for them; you get caught up in it. You have expectations and then those change. Your mom—she's good to the core. She saw the change and encouraged it, but I . . . I was so stuck in my ways, in my vision of what would be best, I drove you away." Looking at my father's face, I see it. It's strange, seeing it there, knowing it's there. That guilt. The remorse. The realization.

"Dad, it's—"

"It's not okay, Ben. It's not." He looks to Tanner. "And you. You've done amazing things over there, and I just gave you shit. You deserve a medal for fixing that mess I made, that your grandfather made. All I did was give you shit about not doing it my way."

Tanner also goes to speak, but Dad interrupts him first.

"That first time I met you, I gave him shit, and you didn't stand for it. Knew you were meant for him then," my dad says to Jordan. Her cheeks go red, and looking from Jordan to Lola, it's kind of funny to see the similarities in who we each chose as ours.

"And you." His eyes move to Lola, her hand in mine tightening.

Her tough Lola shield is up, the one she erected when her father hurt her, the one I worked hard to be left behind, but beneath it, she's anxious. "Thank you for bringing my boy home." He stares at her for a long time, the entire table silent. Lola doesn't speak, and from experience, I know Dad is waiting for her to do so.

But this is Lola we're talking about.

The edges of my dad's lips tip up, realizing this.

"You're good for him. Real good for him, Lola. You're a lot like my Joyce." Lola smiles then, and my dad's face tips to me. "Don't let that one get away," he says.

My eyes move from him to Lola and back before I smile.

"No plans to, Dad."

FORTY-SEVEN

-Lola-

I'm in Ben's childhood bed, and we just debriefed everything.

His talk with his dad after dinner.

How it went better than he expected, regardless of how overdue it was.

How he feels *good* about it.

How his dad is going to talk to his mom, try and set up a weekend at the shore soon.

It feels like the pieces are falling into place for both of us, and it's clearly so heavily-rooted in the fact that we found each other.

I finally had my come to Jesus talk with Dad and Lilah and how his shit will no longer be my responsibility, how it's also not Lilah's.

Regardless of the chaos and the mess—from our rocky meeting, hating each other, the shit with my dad, nearly being kidnapped—falling for each other was meant to be, that much I know.

And deep down, somewhere in my gut, I know Ben is it for me.

Part of me is sad my mom won't be here to celebrate with me, won't be here to fall for him herself. To see what I've done, how far I've come. But another part of me knows she is watching and is beyond proud of me.

"That's so great, babe. I'm proud of you," I say. His fingers comb through my hair, pushing it out of my face.

"I should thank you, really. What you said at dinner . . ."

"No. I meant it all." We're both silent, staring at each other, lost in thoughts and memories.

"It was you, you know. That gave me the confidence. Watching you finally stand up to your dad? Hell, even watching Lilah do it, confess what she knew." He laughs, a deep, almost self-deprecating laugh. "Strange that it took two women in chaos to show me I needed to grow a pair." I smile back at him, brushing a thumb over his full bottom lip, the one I always find myself looking at when he's talking.

"You're tough and brave in your own way, baby." We're silent for a few long moments, me drawing shapes on his bare chest, tracing inked-in lines, him playing with my hair before he speaks. His hand moves from my hair, a thumb going under my chin, tipping it until I look at him.

"You know I love you, Lola," he says, his voice whisper soft, breath brushing my lips, my stomach tumbling in circles with his words.

It's the first time he's said it outright.

I should tell him I love him too, that this is right, that I'm happy we found each other.

But I'm me.

I can't let him do this. So I smile, smile big—I let that much show before I speak.

"Yeah, I know." His lips tip up, and he puffs out a small laugh, rolling his eyes, but that thumb keeps brushing my skin like a metronome.

"Will you ever make it easy on me?"

"Would you love me if I did?" I ask in response.

"Probably not." He presses his lips to mine, soft and gentle, before we fall back into our comfortable silence.

"You know I love you too, right?" I say, wondering if maybe he doesn't. Maybe he doesn't know, and his own gut is unsure.

But Ben knows me. I think he always has.

"Yeah, sweet girl. I know."

EPILOGUE

-Ben-
Four years later

I WALK into a strange mix of cackling laughter and crying.

For a normal household, this would probably be cause for concern.

But Hattie's Beetle is parked out front, and I know Lola's been home all day. Those two together usually call for some chaotic mix of emotions.

My assumptions are confirmed when I enter the living room through the mudroom Lola forced me to refinish and see my girl sitting on our big couch with my best friend.

Hattie is laughing.

Lola is crying.

Sounds about right.

"BABE!" Lola shouts when she sees me, pushing the iPad they were sharing to the side and running toward me. I open my arms and brace for impact.

"Hey, sweet girl. You good?" I ask after she slams into me, hooks her arms around my neck, and lifts her legs. They wrap around my hips, and her tear-streaked face moves back.

"No! There are so many of them. So many, Ben! They need homes!"

"So many what?" I have a sinking suspicion, though, as one arm wraps under Lola's ass and another moves so my thumb can wipe away a tear. I look to Hattie for clarification.

Hattie, who is smiling at me with that fucking look she gets when she knows I'm going to want to kill her after whatever Lola says.

"Puppies!"

"No fuckin' way, Lola."

"Ben, they've been abandoned! They have no mommas! No home! No bed to cuddle into!"

"I told you, Lol. Neither of us is home enough. You hire more and cut back your hours, you can get a puppy," I say, pushing for what I've been begging her to do since I put a ring on her finger.

Three years after that first June 5th, I made Lola Turner mine officially, Tanner's little girl toddling down the aisle and throwing petals to the ground.

She, of course, made her own wedding cake, the psycho she is.

And in the four years since we met, Lola opened a second Libby's location and started wholesaling out some of her cookies.

The business is thriving, but I feel like I never see the woman.

"No. Then you're going to try and knock me up and have me pregnant and barefoot and making cookies in our kitchen while you go off and work."

"I'm gonna do that regardless. You can still work your bakery, babe."

"That's not the point." She shifts gears. "Shouldn't we have a test run? Make sure we're capable of taking care of another being?"

"No."

"Why not?"

"Because you're going to be a great mom, no matter what, Lola."

It doesn't even work. She doesn't soften or smile. Instead, she continues to argue with me.

"Then you need the practice."

And because I fucking love riling her up, I smile and answer.

"Why would I need practice if I have you?" Her jaw goes tight.

"If you think I'm going to bring your spawns into this world and you're not going to be changing diapers, you've got another thing coming, Benjamin Coleman. I've talked to Jordan. Your brother tried to pull that shit." I smile wider then move, pressing my lips to hers.

"Never, baby." Her body melts just a bit in my arms, and I smile again.

"If you let me get a puppy, I will do unspeakably filthy things to you, Benjamin Coleman," she says, a loud whisper in my ear, and Hattie laughs.

"I'm out," she says, a wave to me.

"You good?" I ask, making sure she doesn't need a ride, considering the state Lola's in.

"All good. Lola ate a gummy. I babysat." I fight the urge to roll my eyes, instead flipping off my best friend as she cackles and closes the door behind her.

"I'm serious, Ben. Unspeakably filthy."

"Sweet girl, you'll let me do unspeakably filthy things to you on any given Tuesday. Don't need promises of a puppy to get you to be good for your Daddy." She shivers in my arms before pushing back, her face changing in an instant.

"Oh my God. I forgot. I have a *surprise* for you." She smiles big, her eyes glazed and wonky but so fucking beautiful.

"Yeah?" I say, thumb brushing the remaining tear tracks that look out of place on her now happy face.

"Oh yeah," she says and then, still in my arms, leans back, hands going to the bottom of her loose tee shirt and lifting.

I stand there, holding her, staring in shock.

"What is that?"

"Do you like it?"

"What is it, Lola?"

"It's a . . . piercing." She stares at me, slightly confused, for long seconds. "I thought you'd like it."

Oh, I like it.

I fucking *love* it.

Knowing I can't touch it for months?

Not a fan.

Knowing I wasn't the person to put it there?

Definitely not a fucking fan.

"What did I say about people putting needles to you?" She rolls her eyes.

"Only you can do it. But this—"

"Only *I* get to put a needle to your skin, Lola."

"What if Vic needs to give me a shot?" she asks. I stare at her. She stares back. Her face cracks, a smile bleeding through her annoyance.

My annoyance is still there.

"Hattie knows my rule."

"But Hattie also loves to annoy you almost as much as I do." I start walking, taking her to our bedroom.

"You know what I do when you do something to annoy me?" I ask, kicking the bedroom door shut, taking two steps forward, and tossing her to the bed. She bounces with a giggle and fuck, even though I'm annoyed, I love it when she's like this. Giggly and just a little high and ready to play.

My fucking woman.

Her next words prove that.

"I get punished," she says, a little happy smile on her lips like she can't wait.

Neither can I, baby.

Once she's naked and has moved to the head of the bed, sprawled just the way I like her, I step back and take her in.

Fucking beautiful.

Walking to the side of the bed, I lean in to inspect Hattie's work. Impeccable, as always.

"How does it feel?" I ask, caressing the skin around her nipple, making her shiver.

"Hurts a little. Hat gave me a gummy, which helped." She gives me a sloppy, crooked smile that I love.

"The next one, I do. I do it, and then I fuck you on the table." Her eyes go wide and it takes everything in me not to laugh, to keep my angry facade.

"Hell no. This one hurt like a bitch. Never again."

"Too fucking bad. That's your other punishment."

"What's my first punishment?" she asks with a small smile. I hop onto the bed, situating myself between her legs that open just a bit wider as I do.

"Here's how this goes. Normally, I'd put you over my knee, but your new jewelry means you can't be on your belly for a bit." She pouts at that. *Yeah, didn't think about that one, did you, sweet girl?* "So instead, we're playing a game. I'm going to play with you, enjoy you as much as I want." A shiver runs through her. "But you can't come."

"What? Ben, no!"

"When you get close, you tell Daddy and I'll stop. Let you come down. Then we'll start again." I move, leaning in to kiss her lips, and taste what is indisputably mine. Then I sit back on my heels and wait for her arguments.

"That's not fair!"

"You broke a rule. I don't have many, baby."

"Yes, you do."

"Rules that *don't* involve locking doors and checking in so I know you're safe?" She scrunches her nose but doesn't argue. "Exactly." My finger goes, trailing down her belly, before I run it down her center.

She's already wet.

"Are you gonna be a good girl?" I ask, dipping a finger into her heat, and she sighs out a pleased noise. "Follow my rules to get your reward?"

"Yes," she breathes.

"Yes, what?" I say, my thumb moving to circle her clit.

"Yes, Daddy," she whispers, and fuck if my cock doesn't twitch at that still. I move down the bed a bit so I can bend and be face to face with her pretty cunt. My thumbs open her to me, and I swipe my tongue from her entrance to her clit, using my tongue ring to circle her clit the way I know she likes.

The whole time I lock my eyes with hers.

"Oh, God," she says. But I continue, easing a finger in, pressing it on her G spot as I start to suck her clit. When she's high, Lola is on edge almost instantly.

That's the real reason this is a punishment.

Because just thirty seconds in of me eating her pussy, she's tapping my shoulder.

"I'm close!" she says, and I back off, smiling at her.

"How do you feel, baby?" I ask, loving this form of torture.

"I need you," she says, pouting. I lean in, kissing her deeply, letting her taste herself on my tongue, her wet in my beard smearing on her face, and I know she won't wipe it off until we're done.

"You'll get me, baby," I say, and then I move back again, but before I start, I slap her inner thigh.

Hard.

"Fuck!" she shouts, and from this angle, I can see her pussy clench.

Jesus, this is as much a punishment for me as it is for her.

"That's for not saying anything," I say, looking in her eyes before I'm back, eating her pussy, my tongue fucking her as her hands move to my hair, tugging it, trying to get me closer. My teeth scrape at her clit, and when her hips buck, I back off.

"Ben, no!" She's desperate now, hips still moving like she'd take anything, like anything will get her off at this point.

I get off the bed and start to remove my clothes, looking at her the whole time.

A hand moves, slipping down her belly as I shuck my shirt and start on my pants.

But the woman keeps looking at me as she moves, eyes full of heat and need.

I know, baby, me too.

"Don't test me, sweet girl," I warn, staring at her as my underwear comes down.

Her hand hits curls.

I get back on the bed and she's moaning softly.

As much as I want to see this, I have my own plans.

My hand moves, slapping the opposite thigh as before, then the first thigh, and then her center, right over her hand.

She moans.

"Don't play games, Lola. Listen to me and take your punishment like a good girl," I say, a low growl in my voice.

"I want you."

"And I wanted you to listen to me, but you didn't." Two fingers go inside her and I fuck her with them near brutally, her body moving with the force as I move to graze her G spot.

"Oh, fuck!" she says, head thrashing as she moans.

I love her like this, out of control.

I add a thumb to her clit and feel her pussy clamp on my fingers.

"Daddy!" she says, and I stop, knowing that's my cue.

Then I pull my hand back and slap her wet pussy. The sound is loud, wet skin on wet skin, and her head goes back as she cries out, a mix of pain and pleasure ratcheting through her body.

I do it again, making sure I hit her swollen clit before I leave my hand on it and rub, hard.

"Daddy, fuck, please, God!" She's babbling now, begging for more, for anything.

I pull my hand back and slap her cunt again, then I position and slam into her.

"Fuck!" she shouts, her back bowing.

And then I stop.

"God, Ben, no, please!" she says, looking up at me, tears trailing from her eyes, her hair a disaster, her mouth dropped open with shock and pleasure.

I want to fuck this woman. I want to tear her apart and make her come and fill her up with my come because I need her every moment of every day and it's been that way for four fucking years.

But I need her to know the rules, too.

"Are you going to let anyone put a needle to your skin ever again, Lola?" I ask, pulling out tortuously slowly then slamming back in. A cry drops from her lips but she doesn't answer.

"Answer me," I say, gritting my teeth against the pleasure as I repeat the motion, pulling back and slamming in and staying planted.

"No, no! I'll be good, I swear. Please, fuck, let me come!" she begs, and God, I thrive off of it.

"Hold your legs like Daddy likes, sweet girl," I say, and she does, pulling her legs up and grabbing the back of her thighs, making her impossibly tighter.

"That's it, baby. Now hold on while I fuck you. You come when I tell you," I say, then I pull back and slam in.

"Ben!" she shouts, but I'm not listening. I'm lost in the feeling of her cunt on my cock, on the mental games of not coming and dragging out her punishment longer.

In and out, I fuck her, moving a hand to grab her bare tit, pinching the nipple, and staring at her, hopefully portraying the fact that I'll be making my own mark there soon.

When her pussy clamps on me, I know I got my point across.

"Okay, sweet girl, you can come for your Daddy now," I say in a growl, and then she's moaning, her body shaking with pleasure as she comes instantly.

"Such a fucking good girl, holding out for your man," I say, and then I follow her over the edge, pumping her full of me.

Minutes later, when her words come back, she opens her eyes and smiles.

"Was that supposed to deter me from breaking rules?" she asks, and then I laugh because I know there is nothing in this world that will make Lola listen to me.

The next day we brought home Cooper, a yellow lab mutt.

———

Hey reader!!

In this last section of the epilogue and Lola and Ben's story, there is a mention of pregnancy. If you are struggling with infertility, miscarriage, or if for *any* reason you don't enjoy reading about that topic, you can skip the last few passages and know that Ben and Lola have their own happily ever after.

You are loved, you are important, and you are seen.

Love,
    Morgan

———

-Lola-
Seven years later

I walk through the front door, dumping Cooper's leash and James's helmet that he threw to the ground as soon as we reached our house in the corner.

Looking around, I don't see Ben.

And I don't see Kayla.

"Jay, go upstairs and make sure you tidy up your room, yeah?" I say, directing my seven-year-old up the steps with a tip of my chin.

He rolls his eyes, a new trait that drives me wild (Ben *loves* to remind me where he got it from) before lugging up the stairs, feet slamming with more sound than absolutely necessary.

Just wait until he's blaring music at midnight, I think to myself, catching myself rolling my eyes.

Entering the kitchen, I look toward the family room to see if maybe the rest of my family is there, but nothing. Silence. Sighing, I grab some water out of the fridge and take a deep gulp. My eyes move to the family room, instinctually finding the three frames I love the most. Our entire home is a gallery of art and photos but those three . . . They are my favorite.

Hands on a rolling pin.

A braid.

A collar bone.

Me.

Turns out that the bidding war I saw the day of the auction included Ben's own bids. He paid way too fucking much for his own art because even though he listed it, he couldn't let it go.

"I couldn't stop thinking about some asshole having a part of you in his home forever," he'd said late one night when I'd brought it up.

So Ben bought them, bought them before we were even truly an us.

They are my favorite.

Movement on the back deck catches my eye. The screen doors are closed, but the glass one is open. I move that way, stopping when I see a sight I love even more than those photos.

"Daddy?" I hear her sweet voice say, eyes focused on the paper in front of her where she's swirling colors into a rainbow.

Ben is sketching the trees that line the back of our property.

We picked this house because of those trees, a taste of Springbrook Hills, and the back deck. When I was pregnant with James, and it was time to move us out of the townhouse, I fell in love with the idea of this exact moment.

I've never stumbled upon it until right now, but as I do, I put a hand to my belly—a sister for Kayla.

Five years apart, just like Lilah and me.

"Yeah, pumpkin," Ben says, eyes staying to the trees.

"What happens if I don't like art?" His hand pauses.

"What?"

"If I don't like art the way you do." Kayla's hand starts moving again, dipping in a pot of water to clean her brush before moving back to the watercolors. Ben's hand is frozen. "Like, what happens if I don't want to be an artist? What happens if I want to be a chef or a firefighter?"

"Lala, you will be whatever you want, no matter what." His head turns toward our girl, his eyes soft but holding a knowledge he holds close. The hair at his temple has started to gray, and more art has been added to the arm I can see, but he's still the same man I fell in love with all those years ago.

"Yeah, I know. But art . . . It's our thing."

"Yes," he says then starts moving his hand again, but I see the gears working.

"Like, what if I want to build houses?"

"I bet Uncle Tanner would love your help." She giggles, and I try not to because my brother-in-law would love nothing more than a crew of Coleman girls taking over Coleman and Sons one day, his nieces and his own girls leading the family legacy.

Or not. We've all learned that the futures of our children are not for us to plan.

"Hey, Daddy?" Kayla says again after they're silent for a few more moments.

"Yeah, baby."

"Do you think I'll be an okay big sister?" Ben stops now, setting his brush aside.

We haven't been able to get much out of Kayla regarding her moving from being the baby to a big sister, but it seems she's ready to talk.

"Do you think you'll be a good big sister?" She doesn't stop looking at her paper, adding pink hearts to the edges. He shoulders over, a subtle shrug.

Ben doesn't talk.

Doesn't push.

He does what he does best. He waits silently until she feels safe enough to speak.

Just like he did for me years ago.

"I'm kind of scared. Because babies are delicate."

"Yeah, they are."

"And it's going to be my job to take care of her."

Now Ben turns in his chair to face her.

"And what happens if I'm taking care of her so I can't go to soccer? Or go play at Emily's house?" I hear the concern in her voice, the slight shake and shit. This is what's been eating at her.

And like Ben does, he tugs it out of her.

"Kayla," he says, gentle. She doesn't stop the hearts. "Kayla, baby. Look at me." Our girl does, and I see her light hair tied in braids, a task Ben took upon himself to learn when he realized we were having a girl. "Your job is not ever to take care of your baby sister." My stomach roils, memories popping into place.

"But Grandma—"

"Grandma means well, but she's not Mommy, not Daddy. I'm telling you right now, Lala. Your job will never be to take care of your sister. You'll help us because we're a family. You'll keep an eye out for her because she's your sister. You'll do things for her because you love her, but you will always be Kayla. James still does basketball, right? He's not too busy taking care of you?"

"Yeah, but—"

"No but, baby. Mommy and Daddy will do everything in our power so all of you—all three of you—can do what makes you happy. Sometimes it won't be when you want or exactly how you want. That's life. But your sister will not be your responsibility. Ever."

Kayla scrunches her nose, but I can see that the concern I think she's been harboring for weeks has been eased.

"I don't want to change diapers," Kayla says, and Ben laughs, turning back to his art.

"Yeah, me neither, but your mom makes me do it. It was our deal. I put the baby in her belly and I have to change the diapers." I laugh then, and Ben looks over his shoulder and smiles.

"Hey, Daddy?" my nosy girl asks.

"Yeah, baby?"

"How *did* you put the baby in Mommy's belly?" Ben looks back at me again with wide eyes, and I raise my hands in the air, backing up and laughing.

He can handle that one on his own.

I never did like making life easy for him.

DELILAH

My heels click on poured cement floors.

They're red.

A power color.

In the past, I've worn these to banquets. To meetings to secure fundraising money.

On dates with rich attorneys and richer tech CEOs.

There, the power is in sex. The promise of maybe, but also, the knowledge of probably never. The forbidden fruit. Shane Turner's youngest daughter.

The youngest daughter with a secret my mother nearly took to her grave.

Today, the power needs to stand for something else.

It needs to stand for a woman doing what it takes to take control of her life. To finally pay her dues.

And when I stand in front of Paulie Carluccio in a tight black dress, blonde hair cascading down my tan back, an Italian princess in the making, I decide that red is my color.

Power is my color.

And I'm here to make a deal.

WANT MORE BEN AND LOLA?

Wondering what happens when Lola inevitably gets her first tattoo? Who will do it and what kind of... shenanigans will happen during?

Get your free bonus scene here!

WANT THE CHANCE TO WIN KINDLE STICKERS AND SIGNED COPIES?

Leave an honest review on Amazon or Goodreads and send the link to reviewteam@authormorganelizabeth.com and you'll be entered to win a signed copy of one of Morgan Elizabeth's books and a pack of bookish stickers!

Each email is an entry (you can send one email with your Goodreads review and another with your Kindle review for two entries per book) and two winners will be chosen at the beginning of each month!

ABOUT THE AUTHOR

Morgan is a born and raised Jersey girl, living there with her two boys, toddler daughter, and mechanic husband. She's addicted to iced espresso, chips, and Starburst jellybeans.

Writing has been her calling for as long as she can remember. There's a framed 'page one' of a book she wrote at seven hanging in her childhood home to prove the point. Her entire life she's crafted stories in her mind, begging to be released but it wasn't until recently she finally gave them the reigns.

I'm so grateful you've agreed to take this journey with me.

Stay up to date via TikTok and Instagram

Stay up to date with future stories, get sneak peeks and bonus chapters by signing up for my newsletter here.

HAVE YOU VISITED SPRINGBROOK HILLS?

If you're looking for spicy small town romance, Morgan Elizabeth has you covered! Check out these releases:

Get book one, The Distraction, on Kindle Unlimited here!

The last thing he needs is a distraction.

Hunter Hutchin's success is due to one thing, and one thing only: his unerring focus on Beaten Path, the outdoor recreation company he built from the ground up after his first business was an utter failure.

When his dad gets sick, Hunter is forced to go back to his hometown and prove once and for all that his father's belief in him wasn't for nothing. With illness looming, distractions are unacceptable.

Staying with his sister, he meets Hannah, the sexy nanny who has had his head in a frenzy since they met.

When Hunter's dad gets sick, he's forced to leave the city and move back into the small town he grew up in at his sister's house. Ever since he watched Hannah dance into his life, he's finding himself drifting from his goals and purpose - or is he drifting closer to them?

She refuses to make the same mistakes as her mother.

Hannah Keller grew up watching what happens when a family falls apart and lived through those consequences. When it's time, she won't make the same mistake by settling for anyone.

But when the uncle of the kids she nannies comes to stay for the summer, she can't help but find herself drawn to the handsome, standoffish man who is definitely not for her.

Can she get through the summer while protecting her heart? Or will he breakthrough and leave her broken?

Out now in the Kindle Store and on Kindle Unlimited

He was her first love.

Luna Davidson has been in love with Tony since she was ten years old. As her older brother's best friend, he was always off-limits, but that doesn't mean she didn't try. But years after he turned her down, she's found herself needing his help, whether she wants it or not.

She's his best friend's little sister.

When he learns that Luna has had someone stalking her for months, he's furious that she didn't tell anyone. As a detective on the Springbrook Hills PD, it's his job to serve and protect. But can he use this as an excuse to find out what really happened all those years ago?

Can Luna overcome her own insecurities to see what's right in front of her? Can Tony figure out who is stalking her before it goes too far?

Out now in the Kindle Store and on Kindle Unlimited

She was always the fill-in.

Jordan Daniels always knew she had a brother and sister her mom left behind. Heck, her mom never let her forget she didn't live up to their standards. But when she disappears from the limelight after her country star boyfriend proposes, the only place she knows to go to is to the town her mother fled and the family who doesn't know she exists.

He won't fall for another wild child.

Tanner Coleman was left in the dust once before when his high school sweetheart ran off to follow a rockstar around the world. He loves his roots, runs the family business, and will never leave Springbrook Hills. But when Jordan, with her lifetime spent traveling the world and mysterious history comes to work for him, he can't help but feel drawn to her.

Can Jordan open up to him about her past and stay in one place? Can Tanner trust his heart with her, or will she just hurt him like his ex?

ALSO BY MORGAN ELIZABETH

The Springbrook Hills Series

The Distraction

The Protector

The Substitution

The Connection

The Playlist

Holiday Standalone, interconnected with SBH:

Tis the Season for Revenge

The Ocean View Series

The Ex Files

Walking Red Flag

Bittersweet

The Mastermind Duet

Ivory Tower

Diamond Fortress

Printed in Great Britain
by Amazon

21127219R00234